# The Reliance

LEGACY OF THE KING'S PIRATES | Book Two

# M. L. TYNDALL

BARBOUR
PUBLISHING

© 2006 by M. L. Tyndall

ISBN 978-1-59789-360-2

All scripture quotations are taken from the King James Version of the Bible.

This book is a work of fiction. Names, characters, places, and incidents are either products of the author's imagination or used fictitiously. Any similarity to actual people, organizations, and/or events is purely coincidental.

Cover design by Müllerhaus Publishing Arts, Inc.
Cover Photography by Gloria Roundtree
Cover Illustration by Douglas Miller

Published by Barbour Publishing, Inc., P.O. Box 719, Uhrichsville, Ohio 44683,
www.barbourbooks.com

*Our mission is to publish and distribute inspirational products offering exceptional value and biblical encouragement to the masses.*

 Member of the
Evangelical Christian
Publishers Association

Printed in the United States of America.

## Dedication

*I dedicate* The Reliance *to the one true and faithful God—
the only One on whom we can completely rely.*

## Acknowledgments

Countless people touch a manuscript before it is transformed into a finished novel, too many to name.

To Rebecca Germany and all the talented and dedicated people at Barbour Publishing, I thank you. You have extended to me such grace, style, and professionalism.

Many thanks to Susan Lohrer and Traci DePree, my fantastic editors, who spent hours by my side tweaking and pruning *The Reliance*—and oftentimes me along with it! What would I have done without you both?

To my author friends in San Jose who are always there for a word of support. You guys are great!

To my beloved husband, the pirate captain in my own life, and the six children God has blessed us with. Every one of you fills my life with such joy.

To all the readers of the first book in the series, *The Redemption*, thank you from the bottom of my heart for picking up my novel, and for your notes and words of encouragement and praise.

To all lovers of pirates and romance everywhere, I write these novels for you. May our Lord reveal Himself to you through the daring adventures of Captain Merrick and Lady Charlisse.

And most of all, to God be all the glory!

# Chapter 1
# **Pirates!**

*1668—Porto Bello, Panama*

Captain Edmund Merrick propped his head in his hand and gazed at the angel lying next to him. Reaching over, he eased a curled lock from her face and smiled as she squirmed, snuggling her head deeper into the pillow. How many nights had he spent without her these past three years? Too many to count. Now that he was back in the Caribbean for good, he found he could not keep his eyes off his precious wife.

Charlisse stirred, and her eyes fluttered open. An ocean breeze floated in from the veranda and danced playfully through her golden curls, then drifted over her nightdress, creating waves of shimmering silk in the candlelight. The alluring nightgown was a gift he had brought her from France—a token that in no way could make up for the many months they had spent apart. Now, as he gazed at the way her feminine curves filled out every inch of the silky fabric, he was beginning to think it was more a gift for himself than for her. He smiled and saw her cheeks redden under his perusal. Married for nigh three years, he could still make her blush with only a look.

She shifted her gaze. "What are you thinking, you cad?"

"What this cad is always thinking when he is near his beautiful wife." He caressed her cheek.

An explosion shattered the thick night air, sending violent tremors through the sleeping city. Merrick bolted from the bed. Musket shots cracked like fireworks in the distance. He shoved his legs into his breeches, then barreled onto the veranda. The blaze of torches and the flash of gunfire coming from Fort San Lorenzo, lit up the night sky. From the second story of the hacienda, he scanned the dark waters of the bay swirling below the fort. No enemy lurked there, only the gloomy hulks of dozing ships.

Soft fingers touched his arm. "What is happening?"

A cannon blast boomed across the sky. Charlisse jumped. Merrick took her in his arms. "The fort is under attack."

Charlisse stepped toward the railing and stared into the night. A scream pierced the darkness, followed by another volley of musket shot. She faced him with a look of terror. "Who is it?"

"I don't know." Merrick led her inside. Fear snaked up his spine. He'd nearly lost Charlisse once before and had no intention of ever putting her in harm's way again. Placing his hands on her shoulders, he kissed her forehead. "I want you to get dressed and pack our things." He turned and grabbed his clothes that were strewn about the room. Who would dare attack such a well-defended port? The Dutch? Surely they would not risk a war with Spain when they had just ended one with England. The British? They preferred more surreptitious means of attacking their enemies. He could think of no alternative save pirates—and that option disturbed him most of all.

After buttoning his cotton shirt, he slipped on his waistcoat and plopped into a leather chair to pull on his boots.

"Don't leave me here, Merrick," Charlisse said with a crack in her voice. "In the middle of an enemy town. You know what these Spanish will do if they find an English woman in their midst."

Merrick stood and saw the fear skipping across her wide eyes. He strapped on his baldric as the clang of a distant sword fight and the roar of a cannon blared through the window. Charlisse flinched and turned to face him, swallowing hard.

He approached and lifted her chin. Her crystal blue eyes sparkled with admiration as they shifted between his. "You are my wife, milady. I will never let anything happen to you." Leaning down, he kissed her, exploring the softness of her lips and enjoying the taste of her—a taste of which he knew he would never tire.

Charlisse stepped back and lowered her head. "I'm afraid, Merrick."

Following her gaze, he placed his hand over the slight swelling of her belly. "I won't let anything happen to either of you."

Musket fire erupted outside, and the rank stench of gunpowder drifted in with the breeze.

Merrick grabbed his sword and sheathed it. After checking his pistols, he dropped them into the slots on his baldric. "Get dressed, Charlisse." He took her hand in his. "I'll return soon." He marched toward the door, cursing himself for bringing his wife to this dangerous Spanish city.

Charlisse stared at the door, feeling a sudden chill at Merrick's departure. What had happened to the brave girl who had left the comforts of London three years before and risked everything to sail to the Caribbean alone? Maybe it was the child she carried that caused her courage to falter. Placing her hand over her stomach, she closed her eyes, remembering the sparkle in Merrick's eyes when she'd told him that he was going to be a father.

Pistol shots sliced through the darkness, shattering Charlisse's blissful thoughts. Scrambling to her open trunk, she removed her nightdress and threw on her petticoats, bodice, and a turquoise gown trimmed in satin lace. She pinned her hair up in a loose bun and gathered Merrick's scattered things from around the room, placing them into the trunk before she slammed it shut. They hadn't unpacked yet—they hadn't expected to stay at Don Diego's hacienda for more than a day or two while Merrick sought his latest prey.

Loud voices from the hall drew her attention, and Merrick crashed through the door, followed by Don Diego de Acala. "We must leave quickly." Merrick marched to the bed and grabbed Charlisse's cloak.

Charlisse's insides quivered at his harried tone. "Why? Who is attacking the fort?"

Merrick looked down at her with his piercing dark eyes. He seemed hesitant. His ebony hair had escaped its tie and fell in disarray around his handsome face.

Don Diego stepped forward into the light. The spurs on the heels of his boots rang like warning bells when he walked across the room. A

Spanish saber, its golden hilt glittering in the lamplight, hung at his side. "It's the pirate Captain Morgan. The outer fort has fallen, and he now attacks San Lorenzo. Our courageous governor has barricaded himself within the fort's stone walls and has left his city defenseless."

Charlisse swerved to face her husband. "But don't you know Captain Morgan?"

Merrick helped Charlisse on with her cloak. " 'Tis true, my love, but it won't matter. I'm told he has near five hundred vicious men in his company, and they will give neither care nor concern as to whether I know their captain."

Stepping toward the open window, Don Diego peered out. A tortured scream rose above the tumult, followed by a crisp *pop, pop, pop* of pistol and musket fire—louder this time. "After they take the fort, they will swarm through the city like locusts." The commanding Spanish don turned on his heels, his sword swinging behind him. "If you leave now, you may escape them."

"But you will not. You must come with us, Diego," Merrick said.

Don Diego waved his hands in the air. "And leave my home? No, I'm tired of running."

Charlisse knew little about Don Diego de Acala except that he had once been a pirate and although Spain held his foremost allegiance, his ties of friendship with Merrick, formed long ago, remained strong. He had taken Merrick and Charlisse into his hacienda at great risk to himself. Merrick approached his friend and clasped his arm. "I'll get my wife safely aboard the *Redemption*, and then return to help you."

"No need, *mi amigo*. It is too dangerous for you. I am well armed and have many servants who will fight with me."

Merrick released his hand. "You would do the same for me."

Don Diego sprang for the door and shouted something in Spanish down the hall.

Leading her from the room, Merrick picked up his pace. Another blast from the fort's cannons shook the stone walls of the hacienda, loosening dust that rained down on them from the beams overhead. Charlisse coughed.

"My things." She pointed back toward their room.

"I'll come back for them." Merrick hurried her down the marble stairs, through a tiled entryway, and out the front door into the main gallery—a beautiful garden open to the starry sky and surrounded by thick adobe walls spiked with iron. An iron gate guarded the only entrance, and on the other side of its rusty rods, slaves and commoners dashed through the street while *caballeros* on horseback raced by, ordering them to move aside. A sense of urgency overcame Charlisse. This was no small attack. These murderous vermin would soon overrun the city, and people would surely die.

Charlisse turned for one last look at the grandiose mansion of Don Diego de Acala, a two-story hacienda of wood and stone with exquisite balconies overhanging the gallery. She feared for the people inside and for Don Diego himself. How would they survive such an assault?

From around the corner a servant hurried, leading a magnificent black horse. Don Diego took the reins, and the animal snorted and stomped his hooves into the dirt, stirring up a cloud of dust. "This is my fastest horse," he told Merrick. "A rare Andalusian stallion."

A barrage of musket fire cracked the darkness not far from them, followed by a woman's strangled scream. Charlisse's insides clenched.

"The pirates have already reached the city." Don Diego handed the reins to Merrick. "You must hurry."

Charlisse's breath came in quick spurts. How would they ever make it to their cockboat tethered at the Manzanillo Bay, when five hundred drunken pirates scoured the city? She faced Merrick—suddenly angry with her husband for his insatiable quest for adventure. "If we had only settled in the colonies like I wanted, our child would not be in such grave danger."

Merrick's lips pressed into a somber line as he assisted Charlisse up onto the saddle, her skirts billowing around her. He turned to his friend. "I'll return soon."

Don Diego nodded. "Now hurry."

Taking two full strides, Merrick swung himself up behind Charlisse on the horse's back. The stallion bolted, and Merrick reached around her and grabbed the reins. His warm breath floated down her neck. Despite her anger, she leaned back onto his chest, hoping his strength would ease her fears.

He gave the horse a kick. The powerful stallion neighed and clawed the air with his front hooves, then charged from the courtyard and through the iron gate held open by one of Don Diego's servants.

# Chapter 2
# Death Trap

$M$errick raced the stallion down the cobblestone street. The clopping of the horse's hooves echoed like war drums against the exquisite courtyards lining the roadway. Terror-stricken residents of Porto Bello dashed across the lane, forcing him to drive a chaotic path between them. A man burst into the street. Merrick jerked the reins just in time to miss a woman carrying a baby. The horse bucked, nearly toppling him and Charlisse. A load of pots, clothes, and tools flew from the man's arms, falling to the street with clanks and thuds. The woman screamed. Charlisse shrieked as Merrick tried to control the rattled horse. The man scurried to get his things, grabbed the woman's hand, then fixed Merrick with a level stare before darting into the darkness.

A volley of musket shot saturated the air. Merrick kicked the horse's ribs and drew Charlisse close before the stallion bolted into a gallop. She trembled. He leaned over and whispered in her ear, "Never fear. You are safe."

She squeezed his arm in return. He hated that she was afraid. He hated that he had put her in danger. And he determined to let no harm come to her—not tonight and not ever.

Ornate haciendas, as yet untouched by the savage assault, flew by them on both sides, their galleries guarded by wooden portals pierced with iron bars. *Señores* and *señoras* stormed onto their balconies, shouting in the direction of the noises that dared to disturb their sleep.

Mansions soon gave way to modest stucco homes capped with tile roofs.

Within their iron-grilled windows, inhabitants darted about frantically as they prepared to flee.

Horses piled into the street, along with the gilded coaches of caballeros forcing their way through the crowds. A little boy, lost and crying, strayed into the path of a carriage that was barreling toward him. Charlisse screamed. Merrick jerked the horse in his direction, cringing as he realized he could not reach the child in time. A woman came from nowhere, grabbed the boy, and dragged him to the side of the road just before he would have been crushed beneath the coach's iron wheels.

Letting out a sigh of relief, Merrick patted Charlisse's hand while they swerved around a man pushing an overloaded cart. Don Diego had been right about the horse's speed, but the animal was also very agile for its size. No doubt the don had given Merrick his best horse, knowing he might never see it again. Merrick vowed to return to his aid as soon as possible. But he must get Charlisse to safety first. He looked over the harrowing scene of fleeing people and then toward the bay where smoke from fires clouded the moonlight. A sickening wave of terror welled up from his belly at the thought of anything happening to his wife.

The street narrowed and angled toward the docks, twisting and turning in its descent. Wooden warehouses towered above them on one side, while jacaranda trees created a tangled purple web on the other. Africans and Indians, holding crates atop their heads, rushed up the road away from town.

Merrick glanced toward the bay. The gray walls of Fort San Lorenzo loomed like a skull against the cobalt sky. Ashen smoke, draped in milky moonlight, hovered over the gun turrets that now stood silent.

The pirates had taken the fort. Soon they would overrun the city like a pack of hungry wolves.

A fire blazed by the docks. Clusters of pistol shots popped in nerve-wracking volleys all around him. He would have to go through the center of town in order to reach the pathway leading to Manzanillo Bay, where a cockboat from his ship awaited them. He sped down the cobblestone lane, now littered with people and goods heading in the other direction. A push wagon appeared in front of him, and with a sharp nudge to the stallion's side, Merrick urged the horse into a wide jump over it.

Swerving through the mass of people and animals, Merrick raced down the main street, past shops and taverns, ignoring the screams that assailed him, and berating himself for it. He wanted to help them. He knew all too well the terror they were facing at the hands of these pirates, but he had a family to protect now. Placing one arm protectively around Charlisse's belly, he drove the horse onward.

The jarring sound of shattering glass alerted him to slow down before entering the main plaza. As he turned the corner, a jumbled throng sped across the circular courtyard, and skirted the black marble fountain that stood in the center. Merrick reined the horse to a halt. Oil lamps hanging from wooden posts cast an eerie, flickering glow over the chaotic scene. One man clubbed through the wooden doors of a silver shop, and a hoard of peasants followed him inside. Others barreled out of storefronts, their arms brimming with candleholders, silver sconces, and fine fabrics of silk and lace. They sprinted across the plaza, dropping goods as they went.

"What are they doing?" Charlisse asked.

Merrick tightened his hold on the reins, preventing the jittery horse from proceeding any farther. "They're stealing."

Charlisse shook her head. "When their neighbors are being butchered, they steal from one another?"

"I'm afraid so."

The horse threw its head into the wind and snorted, striking its metal-shod hooves onto the cobblestones with clips and clops. A man shot into the plaza. His chalky-white face held wild, darting eyes. Splotches of red stained his shirt. "*Los piratas están aquí!*" he shouted. "Los piratas están aquí!" His gaze met Merrick's. Horror and shock sparked in his eyes. Guilt weighed upon Merrick's heart as he watched the man cross himself before he sprinted to the right and disappeared between two buildings.

Pirates swarmed into the courtyard like rats, lust and greed glinting in their eyes. With drawn swords and pistols, they growled at the mob, who scattered in all directions, people climbing over each other to get away. Pistol shots exploded and men dropped to the ground. One pirate, a huge, brutish-looking fellow, grabbed a woman and dragged her behind a cobbler's shop. Her terror-filled eyes held Merrick's until she disappeared from sight. His heart sank.

Charlisse clutched Merrick's arm. "You must help her!"

To his right, another woman screamed. More cries for help roared across the plaza. A few men stood their ground and fought bravely to defend their women and shops, but their efforts were useless against the ruthless onslaught. Wrenching their bloody blades from the lifeless bodies of their victims, the pirates laughed and moved on to the next man foolish enough to resist them.

Merrick's blood boiled. Every nerve ignited within him, pushing him to jump from his horse and join the fray. Like the stallion beneath him chomping on its bit, Merrick clenched his jaw. But he could not get involved—not with Charlisse in his arms.

He waited for a clear path and then kicked the horse. They bolted across the plaza. Hands clawed at them as they passed, pulling on their legs. Merrick drove his boot into one pirate's face, knocking him backward onto the street. He drew his pistol and shot another, then swerved the horse quickly to the left to dislodge a third pirate's grip on their saddle.

Two grisly men charged into the court and blocked Merrick's exit. Upon seeing Charlisse, they plodded toward them, waving their swords in the air and throwing the stallion into a panic. Merrick reined the unruly beast to a halt.

"What 'ave we here?" One of the men gave Charlisse a toothless sneer. The other man approached from the other side and snickered.

Slipping his hand behind Charlisse, Merrick dropped the pistol and slowly withdrew the other from his baldric, keeping it hidden behind the folds of his wife's dress.

"What say we take this pretty *señorita* off yer hands, mate?" One of the men lifted the tip of his sword to Merrick's neck.

"And yer horse, too, if ye don't mind."

"I'm afraid I do mind." Merrick's voice was calm and steady. "Now, begone with you or suffer your due fate."

"An Englishman, are ye?" the bald man on the right said, grinning at the challenge.

Charlisse straightened her back. "I'll have you know, sir," she said, "this is Captain Edmund Merrick, the most notorious pirate on the Caribbean."

Merrick nudged her in the back. With more enemies among pirates than friends, he doubted that information would aid their cause.

A flicker of awe passed across the eyes of the pirate on the left—the one with eyebrows as thick as his beard. He lifted the hairy arcs and stared at Merrick.

Charlisse put her nose in the air. "So if you know what's good for you, you'll take your leave."

"Is that so?" The pirates exchanged a quick glance and chuckled. "I've heard of ye, Cap'n," one of them said. "Heard ye went yellow-livered and quit piratin' fer good, that ye found yerself religion and a wife"—the man gazed at Charlisse and licked his lips—"and that ye ain't nothin' to be feared no more."

Merrick curved his mouth in a bold grin. "I wouldn't believe everything you hear, mate."

The pirate on the left pointed his sword at Charlisse. "Enough o' this! Get off yer horse, or I'll run 'er through." Charlisse stiffened as the sharp tip touched her chest.

Rage sent flaming arrows through Merrick.

"First, hand over yer pistols," the other pirate said, still holding his sword to Merrick's neck.

With his right hand clutching the loaded pistol, Merrick eased his left hand down his thigh. "Of course," he said, smiling. His fingers found the dagger and circled around it.

Allowing his pistol to swing by the trigger guard, he offered its grip to the pirate.

More pirates entered the plaza.

Charlisse trembled.

The stallion snorted and stomped its hooves.

Before the pirate could grab the pistol, Merrick swung it around on his finger and fired on him. He kicked the sword from the pirate's grasp on his left, and flung his dagger straight into the man's heart. Both men stumbled backward, clutching their chests, eyes wide in horror.

Charlisse gasped.

Three more pirates rushed toward them. Merrick steadied Charlisse and raced the horse out of the courtyard and up the street leading away from the docks, not slowing until he was sure they were out of danger. Easing the horse to a trot, he shook his head, disgusted by the violence. He nestled his face into Charlisse's neck, not only to comfort her, but himself, as well. Hadn't he been just as wicked as these men? How many raids such as this had he partaken of before God had rescued him? It seemed a lifetime ago. Memories of a man he no longer knew or recognized haunted his nightmares, taunting him into thinking he really hadn't changed at all. But he knew differently.

"We should have helped those people." Charlisse sniffed, still shaking.

Merrick squeezed her. "We can't save everyone."

"But you could have done something."

"I saved you, and that's all that matters right now." Even as he said the words, they fell flat on his conscience. But he could not risk Charlisse. He would not lose her again.

Urging the horse forward, he headed up the road, away from the main part of town where most of the pirates would be looking for plunder and women. The stones beneath them gave way to dirt, and small farms appeared on either side. They were nearly at the edge of the city. Fewer people crowded the roads. Groups of families, their backs overloaded with blankets, pots, clothes, and sacks of grain, scurried out of town. Merrick's taut nerves began to loosen.

He leaned toward Charlisse. The scent of lilacs from her hair teased his nose as her curls tickled his cheek, reminding him she was finally at his side for good. Merrick had been called to London soon after their marriage to help his father flee to France during a political crisis. He and Charlisse had spent only half of their three-year marriage together, and only in short months or weeks when Merrick had been able to steal away from England. Their time apart had been unbearable. Charlisse was his life—his precious gift from God, and he did not intend to leave her again.

Up ahead, two church towers pierced the starlit sky with their coral bricks and iron steeples. Between them rested a rectangular sanctuary with arched windows and a massive wooden door guarded on both sides by angelic bronze sculptures.

A feeling of reverence emanated from the building. Merrick kicked the stallion, anxious to pass by and flee the perilous city, when one side of the door flew open, and a small child darted out. "*Ayúdenos, por favor!*" he shouted. The boy, with black hair flopping, could have been no more than six or seven years old. He rushed toward the horse, arms flailing, repeating the same phrase, "Ayúdenos, por favor!"

"What is he saying?" Charlisse asked. She placed her hand on Merrick's and pulled back on the reins. The horse slowed.

"He's asking for help."

"Then we shall help him." Charlisse turned her head. "Stop the horse at once."

Merrick sighed and eased the horse to a stop. A group of children crowded the open door of the church.

He leaned to Charlisse's ear. "I must get you to safety immediately."

"But look at all the children." She squeezed his hand. "They need us."

The boy yanked on Charlisse's foot, looking up at her with wide, pleading eyes.

Charlisse jabbed Merrick with her elbow. "Let me down."

He didn't want to let her down. He wanted to kick the horse into a gallop and take her to his ship, where she would be safe. Every minute he delayed put her in more danger. But he knew his wife—knew her tender heart. She would never forgive him if he didn't at least stop and see what the children needed.

Merrick swung himself to the ground, then reached up for Charlisse. "As you wish. Let's see what they need and then be on our way."

As soon as her feet touched the earth, Charlisse knelt, and the boy flew into her arms.

An older boy headed their way. "Miguel. Get back here."

With a shake of his head, Miguel snuggled his face against Charlisse's cheek.

Merrick turned toward the boy who approached. The young man glanced at the cutlass at Merrick's hip and froze. "Sorry to trouble you, milord. Miguel, come here."

"You speak English," Merrick said.

"Yes, milord."

Merrick took a step toward him. "Who's in charge here?"

"I am." The boy lengthened his stance. "We are orphans, milord. Our priest and the sisters were taken away by the pirates hours ago." He peered anxiously over his shoulder at the church.

Merrick glanced at the other children who slowly inched their way from the shadows—a disheveled group of kids ranging from toddlers to adolescents all with wide, fearful eyes. His chest constricted. They wouldn't stand a chance against the pirates. "And they left you and the church unharmed?"

The boy nodded. "I overheard the pirates say they needed the father and the sisters at the fort."

Merrick guessed he was around twelve or thirteen; he stood tall and lanky, his brown hair sticking out in all directions, but the features of his face were handsome and his eyes sharp.

"They said they would return, milord." Fear quivered in his voice, and he shot a glance back at the church. When his eyes met Merrick's again, they transfixed upon him with horror.

A spark of alarm tore through Merrick. He shook it off, attributing the boy's apprehension to the atrocities he had recently experienced.

Charlisse stood, holding the little boy's hand, and gazed upon the orphans. Her eyes moistened. The children crept toward them with bare, dirty feet, their clothing torn and ragged, and all thin—so terribly thin.

The young man glanced behind him. "We. . .the children are frightened. We don't know what to do."

A girl, no more than two years old, ran to them. Stooping, Charlisse swept her into her arms and squeezed her. Her swimming eyes swerved to Merrick's.

A wave of trepidation swept over him. How would he be able to draw Charlisse away now? But he must. They could not stay here, and there were too many children to take with them.

Grabbing the horse's reins, Merrick held his hand out for Charlisse and turned to the young man. "Go back in the church and hide."

"Surely you do not intend to leave them." Charlisse refused his hand.

"There is no time. I'll come back for them after you're safe."

"You know as well as I, it will be too late then." Her voice cracked.

Merrick looked into her wide, beseeching eyes—eyes challenging him to disagree—then scanned the terrified faces of the children. Some sobbed, some trembled, and some—the older ones—stared at him with hopeless expressions that told him they did not expect him or anyone else to help them. The toddler wrapped her chubby arms more tightly around Charlisse's neck.

Looking out toward the bay, Merrick ran a hand through his hair. Pistol shots and the clang of swords continued to ring through the night—the sounds of a pirate raid. He had partaken of one too many in his life, and the blaring cacophony of wickedness taunted him with hellish nightmares. How long before they got there? *Lord, what do I do?*

*Save the children.*

Merrick tied the horse's reins onto a fence post and grabbed two orphans, ushering them toward the church. "Let's get them inside."

Charlisse followed his lead. "Come, children." Still carrying the girl, she clasped the boy's hand and pulled him along beside her.

As they passed through the door, a moldy darkness enveloped them. Wooden arches climbed up both sides of the church to form a domed ceiling that stretched the length of the building. Colorful paintings of biblical figures lined the walls, and rows of pews extended toward the back, where all was lost in the gloom except a gold crucifix that glittered in the light of one candle.

An uneasiness lifted the hairs on the back of Merrick's neck. He scanned the shadows, searching for the presence he was certain he felt, but saw no one.

Charlisse stepped toward him. "What are you going to do?"

The young man who'd spoken to them outside shook his head. "You're going to leave us here, aren't you?" The muscles in his pale face twitched.

"My wife and I will get a wagon." He glanced at Charlisse. "We'll return to take you to safety."

"Let me stay," Charlisse said. "You can ride faster without me."

The two-year-old whimpered and buried her head deeper into Charlisse's neck, clinging to her as if her life depended on it. Charlisse rubbed her back. "It will be all right, little one. You are safe," she whispered.

"Please, Merrick." Her eyes scanned his.

Conflicting emotions surged through him. How could he leave her? Yet taking her back into town would be just as dangerous. Most likely, the pirates wouldn't make it up this far for another hour. With all the spoils in town to occupy them, they might not come this way again for days.

"Where do you stay?" he asked the young man.

"We have rooms upstairs, and our schoolhouse is in the back."

Merrick turned to Charlisse. "Hide the children here in the church."

He kissed her cheek, noticing the smile she threw his way. "Keep them quiet. I'll be back soon." After nodding at the young man, he swung about and rushed out the door.

Apprehension gnawed at his insides. Was he doing the right thing? With every step he took away from Charlisse, his heart shrank. But surely it was God's will to risk their lives in order to save all those children. Then why were doubts piercing his soul from every angle?

He untied the horse's reins from the fence and patted the stallion's neck, hesitating. The beast snorted and jerked his head back with eyes aflame. "Whoa, whoa." Merrick tugged on the reins and stroked the animal's neck again, then eased him around the fence and onto the dirt road. "You're as jumpy as I am tonight, my friend."

Swinging onto the horse's back, he glanced over his shoulder toward the church before a kick sent the stallion speeding down the path. *Please keep them safe, Lord.*

A deafening blast erupted behind him. The force of the explosion pounded against Merrick and threw him to the ground. Even before he hit, everything inside of him screamed.

*NO!*

Pain speared up his legs and across his back.

He tried to get up. His head pounded. Hot blood trickled down his forehead. Turning, he looked at the church, knowing what he would see before he did. A blazing inferno of charred rubble. No towers, no steeples, no sanctuary, no angelic statues guarding a doorway that no longer existed. Only fire, crumbled stone, and splintered wood. His gaze landed on the back of the building where some of the walls remained intact.

*Maybe she survived.*

As he stumbled to his feet, pain shot up his leg. A spike of wood from the explosion protruded from his thigh. Grabbing it, he yanked the wooden lance from his flesh and tossed it aside. Ignoring the flow of blood and the excruciating spasms, he hobbled toward the flaming building.

Chunks of brick and pebbles rained on him like flashes of memories: Charlisse's curls, her smile, the child nestled on her shoulder, the spark of love in her eyes. All crumbled and broken into bits, falling to the dirt around him along with every piece of his heart.

"Charlisse! Charlisse!" he screamed.

Nothing but the crackle of flames.

Dragging his leg, he angled around toward the back of the church.

Nothing—just a smoking hole of flaming wood and stone.

Holding a hand up against the searing heat, Merrick dared to peer within the burning chasm. No charred bodies. No screams for help. Had they already been consumed? Could they have escaped?

"Charlisse!"

Nothing. No, there had not been time. Falling to his knees, Merrick pounded the dirt with his fists and screamed. "God, no! No!"

Charlisse writhed in the grasp of two burly pirates as she watched her husband limp around the corner of the church. The visage of his body blurred through the scorching heat, but even so, she saw the agony twisting his face. He screamed her name over and over. She tried to reply but the tight cloth between her lips allowed only muffled grunts—inaudible above the crackle of the flames. She shot a glance behind her. The children huddled in a group on the forest floor, whimpering. Three men surrounded them with pistols aimed at their heads.

The man on her right leaned toward her ear. "Another peep out of you, and we'll shoot one of the brats," he whispered.

Somehow she had no doubt they would do just that.

She returned her gaze to Merrick. He peered into the burning church. Blood oozed from his right thigh—she could see its red stain even from here. She started toward him but winced when one of the pirates tightened his grasp on her arm. Desperation squeezed every nerve. Her eyes burned with tears. She must get Merrick's attention. But how could she when the children's lives were at stake? Unless her husband entered the forest, he would never see them hidden in the shadows of the trees.

Merrick slunk to the ground in a heap, and Charlisse's heart sank with him.

He believed they were dead. He would never search for her now.

# Chapter 3
# Captured

Hands bound behind her back, Charlisse sat in a longboat and watched the black water swirl with each foamy intrusion of the paddles into its depths. Two pirates sat in front of her and three behind. They had refused to tell her where they were taking her, but she could only assume her destination was one of Morgan's ships. Whatever could they want? And why go to all the trouble of blowing up a church to capture her?

Thank God the children had not been harmed. After Merrick left, the pirates had ordered the orphans to run deeper into the woods, threatening them with death if they came out before sunrise. Charlisse had encouraged them to obey, telling them not to worry. All would be well. As they scampered off into the night, casting frightened glances back her way, she'd said a silent prayer for their safety.

Afterward, the pirates dragged her to a shack near the coast where they'd kept her prisoner for three days, waiting for their captain to return to the ship—as least, that was what she'd overheard them saying. They'd left her alone, save for bringing her food and water, and although now relieved to be finally out of the dark hut, a new terror consumed her as she pondered what fate awaited her when they reached their destination.

Regardless of her immediate peril, Charlisse thanked God that Merrick had survived. If he had not left the church when he did, the pirates would certainly have killed him. She was the prize they were after. The band of ruffians had used the children to lure her into the church. But why? What was so special about her compared to all the other women in town? She shuddered, despite the warm night, and said a silent prayer that Merrick would realize she still lived and come for her. Glancing up into the night sky, she also prayed for strength to endure whatever these men had planned.

The dark hull of a ship loomed ahead, lit by two lanterns, one on the bowsprit and the other swinging from a hook on the mizzenmast. Dim light shone through a porthole below the quarterdeck. Three masts covered with tangled rigging towered against the moonlit sky like webbed claws ready to snatch Charlisse from the boat. Most likely an ex-merchant vessel, the three-masted, square-rigged ship could hold up to forty guns. Charlisse wouldn't have known or cared about such things three years ago if she hadn't married a privateer and chosen a life at sea.

The longboat scraped and thudded against the hull of the larger ship, and the pirates secured it with cords that dangled from the bulwark. A rope ladder flew down the side, and Charlisse's heart dropped with its descent. The smell of damp wood and gunpowder drifted past her nose.

"Come on, littl' missy, up ye go." One of the pirates grabbed her arm and lifted her. He untied the rope binding her hands, then pushed her toward the ladder. When she didn't move, he leaned over, showering her with his foul breath, and hesitated, his slobbering lips smacking near her ear.

Charlisse cringed and clutched the rope, desperate for any escape.

The man took a step back and swatted her bottom. "Begone with ye now."

The pirates chuckled.

Charlisse whirled. "How dare you?" She slapped him full force on his right cheek, but his thick beard softened the sharp impact.

Shock claimed the pirate's wicked features. He raised his arm to strike her, but a deep voice from above halted his hand in midair. "What goes on down there? Bring her up, or I'll have you stretched and scaled alive!"

That voice. Charlisse knew that voice. Tremors of dread etched their way down her spine. Gazing upward, she saw nothing but darkness and the eerie outline of an immense storm cloud drifting in over the ship.

A wave hit the longboat, and she nearly toppled overboard. The sea beckoned. *Come. Jump in. Anything but go up that ladder!* Laying a hand on her stomach, she thought of the growing life within her and glanced back at the rolling indigo water. Although she had only recently learned to paddle—at Merrick's insistence—she might indeed make it to shore. But could she risk it? She had more to consider now than her own life.

The pirate shoved her, and she clambered up the ropes despite the quivering in her knees.

At the top, a strong arm grabbed hers and assisted her on deck. Her silk brocade shoes hit the wooden planks with a slap. A salty breeze tossed her wayward curls about her face. She looked up. Dark, sinister eyes bored into hers. A crooked grin spread over his lips.

"Ah, my sweet, we are together again at last."

He sauntered toward her. The thud of his tall leather boots ground away at her courage. With one hand on the hilt of his cutlass, he waved the other through the air, his fingers nearly hidden by a burst of white lace that bulged from the wrist of his black camlet suit. "I have dreamt of this moment for quite some time."

"Kent," Charlisse hissed between clenched teeth.

He flashed a stern look. "Captain Carlton, if you please."

Doffing a black hat with a sweep of ostrich feather, he bowed. "Welcome to my ship, the *Vanquisher*, miss."

"Lady Merrick Hyde to you."

"Ah yes. I heard you married that buffoon, Merrick." He shook his head. "Such a waste of your exquisite beauty."

Charlisse lifted her chin. "And your charm, sir, is wasted on me. You forget. I know you."

The rest of the pirates had climbed over the rail and shuffled off to their posts, casting quick glances her way.

"What do you want with me?" Charlisse could hear the crack in her own voice despite her efforts to appear calm. She inched her way toward the railing.

Kent leered at her from under heavy lids, following her movements. "What I have always wanted with you."

The effect of his licentious comment crept up her spine like a poisonous snake. Charlisse glanced at the swirling water. Perhaps it was better, after all, to risk her life and her child's rather than endure the advances of this madman.

Before she looked up again, Kent pounced on her and clamped her arm in his firm grasp. "Gibbons, weigh anchor, unfurl the topsails and topgallants," he said over his shoulder.

A short, stout man, who appeared to be in his midthirties, shouted, "Aye, aye, Cap'n," and boomed the order to the crew on deck.

"Where are we going?" Charlisse squirmed and tried to yank her arm from Kent's grip. Fury mixed with fear surged through her heart, causing it to pound violently. "Release me at once!"

Kent jerked her toward him and squeezed his grip on her arm until Charlisse buckled under the pain. She looked up at his red, seething face. Fiery sparks of anger boiled in his eyes. Charlisse knew he would not relent. Hopelessness sapped her strength, and she ceased struggling.

He loosened his grip. The right side of his upper lip twitched. "You will learn to behave on *my* ship, milady." Turning, he dragged her across the deck.

A pirate with a long gray beard ran up to him. "But, Cap'n. There's booty for the takin' in Porto Bello. Why are we leavin'?" Several more men gathered behind him.

Kent studied Charlisse. "I have what I came for." Then turning to the men, he bellowed, "Now do as I say, you jackanapes!"

A low rumble of murmurs rose from the motley group.

Kent drew his cutlass. "I'm the captain aboard this ship, and I'll be deciding when and where we plunder." His anger spread to his fingers that clenched Charlisse's arm. She winced. "Haven't I done good by you so far? Aren't your pockets full of doubloons?" He scanned the crowd and shifted the tip of his sword between two of the men. "Max, Python, what say you?"

"Aye, Cap'n, that ye have."

"Then be gone with you! All of you, back to work before I swab the deck with your carcasses."

Grumbling, the pirates dispersed.

Kent sheathed his sword and proceeded.

"You can't take me away from here," Charlisse begged, her feet dragging over the wooden planks. "Please."

"Why? Because your precious Merrick is here?" Kent tugged her down a flight of stairs and into a dark companionway. "I assure you, milady, he won't be looking for you."

Kent's statement blasted her like a cannonball. Although she'd already come to the same conclusion days ago, hearing it so forcefully declared sent waves of hopelessness over her.

Releasing her arm, he retrieved a set of keys from his pocket and unlocked an iron padlock on a wooden door. He pushed it open and thrust her inside. "I am sure by now, your husband believes you are dead."

Charlisse stumbled backward over a padded, high-backed chair. The warmth drained from her body, leaving a cold numbness in its place. As she turned to face Kent, her gaze covered the modest decor of the small cabin and landed on a woman. Elegantly dressed in an emerald satin gown, she rose from the chair she'd been sitting on, a horrified expression marring her delicate features. A book slid from her hand onto the floorboards, and Kent stooped to pick it up, his soft gaze never leaving the woman.

Placing the book on a table, his eyes shifted to Charlisse and hardened. "So you see, there will be no heroic rescue from your beloved Merrick. You are mine now," he said, a faint smirk on his mouth.

His attention swung back to the woman. He smiled and shifted his stance. "I have brought you a companion, since you find my company so appalling."

The woman said nothing, only stared at Kent with proud eyes the color of jade.

His face paled.

Charlisse took a step toward him, clenching her fists. This couldn't be happening. Not when she finally had a chance of happiness with Merrick—of raising their child together. "You are wrong. I'm not yours. I'm Lady Charlisse Merrick Hyde, wife of Lord Edmund Merrick Hyde, and he *will* come for me, you'll see." Terror set every nerve on fire. She glanced out the door, her instinct to flee at full force. "Release me now, and I promise Merrick will be merciful to you when he finds you."

A wicked chuckle burst from his mouth. "Egad, you are a daft woman." He leaned toward her and lifted one dark eyebrow. "Do you think I have not been planning this very day for years? Even the news of your marriage did not deter me—in fact it made my revenge all the more sweet. There will be no doubt in your lover's mind as to your demise. I have a man in place who will swear to have found a woman's remains in the fire."

Charlisse heard the words but refused to believe them. Panic seized all rational thoughts and squeezed the hope from each one.

Tugging at the foam of white lace flowing from his sleeves, Kent straightened his silk shirt, then brushed dust from his doublet. "Who is the better pirate now? Who has the bigger ship, the most ruthless crew, the most gold? Hmm? And now that I have you—his most prized possession—I have won. He has nothing left but a silly ship and a worthless crew of ninnies."

Horrified by his jealous declarations, Charlisse was unable to speak.

He fixed her with a smoldering gaze. Purple veins throbbed on his forehead. "No one makes a mockery of Captain Kent Carlton, not you and not your husband." Regaining his composure, he lengthened his stance and grabbed the door latch.

"You will never see Merrick again."

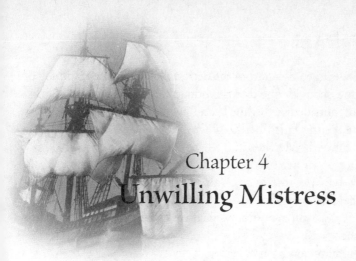

# Chapter 4
# Unwilling Mistress

Charlisse stepped back, grabbed onto a chair to keep from falling, and slowly lowered herself into it. She took deep breaths, trying to settle her tattered nerves and quell the dizziness in her head. For the baby's sake, she must remain calm. She must put her trust in God. But what if Merrick truly believed she were dead? What if he did not search for her? No one knew where she was. An arrow of panic pierced her heart, and she placed a hand over her chest, hoping to stop the pain. Bowing her head, she tried to pray but could find no words to utter, save *Why?*

The creaking of a chair to her left broke through her dismal thoughts. She had forgotten she was not alone. She looked up into green eyes brimming with tears.

The woman slumped back into her seat. A tentative smile lifted one corner of her mouth. "My name is Isabel." A tear escaped her eye and slid down her fair cheek. Wiping it, she sniffed and tucked a wayward auburn curl back into her bun.

Showered with guilt at her selfishness, Charlisse stood, approached Isabel, and eased into the chair beside her. "As I'm sure you heard, I'm Charlisse." She smiled and gazed at Isabel's tear-streaked face. Her rosy skin carried a touch of baby fat around the edges. "Why, you are just a girl."

Isabel shot her a look of indignation. "I am eighteen!"

"My apologies." Charlisse smiled and squeezed Isabel's hand.

The ship lurched, and Charlisse grabbed the chair arm. Kent's bellowing voice echoed down from the deck, followed by the tramping of boots as his crew scrambled to do his bidding. Water gushed and gurgled against the hull outside the tiny oval window.

They were leaving Porto Bello.

They were leaving Merrick.

Swallowing down her sudden fear, Charlisse gazed at Isabel. "Who are you? How did you come to be on this horrid ship?"

Isabel inhaled a deep breath, and her eyes filled with tears again. "I am a captive just as you are—imprisoned by that blackguard." Her lips trembled as she spoke.

"How long have you been here?"

Isabel shook her head. "I don't know. Months, perhaps."

"Months!" Charlisse shot up. Months imprisoned on a pirate ship—especially Captain Carlton's ship. Horrifying thoughts shot through her mind. She almost dared not look back into those glassy eyes, but when she did, she knew. She knew this poor woman had been ravished by Kent just as Charlisse nearly had been three years before.

She sat back down. Grabbing a handkerchief from the table, she dabbed at the tears streaming down Isabel's cheeks. "It's all right now."

"I know 'tis selfish of me," Isabel sobbed, "but I'm so glad you are here. I haven't had a soul to talk to besides that monster."

"How did you come to be his prisoner?"

Isabel whisked tears from her eyes and patted her hair into place. "He attacked Charles Towne, he and that villain, Morgan. Those vile creatures ransacked the whole town, plundering, murdering. . . ." Isabel hesitated and closed her eyes.

Charlisse's heart sank. She knew exactly what Isabel was talking about. She had observed that very thing only days earlier. It was too much for any gentle lady to discuss, let alone live through.

"Is that where you live, Charles Towne?"

Sitting up straight, Isabel gazed across the room. "Yes, we moved our estate from England to New Providence a year ago. . .or has it been longer? I'm afraid I've lost track of time." She cast a sheepish glance at Charlisse.

"Is your family still there? Do they know where you are?" Charlisse placed the handkerchief in Isabel's hand and leaned toward her.

"I don't know." Isabel sniffed. "My parents are Lord and Lady Ashton of Hertfordshire." She glanced at Isabel as if expecting some reaction, but then her shoulders slumped and she dabbed at her nose with the cloth.

"I shouldn't have been out that night," she continued. "Only servants should be sent on menial errands, but when my mother sent Margaret—her lady in waiting—to purchase some Mechlin lace, my father insisted I accompany her. I was the only one who knew the exact hue my mother desired. My mother is a countess, you know." She lifted her chin. "The Countess of Dorset." She sighed, then shifted her brimming eyes to Charlisse. "In any case, Margaret and I were at the mercantile when that ruffian Kent walked into the store with five of the filthiest men I had ever seen. He took one look at me, and just as if I were a piece of cloth on the rack, he hoisted me over his shoulder and dragged me to his ship. I've been here ever since."

A lump of disgust rose in Charlisse's throat. "Does the captain say nothing of releasing you?"

Isabel shook her head and sobbed.

Charlisse took the young girl in her arms. "There, there." She patted her back. "It will be all right." Isabel fell against her shoulder and clung to her. Shudders rippled through her body, rising to break free in heart-piercing wails.

"He—he—ravished me," she stuttered between sobs.

Rage churned in Charlisse's stomach. "I know."

Isabel pulled back, her red-rimmed eyes teeming with tears. "How do you know?"

Charlisse sighed. Should she tell her what atrocities Kent had orchestrated upon her and Merrick? Or would it serve only to terrify her further?

"I was in your position once—a captive of Kent's," Charlisse began, deciding to disclose only the portions of her ordeal that might bring comfort to Isabel.

The young girl's eyes widened. "Surely not?"

"Yes, I'm afraid so." Charlisse stood and paced across the tiny cabin, calling the painful memories out from hiding. "He was not a captain then. He kept me in a room similar to this one, only smaller." She gazed around, noting the oak bed, the two teakwood trunks overflowing with silks and lace, the comfortable leather chairs, the desk, and the bookshelves lined with books. A ceramic basin and a pitcher of water sat on the desk.

"Where was your husband, the man he spoke of earlier?" Isabel sniffed. "Merrick, was it?"

Charlisse nodded and turned to face her. "Yes, Captain Edmund Merrick." With just the mention of his name, grief at their separation tugged at her heart, and she looked away, wondering where he was. Was he thinking of her? "We were not married at the time. In fact, he was in prison, thrown there as a result of Kent's scheming."

Isabel scooted to the edge of her seat. "Did he. . . ? Did Kent. . . ?" Her cheeks reddened.

"No, he didn't." The ship swung abruptly to the larboard side, and Charlisse clutched the bedpost to keep from falling. She sat on the bed and ran her fingers over the silk bedcover, surprised to find such luxury on a pirate ship.

"However did you avoid his advances?" Isabel asked.

"It wasn't me." Charlisse forced herself to remember the endless days she had spent locked in the hold of the ship—the excruciating heat, the noxious stench, and the rats, hundreds of them nipping at her flesh. When Kent had dragged her up to his cabin with the intention of making her his mistress, the Lord had prevented him. "God protected me," Charlisse said.

Isabel lifted one eyebrow, then instantly narrowed her eyes. "I suppose this God of yours doesn't find me worthy of His efforts."

"That's not true." Charlisse bolted from the bed and rushed toward Isabel, sitting beside her. "Of course He does. God loves you. You are His child."

Isabel shot her a cynical look and turned away.

"Don't you believe in God?" Charlisse took her hand.

With eyes flashing, Isabel pulled her hand back and stood. "Why should I, when He has abandoned me?" She stomped toward the window, her green satin dress swishing with each step. Two silver combs inlaid with pearls sparkled from the auburn curls of her hair as she stood gazing into the darkness with head held high.

Charlisse's stomach tightened in a nauseous twist. Not three years ago, she had believed the very same thing—that because God had allowed her to be abused as a child, He did not love her, nor was she worthy of His love. *How do I help her, Lord? What shall I say?*

"I know 'tis hard to understand why God allows such tragedies in our lives," Charlisse said, "Trouble comes to all of us, but why should you endure your problems all alone when you could be under the protective care and guidance of a God who truly loves you?"

Isabel shook her head but said nothing.

Charlisse rose and began to search the drawers and the shelves, behind books. She would not sit still and do nothing.

Isabel's icy voice shattered the silence. "If your God has not abandoned you, then why are you on board this vile ship, suffering the same fate as I?"

The question unearthed doubts long since buried and forgotten. Why *had* God allowed this to happen to her—*again*? Charlisse had no explanation—could not imagine what good purpose could come of any of this, but she must believe God had a plan and that He was still in control. With a huff, she continued searching the shelves in silence.

"What are you doing?" Isabel demanded.

Charlisse turned to see Isabel's features twist into a frustrated pout. "I'm looking for weapons." She spun back around and sifted through the remainder of the books, peering behind each one. Nothing.

Frustrated, she plodded to the bed and sank onto the plush bedcover. The ship had settled into a gentle roll reminding her exhausted body of the late hour. She motioned for Isabel to come sit with her. Hesitant at first, she finally gave in and sat, glancing at Charlisse. Her tears had dried into a cold shield that guarded the emotions behind her eyes.

Charlisse leaned toward her. "Whatever you believe about what has happened, you are not alone now. I am here with you." She placed her arm around Isabel's shoulder.

The young girl's smile faltered on her lips. "What on earth were you doing in Porto Bello? And you are with child." She nodded toward Charlisse's belly as if she'd just noticed.

"Yes, five months along." Charlisse slid a hand over her rounded stomach. "My husband is a pirate—or he used to be." She chuckled. "Now he works as a privateer for the British, but he has his own mission to rid the Caribbean of wicked pirates and bring as many of them to God as he can. We were in Porto Bello hoping to find the Portuguese pirate,

Manoel Rivero Pardal, visiting his mistress who lives there." She sighed, remembering she'd insisted on accompanying Merrick despite his fears for her safety. When she looked up, distress creased Isabel's brow. "Don't worry," Charlisse said, "my husband will come for us."

"But doesn't he believe you are dead?"

"He is far too smart to fall for one of Kent's tricks. I know him. He's looking for me right now." She glanced away, desperately hoping it was true. Then, smiling at Isabel, she gave her hand a squeeze. "He is a fierce warrior, and he has already beaten Kent both on land and at sea."

If Charlisse had comforted Isabel at all with her words, she could not tell from the young girl's blank expression. Charlisse opened her lips to further encourage her, but the clank of a latch sounded, and the door burst open, startling them both.

Kent stomped inside, his gaze first landing on Isabel and lingering there before jumping to Charlisse. "I see you two have become friends already." His massive body swayed, and the pungent odor of rum wafted over them.

Charlisse sprang from the bed. "You deceive yourself, sir, if you believe that commanding a bigger ship, brandishing more powerful cannons, and even capturing me will ever make you more of a man than Merrick!"

Isabel grabbed Charlisse's hand and tried to pull her back even as Charlisse took another bold step toward the intruder. The glowing tan on Kent's face colored to a flaming burgundy. His upper lip twitched.

"In fact, you are nothing but a spineless, ill-tempered cur," Charlisse added, "and no amount of trinkets or trophies will ever alter that."

"No, don't. . . ," Isabel said in a small voice as she tugged on Charlisse's sleeve.

Charlisse glanced over her shoulder at the young girl who shook her head in warning and returned Charlisse's gaze with a wide-eyed stare. Strong arms snatched Charlisse's shoulders and spun her back around.

"I will not suffer your impertinent tongue, woman!" Kent roared. A sardonic expression drove his fury into a wicked grin. "Ah, but perhaps you are correct. Perhaps I am the rogue you insist I am." His glance moved to Isabel. "Miss Ashton seems to share your opinion, do you not, milady? Perhaps you should instruct Lady Charlisse Hyde on the benefits of stilling her sharp tongue. But nevertheless. . ." He tossed his other hand through the air while Charlisse struggled against his grip. "I believe a lesson must be learned."

With a twist of her arm, he dragged her out the door. She cast an uneasy glance at Isabel, before the solid oak door cloaked her from view.

After Kent bolted the lock, he wrenched her arm behind her and forced her down a long hallway. Kicking open a hefty door, he thrust her inside. He followed her in, closed the door, and began unbuckling his baldric.

"Now, for unfinished business."

# Chapter 5
# Memories

Captain Merrick stood at the bow of the *Redemption*, arms crossed over his chest. The sliver of a moon frowned down on him from a night sky as stormy as his raging thoughts. With each heave of his mighty ship, sea spray blasted over him. The shot of rum he had downed a minute ago was having no effect, either in warming his belly, or in numbing his pain. Perhaps he needed another.

Images of the blazing church—the last place he had seen Charlisse—consumed his visions day and night. Was it only the church that had burned? For as he'd stood and watched the fire consume the last timber of sacred rubble, the blaze of bitterness in his soul seemed to consume the last of his faith along with it. Unable to pray, unable to utter even a word to the God who'd allowed this to happen, he encased himself in a lonely shell of self-pity.

"Charlisse." Just the sound of her name coming from his lips flung spikes of agony through every part of him, more painful than any sword thrust had ever been. Was she truly gone? His mind believed she was, but his heart was not yet convinced.

Yet it was for her that he had gone back, as promised, to assist the don in the defense of his hacienda. It had taken two days, and he had fulfilled his obligation.

Charlisse would have liked that.

Those two days seemed like a dream to him now, events that had happened in the dark recesses of his mind during fitful slumber. A dozen pirates had lost their lives at the tip of his sword, and he had felt nothing, not anger, nor even hatred—just a pervasive numbness that had invaded his soul the day Charlisse died and spread outward like a plague.

Afterward, when he had returned to the church, a priest rummaging through the smoking debris assured him they had found the charred remains of a woman and several children and had given them a proper burial. Because of the priest's despondency over the loss of the orphans, and the evidence of the gravesites themselves, Merrick had no reason to doubt him. Yet deep within his heart, a spark of Charlisse remained lit. It would not go out, no matter how hard his mind tried to extinguish it. Was she still alive? Or was it only a foolish husband's hope?

He would have stayed by her grave, would have been there still, if Morgan's pirates had not continued their rampage of the city. Even then, he intended to fight until the blood of every last one of them poured out on the streets of Porto Bello in retribution for what they had done to Charlisse. It was Sloane, his friend and quartermaster, who had finally pulled Merrick away, convincing him that he and his crew would die in the attempt. Not that it mattered to Merrick whether he died, but then how could he get his revenge from the grave?

*Vengeance is mine. . .saith the Lord.* The words swept through his thoughts, shining light into the dark corners already smoldering with hatred. Merrick shook his head, trying to dislodge them.

Heavy boots thumped across the deck behind him, but he could not force himself to turn and see who it was.

"Cap'n." Jackson's deep voice filtered to Merrick's ears. His tone was softer than the man's usual thunderous baritone.

"Cap'n, beggin' yer pardon, but where should we be headin'?"

Merrick scanned the darkness, the chaotic sea barely distinguishable from the night sky save for the flecks of silvery foam reflecting the moonlight. "Continue on our present course," he said without turning.

"But, Cap'n, that'll lead us straight through the storm's path."

Sloane appeared beside Merrick, his pet monkey, Solomon, perched on his shoulder.

Annoyance pricked at Merrick's skin. He just wanted to be left alone. "Then into the storm we will go!" he bellowed and lifted his hand in dismissal. The massive, dark man retreated. Guilt assailed Merrick. He didn't mean to be so harsh. Jackson had proven his loyalty as first mate on more than one perilous venture.

Sloane shuffled his feet. The monkey squealed.

"What?" Merrick asked.

"I didn't say nothin', Cap'n."

"But you wish to."

Scratching his beard, Sloane looked at Merrick. "I knows ye feel like yer innards been sliced open and left t' dry on the sand, but it's jest that ye aren't normally as hard on the men as ye been as of late."

Merrick gritted his teeth, stomped to the railing, and clutched it with both hands. He gazed down as the bow rose and plunged in the sea, slicing a frothy *V* into the dark, murky waters. The *Redemption* sped onward to her next adventure as if nothing had happened—as if the most precious angel ever to grace the planet had not been taken from him. Did life truly go on after such a loss? He couldn't imagine it.

He knew Sloane meant well, but the hollow ache in his chest left no room for anything. . .not for his men, not for his ship, and not for himself. A chill came over him though the night was warm. Icy fingers raked down his spine, urging him to fling himself into the peaceful oblivion of the sea—to end the pain and emptiness. But no. He had unfinished business. Someone must pay for Charlisse's death. He pounded on the rail and swung around abruptly. "I need more rum."

"Naw, Cap'n." Sloane stepped out of the way of Merrick's advance. "That won't do ye no good."

Ignoring him, Merrick leapt down the foredeck steps and stormed across the main deck. A puff of rain-laden wind tugged at his hair. A rumble of thunder protested in the distance. Down the companionway, he burst into his cabin and headed straight for his desk, opening and slamming drawers. He ran his hand across the back of his neck, sprang to the shelves that lined the wall, and tossed books to the floor. A sparkle of amber flickered in the corner of his eye, and he swerved to see a half-empty bottle of rum on a table to his right. Grabbing the flask, he uncorked it and took a deep swig, then sank into one of the leather chairs, clutching the bottle as if it held the remedy to all that ailed him. He hadn't allowed the pungent liquor to touch his lips in quite some time, years in fact. After he'd given his life to Christ, he'd only had a few swigs now and then, but with each year that passed, his thirst for the vile liquid had lessened. It did naught but weaken him and dull his senses—a fool's drink, to be sure. But tonight, he felt like a fool, and he feared if he didn't numb the pain in his heart, it would kill him by morning.

Tipping the bottle again, he allowed a large gulp of the dark, potent liquid to slide down his throat, radiating warmth to everything it touched. He leaned his head back and closed his eyes. A slight hum began to mute the cry of his heart, followed by a callous sensation that pounded through his veins, offering a deception of euphoria.

When he opened his eyes, a blur of red satin teased his vision. Charlisse's gown peeked from the half-closed armoire. He shifted his gaze over to the bed draped with the silk sheets she had chosen from a mercantile in Barbados. A cautious smile lifted his lips as he remembered their argument that day.

"Pirates don't have pink silk sheets on their bed!" he had protested.

"They do if they are no longer pirates and want to please their new wives." She sidled up to him, pressing her soft curves against him, and offered him those wide blue eyes in a look of playful entreaty. "And they are not pink," she'd insisted. "They are coral." As soon as he gazed at her, he knew he was lost. Coral sheets it would be—anything to keep her smiling at him like that forever.

*Have some more rum. It will ease your pain.*

He raised the bottle to his lips again and gulped down a long swallow. His eyes landed on the mahogany vanity in the corner. A carved Italian mirror sat atop it. French bristle brushes, bottles of scented oils, and Charlisse's favorite hair combs lay scattered across it. She had never been very tidy.

Feeling his heart jump to his throat and threaten to suffocate him, he ripped his gaze from the spot, but found it migrating to a pair of her silk slippers sitting underneath the bed. The embroidered details blurred as his eyes filled with moisture. He jumped up. Her gowns, her shoes, the sheets, the vanity, all twirled around him, laughing at him, taunting him. Charlisse's smiling face floated around amidst them all. He could even smell her scent—sweet lilacs.

All she had ever wanted was to settle down someplace safe and have children, but in his selfishness, he had delayed her wishes, seeking the adventures of the sea and wanting to fulfill his promise to God that he would rid the Caribbean of wicked pirates. Now, what he wouldn't give to have her and their child nestled in a safe, comfortable home. Why was he always so stubborn?

He lifted the flask in his hand, intending to throw it at the vanity, to destroy the memories forever, but couldn't. Instead, he hurled it against the far wall, sending an ear-piercing crash through the room and showering rum and glass over the bed. Drops marred the satin pillow where the indent of her head remained. Was that a strand of her golden hair still lying there? He shook his head, hoping for the rum to swallow him up and drown the agonizing images. Crumbling to the floor, he wished he could shatter like the bottle of rum and blast himself all over the room until bit by bit he seeped into the wooden planks. Then he would forever be a part of the place where her memory lingered so strong.

"Why, God?" he wailed, "Why?"

Charlisse froze in place and glanced around Kent's cabin. A chill fell over her and bristled the hair on her arms. Kent smirked and tossed his baldric onto a table. Terrifying images emerged from Charlisse's memory—all-too-familiar pictures of Kent tossing the same baldric aside, wearing the same sneer on his lips. Only the surroundings differed. Now, she stood in the center of a plush captain's cabin. Then, he had dragged her down into the dank hold of the *Redemption*.

Charlisse took a step back and gazed over the room, searching for a pistol, a knife, a cane—anything with which she could defend herself. A broad stained-glass window peered out upon an onyx sea. In front of it stood an imposing mahogany desk covered with charts, books, quill pens, and a sextant, all organized in a methodical fashion. Three velvet-covered chairs cornered a small table on which two bottles of rum, one half-empty, waited. Behind Charlisse, Kent's four-poster bed consumed the port side of the room, save for a French armoire with dark walnut-paneled doors. She saw no weapons—only the cutlass and pistols stuffed in Kent's baldric. A whiff of leather and rum assaulted her nostrils.

"Oh God, help me," Charlisse whispered. She closed her eyes and held back the tears that threatened to fill them. Cradling her stomach in her hands, she thought of her innocent child growing within her—Merrick's child.

Kent took a step toward Charlisse. A look of terror consumed her face—the same look of terror he'd seen contort her features on Merrick's ship three years ago. But something else flickered in her expression, a strength and determination that had not been there before. Grabbing a bottle of rum from a table, Kent tipped it to his lips and took a full draught, allowing the caustic liquid to burn his throat and further dull his senses. The room swirled around him, and he plunged into a chair. What was he doing? He didn't want Charlisse—had no desire to harm her. He gazed at her as she backed against the far wall. Her eyes darted about the room.

Belching, Kent leaned forward on his knees, examining the cracks and stains marring his wooden floor. How long had he waited to get his revenge on Captain Merrick—how long had he planned this very night? Of course he hadn't planned on Lady Ashton being on board—or in his life for that matter. But since his plan to capture Charlisse had been successful, he hoped she would provide some comfort for Isabel.

But why had he dragged Charlisse to his cabin? Now Isabel would surely see him as the scoundrel she believed him to be. He'd only wanted to still the woman's insolent tongue, and his temper had gotten the best of him—as it always did when emboldened by rum.

"I won't hurt you." He gazed up at the blurred vision of Charlisse as she fingered a lock of her hair.

"Why should I believe you?" she snapped.

Indeed why should she? But how could he explain to her that he had no desire for any woman save Lady Ashton. How could he tell her that something had changed inside him when he couldn't explain it to himself?

"Believe what you want." Kent stood, and the ship pitched hard to starboard. Charlisse stumbled and grabbed the bedpost. Her features twisted in alarm. Two lanterns swung from their hooks above them, squeaking and casting eerie shadows across the room.

"Never fear, milady, 'tis only a storm up ahead." He staggered, catching his balance. "We shall miss the brunt of it, but the strong winds will hasten us to our destination."

"And where might that be?"

"To Port Royal, of course. I have business to attend to." He grinned. "Ah, isn't that where you and that jackal, Merrick, got married?" He tilted his head and smirked. "How quaint."

"What do you truly want with me, Kent?" A quiver tainted her voice. He sauntered toward her.

Charlisse backed away.

"Captain Carlton, if you please." He peered down his nose at her. She was beautiful, she'd always been beautiful, but he realized now that he'd only wanted her because she'd chosen Merrick and not him. "I want nothing from you save the pain your absence causes your husband."

He reached up to brush a lock of her hair from her face. She flinched, her nose crinkling, and glared up at him. "Please, it's over. You're a great captain now. You command your own ship. You sail with the notorious pirate Morgan. You have nothing more to prove."

Kent turned, stormed to the window, and gazed out upon the black night. "Indeed, I need prove myself to no one, especially not a pirate's whore like you." Then why did her words sting him so much? He was a great pirate—respected and feared, a commander of men. If only his father could see him now. *I am not the incompetent buffoon you thought I was, Father. I possess more power, more wealth than you ever did, or my favored brother, and especially more than the infamous Captain Edmund Merrick.* Yet somehow the success did not feel as sweet as he'd hoped it would.

"What do you intend to do with me?" Charlisse asked. Her slippers scuffed over the floor, but Kent did not turn around. He did not want her to see the mist clouding his eyes.

"I haven't decided. I suppose it depends on your behavior."

"Merrick will never stop looking for me."

"Indeed?" Kent swerved around and strutted to the table. "Why search for the dead? He'll soon move on to the next trollop."

Charlisse swallowed hard, her lip trembling.

Kent allowed his gaze to rove over her and noticed the swell of her abdomen. He grinned. "Putting on weight, I see?"

"I carry my husband's child." She threw back her shoulders.

"Merrick's brat? What good news! Alas, I've stolen two precious things from him instead of only one." Kent's fortune seemed to be improving.

What horrors poor Merrick must be suffering, having lost both wife and child! He only wished he were there to watch his agony.

"I demand you release me at once." Charlisse bunched her fists, eyes blazing, surprising him with her courage. "And Lady Ashton, as well."

"You? Demand? Faith, woman, you grate on my nerves nearly as much as Merrick did." He grabbed the bottle of rum and tossed his head back. "Besides, Lady Ashton remains with me." Forever if he had his way, for he could not bear the thought of losing her. "And you therefore must remain to keep her company."

Charlisse huffed. "She is a lady and should not be forced to be your mistress."

So Isabel had told Charlisse what he'd done. Unfamiliar shame dragged his heart down and he looked away. He gulped another swig of rum and slammed the bottle on the table. He'd not meant to hurt her. Memories of that night swirled in a blurry mass in his mind. Caught up in the thrill of a successful raid and an overindulgence in rum, he barely remembered capturing her and bringing her on board. After that night, he'd done everything to make it up to her—showered her with gifts, fed her the best food—but she'd shunned his every attempt to make amends. Instead, after spending hours with her, he found himself mesmerized by her—her intelligence, charm, kind heart, the soft tilt of her head when she gazed at him with those green eyes.

As he thought of Isabel, a smile began to form on his lips, and he immediately replaced it with a sneer. "She will be my mistress if I so desire it." Kent tore away from Charlisse's accusing glare and marched to the window again, turning his back to her. Forcing down his emotions, he regained a stoic expression. Feelings were a sign of weakness, and he would not be weak—never again.

Scuffing sounds came from behind him. The poor lady no doubt made her way to the door in hopes of escaping. But where could she go? He must decide what to do with her. He had no desire to keep her on his ship forever.

A bell sounded, indicating the change of the night watch, but no sooner did the chiming end then the cock of a pistol cracked the air. Kent spun around to see the shaking barrel of a gun pointed straight at his head.

# Chapter 6
# The Tempest

Pain throbbed through Merrick's head, calling to him. He ignored it. Another jab struck him from the left and beckoned him from his stupor. He didn't want to come out. For in this place, there was peace—if only temporary—and he hadn't been here long enough to stifle the agony of his heart. Wood scraped against his skin, and something hit him in the thigh. Opening one eye, he saw an oak table swinging toward his face. Shock jolted him awake, and he reached up to grab the wooden leg before it struck him. Sounds of creaking wood and howling wind barged into his placid mind, bringing him out of his trance. He hobbled to his feet and clung to the bedpost to keep from falling. His door swung open.

"Cap'n!" Sloane's drenched frame filled the doorway. "We've lost the top gallant and rigging in the storm."

Angry determination swept away the remaining haze in Merrick's mind. Pushing his friend aside, he barreled up the companionway steps. A blast of seawater struck him and tore the breath from his throat. His feet flew off the deck, and he slid across the slippery wood on his back, arms flailing in the tempest of wind and rain. He crashed into the bulwarks and grabbed the edge as he toppled over the side. The angry sea licked hungrily at his boots. A rope flinging in the wind zipped in front of him, and he grabbed it, hoisting himself back onto the deck. *Thank You, Lord.*

Yet why was he grateful? Surely, a watery grave would drown his pain. He glanced across the ship and saw the blurred shapes of his men struggling—men who had put their trust in him as captain. Concern for their safety raged against his apathy.

Pulling himself up, he lunged toward the main deck railing and hung on as the ship lurched first in one direction then the other. A river of water cascaded over the deck, carrying Jackson in its torrent, and Merrick reached out just in time to save him from tumbling into the angry sea. The black man nodded in appreciation. Merrick helped him grab the railing and glanced upward. Bare top yards, void of sails, pierced the charred sky. The broken riggings zipped through the air like deadly whips, nearly striking one of his crew. The man slipped and fell, colliding with the capstan.

Panic exploded into fury. "I want every man tied to a lifeline!" Merrick yelled to Jackson over the din. "Strike lower yards and top masts!"

Jackson nodded and clawed his way to the main deck stairs, howling orders to the crew.

The ship leveled again. Sloane approached, bracing himself against the wind. The gale whistled through the riggings and sails with a hideous moan that sent a shiver through Merrick.

Wiping the rain from his face, he turned to Sloane. Saltwater stung his eyes, and a sharp pain emanated from his chest where he had hit the bulwarks. Lightning etched a ragged sword across the sky, followed by a boom of thunder that shook the ship to its keel. Yet Merrick felt no fear—only a fierce determination to save his crew and his ship.

"Cap'n, the water's rising in the hold."

"Tell Smack and Gunny to man the pumps!" Merrick bellowed. The ship plunged over a massive wave and pitched to the port side. Sloane strained to maintain a grip, and Merrick leaned toward him. "Tie on a lifeline." The quartermaster nodded, spitting seawater from his mouth.

Merrick stomped across the glassy deck, bracing himself against the death tilt. He stared up into the black swirling clouds.

Sloane came up beside him and held out a rope. "A lifeline for ye, Cap'n."

Ignoring him, Merrick pulled the fallen man up from the capstan, where he lay dazed from the storm. A wall of water struck them from the side, stinging Merrick's face. He shook it off and grabbed Sloane and the other man just as a fierce gust of wind blasted over them. The three men locked their arms over the capstan. Their feet left the deck when the ship lurched to the starboard side, groaning under the strain.

When they were able to stand again, Merrick recognized the third man as Mason, the ship's carpenter. Streams of water plunged off his wide-brimmed hat. His long hair hung in saturated strands. Between blasts of wind, Merrick saw fear skipping across his eyes. The man had just turned eighteen, and this was his first sea voyage—probably his first storm, as well.

"Get below and help with the pumps, Mason." Merrick slapped the young man on the back. Mason nodded, relief upturning his lips, and jumped down the companionway stairs.

A rod of lightning arrowed toward the ship, and thunder bellowed its warning of doom, sending a tremble through the hull that reached Merrick's boots.

The captain marched up the quarterdeck steps. Rusty, his helmsman, clung to the whipstaff in a tight grip with both arms, but managed a slight smile at the sight of his captain.

Through the tempest, Merrick made out the blurred shapes of four of his crewmen climbing the swaying ratlines to detach sections of the masts. Only then would they be able to hoist the storm sails on the lowered gallants and royals and achieve some maneuverability in the agitated sea. One of the men slipped and dangled for a moment before the wind picked him up and tossed him about as if he were a paper doll. Merrick's heart leapt. *No.* He would not be responsible for another death! The ship pitched and tossed the man back into the ratlines, where he found his footing once again, and Merrick released a sigh.

Giant swells of indigo capped in ivory surged and fell, crashing into the depths with the boom of a cannon blast. The power of the sea, untamed, unpredictable. Merrick had both craved and feared its strength and supremacy. A storm such as this one had brought Charlisse to him. Perhaps it would be this storm that would sweep him away to join her.

Merrick braced himself against the fierce wind and frowned at the seething clouds. "What do You want from me?" he spat under his breath, feeling his own rage rise to match the violent squall surrounding him.

The dark, riotous mass swarmed above him, but no answer came.

When he looked down, Sloane stood next to him.

The ship lunged to the larboard side with masts creaking and wailing. Several of his men clambered up the quarterdeck stairs, hunched against the pounding rain. They stopped before him and steadied themselves on the rocking ship. "Cap'n," one of them shouted. "What are yer orders?"

Merrick scanned their faces as they waited his instruction. Fierce pirates all, yet despite the fear burning in their eyes, they trusted his expertise and relied on him for their safety. He couldn't let them down, no matter how little he cared for his own life. He must save his crew.

Giving each of them an affirming nod, he bellowed orders over the roar of the storm, sending the crew lumbering over the deck to do his bidding.

A shard of lightning flashed across the sky. Merrick glanced up. *All right, Lord. It is Your will I want. . .it has always been Your will.*

Thunder boomed through the ship and threatened to tear it asunder. Was that the Almighty's angry reply?

Sloane teetered upon the swaying ship and nearly lost his footing.

"Get below, my old friend!" Merrick yelled.

The quartermaster shook his head and nearly fell. "Naw, Cap'n, my place be next to ye."

"Then at least hold onto the railing, you old fool." Merrick grabbed his friend as a mighty wave crashed over them. When the water receded, Sloane coughed, gasping for air.

Muted light drew Merrick's attention upward, where a section of the dark sky had brightened. Gray clouds swirled in a chaotic dance of twisted shapes that seemed to calm the sea beneath them. Mesmerized, Merrick stared at the whirling mist until his vision began playing tricks on him. He thought he saw Charlisse. She smiled at him, but the wind picked up again, and the image dissipated.

Swinging about, Merrick helped Rusty wrench the whipstaff to the correct position.

A flash split the sky in two, and the bulging clouds uttered a defiant clap of thunder. The muscles in Merrick's arms strained. He watched the shadowy figures of his crew swaying with the teetering of the ship.

A ray of sunlight broke through the dark mass above them and landed upon the ship like an arrow of hope. The sting of the rain on Merrick's arms lessened as the growl of the storm dulled to a mere groan.

Releasing the whipstaff to Rusty's care, Merrick stomped to the railing and scanned the brightening horizon. Up ahead, the seas quieted.

He glanced over his shoulder at the black, retreating clouds. They spit one final blast upon the ship, and Merrick gripped the railing as the crest of a wave reached over the deck, searching for a victim, before tumbling back over the side. The wind died down and only a sprinkle of rain showered upon them. The massive swells decreased into rolling waves, and the ship ceased its violent tottering.

Sloane winked at Merrick. "Seems to me like He still hears ye." He nodded up toward the clearing sky.

"Humph." Merrick shook his head, unimpressed. "Perhaps."

Jackson plodded up the steps, his bulky form slick from rain and his bald head shining in the emerging light. The three gold earrings in his left ear shimmered against his dark, wet skin. "Good job, Jackson," Merrick said when the first mate halted before him. "Report."

The huge man grunted. "No casualties, Cap'n. Jest a few repairs needed to the top gallants and riggings on the main mast."

Merrick nodded, feeling suddenly calm. He shoved his wet hair back from his face. "Then let's get to it."

He fixed his gaze on the gloomy horizon, remembering the vision of Charlisse in the clouds, and thought of their wedding day. He pictured them kneeling before the altar in the tiny church at Port Royal with only slaves, orphans, and pirates in attendance. Reverend Thomas—Merrick's longtime friend—had stood in front of them, open Bible in hand, as they repeated their vows. Perhaps the reverend could help Merrick make some sense out of Charlisse's death.

"Where to, Cap'n?" Jackson asked.

"Port Royal," Merrick said. "Let us make haste to Port Royal."

As soon as Kent turned his back to her, Charlisse took a tentative step toward the chair on which his baldric and pistols lay. With every nerve ignited, she stepped forward again. The floorboards creaked beneath her silk shoes. She held her breath and looked up. Still, he did not move. Spikes of terror shot through her heart, sending a dizzying rush of blood to her head. No, she could not faint now! Her stomach rumbled, and a pool of nausea threatened to rise in her throat.

Another step. Somewhere on the ship, a bell rang. One more step and she would have it.

Kent coughed and put his hands on his hips.

Charlisse sprang forward, grabbed a pistol, cocked it, and aimed it at his head.

He spun around, his eyes widening in shock, but then a brazen smirk overtook his features. "You won't shoot me." He took a step toward her.

With a gulp, Charlisse forced down a burst of nausea that had jumped into her throat. The gun weighed heavily in her sweaty hands and threatened to slip between her fingers and drop to the floor. She knew it was too late to turn back. Could she really fire upon a man?

"I will shoot you if you force my hand," she said in her most courageous voice, but her quivering hands gave away her fear.

Kent stared unmoving at her, his dark, fuming eyes shifting between hers and the barrel of the gun.

Charlisse took a step back. "You will escort Miss Ashton and me to the nearest civilized port."

"And what are your plans after you kill me? Taking on the whole crew with one pistol?" His mouth curved into a disarming smile.

The gun shook in her hands, oscillating its aim across Kent's massive chest. She had not thought that far ahead. If she shot him, she and Isabel would be at the mercy of these ruffians.

"If I have to," she said. "Besides, I'm not alone. God is with me."

"Ah yes, you and your husband's weak God. Where is He now?" Kent sneered and waved a jeweled hand in the air. "It seems He has abandoned you along with Merrick, milady." He leaned toward her. "Perhaps they are together somewhere, enjoying their freedom."

Raw anger ignited within Charlisse, lit by childhood memories of being abandoned—being unloved. Her trembling ceased as the rage spread from her heart to her fingers. "And what of you? Does it make you feel like a big, powerful pirate to capture and assault innocent women? Why Lady Ashton is but a young girl. You should be ashamed of yourself."

Kent grimaced. "She is none of your concern."

Charlisse lifted a brow. "Yet you have made her my concern by throwing us together."

"Then I shall toss you in the hold where you belong." He darted forward and seized the bottle of rum from the table, keeping an eye on the gun in her hand. "If I recall, you are quite fond of rats."

Charlisse shivered at the memory of the voracious rodents, but she ignored his threat, curious at his reaction to Isabel's name. The pistol slipped in her sweaty grip. She quickly leveled it again, her arm aching under the weight. "Why should a young lady cause you such discomfort?"

Kent gulped the amber liquor and wiped his mouth. He fixed her with a hard gaze but quickly shifted it away.

Was it possible he cared for this woman? Charlisse found it hard to believe that he could care for anyone but himself. "Perhaps you'd have more success with women if you didn't capture and ravish them."

Kent pointed the flask of rum at her. "I have no trouble acquiring women!" Then slamming it on the table, he blared out a string of curses.

Charlisse gulped and tightened her grip on the wavering gun. "Women are not spoils of your trade. Must you win at everything?"

"Yes," he barked. "Pray tell, what else is there?" His lips twitched below eyes seething with bitterness.

"Enough! What must I do to curb that shrewish tongue of yours?" Fury flamed from his gaze. He lunged at Charlisse and grabbed the pistol, twisting it in her grip.

Charlisse struggled, clinging to it with all her strength. The gun fired. A cloud of smoke enveloped her, and the acrid smell of gunpowder stung her nose. The pistol fell from her slippery hands. Kent threw the smoking weapon into the corner and clutched his side. Blood oozed between his fingers. Shock and anger twisted his features.

Without warning, Kent slammed his hands into Charlisse's shoulders. Her body flew backward. She lost her footing over the legs of the fallen chair and tumbled into the bedpost. Sharp pains bolted through her back and into her head. She fell onto the hard wooden floor, dazed.

A burning spasm shot through her belly.

# Chapter 7
# With Child

Something cold and moist touched Charlisse's forehead, and the sensation radiated through her mind, prying open the doors of her slumber. She heard the creaking of wood and the swish of satin. A bright light darted across her eyelids, taunting her to open them. She didn't want to open them, for she feared if she did, the dull ache in her abdomen would only increase. A moan escaped her lips. Another rustle of satin, and then a soft hand enfolded hers. Charlisse cracked open one eye to see Isabel's concerned face leaning over her.

Taking the cool cloth from Charlisse's head, Isabel dabbed it across her brow. "How do you feel, Lady Hyde?"

"Plea. . .please call me Charlisse," she said in a scratchy voice.

Isabel's lips curved in a weak smile. Placing the cloth on a table, she grabbed a pitcher and poured water into a mug. "You must be thirsty." She held out the cup and reached behind Charlisse's back to assist her.

Charlisse slowly forced herself to her elbows, fighting a wave of dizziness that threatened to plunge her back onto the bed. Clasping the mug, she drew a long gulp of the refreshing liquid, hoping to soothe the desert in her mouth. She glanced around the cabin where she had first met Isabel and noted the glaring sunshine angling through the porthole, scattering its shimmering rays over the bed and down onto the floorboards.

"How long have I been asleep?"

"For hours, I'm afraid." Isabel took the mug, placed it back on the table, and rose. "One of Kent's odious men carried you here—"

Charlisse widened her eyes. "I shot Kent."

Isabel's gaze darted to hers. "You shot him?" Her hand flew to her mouth; a sudden fear clamped her heart. "When? How?"

Charlisse threw her feet over the side of the bed and sat up. Wincing, she clutched her stomach and bent over.

Isabel clasped her arm. "Are you ill?" She helped her lean back onto the pillows and touched the back of her hand to Charlisse's cheek. "You're feverish." Grabbing the moist cloth, she patted Charlisse's forehead. "You must rest—for the baby's sake." The thought of losing her new friend so soon and being all alone on this ship again sent waves of panic through Isabel.

Charlisse took a deep breath and caressed her stomach. Tears filled her eyes.

Isabel clutched Charlisse's hand. "Did you kill him?"

"I don't think so." Charlisse pressed her temples. "Truthfully, I don't remember."

Isabel sat beside her friend, adjusting her skirts in an elegant curve around her feet. Why did she care if the rogue were dead—especially after what he'd done to her? She gazed at Charlisse. Tears slid down her friend's cheeks. "What happened? Did he—?"

"No." Charlisse shook her head. "He has no interest in me."

"Your God seems to favor you." Isabel rose from the bed and turned away, bitterness gnawing at her heart.

"God has no favorites."

With a snort, Isabel paced to the window and scratched a rising itch on her arms.

Kent's low, growling voice roared from above them, drawing her gaze upward. He was alive. Relief filtered through her. But why? Surely, it had nothing to do with Kent and everything to do with the fact that he alone stood between his crew of cutthroats and her and Charlisse.

"You have your answer, then," Charlisse said.

"So it seems."

The clomping of heavy boots sounded from outside in the companion-way, followed by the clank of key and latch in a tangled battle for entrance.

The door burst open, and Kent stomped in, stylishly dressed in leather breeches, a white silk shirt, and a black lace neckerchief. He stood fully armed, an impertinent smirk plastered on his lips.

Isabel swung about to face him.

"Ah, I perceive your displeasure at seeing me alive and quite vigorous, milady," he said to Charlisse.

"My only displeasure is in seeing you at all," Charlisse snapped.

Kent took a step forward and winced.

"How's your side, sir?" Charlisse asked with a tilt of her head.

"That's *Captain*, if you please." Kent's upper lip twitched. "And 'tis only a flesh wound. Nothing to trouble yourself with."

Charlisse smiled. "Never fear, I won't give it a second thought."

Isabel shifted her stance, pulling Kent's attention in her direction. He made a deep bow with a sweep of his jeweled hand and extended her a rakish grin. "Lady Ashton, you look as charming as ever."

Offering him a smug look, Isabel took a step backward and stumbled over one of the teakwood chests.

Strong arms grabbed her waist, assisting her upright. She looked up to see Kent's brown eyes warmly perusing her. Jerking from his grasp, she backed against the wall, confused by both the attraction and fear battling within her.

Kent's face drained of color. Straightening his neckerchief, he lengthened his stance with a huff. Finally, he retreated and cleared his throat. "I would be honored to have you join me for supper in my cabin tonight," he said to Isabel.

"Does she have a choice?" Charlisse asked sharply.

Kent's gaze swerved to the bed. "As I have said, this is none of your affair." With a hand on the pommel of his sword, he sauntered toward Charlisse. "If you hadn't swooned, I would have thrown you in the hold where you belong."

"I will join you in your cabin, Captain." Isabel cut in, hoping to draw his attention away from Charlisse. "If you will do something for me." Truth be told, the evenings spent in his company had not passed so unpleasantly, and she might as well use his desire for her company to her best advantage.

"At your service, milady." Kent nodded with a grin that seemed to bring the color back to his cheeks.

"Lady Hyde suffers from a fever." She nodded toward Charlisse. "Please have some decent food sent to us at once."

Kent's nostrils flared at her commanding tone. "I'll see to it immediately."

"And a walk up on deck," Isabel added. "This cabin reeks of perspiration and filth." She raised her chin in the air.

"As you wish." Kent fumbled with his baldric as he stared at Isabel, then dropped his gaze uncomfortably. "Until tonight, milady," he said without looking up. Turning, he headed out into the hallway and tripped over the rug before he slammed and locked the door behind him.

Charlisse coughed. "You shouldn't have done that for me."

Isabel shook her head and lowered herself into a leather chair. "He would force me to join him in any case. Better to get some food and a jaunt on deck for my trouble."

Moaning, Charlisse crawled off the bed and took the chair next to Isabel, a look of pain piercing her eyes. "There must be something we can do to stop him. No lady should have to endure what you suffer every time you are summoned to his cabin."

Isabel sighed. " 'Tis not so bad, really. He has not touched me since the first night."

"Not touched you?" Charlisse's brows lifted. "Then why does he summon you? What do you do when you are there?"

"We dine." Isabel shrugged. "And quite well, I might add."

"You have dinner?"

"And he talks to me," Isabel said.

"Whatever about?"

Isabel stood and patted the combs in her hair. "His ship, his plans, his adventures. I don't know, many different topics." Despite his vocation, Kent possessed a stimulating intellect and an abundance of interesting stories that had kept her well entertained. She'd never met anyone like him—especially not in Hertfordshire. "It's as if two people exist within him. I don't know what to make of it."

"Be careful, Isabel. He is not to be trusted."

Isabel knew she was right. Captain Carlton was not a man to contend with. Memories of that night still gripped claws of terror around her heart. Yet something in his eyes told her that he would not hurt her again. That he was sorry he'd hurt her. Was it only wishful thinking?

"So, you grew up in Hertfordshire?" Charlisse asked. "I spent my childhood in London."

"Yes, my father had a grand mansion." Isabel pictured the huge manor perched on rolling green hills surrounded by oak and beech trees. "We were very happy there."

*"Had?"*

"Yes, we lost our fortune in the Great Fire." Isabel sank into the chair, the strength suddenly draining from her legs. "My father's profitable mercantile business and all his merchandise went up in smoke that night in London. All we had left was our home and the land it stood upon."

"Oh my, I'm so sorry." Charlisse leaned over and placed a hand on Isabel's arm. "But isn't your father an earl? Surely he inherited his family's money?"

Shame drew Isabel's gaze downward. She didn't want to tell Charlisse her scandalous family history, but as she looked into her friend's caring eyes, for the first time in her life, Isabel felt as though someone cared. "Nay, I'm afraid my grandfather was a lazy man who gambled away his inheritance. All we had left was the land on which we lived and a horde of gambling debts. So my father sold everything and sailed to the West Indies to start anew."

"I take it you were not pleased with the move?" Charlisse blinked. Pain etched across her eyes.

"Pleased? I was horrified. I had to give up everything—my gowns and jewelry. I lost all my friends. Even my betrothed abandoned me." An arrow of agony clipped Isabel's heart. "Yes, I was promised to William Herbert, Earl of Pembroke. Can you imagine, an earl?" Isabel couldn't help but smile as she remembered him. "He was rich and handsome. My father arranged the marriage, but I was quite pleased with the match." Her elation abruptly dissolved into grief. "Of course once he found out we were no longer wealthy, he broke off the engagement. Last I heard, he was courting Lady Katherine Henworth." She spit out the name with disgust as she remembered the pretentious, spoiled girl. "These combs are all I have left to remind me of William." Isabel slid her fingers over the smooth silver. "Aren't they lovely?"

"They are indeed." Charlisse gave her a weak smile. "But don't you like New Providence?"

"Nay, 'tis a heathen place filled with ignorant savages. The food is bland. The sweltering heat and blaring sun wreak havoc on my skin, and due to a lack of servants, I am forced to work alongside my mother." Isabel huffed remembering how she'd had to cook in the hot kitchen and clean her own clothes—things a proper lady never should be expected to do. "Can you imagine? I have no friends, no prospect for marriage. Why I'll probably shrivel up in the sun and die an old maid."

Charlisse giggled but instantly stopped when Isabel shot an angry glance her way. Then, clutching her stomach, Charlisse bent over, gasping.

Isabel leaned toward her, placing a hand on her arm. "What is it?"

Charlisse looked up, her eyes swimming. "It's the baby," she said. "I fear something is amiss."

Panic tightened over Isabel. "What can I do?" Whenever anyone had been sick in her family, they'd simply called for the doctor. She knew absolutely nothing about babies. "You should be lying down, milady." Easing an arm around Charlisse's back, she helped her to her feet and back to the bed.

Letting out a ragged sigh, Charlisse leaned back on the pillows. "It's subsiding now." She rubbed her stomach.

Isabel drew a quilt over her. "Forgive me. There I am going on and on about myself, and you are suffering. Sometimes I can be so selfish." Isabel sat on the bed beside her and pressed a hand over her own stomach. "It's just that I'm so frightened."

"I know." Charlisse nodded. "I am, too."

Tears filled Isabel's eyes and spilled onto her cheeks. Should she tell her? If she said it out loud, would it make it any more real?

"It will be all right." A weak smile lifted the corners of Charlisse's lips. "We'll find a way to escape."

Isabel gulped. " 'Tis not only that."

"What then?"

"I, too, am pregnant."

Charlisse's mouth dropped open. "You? But—"

"I carry Kent's child."

# Chapter 8
## Divine Meeting

Captain Merrick flipped the iron key fitfully between his fingers as he held his hand over the frothing wake of the ship. It was the key to his cabin—their cabin—where he and Charlisse had spent many blissful hours together. Merrick could not force himself to enter that room again, so he had instructed Sloane to remove his clothes and weapons, fasten a heavy latch to the door, and bolt it shut. Now Charlisse's things would be locked up forever—along with his heart. He wished he could do the same with the torturous memories invading his mind.

The blazing sun hung halfway in its descent, sending shimmering reflections over the turquoise sea. It had been a beautiful day, but for Merrick, it might as well have been dark and gloomy. Feeling his eyes moisten, he swung his arm back, flung the key high into the air, and watched it fall, then disappear into the white foam seething off the stern. He closed his eyes and tried to pray, but all he envisioned was an angry God with arms crossed and face turned away.

"Cap'n," a scratchy voice sounded from behind him.

Opening his eyes, Merrick turned to see Brighton, the ship's cook and ad hoc doctor.

The pirate adjusted the patch over his left eye. "Mebbe I should be checkin' the wound on yer thigh?"

Merrick shook his head. "No need." He tested it with his full weight and winced. Brighton had cleaned it out and patched up the gaping slash caused by the flying chunk of wood from the explosion. Although it still pained him, he found he preferred the suffering for the time being.

"Thank you, Brighton." Merrick nodded, but the doctor didn't leave. "Anything else?"

Brighton scratched his hairy chest through a torn, yellowish-brown shirt that surely had once been white. The smells of sweat, tobacco, and rancid meat emanated from him.

"Well, I was thinkin' of makin' yer favorite meal, roast pork." He smiled through dingy teeth. "Some o' the men caught a wild boar when we was at Porto Bello."

The sound of that city's name sent a lance of pain into Merrick's heart. Shrugging it off, he stared at Brighton. The doctor had never been this accommodating before, and Merrick hated being coddled. "Go ahead and make it for the men," he replied, feigning politeness. "I'm afraid I've no appetite as of late."

Sloane hopped up the stairs, shoving a biscuit in his mouth just as Jeremy up in the crosstrees yelled, "Sail ho!"

Shielding his eyes from the sun, Merrick scanned the horizon but saw only a fuzzy line of blue between water and sky. He grabbed the spyglass stuffed in his belt and held it up to his eye. "Where away, Jeremy?" he bellowed.

"Two points off the larboard bow, Cap'n."

Merrick swerved the glass to the left and adjusted it until he saw a touch of stark white sail against the azure skyline. Too far yet to determine whether it be friend or foe. Not that it mattered. Merrick was in no mood for either company or conquest. The best he could hope was that the other ship would pay him no mind and be on its way.

Sloane stood beside him, his mouth full of biscuit. "Who d'ye suppose she be?" A crumb flew from his mouth, and the monkey on his shoulder snatched it out of the air and chortled with glee.

Merrick shook his head. "It's none of my concern."

Rusty shifted his stance behind the whipstaff and looked toward Merrick. "Cap'n, where should I point 'er?"

"Hold our present course."

"Aye, aye, Cap'n."

Snapping the spyglass shut, Merrick turned and marched down the quarterdeck steps.

"What if she be Spanish?" Sloane asked, quick on Merrick's heels.

The captain's boots slammed onto the main deck. Jackson's booming voice sped on the wind as he ordered the raucous crew to their tasks.

"I have no further interest in the Spanish." Merrick glanced over his ship. Two pirates sat on kegs near the foremast repairing ropes. Five more hovered in a shaded corner under the foredeck, betting their coins on a game of cards. Drake, one of the younger pirates, pushed a sopping mop across the deck while he trudged behind it, frowning. He looked up, gave his captain a half smile, and continued his work. Jackson stood by the capstan, gazing upward at three pirates adjusting the topsails in the shrouds.

Merrick continued across the deck, nodding at Jackson, who looked down as he passed. He heard Sloane still following him and wished his friend would leave him alone.

"But what if she's a merchant ship loaded with pieces o' eight?"

Irritation clawed at Merrick's fraught nerves. "Then this is her lucky day."

"But what if she attacks us first?"

"Then I shall engage her."

"But what if—"

"Still your tongue, man!" Merrick snapped, sending Solomon leaping from Sloane's shoulder into the ratlines. "You sound like a cackling old hen." Merrick jumped onto the foredeck steps.

"I'm just thinkin' a littl' fight might be puttin' ye back into yer old self."

Merrick stopped halfway up the stairs and swerved to his friend, fixing him with a cold eye. "I will never be my old self again."

A strong breeze struck him from behind, and a strand of his hair loosened from its tie and fell across his cheek. He turned to face the blast of wind and took in a deep breath of the salty air. Charlisse had loved the smell of the sea. With one jump, he leapt up the remaining steps. Sloane followed him but said nothing further.

Planting his feet near the foredeck railing, Merrick crossed his arms over his chest and allowed the sea spray to shower over him. The setting sun shot its last warm rays across the choppy waters, yet he felt chilled. Should he be going to Port Royal—the place where Charlisse had spent most of the past three years—the place where they had been married? What could Reverend Thomas possibly do to ease Merrick's pain?

Merrick shivered. *Why torture yourself with such agonizing memories?*

The wind shifted, and Merrick heard Jackson bellowing to the crew up in the ratlines to adjust the sails. Merrick glanced toward their larboard horizon. The ship they had spotted earlier loomed larger. Clearly, by her soft lines and square sails, she was not a Spanish vessel. Most likely a British ship or pirate, and Merrick wanted nothing to do with either.

Jackson and Sloane approached. The sun dipped its flaming curve into the cool ocean, sending slices of orange, red, and gold over the darkening sea.

After asking for the spyglass, Jackson peered intently through it for several seconds. " 'Tis the colors of the *Vanquisher*," the first mate stated, closing the glass.

Sloane scratched his thick beard. "Sink me sails, that be Cap'n Carlton's ship, don't it?"

Merrick clutched the hilt of his cutlass in a tight grip. Anger bubbled hot in his chest. "Kent," he hissed.

"The nerve o' that littl' jackanapes," Sloane spat. "Pretendin' to be a pirate cap'n."

Visions of the traitorous man Merrick had once trusted flooded his memory. How young and naive the boy had seemed when Merrick first met him at port in Barbados. He had begged Merrick to allow him to join the crew of the *Redemption*, so Merrick took him on, trained him, and finally, after he had proven himself, promoted him to first mate. Only then did the man's true nature come forth when he blackmailed Merrick, had him thrown in prison, and absconded with Charlisse.

"I heard he joined up wi' Cap'n Morgan and the Brethren o' the Coast," Jackson added.

"Indeed?" Merrick narrowed his eyes like a hawk closing in on its prey. At one time Merrick had considered Morgan a friend, but no longer. The perfidious old commander should know how to keep a rein on the cutthroat pirates under his command, and Merrick held him entirely at fault for the atrocities his men committed, including what had happened to Charlisse. A jab of pain thrust in his gut, twisting and turning his agony into hatred.

Merrick snatched the telescope from Jackson and scanned the ship—a square-rigged, three-masted vessel carrying at least forty cannons. Outgunned by less than half and much smaller, the *Redemption* still had the advantages of speed and maneuverability. Swinging the glass across the horizon, Merrick searched for other vessels.

" 'Tis suspicious that he sails alone," he said. "And that he left Porto Bello so soon—just four days—after the attack. Surely if he'd taken part in the raid, he'd still be there rampaging the city with the rest of Morgan's men." Even so, the rapscallion was near the top of Merrick's list of pirates he deemed the cruelest on the Caribbean—and those he had promised God he would bring to justice.

Sloane shifted his stance. "He be offerin' a sore temptation, flaunting his sails at us like that."

"I says we send him a welcome from our broadside." Jackson's deep voice rang. The gleam on his shaved head nearly matched the one from his earrings in the setting sun. "I ne'er much liked that fancy dawcock."

Merrick grabbed the rail and turned his face to the wind. The thought was not without appeal, to be sure.

Charlisse stood at the starboard railing, allowing the warm tropical breeze to waft over her. She inhaled a deep breath of the sweet, salty air and closed her eyes. Isabel stood beside her, silent for a moment, and Charlisse took advantage of the peace to converse with her Father and ask Him for wisdom and guidance. Yet the heavenly realm seemed strangely quiet despite her pleas for help. *Where are You, Lord? Why is this happening to me?*

Nothing.

The breeze turned cold. *He has abandoned you like every man in your life.*

No, she refused to believe that. A verse filtered into her mind from the book of Matthew. *"I am with you alway, even unto the end of the world."* The Lord had delivered her once before, and He would surely do it again. But in place of the peace she normally felt, a silent chill threatened to freeze her heart with fear—fear of losing Merrick, fear of being alone and unloved, and the agonizing fear that she would lose the precious child she carried. Adding to her anxiety, she had discovered drops of blood on her undergarments just hours earlier.

She cast a glance at Isabel, who continued to fight back tears after her declaration in the cabin. The poor girl. It was unimaginable. Charlisse had no words with which to comfort her. Nevertheless, she could do something. She could plan their escape.

Renewed determination swept through her. God had placed four precious lives in her hands—two unborn children, Isabel, and herself—and with His help, she would do all she could to save them and escape this ghastly predicament.

Glancing behind her, Charlisse saw the sun hovering over the horizon, sending a bouquet of warmth across her back and shimmering golden highlights over the waves. The *Vanquisher* flew through the ocean with all her sails set to the breeze, plunging over the rolling swells. Charlisse smiled at the familiar silken rustle of water against the hull of the ship. She loved the sea.

"How can you smile at a time such as this?" Isabel turned to her, squinting in the sunlight.

"Because I have hope."

Out of the corner of her eye, Charlisse saw pirates bursting up from the hatches and swarming over the deck like wasps from a hive. Repulsion curdled in her belly at the sight of them—filthy, unscrupulous fiends, unfettered by morality and conscience as they sought to attain their only goals of money and pleasure. Not that she wasn't used to associating with such men—an unavoidable occurrence when married to a privateer. Even though Merrick worked for the British government, he'd been forced to hire such men due to a shortage of decent men in the Caribbean.

Several of the ruffians huddled in a cluster on the other side of the deck, whispering and breaking into occasional bursts of laughter while casting glances at the women. A few pirates clung to the shrouds, working the sails. One watched from the crosstrees, and another group played some sort of game up on the quarterdeck. Armed with knifes, cutlasses, boarding axes, and pistols, they presented a frightening sight. All she could hope for was that Kent had more control over his crew than he had over his own appetites.

As if reading her thoughts, Isabel remarked sharply, "Your hope is ill-founded, for in case it has escaped your notice, we have been captured by pirates." She lifted one hand to her nose. "The stench of these beasts.

I cannot bear it."

Charlisse attempted a smile. "Don't you believe God can handle a few pirates?"

"Humph, no doubt, but I fear more pressing matters draw His attentions elsewhere, for it appears He has left us to our own devices." Isabel continued to stare out over the darkening sea.

A loud *clank* sounded behind them, and Charlisse turned to see a man emerge from the hatch carrying a bucket. A thick chain linking his ankles scraped the deck as he walked. The stark white of his eyes against ebony skin met Charlisse's, but he quickly looked away and staggered forward. Dropping to his knees, he took a brush from the bucket and began scrubbing the boards.

"A slave," Charlisse said in a sour tone, disgusted by the sight.

Isabel darted a glance over her shoulder before returning her gaze forward. "Yes, I know, loathsome, ignorant creatures, aren't they?"

"How can you say such a thing?" Charlisse gave her a scorching look. "He's a man, just like any other."

Isabel threw her shoulders back. "Some men are destined to serve others."

"Indeed? Pray tell, enlighten me."

"You mock me. Surely you feel the same way, being a lady of noble birth?"

"I believe no such thing." Charlisse gulped down a burst of rage that threatened to rise to her lips. She had spent the past three years working with Reverend Thomas at Port Royal, feeding and caring for the orphans of slaves whose masters saw it fit to work them to death. "No man should have the right to enslave another."

Isabel raised her nose in the air but said nothing, and Charlisse sighed. She, too, had once been apathetic on the issue of slavery. But that was before she had given her life to Christ and before He had revealed to her the value of a human life—all human lives.

"I beg you to hear me out on this," she began, but a deep thud of boots echoed behind them, and Isabel whirled around. Following her gaze, Charlisse saw Kent at the head of the companionway talking with one of his crew. He pointed toward something aloft and ordered the man away before nodding in the women's direction.

A deep red hue rose on Isabel's creamy face. She darted her gaze back onto the water and tucked a wayward curl into her bun.

Charlisse turned her back on the captain and whispered to Isabel, "I've never seen Kent look at anyone the way he looks at you."

"He looks at all women in the same fashion—only as objects."

"No, you are mistaken. He looks at me in such a way, but when he sees you, something softens in his countenance."

Angry shouts blared from the quarterdeck, and Isabel glanced over her shoulder. Fear tightened the features of her face. Charlisse turned to see that a brawl had broken out among the pirates who'd been playing cards. Two of the men had drawn knives and one man a pistol. They growled at each other through muddied teeth. One grotesque man with matted hair and grimy breeches headed toward the stairs and smacked his lips together when he spotted the women.

Charlisse put her arm around Isabel. "Turn around. Don't look at them." The young girl trembled beneath her grasp, and Charlisse gave her a squeeze. "Kent will keep his men at bay. Never fear. And we *will* escape."

Isabel sniffed. "How?"

"I don't know yet, but I promise you, we will." Charlisse smiled and looked out over the Caribbean. She spotted a ship on the horizon, but heard no alert from the crosstrees. Excitement coursed through her. When she glanced over at Kent, he stood, arms crossed, facing off the port bow. Squinting, she yearned for a spyglass to bring the flag that flew from the ship's mainmast into clearer view.

Charlisse leaned toward Isabel. "Say nothing, but there's a ship approaching off our starboard quarter."

Lifting her face, the young girl peered over the choppy water. Her eyes widened. "Who is it? Will we be rescued?" She darted a glance at Charlisse.

"Difficult to say, but let us remain hopeful." Bracing against the wind, Charlisse studied the ship's shape. "Pray she is neither pirate nor Spanish, and that she has enough honor to challenge this vessel of brigands."

"I shall leave the praying to you." Isabel scowled. "If you don't mind."

Charlisse cast a fleeting look over her shoulder and returned her gaze to the ship. With most of the pirates' attention focused elsewhere—on their drink or their greedy altercations—and Kent staring off in one of his melodramatic musings, this fast-approaching ship might have a chance at overtaking them unaware. "Another minute and I will be able to make out the colors she flies," Charlisse declared.

Isabel twisted her arm around Charlisse's and squeezed her hand, the contagion of her excitement drifting over to Charlisse.

The sun descended in its usual vainglorious exit, sending fingers of crimson and saffron curving along the horizon from behind them. "Hurry," Charlisse whispered to the ship. *Oh Lord, please help us.*

Minutes passed and still no shout from the crosstrees. The sun flung its last blazing rays onto the swift-flying ship as if to aid Charlisse in determining whether it be friend or foe. As the details of the flag grew sharper, her heart leapt into her throat. The white cross of Christ, crisscrossed by two golden swords against a black background—the flag of the *Redemption*.

"Merrick!" she gasped and covered her mouth almost instantly. " 'Tis my husband," she whispered to Isabel, trying to keep from jumping over the rail and swimming to him.

Isabel beamed, her eyes flickering with excitement. "Truly?" She turned toward the approaching vessel. "Make haste, dear sir, make haste."

"I knew he would come for me," Charlisse said just as "Ship ahoy!" rang out above them.

Kent's heavy boots pounded down the stairs. Charlisse heard the metallic snap of his spyglass. After a few seconds, a foul curse shot from his mouth, and his beefy hand clamped around her arm. Isabel shrieked as he grabbed her arm as well and hauled them both down the companionway stairs and shoved them into the cabin.

"Know this, milady. If that fish-brained husband of yours dares to attack me, I will sink him to the depths of the ocean."

Isabel cringed, rubbed her arm, and sank onto the bed.

Charlisse marched toward Kent, emboldened by the sight of Merrick's ship. "If my husband attacks you, you insufferable boor, 'tis you who will find yourself in a watery grave."

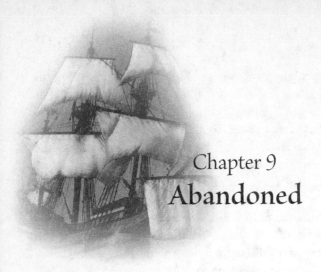

# Chapter 9
# Abandoned

Exhilaration coursed through Merrick's veins. Kent's ship, the *Vanquisher*, sailed on a tack that took her brazenly within range of the *Redemption*'s cannons. The urge to take on the arrogant menace and pummel him with grapeshot filled him with a dark desire for revenge.

"Should I 'ave the guns run out, Cap'n?" Jackson asked, taking a step toward the stairs.

Bracing his fists on his hips, Merrick squinted against the piercing rays of the setting sun and stared at his nemesis. An evening breeze picked up from the west and filled his lungs with the sweet smell of impending conquest.

"Come on, Cap'n, we got the weather advantage of 'im." Sloane cocked one eyebrow. "Ne'er such a chance as this will come again soon. Ye don't need to be killin' 'im, since I knows yer faith frowns on such things. Let's just teach 'im a lesson, to be sure."

"My faith." Merrick snorted. "What difference does that make now?"

"Ye don't be meanin' that, Cap'n."

Merrick gave a humorless snarl and clasped the hilt of his cutlass. Had he meant it? He wondered. What difference did anything make now—without Charlisse? Yet he could not deny the intoxicating thrill surging through him at the thought of besting that young dawcock.

An icy chill raked his spine. *It's Morgan you want, not Kent.*

Merrick rubbed the back of his neck, where a brisk needling pricked at his nerves.

*Morgan's the one who killed Charlisse.*

Was he? Confusion spread through him. "The spyglass," Merrick ordered and seized it from Jackson. No, as much as he'd love to blame Kent for Charlisse's death and sink him to the bottom of the sea once and for all, Merrick knew Kent. If he'd been at Porto Bello, he would not now be missing the drinking and pillaging that went on for days after the city was taken.

He peered toward the *Vanquisher*. Adjusting the focus, he brought the sails into clear view and scanned the deck of the ship. A flicker of blue fabric and blond hair flashed across his vision. The *Redemption* bucked over a rising wave, and the image jumped out of view.

"Blast." Merrick brought the glass back into position. Squinting one eye, he focused the instrument and surveyed the ship from aft to stern. Nothing. Just pirates rushing to their posts. They had spotted him.

Sloane scuffed his boots across the deck. "What d'ye see, Cap'n?"

Merrick sighed and lowered the glass. "I thought I saw. . ." He gazed at the ship, a dark outline against the setting sun. His heart sank lower with each heave of the bow over the rising swells. Nothing but a wicked trick on his senses. "Impossible," he muttered.

"What's that?"

"Nothing." He slapped the spyglass into Jackson's hands. "Set a course around the *Vanquisher*, ten degrees north by northeast." Turning on his heels, he stomped away.

"But, Cap'n," Sloane's urgent voice followed him.

A flood of despondency spread through Merrick, smothering the anticipation he had felt only moments ago and replacing it with a burning hatred for Morgan.

*Why should you honor a promise to a God who doesn't keep His?*

Indeed. God had promised Merrick a wife and children. He had promised him that He would protect Charlisse and watch over her, that all things would work out for good—promises that now seemed nothing more than a vanishing mist before the hot sun.

"My business with Kent is completed. Morgan's the one I'm after."

"Cap'n." The thud of Sloane's boots sounded behind him as Merrick took the stairs down to the main deck. "Ye can't be blamin' Morgan fer what happened to Charl—"

Merrick swung about. "Silence!"

A deep growl of thunder rumbled in the distance.

Shock lifted Sloane's furrowed brows, and a flicker of pain crossed his blue eyes.

Merrick sighed and raked his hand through his hair. "I am your captain. You do as I say." He turned and took the remaining steps in one leap, his leather boots pounding across the main deck. Two pirates scurried out of his way as he barreled toward the railing and gazed at the rising half moon in the east.

A breeze twisted shivery fingers around him. *Tortuga.*

Tortuga? Why was he thinking of that wicked city? Shaking his head, he watched as the sun sucked its last remaining rays across the black chaotic sea, pulling them down below the horizon. *Lord, are You there?* Merrick felt his eyes moisten. *I have lost the will to fight.*

*Trust Me, son.*

Trust. Merrick hung his head. Frigid mist wafted up from the sea, hardening the remainder of his conscience. *Morgan must pay.*

Swinging about in disgust, Merrick stomped to the foredeck stairs, nearly toppling Sloane. He looked up. "Belay that order, Jackson. We make for Tortuga."

"Aye, Cap'n," Jackson said, then consulted a chart spread before him on a crate. Raising his gaze, he bellowed to the helmsman. "Ten degrees east by north, Rusty. Steady as she goes."

"Ten degrees steady east by north," Rusty repeated.

Sloane kept in step with Merrick as he marched toward the companionway stairs. "Tortuga? But what about the reverend, Cap'n?"

"Confound it, man!" Merrick roared. "Must I suffer your constant second-guessing?" He glared into Sloane's aged eyes. Disappointment flickered within them.

"My apologies, Cap'n." Sloane scratched his beard and looked away. "It just be that I thought seeing the rev would do ye some good, 'tis all."

"When are you going to get it through your thick skull"—Merrick spat, annoyance fueling his temper—"that there is neither a person nor a thing that will do me good any more!" Turning his back on Sloane, he took the first step down the companionway, hoping his friend would give up and leave him be.

"But Tortuga, Cap'n. 'Tain't no worse place for ye to be right now."

Merrick spun about. "What do you know about where I should and should not be? You're nothing but an old fool!" He barked the words before he saw the look of concern in Sloane's eyes, before he saw the pain etched on the old pirate's face.

Ashamed, Merrick turned away. How could he treat his oldest friend this way?

"Beggin' yer pardon, Cap'n." Sloane said, and Merrick heard the thud of his boots fade across the deck.

Charlisse raced to the cabin window and flattened her face against it, desperate to catch a glimpse of the *Redemption* and to watch Merrick sweep in and rescue her. She saw the faint outline of his ship against the darkening horizon, highlighted by an occasional burst of foam over the bow. Excitement tickled every nerve as her heart throbbed with love and admiration for her husband, who she knew would never desert her.

"Isabel, come here and witness our rescue," she said to the girl, who sat despondent on the bed.

Isabel sniffed. "But you heard Kent. He will sink your husband's ship. I've seen him do it before."

"Perhaps you've seen Kent sink other ships." Charlisse approached Isabel, grabbed her hand, and pulled her from the bed. "But you will never see him sink the *Redemption*—not with Merrick at the helm." She led Isabel to the window, and they sat on the ledge, peering out in anticipation.

The *Redemption* grew smaller.

A twinge of pain pinched Charlisse's belly. She fidgeted in her seat and gave Isabel's hand a squeeze.

The young girl looked at her, eyes moist and face paling. "Why doesn't he sail in closer?"

Charlisse swallowed hard and stared at the retreating ship, now just a dark circle against the indigo sky.

Where was he going? Why was he leaving?

Terror spiked through her heart. "He must be circling around. . . perhaps coming from a more advantageous position." She tried to reassure Isabel, but she knew that wasn't true. Coming from the windward side, he already had the advantage.

A cold fog settled on her heart. *He's left you.*

One more glance out the window confirmed her darkest fears. A half-moon rose over the turbulent black waters.

The *Redemption* was no longer in sight.

Charlisse gasped for air that seemed to escape from all around her. She tore off from the window ledge and stumbled across the cabin, her heart trying to grasp what her mind already knew.

Her husband had abandoned her.

Wringing her hands, she paced the room and crashed into the table, stubbing her toe. Ignoring the pain, she threw a hand to her chest. Her breath came in quick bursts. Heat enveloped her and the walls began to spin. How could he do that? She pressed a hand onto the back of a chair to steady herself. Wracking cramps seared her abdomen, and she slumped over.

"Charlisse!" Isabel helped her to the bed. Lying back on the pillow, Charlisse closed her eyes and felt a cool cloth on her forehead and Isabel's soft hand caressing her cheek. "You have a fever again. What can I do?" the young girl asked. Fear quivered in her voice.

Charlisse panted as the last of the clenching pain eased. "I'm afraid there's naught to be done, save pray."

The door flew open. A burst of wind hit Charlisse with the scent of salt and leather, and she opened her eyes to see Kent. Amusement flickered in his lofty smile.

"Perchance, did you observe your husband's tail tucked neatly betwixt his legs as he limped off into the night?" He sneered.

Charlisse struggled to sit and returned his hard gaze. "Indeed, I saw no such thing. Merrick tricks you. He will return."

Kent took another step toward them, his leather breeches creaking in time with the thump of his boots. "It pains me to inform you, milady, that your skittish husband, upon perceiving himself both outgunned in weaponry and outmatched in wit and skill"—Kent gestured toward himself—"has fled into the night like the coward he always was, preferring to leave his beloved wife in the hands of pirates than risk his spineless neck."

A piercing pain shot through Charlisse, inflaming the hatred in her heart. "You loathsome knave."

Kent gave a mocking bow. "At your service." When he lifted his eyes, they landed on Isabel and their harshness dissolved.

The young girl averted her eyes.

"I will have Smithy come and escort you to my cabin for dinner within the hour, Miss Ashton," he said softly.

"Begging your pardon, Captain." Isabel looked up. "But Lady Charlisse is not well. I should not leave her tonight."

"Lady Charlisse will recover from the shock of her husband's abandonment with or without your presence."

"I do protest, sir. She is ill."

Kent flexed his jaw and glanced at Charlisse. Was that a spark of concern in his eyes? "Nevertheless, you will do as I say." He turned and left.

*Abandoned. . .abandoned.* The word repeated in Charlisse's mind like a chant of doom. She fell back onto the bed.

Isabel stood and paced, scratching her arms.

"He fancies you," Charlisse said. "We may use it to our advantage."

"To our advantage?" Isabel shot her an incredulous look. "Are you suggesting I encourage his advances?"

"No, of course not. That he wishes to please you is obvious, however misguided his intentions may be. Perhaps you can use that to gain more freedom so we can better plan our escape." Charlisse reached for a handkerchief on the table and dabbed at the perspiration on her brow. "After all you've already bartered with him for food and a walk on the deck, who knows what other desires of yours he may grant."

Isabel dropped into the leather chair and placed a hand over her stomach. Her eyes misted and she looked away.

Minutes passed, and in her own pain, Charlisse found no words to comfort the girl. At least Charlisse carried the child of the man she loved, not the product of an attack. Her heart broke as she watched a sob wrench over the girl. With effort, Charlisse hoisted herself up and eased to the edge of the bed. "If you gain enough of his trust, perchance you may even convince him to release you to the safety of your family."

"I fail to see why he would perform such a kindness," Isabel snapped.

"Because if he thinks he may have a chance to win your affection, he may choose to release you."

Isabel gaped at Charlisse. "I would never marry a man such as he—a *pirate*." She said the word with disgust, then adjusted her flowing skirts and raised her chin. "I will marry a gentleman, a nobleman—a man of great wealth and power."

"I made no mention of marrying the villain." Charlisse straightened her back and eased a hand over her stomach. "But what about love? What about character? Surely these things matter more than money."

"I beg to differ. Such things are trivial compared to wealth." Isabel patted her hair in place.

A light tap at the door signaled Smithy's entrance. The burly, shaggy-haired pirate grinned. "The Cap'n's callin' fer ye, Miss."

Isabel rose, released a shaky breath, and followed Smithy out the door.

As soon as Isabel had gone, Charlisse doubled over and sobbed. *Oh God, what is wrong with me?* She cautiously lay back on the bed and tried to pray—pray for Isabel's safety and for her own baby as he fought for his life within her.

*He.* Perhaps it *was* a boy.

A sudden chill shivered over her, despite her fever, and she tugged a blanket over her chest. *Merrick has deserted you. . .abandoned you.* The dark words echoed like death tolls through her mind.

"No," she whispered, lifting a hand to her aching head. "I don't believe it." But a gnawing fear etched uncertainty into her resolve, bringing back feelings of unworthiness long since buried. Visions of her uncle hovering over her, his ostentatious crucifix gleaming against his brown cowl, flashed across her feverish brain.

*"You filthy trollop. You think any man would want you?"* A glob of white spit sat at the corner of his cracked lips as his gaze scoured her. *"Why, your own father couldn't even stand the sight of you."* His venomous voice rang through the cabin as if he were there, standing beside the bed.

"No," Charlisse sobbed. "That's not true." She tossed her head across the pillow as the haze of fever consumed her. Images of her father, Edward the Terror, floated through her scattered thoughts. True, he had kidnapped her and locked her in the rat-infested hold of his ship. But in the end, he'd declared his love for her.

Hadn't he?

Somehow, in the fiery jumble of her mind, she could not remember.

In any case, certainly Merrick loved her.

A cramp clutched her abdomen, squeezing every tissue and fiber of her until she curled into a ball on her side. *He left you.*

"No," Charlisse sobbed. Warm moisture poured from her body, and she pressed her eyes shut, fighting back the terror that threatened to spill from them in a flood of tears.

A whirl of icy wind drifted over Charlisse, and she popped open her eyes, wondering from whence it came and why she suddenly felt as if insects crawled over her skin. *Everyone has betrayed you. Everyone has left you.*

"No!" Charlisse gulped down a surge of nausea. "God still loves me."

*Hmm. . .Where is He, then?*

The cabin walls swayed under the gentle rocking of the ship as lanterns cast shifting shadows across them. Stars drifted lazily past the window, taking turns peeking at her. But no one was here. She was alone.

*Always alone, always abandoned, poor Charlisse.*

"Leave me alone. I don't believe you." Charlisse turned her face into the pillow. Another sharp pain surged through her, shooting out in waves of agony across her whole body. *Lord, please help me.*

Some time later the thick oak door thudded shut, and soft footsteps approached. But through the sizzle of her mind, Charlisse couldn't be sure whether she was dreaming. A soft touch to her forehead confirmed that Isabel had indeed returned.

"You are burning up with fever!" With a rush of silk, something cool touched Charlisse's forehead. Peering through half-closed eyes, she saw the concern wrinkling Isabel's otherwise flawless features. "How was your dinner?" Charlisse asked in a feeble voice.

"My word, milady. You are beyond ill, yet you inquire about me?" She dabbed the cloth over Charlisse's brow and tossed the blanket aside. Her face faded to ashen white. With wide eyes, she stared down at Charlisse's gown.

Lightheaded with pain, Charlisse rose on her elbows and followed Isabel's gaze to a slick red stain spreading out from her lap and soaking her dress.

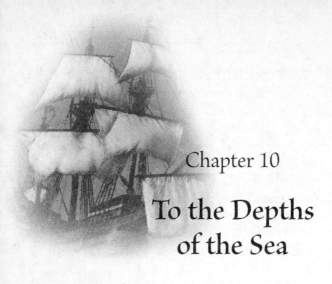

## Chapter 10

# To the Depths of the Sea

Charlisse clawed her way through a dark tunnel, groping against the hard, cold walls as a moist chill covered her. She saw nothing ahead or behind, yet somehow she knew if she kept moving, she'd reach the end. The pain had dissipated, replaced by the ache of a barren void that encompassed her heart in its icy grip. A pinprick of light appeared in front of her, and she stopped, knowing if she continued and reached it, she would have to face something she did not think she could endure.

*That's right. Stay where you are. Better to die here than face the truth.*

Charlisse dropped to the stony floor of the tunnel and sobbed. Maybe she was better off in this dark, peaceful place. Here, she did not have to undergo the pain of abandonment, the agony of betrayal, or the loss of. . .

*My child, I am with you.*

Lifting her head, she listened for that soft, kind voice. She'd heard it before, and it always brought her peace.

The light grew brighter, and Charlisse heard her name echoing in the darkness. She rose and continued inching her way toward the glow.

Her eyes popped open.

Isabel's auburn curls fell loosely across the shoulders of her crimson gown, having escaped the silver combs that clung stubbornly to her hair. Her delicate head—facing away from Charlisse—leaned in one hand, while the other hand held Charlisse's.

Charlisse moaned, and Isabel's brimming jade eyes swung to hers. "Oh, milady," she sobbed. "How do you feel?"

"Tired."

Isabel pressed the back of her hand against Charlisse's forehead. "Your fever is gone." She sighed and looked away.

Charlisse swallowed the terror that threatened to squeeze her heart into her throat. Pushing herself up on her elbows, she ignored the throbbing ache in her abdomen and glanced down, searching for the reddish-brown stain she remembered seeing on her gown. But her dress was gone, replaced by a faded petticoat. Had she only dreamed of the blood?

"Where's my dress? Whose petticoat is this?"

Isabel rose from the bed and moved toward the window. She lifted a hand to her breast and turned to face Charlisse. "Oh, milady," she gasped. Her eyes filled with tears until one spilled over its lashed boundary and slid down her cheek.

Despair tugged on Charlisse's hope. She passed her hand over her stomach, searching for the slight mound so familiar to her now that it seemed it had always been there.

Flat.

Flat and lifeless like her heart suddenly felt. Squeezing her eyes shut, she wished—begged—for that beating organ that kept her alive to cease its endless thumping and drop her back into that dark tunnel.

"Oh God. . .I'm sinking," she sobbed.

*Grab hold of Me, daughter. I'm here.*

Charlisse lay back and opened her eyes, trying to focus on Isabel's face through her blurry vision. Sunlight streaming in through the window highlighted the tracks of tears staining the young girl's cheeks and dark circles hanging beneath her eyes.

"How long have I been asleep?" Charlisse asked.

"I'm not sure. Ten hours perhaps."

Charlisse swallowed. "Was it a boy?" She had to know, no matter how painful.

Isabel attempted a weak smile and nodded, rushing to the bed. Her eyes flooded again, and Charlisse grabbed her hand. "Where is he?"

Isabel shook her head. "He was so small." She settled on the bed and sniffed. "I insisted he be wrapped in a clean cloth and put below."

"Who. . .who. . .was here?" Charlisse choked, wondering if this innocent girl had faced such an overwhelming task alone.

"You don't remember?"

Charlisse shook her head, fighting back a new wave of tears.

" 'Twas only me, milady. You fought so hard! There was so much blood. But it was over quickly." Isabel bowed her head and gulped. Then grabbing a handkerchief off the table, she dabbed at her face.

Charlisse wanted to comfort her, but could not find any words to ease either of their sufferings.

"Your screams brought Kent," Isabel continued. "He called the ship's doctor." She glanced at the door, then turned to Charlisse and raised her quivering chin. "I didn't let them touch you. They brought water and fresh clothes, and I cleaned you up."

"You were very brave," Charlisse said. "Thank you." In truth, she could not imagine the horrors Isabel must have endured, or even where the girl had found the strength to handle such a gruesome burden. But none of it really mattered anymore. She had lost Merrick's child—her son—and the emptiness inside her was beyond bearing.

She shivered as a chill drifted over her. *Merrick abandoned you, and now your child has left you.*

Charlisse curled up on her side and hugged herself, praying for her own death to come quickly.

The door opened, and in stepped Kent, followed by a tall, lanky pirate whose left arm hung withered and scarred. The limb trembled as he walked, and one side of his upper lip twisted in a snarl of red and purple flesh.

Kent's gaze lingered over Isabel before it settled on Charlisse. He bowed. "I trust you are recovering, milady?"

*Recovering?* Charlisse would have laughed if she had an ounce of joy left within her. How did one recover from the loss of a child? She returned his gaze with a silent, hardened scowl.

Isabel stood and wiped the tears from her face. She took a tentative step toward him. "Losing a child is not a trifling illness you recover from, Captain."

Kent's eyes shot to Isabel's, and a spark of softness broke through the usual hard sheen. "No. I would not imagine so. Nevertheless, I have brought the doctor to examine her." He nodded at the tall pirate, who proceeded toward the bed.

Charlisse sprang up, clutching her stomach against the throbbing pain. "I assure you, I have no need to be examined." She held up her hand.

Kent took a step toward Isabel but glanced at Charlisse. "Curb your fears, madam, Cutter means you no harm."

"Cutter?" Charlisse gasped. The square-shouldered man approached her. Dressed in a black sleeveless waistcoat over a ratty cotton shirt and canvas trousers from which the handle of a pistol protruded, he looked like every other pirate she had seen. Yet there was something refined in the way he crossed the room.

A rush of blood stormed Charlisse's head, and she feared she would pass out.

Kent chuckled. "Yes, a nickname we gave him."

"Leave her be!" Isabel spun around to intercept the doctor, but Kent reached out and yanked her to the side.

"Be still, milady," he said, pulling her close to him.

Isabel wrenched from his grasp and backed away. "Haven't you done enough damage?" the girl spat. "Now you're to frighten her to death, as well?"

The doctor placed long, slender fingers on Charlisse's cheek, and the odors of tobacco and fish assailed her. Repulsed, she backed away, but his firm hand followed her until the headboard prevented her retreat. She glanced up into his gray eyes—the color of a thundercloud—as they perused her beneath thin, cultured eyebrows the same sandy color as his hair. He grinned, and an intelligence shone from behind his disfigured expression. Placing two fingers on the side of her throat, he winked at her as if they shared a secret.

"Are you dizzy?" he asked.

"A bit."

"She lost a lot of blood," Isabel interjected.

A heavy wave crashed against the hull, and a breeze thick with saltwater blew in through the open door, freeing some of Kent's dark locks from their tie and reminding Charlisse of Merrick, whose ebony hair always flew wildly about him when they were at sea.

Unable to restrain her agony, Charlisse felt her eyes fill with tears.

Cutter, his shorter arm still trembling, placed his open hands over Charlisse's belly and glanced at her. "With your permission, milady?"

Charlisse shook her head. Tears spilled down her face. "He's gone," she sobbed. "Can't you see that?"

The doctor withdrew his hands and turned to face the window, but not before Charlisse thought she saw a mist cover his eyes.

Isabel rushed to her side.

Cutter stepped back. "She is weak, Cap'n, but she'll recover in a few days. Give her some rum for the pain."

"This is all your fault!" Isabel spun around and shot an accusing glance at Kent.

Kent nodded for the doctor to leave. "That will be all, Cutter."

"Aye, Cap'n."

Shifting his stance, Kent looked down.

Charlisse swiped at the tears endlessly flowing down her cheeks and stared at him, waiting for the flare of anger and sadistic witticisms to spew forth from his mouth. She had never seen anyone accuse Kent without receiving the brunt of his retaliation.

The crisp snap of the mainsail, followed by the gurgling rustle of water against the hull, told Charlisse the ship had made a slight turn and caught the wind for a speedier course. The streams of sunlight spilling in through the window shifted their beams across Kent as if trying to wake him from his thoughts.

Finally, he looked up at Charlisse and folded his arms over his violet doublet. "It was never my intention. . ." For a moment, the impenetrable, cold shield fell from his eyes, and Charlisse caught a glimpse of a vulnerability she could never have fathomed in such a villain. "No matter." He waved his hand in the air and headed toward the door.

"Kent," Charlisse said, drawing him back around.

His lips formed a line of annoyance, and she realized she had not used his title.

"Captain," she corrected, noting the coldness had returned to his eyes. "If I may beg a favor of you?"

He nodded, waiting.

"I would like to say some words over my son." Charlisse drew a shaky breath. "And give him a proper burial at sea."

"Impossible." Kent braced his hands on his hips. "The crew would think me soft, and I will not be made a fool for the likes of you."

"How can you deny her this one small service," Isabel stormed, her face growing red, "after what you have done?"

Kent's eyes widened. "If the wench is not strong enough to carry a baby that is no fault of mine."

Charlisse hung her head, squeezing her eyes shut against the deluge of agonizing tears.

"Merciless knave." Isabel turned her back to Kent, her face twisted in anger.

Kent stormed out, slamming the door behind him.

Charlisse sipped the rum-laced tea Smithy had brought her and watched Isabel sleeping curled up on one of the leather chairs. Although it was the middle of the day, the poor girl had sunk into the seat after Kent left and quickly nodded off. Drawing one last gulp of the pungent tea, Charlisse lay back on the pillow, hoping either the rum or her own exhaustion would transport her into unconsciousness. But the torment of her soul forbade any rest. Weak from loss of blood and now dizzy from the liquor, she could not even pace the room in her distress, but was confined to the bed like a condemned prisoner chained to her coffin.

*Alone and abandoned. . .even by your own son.*

"No," Charlisse gasped, hugging herself against a sudden chill. "That's not true."

The rum swirled through her thoughts, knocking each rational one senseless until nothing but a muddled band of flailing notions remained.

"Please, God, help me. Why? Why did You take my son?" Charlisse buried her face in the pillow. "Oh, my precious boy!" she wailed. Uncontrollable heaves of anguish wracked her body as she released the torrent of misery she had fought to control. But now, with no one save God to see her, she abandoned all propriety and cried for what seemed like hours. She cried until her head ached and her eyes were nearly swollen shut. She cried until she had no tears left. Then she stopped and listened as her jagged breathing slowed to match the quiet rhythm of Isabel's deep breaths.

The ship creaked and groaned its way across the pounding sea as if nothing had happened. But something had happened. Merrick was gone. She was imprisoned by a vindictive pirate, and now her son was dead—never even given a chance to live.

*Trust Me.*

An icy breeze raked over her. *Trust Him? He doesn't love you. Would a loving Father do this to His daughter?*

Doubt clambered up the steps of faith Charlisse had so tediously built over the past three years. Why would God allow these things if He truly loved her? She rubbed her temples. She had given her life to God—had trusted Him. All she ever wanted was to settle down with Merrick and raise a house full of children.

Frosty air showered over her. *Now you probably can't have any more children.*

"Be quiet. I don't believe you," Charlisse snapped.

*Trust in My love, daughter.*

Opening her swollen lids a crack, she watched the shifting patterns of sunlight on the cabin wall. "Father," she whispered, "help me to trust You."

Isabel jumped to her feet as the door creaked open. Kent strode inside, a wide grin on his mouth. "You wished to see me?"

"Shhh." Isabel held a finger to her lips and glanced over her shoulder at Charlisse asleep on the bed. "She needs her rest."

Kent nodded. "How may I be of service, milady?" He lowered his voice and raised his dark brows.

His umber hair was tied behind him, revealing a strong jaw—clean-shaven for once. Wearing a spotless shirt and neatly pressed damask waistcoat, he glanced at her, expectation flickering in his dark brown eyes. For a moment, he appeared more like an anxious boy than a cruel pirate.

"I beg you, Captain. Please allow Lady Charlisse to give her son a Christian burial." Isabel didn't know if she could convince him to change his mind, but for Charlisse's sake, she had to try. Isabel drew in a deep breath. She walked a fiery line between his affections and his temper by demanding anything from him.

He frowned and let out a disappointed sigh. "I have already told you I cannot."

"You mean you will not, and to what purpose? Simply to maintain your fierce reputation? Is that more important than this lady's peace?"

Kent pursed his lips, and his gaze wandered over to Charlisse then back to Isabel.

Isabel took a brazen step forward. "Since you are the cause of her losing the baby, 'tis the least you can do," she hissed, instantly regretting her demanding tone as the features of his face twisted into knots. Fear swept over her, and she retreated.

"I am not the cause. . . ," Kent stormed, then fell silent, grimacing. His shoulders dropped and he scratched his chin.

A moan escaped Charlisse's lips.

Kent shifted his gaze back to the bed. "She may have lost the child anyway. However, I take no pleasure in the tragedy."

"Then allow her to read a passage from the Bible over her son and bury him properly." Isabel softened her tone and gave him her most pleading look.

The hard shield over Kent's eyes melted, and for a moment Isabel saw a glimmer of remorse in them. He turned away. "I have no Bible."

"I fear you are incorrect, Captain."

He eyed her with suspicion.

"I've seen it in your cabin—on your shelf. Though I must admit I wondered what use a man like you could possibly find for it."

"A man like me? A vicious scoundrel, you mean?" He tilted his head and his lips flattened, but there was no anger in his tone. "The Bible was a gift—the contents of which I have found most intriguing."

Amazement flooded her. Kent, reading the Bible? She studied him. "Simply being intrigued with the moral standards one should aspire to is not enough to change the vicious scoundrel into a gentleman."

Kent fumbled with the lace on his neckerchief. "Have you not found in me a mor. . .morsel of anything worthy of your regard all this time?" he stuttered.

"Grant my wish and give me a reason to, Captain."

Grabbing the door latch, Kent stepped out into the hallway. "Very well." He smiled. "When she recovers." He closed the door with a quiet snap.

Charlisse tried to focus her teary eyes on the sacred words, but a humid breeze fluttered the pages of the old Bible. She scanned the bedraggled assemblage standing on deck around the wooden plank where the tiny bundle wrapped in white linen lay. Kent stood across from her, plumed hat pressed against his chest. He wore a solemn expression that was at odds with his usual insolent smirk.

Six days had passed. Charlisse and Isabel had remained locked in their cabin—their only visitor being Smithy, who brought them food and water and freshened their chamber pot. From the changing sounds of surf, sail, and seagulls, plus Isabel's brief descriptions from the window, Charlisse determined that they had made two stops: one at a port and the other at an island inlet.

Unwilling to leave her bed, Charlisse had battled a growing despondency even as she felt her body heal and her strength return. Kent's announcement that she could bury her child had provided the spark she needed to shake off her despair and rise from the stale berth that held her down. She had no idea what had changed the captain's mind regarding her requested ceremony, but she craved the finality it would bring as she offered her child to the depths of the sea and her dreams along with him.

Five other pirates gathered around, whether by compulsion or desire, Charlisse neither knew nor cared. The doctor was among them, standing across from her, wearing a somber expression on his gnarled lips. Oddly enough it was Kent who'd handed her the Bible—the one from which she now intended to read over her son.

*My son.*

Furious black clouds boiled on the horizon, flashing sparks and bursting in deep grumbles that matched the anguished pangs of her heart. Taking in a deep breath of the tangy scent of oncoming rain, Charlisse read:

"And I saw the dead, small and great, stand before God; and the books were opened: and another book was opened, which is the book of life: and the dead were judged out of those things which were written in the books, according to their works. And the sea gave up the dead which were in it; and death and hell delivered up the dead which were in them: and they were judged every man according to their works."

Charlisse sobbed, flipped some pages backward, and continued:

"For he knoweth our frame; he remembereth that we are dust. As for man, his days are as grass: as a flower of the field, so he flourisheth. For the wind passeth over it, and it is gone; and the place thereof shall know it no more. But the mercy of the Lord is from everlasting to everlasting upon them that fear him, and his righteousness unto children's children."

Charlisse kissed her hand and laid it upon the bundle. "Farewell, my precious son. Until we meet again."

Raising a handkerchief to her eyes, Isabel wept.

Swallowing hard, Charlisse lifted her gaze to Kent's. He flexed his jaw, but the flicker of emotion she saw in his eyes instantly vanished behind a curtain of sober indifference. He gave Smithy a nod. The pirate lifted the plank, and the tiny bundle slid into the sea with a splash that sent a chill through Charlisse.

The men dispersed, and Charlisse stepped to the railing and looked down to the churning waters, where a few fading bubbles marked the spot where her son would rest until the Lord returned to claim him.

Isabel appeared beside her and put her arm around Charlisse's shoulders. "How can you bear it so well?" she asked, looking at her curiously.

Thunder bellowed in the distance as the wind scattered ominous clouds, blotting out the remaining sunlight. Charlisse wiped a wayward tear from the corner of her eye. "Because I have no choice."

"Seems neither of us have much choice as of late." Isabel murmured, then turned with moist eyes to Charlisse. "You said God loves you and protects you. Why doesn't He come to our rescue? Why did He take your son?"

A frosty breeze raised goose bumps on Charlisse's arms. *She's right. You've lost everything. What kind of God would do that?*

Closing her eyes, Charlisse lifted her face to the wind, allowing the salty gusts to dry her remaining tears and caress her skin. Truly, she didn't understand. How could the Father she had come to trust allow such tragedies? It made no sense. What happened to His words in Romans when He said, "All things work together for good to them that love God, to them who are the called according to his purpose"? *Lord, I cannot feel Your presence through my pain. Where are You?*

Isabel removed her arm from Charlisse and clutched the rail, staring out over the tumultuous sea. "Perhaps we humans are foolish to believe that God gives us any consideration at all." Groaning, her fingers fluttered to the silver combs in her hair then fell away.

Charlisse studied Isabel's despondent expression and cringed, remembering how it felt to be without hope in a world gone mad. How could she persuade this young girl that God loved her when Charlisse was beginning to doubt His love herself?

Wicked chuckles echoed in the stormy breeze, and Charlisse glanced over her shoulder to see clusters of pirates gawking their way. Her eyes locked on Kent's as he leapt down from the quarterdeck, shouting aloft for the men to furl topsails and gallants for the upcoming storm. Why he allowed her and Isabel to remain on deck, she had no idea. His moments of civility she could attribute only to his attraction for Isabel, surely not to any ounce of kindness in his soul. Yet she had detected a change in him—ever so slight, but there, nonetheless, in fleeting, unguarded looks and brief moments of accommodation.

Swirling black clouds swarmed over the ship, blocking out the last rays of sunlight and offering flashes of lightning in their place. An angry gust fluttered over them, and Isabel plucked out her combs and sighed.

Charlisse smiled at the girl's attempt to maintain a neat coiffure despite the savage ocean blasts that constantly fought to dislodge her auburn curls. Charlisse had given up on her own hair and simply tied it behind her neck, no longer concerned with her appearance. She must concentrate on more important things now—like gaining her strength and planning an escape.

Already she felt stronger physically. Would that she could heal as quickly in her spirit and soul. Now that her son, Edward—she had named him after her father—had been put to rest, she knew she must move on, despite the ache in her heart that would remain forever. Her trust in God was another matter. She'd been discarded by every man in her life. Was He just another? No, He was not a man, but God. She must ignore the doubts and accusations assailing her and reaffirm her faith in His love. She must. But how?

A thick, heavy cloud overhead broke open and flung sheets of rain down upon them. The refreshing drops showered over Charlisse, and she closed her eyes and tilted her face upward, allowing the water to wash away the horrors of the past week.

Isabel grabbed Charlisse's arm. "Let's go to the cabin before we get drenched."

"Oh, I do love the rain, don't you?" Charlisse said without looking at her.

"Are you daft?" Isabel asked. "You'll catch your death of cold. Not to mention ruin your hair."

The *clomp* of heavy boots sounded behind them, and Charlisse pried open her rain-sodden lashes to see Isabel's lips tighten.

"Ladies." Kent's deep voice rang through the rain.

They turned to see his muscular frame looming over them, the ends of his dark hair curling in the moisture. His gaze covered Isabel, and she wrapped her arms across her chest and looked down, a red hue rising on her cheeks.

"What do you want, Kent?" Charlisse said, pulling his attention toward her.

As if in answer, a growl of thunder rumbled. The downpour ceased, replaced by a gentle sprinkle of warm rain.

" 'Tis *Captain*, if you please." His growl matched the retreating thunder. "I wish to speak to you, Lady Charlisse." He turned toward Isabel. "Would you excuse us?"

Charlisse searched his shifty eyes under the brim of his hat, but found no indication of his intentions. She nodded for Isabel to go.

"But, Char—"

"I'll be fine," Charlisse reassured her, gently touching her arm.

Isabel swung around, cast a cautious glance over her shoulder and disappeared below.

Kent returned his gaze from the retreating girl, approached the rail, and gripped it with both hands. Sighing, he peered toward the horizon.

Charlisse stood silently watching him.

"Lady Ashton," he began then swallowed hard. Though he tried to meet Charlisse's gaze, he could not. Instead, he focused on the agitated sea. "How does she speak of me?"

From the corner of his eye, he saw Charlisse flinch. "Speak of you?" she asked in a quizzical tone.

Kent leaned one arm on the rail and raised his dark eyes to hers. How he abhorred debasing himself in front of this woman, but she was the only one to whom Isabel would confide. "Does she hate me?"

Charlisse gave him a puzzled look. "Would you blame her? You ravished her."

"I was drunk. I didn't know what I was doing." Truth be told, he regretted that evening more than anything else in his life. "I never touched her after that night."

"Your inebriation is no excuse, sir, and when it comes to being forcibly violated, I believe once would be enough to cause any woman to hate you, wouldn't you say?" Charlisse wiped the raindrops sliding down her forehead and thrust her chin in the air.

"Always the pompous wench." Kent grimaced at her blunt candor and lengthened his stance.

"I beg your pardon." Charlisse threw her hands onto her hips.

He shook the water from his hair and flicked it behind him. Why couldn't he make her understand how sorry he was for what he'd done to Isabel? Words of remorse formed in his mouth but faltered upon his lips. Apologies were for the weak, and he was not weak.

"Good day, Captain." With a lift of her nose, she started toward the companionway stairs.

Kent clasped her arm. She winced and glared up at him.

"I must have her," he demanded.

"I believe you already do."

He pulled her back then loosened his grip. "Willingly."

"If you speak of her love, I'm afraid you will never have it. 'Tis the one thing no amount of threatening can gain you." Charlisse turned and stomped away.

"I have not dismissed you!" Kent stormed. The woman's impertinence was not to be borne. But how could he expect her to help him after what he'd done to her and Merrick?

Charlisse faced him. A few strands of her hair had loosened from its tie and fell in wet coils around her face.

He closed his eyes, forcing down his rage and momentarily his pride. "Tell me what to do."

"You want my help?" Charlisse snickered.

Her laughter fumed his blood to a rapid boil, but he held his temper in check. He did have one card to play in this game. "If you wish to see your husband again." Of course he had no intention of allowing her to win the hand should she accept his play.

By the yearning that writhed upon her face, he could tell he'd made his move well.

The gloomy clouds retreated, sending a blast of wind over the deck. Charlisse hugged herself and studied him with those eyes—those piercing blue eyes that always made him feel ashamed. "You are sorely mistaken, Captain," she said, "if you think I would help you in any way—especially when it comes to Isabel."

Kent bunched his fists, digging his nails into his palms, infuriated at this woman's moral defiance. Forcing his expression into a smug grin, he glowered at her. "You will soon wish you had been more agreeable, milady."

"What do you intend to do with me?"

"Let's just say I know of someone who would pay handsomely for a beauty such as you."

Charlisse's chest heaved. "How unfortunate for him that I am not for sale."

"Ah, but there are so many lonely men here in the Caribbean in need of a mistress."

"And there are plenty of willing trollops to accommodate them, I'm sure. I, however, am not one of them. I am a free woman."

"On the contrary, milady, you do not appear to be free at the moment." Kent crossed his arms over his chest and grinned, happy to have the upper hand once again. "Yes, I do believe you shall live out your days warming the bed of a fat, old, flatulent man."

# Chapter 11
## Ominous Meeting

Merrick slammed into the Drunken Skunk, his leather boots thumping over the spit-laden floor. Sloane and Rusty followed quickly on his heels. After the *Redemption* had made anchorage at Tortuga, Merrick's two comrades had begged to accompany him onshore. Finally, he had relented, though he much preferred to be alone. Merrick tore off his tricorn and slapped it across his thigh, shaking the rain from its brim. Thunder ripped across the night sky, sending the beams overhead rattling down dust and rat feces. The putrid reek of alcohol, sweat, and tobacco assaulted Merrick's nose, old familiar odors that soured his stomach along with his mood. Lanterns swayed overhead, and candles flickered in the stormy wind gusting in from open windows, but nothing disturbed the mob of degenerates in the midst of their nightly debauchery.

Spotting his first objective, Merrick marched toward the back of the large rectangular room, pushing his way through the crowd of inebriated men. He kept his hand on the hilt of his cutlass as a warning that he was in no mood for a trifling brawl. A few pairs of eyes met his and the pirates nodded as he passed.

"Why, 'tis Cap'n Merrick," one burly man stated, pointing at him with a mug of sloshing liquor.

Other men peered over their drink with squinted eyes, then turned to those around them and muttered.

Ignoring their stares, Merrick stopped in front of a long wooden bar, behind which three men worked furiously filling mugs from two huge kegs sitting atop crates. A row of bottles lined the shelves above them.

"Rum," Merrick bellowed, drawing the attention of one of the workers. He grabbed a bottle from the top shelf and tossed it to Merrick, who flipped two coins into his hand. The man swiped an ale-saturated hand across his forehead and grinned his appreciation.

A woman's scream pierced the air from the left, and the clash of swords echoed over the shouts and curses pounding at Merrick's ears. Disregarding the skirmish, Merrick searched for a vacant table, preferably one in a dark corner. Rusty ordered a pint of ale, and with Sloane, followed along behind him.

"By the powers, Cap'n Merrick," a beefy pirate said as Merrick passed. "I heard ye gave up the trade an' took up the priesthood." He chuckled, joined by several pirates around him.

Halting, Merrick shot the man a probing look. The pirate slammed down his mug and returned Merrick's level stare. Soiled lace bubbled out from a purple doublet onto his furry chest. One silver earring hung from his left ear, and scales of unwashed dirt crusted his thick neck. Merrick recognized him as a man he'd sailed with years ago—a furtive fellow with a reckless tongue and a propensity to fight.

"Is that holy water yer carryin' there, Merrick?" He glanced at his friends and crossed his arms over his chest, keeping his hands close to the pistols housed in his baldric. "Perchance, can ye anoint us lowly sinners?"

Merrick twisted his lips into a mocking grin. "It would be my pleasure to anoint you, sir, but please step aside so I don't splatter the precious fluid on your friends." Merrick lifted his bottle of rum in the air to crash it down upon the man's head when, as Merrick expected, the stout pirate drew his pistol. In a flash, Merrick tore his cutlass from its scabbard, knocked the man's weapon from his grasp, and threw the sword in the air. It wheeled, glittering, and he caught it by the hilt. Without spilling a drop from his bottle, he positioned the sharp point at the pirate's chest. A spot of red formed at the blade's tip, creating a brown smudge on the pirate's sullied, ragged shirt.

Gasps drifted over the crowd. The man's bloodshot eyes bulged, and his mouth hung open. One deep voice from the mob yelled, "Run 'im through!" and Merrick was reminded of how vacillating the loyalties of this loathsome band were.

A rage seething deep within Merrick forced the point of his cutlass a breath farther into the pirate's skin despite the imploring look in the villain's flashing dark eyes.

A cold blast of wind blew over Merrick. *Slice him.*

He wanted to, if only to appease the wrath that tormented him day and night. His hand trembled, and the pirate closed his eyes.

"Kill 'im, ye yellow-livered carp," a slurred voice blurted out over the boisterous crowd.

Tightening his muscles for the final plunge, Merrick hesitated as a part of his conscience woke from its slumber and shone a light over the darkening areas of his heart. He dropped his sword, sheathed it, and took a swig from the bottle. The pirate opened his eyes and breathed a sigh of relief, then took a step back. Moans of disappointment emanated from the surrounding men, who soon returned to their drinks and trollops.

Merrick sauntered through the mass of sweltering humanity that now parted for him, and he came to a table in the corner from which he could view the whole tavern. The scrawny man who occupied it gave Merrick a cursory glance and continued his activities with the vixen on his lap. Suddenly, he returned his gaze, wide-eyed, to Merrick.

"Begone with you," Merrick ordered.

The man stood, dropping the woman to the floor, and scrambled off like a rat running from sunlight.

Stumbling to her feet, the woman spewed profanities after the man until she turned and saw Merrick. A sensual smile replaced her scowl, and she sidled over to him, cooing like a diseased dove.

Momentarily distracted by her bosoms abounding from her tight bodice, he gaped at her, but the closer she came, the more powerful grew the stench of body odor and cheap perfume, and he waved her away.

Feeling a surge of power, Merrick smiled, remembering the sense of authority and control he once had before giving his life to Christ. He liked this sensation, being autonomous again, back at the helm of his ship, where he belonged. Before his commitment to God, Merrick had been the most respected pirate on the Caribbean—well-known for his daring and skill in battle and for his cunning savvy in acquiring hordes of treasure. He had been feared and admired by all, and apparently, he still had the efficacy to rise to the top again.

A sudden chill clawed at his spine. *If you had been in control, Charlisse wouldn't have died.*

The sound of her name, even in his thoughts, stabbed him like a knife. He took another drink, kicked out a chair, and sat down.

Sloane dropped onto a bench beside him and scratched his beard. "Good thing ye didn't kill that slimy crawfish, Cap'n, though I knows ye wanted to."

"Why is that good?" Merrick asked as Rusty settled into a seat next to Sloane.

Sloane cocked his head, and a furrow deepened the crinkle between his brows. "Ye knows why, Cap'n. 'Tis not right. The Good Book says—"

"The Good Book says many things, but I'll not hear of it now." Merrick slammed his bottle onto the wooden table.

"Been awhile since I been in a place like this," Rusty declared, scanning the room with glee. "But I feel a mite easier with ye at me side, Cap'n."

Merrick shot him an approving nod but continued directing his gaze across the mob, searching for that truculent rogue Morgan whom he heard often came here to celebrate after a victory. Having put the word out on the street that he was looking for him, all Merrick had to do was wait for the villain to make an appearance.

Sloane leaned across the table toward Rusty. "Then yer a fool's fool mate. 'Tain't nobody safe amongst these blackguards—especially when they been drinkin'."

The smile fell from Rusty's face as he slumped back into his chair and gulped his ale.

"Ah, leave the boy alone, Sloane," Merrick said, sliding the bottle of rum over to him. "You squawk like an old woman. Have a drink."

"Naw, ye knows I don't partake no more, Cap'n. I seen that vile liquid turn honorable men into half-masted monkeys far too often for the likes o' me to indulge."

Merrick took another swig and glared at his friend, regretting his decision to allow him to come along. "If this place offends you so, perhaps you should return to the ship."

Sloane scratched under his purple headscarf and a disgruntled smile spread upon his lips. "Naw, I won't be leavin' ye, Cap'n. I needs to be here to help ye keep a level head about ye." He grabbed the bottle of rum, shifting it nonchalantly across the pockmarked table.

"There's naught to concern ye," Rusty piped up, emboldened by the ale. "The cap'n don't be needin' nobody's help." He took one more gulp and smacked the empty mug onto the table.

Merrick grinned, allowing the boy's confidence to feed his resurging pride. He retrieved a coin from his pocket and flung it at Rusty. "Go get yourself another one, son."

"With smiling pleasure, Cap'n." The boy sprang from his seat, and Merrick watched his shock of red hair bob through the crowd.

Lightning flashed outside the window, transforming the dark interior of muted, swaying colors into stark grays and whites. Even Rusty's hair turned to dark gray as he faded from Merrick's view. A roar of thunder shook the table, and Merrick reached for his bottle as a blast of cool air charged with rain lifted the hair from his shoulders.

"The boy looks up to ye. Ye shouldn't be encouragin' 'im to drink."

"Spare me your lofty opinions, Sloane, and remember from whence you came." Merrick instantly regretted the insulting reminder of Sloane's humble beginnings as an orphan on the streets of Aruba. He drew another long gulp, allowing the sharp fluid to numb his biting conscience.

Sloane cringed, sorrow tugging at his eyes. "Cap'n, what are we doin' here, if I might ask?" He inched his gnarled fingers toward Merrick's bottle and began sliding it across the table. "This ain't yer kinda place no more."

Was it? Merrick wondered. He peered across the mob of pirates, merchants, and harlots. To his right, four men played a game of cards. Accusations flew and tempers flared as stakes were raised and mugs filled. Up ahead, two men fought fist to fist as a crowd grew around them, placing bets. One merchant to Merrick's left had passed out in his chair, and the woman who had kept him company now relieved him of his money purse and jewelry. Curses flew through the air like grapeshot, and doxies sauntered about displaying their wares, leading men upstairs to their destruction. He knew well what the Bible said about such women.

*"For her house inclineth unto death, and her paths unto the dead."*

Merrick's nose burned from the rank stench of sweat, vomit, and ale. This sort of place had been his haven for many years before the Lord got hold of him. In here, he was master, *he* was lord—respected and feared by all. He could drink as much as he wanted and have as many women as he wanted. But as he surveyed the room, nausea churned in Merrick's stomach. The tavern oozed with nothing but wickedness, greed, and pride; even in his grievous state, he wanted no part of it.

*You are My son, now. You are being transformed into My image.*

Merrick nodded. He knew he was a better man than he once had been.

An icy breeze flowed over him. *But what good has it done you?*

He shook his head and rubbed his temples, trying to dislodge the conflicting thoughts.

"I'm searching for Morgan," Merrick said plainly, avoiding Sloane's piercing gaze.

"You'll be seein' 'im here eventually, I'm guessin'." Sloane dug his long nails into the soft wood of the table and fidgeted in his seat. "But what'll ye do with 'im when ye finds him?"

Merrick leaned over and swept his bottle up from the far end of the table, giving Sloane a sideways glance. A flash of red silk burst from amongst the haze of dingy, tattered clothing, drawing Merrick's attention. He stared at it, fascinated, as the soothing liquor began to deaden his senses. When he lifted his gaze, it met a pair of blue eyes—the color of Charlisse's—but the face that held them was nothing like the soft, alabaster skin of his wife. In place of her high, rosy cheeks were two round spots of pasted-on rouge. Instead of golden curls dancing over the woman's shoulders: the dreary brown mass that grazed them seemed as stiff as the corset she wore. Placing one hand on her hip, she shifted her weight and winked at him. "Want some company?"

"Thank ye, but no, he don't," Sloane snapped.

Merrick chuckled and squinted at the vision before him. *Charlisse.* How he missed holding her—the feel of her soft skin in his arms, the tickle of her silken hair on his face. If he didn't look too hard or for too long, this girl could remind him of her. "Come here." He motioned for her to approach.

Sloane groaned.

The girl sashayed over, plopped down on his lap, and wrapped her arms around his neck. "I thought you looked lonely." She giggled.

Closing his eyes, Merrick put his arm around the girl's waist and begged for the haze of rum to transport him to another time and place where Charlisse still lived—where she smiled at him and loved him and where he could never lose her again. His eyes burned, and he squeezed them, forcing back the agony. When he opened them, he grabbed the bottle and downed another gulp, but as the scent of liquor and sweat rose from the woman, he realized no amount of alcohol would deceive his senses into believing she was Charlisse.

He shivered, despite the mugginess of the tavern. *She will ease your loneliness.*

The woman burped and snuggled against his chest. Her brazen fingers inched inside his shirt. A putrid bubbling churned the rum in his empty stomach, forcing it to his throat. Merrick shot to his feet, holding onto the woman only to ensure she wouldn't fall. He set her on her feet and bowed. "My apologies, milady, but I fear I was mistaken in my need for companionship."

The woman huffed and flung him a doleful glance before shrugging and sauntering away.

"Good for ye, Cap'n," Sloane said.

Merrick shot him a patronizing look as Rusty returned with another mug of ale, already half empty.

"Cap'n," Rusty said. "Methinks I saw Cap'n Collier o'er there by the bar."

"Collier?" Merrick squinted into the smoky room. "You mean, Captain Edward Collier?"

"Aye, that be the one." Rusty leaned toward Merrick, wiping the beer from his prickly chin. "I hear he's one of the fiercest pirates on the Spanish Main."

" 'Tis him o'er there." Rusty glanced over his shoulder, and Merrick followed his gaze to the table where the brutish English pirate had just sat down, flanked by his minions. He dusted off his silk doublet, then waved an arm through the air, lace fluttering in the breeze, sending one of his men scampering away. Yanking a velvet pouch from his belt, he shook it in the air and tossed it onto the table, drawing the eyes of every greedy soul within hearing's reach of the coins clanking inside. His beady eyes met Merrick's as he twisted his thin mustache between two fingers. Merrick returned his glare, unflinching. Yes, Merrick had been on the hunt for Collier for months. Tales of his barbarous torture of innocent victims sped across the Spanish Main, evoking fear wherever they landed. He needed to be stopped—at least that's what Merrick had once believed.

"He knows ye?" Rusty swerved back, his eyes were flickering with excitement.

"He knows *of* me."

"Ye best be stayin' away from 'im," Sloane added sharply, pulling the bottle toward him. "You may lay to it, the man is as cruel as they come. They don't be callin' 'im the Scourge of the Spaniards for nothin'."

Merrick studied the vile pirate and his ostentatious display, but found him to be nothing but a gaudy boor. He reached for his rum and saw the bottle perched on the other side of the table. Merrick turned toward Sloane. "Blast, man, will you stop moving my rum away!" He leaned and clutched his bottle, then took another swig.

Sloane frowned at Merrick with harsh blue eyes as stormy as the sea.

"Do you think to keep me from my drink?" Merrick asked.

Shaking his head, Sloane looked away.

Thick drops of rain pelted the rooftop, sounding like the march of soldiers, pulling the gazes of several pirates upward. Closing his eyes, Merrick allowed his thoughts to swim freely through the numbing haze of his mind, searching for a quiet place where he felt no pain.

*Go to Port Royal.*

"Confound it, man," Merrick popped his eyes open and scowled at Sloane. "Must you nag me like an old woman?"

"But, Cap'n," Sloane said, brows knit. "I didn't say nothin'."

"Wha..." Merrick passed a hand through his hair. Was he going mad?

The thud of heavy boots echoed above the clamor of the storm, and a shadow fell across the table. Merrick looked up into dark, sinister eyes.

"Captain Collier at your service." The man bowed with a sweep of his plumed hat. "I understand you are looking for Morgan."

"Indeed I am, Captain." Merrick nodded, a shiver lifting the hairs on the back of his neck. "You have news of him?"

"I have just left him at Porto Bello."

A fiery shard passed through Merrick. "You were with Morgan?"

93

Sloane scuffed his chair back and laid a hand on his thigh next to his cutlass.

"Aye, I was. But he has been detained." A devious grin twisted the man's otherwise noble features. "Shall we say he's enjoying the hospitality of the Spaniards."

Having witnessed Morgan and his men's social graces firsthand, Merrick felt his blood surge to his hands, and he toyed with the handle of the dagger strapped to his thigh. With one quick flick, he could plant it in this monster's heart. Pulling it from its scabbard, he rubbed the carved handle between his thumb and forefinger and glared at the pirate.

Collier gestured toward a chair. "May I?" he asked.

Rusty pulled out a chair. "Why o' course, Cap'n Collier," he said with a cracking voice, eyeing the newcomer with admiration.

Sloane narrowed his eyes and shot Rusty a smoldering look.

Merrick eased his grip on the dagger. Perhaps he could use this man. "Would you know in which direction Morgan intends to sail when his business is concluded?"

Collier sat and gestured for one of his men to get him a drink. " 'Tis difficult to say, Captain." He leaned back and folded his arms over his chest. "But I have plans to meet with him in a few months at Port Royal."

Sloane cleared his throat. "Beggin' yer pardon, Cap'n, but shouldn't we be gettin' back to the ship?"

Ignoring him, Merrick studied his opponent, noting his cold, dark eyes, high cheekbones, and prominent forehead. His chiseled nose stood slightly skewed—perhaps from receiving too many angry blows—yet it did not deter from his aristocratic looks. This was the face of a man who beguiled and charmed his way into a person's good confidence, then ripped the heart from their chest when they weren't looking.

"I have a proposition for you, Captain." He grabbed a mug one of his men brought him, gulping down a long draught of the foamy liquid. "You seek Morgan. I could use another ship to assist in my raid on Barracoa—especially one captained by a man of your caliber and skill. Sail with me, and I'll make sure you and Captain Morgan meet."

"Why should I join forces with you when I can find Morgan on my own?" Merrick cocked his head.

"Because, sir, you look like a man in need of. . ." Collier raised his brow at Merrick's bottle of rum. "Shall we say, a diversion."

Sloane shot to his feet. "Cap'n, let's be going."

Merrick fixed him with a cold eye. "Take Rusty and return to the ship. I have some business to discuss with Captain Collier."

"But, Cap'n—"

"I said *go*."

"Aye, Cap'n," Sloane grumbled and motioned for Rusty to follow.

The young pirate rose and trudged after Sloane, mumbling in discontent.

"Get my new friend here a drink," Collier bellowed over his shoulder to one of his crew. He glanced back. "Make it a bottle of rum," he yelled after the man who headed toward the bar. Collier put his arms on the table and leaned in toward Merrick. "Now, let's talk about making you a real pirate again, eh?"

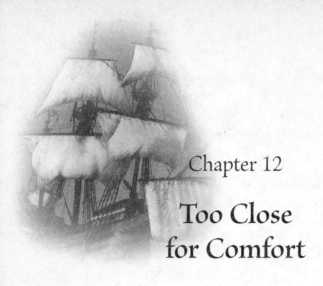

# Chapter 12

# Too Close
for Comfort

Kingston Bay!" Charlisse pressed her nose against the colored glass of the porthole and felt the warm sunlight stream across her face. When she'd heard the commands to lower sails and the ship heaved to and slowed on its tack, she knew they must be approaching a port, but she had no idea it would be the town she had called home for the past three years. Elation lifted her sagging hopes, her mind reeling with plans of escape. The sands of the shore around the port glowed like embers of a fire in the afternoon sun—so close, she could almost feel their warm grains against her bare feet. If she could only get Isabel and herself across the bay, they could flee to Reverend Thomas and be safe. *Lord, help me.*

Isabel moaned from the bed, where she had lain all night and half the day. A pail sat on the table next to her, issuing its putrid odor throughout the cabin. "What does it matter?" she whispered, lifting her hand to her forehead. "Kent frequents Port Royal. If you think he'll allow us to leave this ship, I fear you are misled."

Charlisse crossed to the bed and sat beside her friend, taking her hand in hers. "The sickness will pass soon."

Isabel curled on her side and stared at the bucket. Taking several deep breaths, she reached for it, but then withdrew her hand. "How long must I endure this?"

"Only a few months." Charlisse smoothed back the damp tendrils on Isabel's forehead. Her heart broke for the young girl. She had endured so many horrors during her captivity aboard the *Vanquisher*, and now to suffer sickness from the child she carried. . . It was too much. *Lord, how can You allow so much suffering?*

A blast from the *Vanquisher's* cannons thundered through the ship, shaking it to its keel. Isabel jumped just as a booming volley erupted in the distance. "Why must they greet each other with cannon fire? It is so barbaric."

The ship jolted as the anchor released, and Charlisse heard it splash into the calm, crystalline waters as she rushed back to the window. From her angle, she could see a narrow slice of the main docks. Merchants and slaves swarmed across them, loading and unloading goods from the cockboats rowed in from ships anchored in the bay. The surrounding taverns and shops stood like beacons of hope, igniting her memory with yearning.

She was home.

The oak door flew open, and Kent strutted in, dressed in a fine coat of biscuit-colored taffeta, leather breeches, and a black silk neckerchief. His hair was slicked back and tied behind. The smirk on his face faded when he saw Isabel lying on the bed.

"Are you ill, Lady Ashton?" Taking a tentative step toward her, he removed his plumed captain's hat.

Isabel cast an anxious glance at Charlisse and shook her head.

"Just a bit of seasickness, I'm afraid." Charlisse must keep the young girl's pregnancy secret at all cost. God only knew what further obsessive attachments Kent would form toward Isabel if he knew she carried his child.

"Hmm. . ." Kent eyed her with suspicion. "After so long? Seems unlikely."

Charlisse grabbed a lock of her hair and wrenched it between her fingers. She approached him. "What is your business at Port Royal?"

His lips curved in a jeering smile. "So you recognize your old home? Isn't this where you and your precious Merrick were married?"

Charlisse narrowed her eyes and tossed her hair behind her.

"And the place where I first stole you from Merrick?" He lifted one eyebrow. "Ironic that we are here again, and I have once again stolen you from that gutless imbecile."

Charlisse swallowed a burning lump of rage.

"I can feel your animosity from here, milady, and I assure you it only fuels my intentions toward you."

Isabel sat up, and Kent's eyes darted in her direction. "Leave her be," she said in a feeble voice.

Kent fumbled with his hat and dropped his gaze. "I came only to escort you ladies on deck for one last breath of fresh air before I must depart on business."

"Why should we accept any favors from you?" Charlisse spat.

"Because, milady," Kent's sharp eyes darted to Charlisse's. "You are completely dependent upon my graces, whether they be good or evil. And as it happens, my mood is favorable today."

Charlisse's pride held her feet in place, but after glancing at Isabel and realizing the fresh breeze would do her good, not to mention afford Charlisse a better view of the city, she nodded. "Then we accept your offer," she said, feigning a politeness that nearly stuck in her throat.

"Very well." Kent approached Isabel, offering her his hand, but her hard glare stopped him in midstep.

"I can manage." She coughed and reached toward Charlisse, who inched to her side.

Scowling, Kent swerved on his heels.

Taking Isabel's arm in hers, Charlisse patted her hand, and they followed Kent up on deck.

The sweet fragrance of roses and hibiscus tickled her nose, intertwined with the odors of burning coal, fish, and human sweat. Charlisse drew in a deep breath of the familiar scents that brought back happy memories of Merrick, the reverend, and the orphans whom she'd grown to love.

Pirates clambered up and down the ratlines, furling the remaining sails and leaving the yards and masts stark against the afternoon sun. Four crewmen lowered one of the cockboats into the water below. The doctor stood overlooking the scene with a pipe in his mouth.

Keeping Isabel snug by her side, Charlisse approached the railing and scanned the bay. Streams of sunlight scattered like diamonds over the rippling turquoise water. Seagulls flapped heavy wings overhead, shrieking their welcome to the new visitors. The massive stone walls of Fort Charles towered over the harbor, pierced periodically by the gaping black muzzles of the fort's twenty cannons that protected the ships and the town from intruders.

Kent took his place beside Charlisse and seemed to be studying her as she glanced over the other five ships rocking idly in the harbor. Her gaze flitted over each one, noting the names, if visible, the position and number of masts, the colors and lines of the hulls—an interest of hers since she had become a privateer's wife. A skip of her heart caused her eyes to lock upon one in particular. She examined it until, with unavoidable glee, she jumped from her spot.

"Ah, I thought you'd be overjoyed at the sight," Kent said.

"The *Redemption*." She faced him with a patronizing look. "Merrick's here. And you, sir, are done for."

"Is that so?"

Isabel gave Charlisse's arm a squeeze.

From over Kent's shoulder, Charlisse saw the doctor take a puff from his pipe and glance their way with interest.

"Yes, and you well know it." Charlisse met Kent's intense gaze with her own, then turned to look upon that mighty ship—her husband's ship. "Why do you show me this?" she asked him, knowing she would never have seen the *Redemption* from her cabin window.

"To be sure, I thought it quite ironic that your wayward husband be anchored here in the very city where I intend to sell you off as mistress to one of his sluggard compatriots." He leaned toward her, and the smell of rum wafted over her. "Do you really think he will rescue you? He still believes you dead, milady. Why, I wouldn't be surprised if he had moved on to another pretty trollop. The town's full of them, you know."

Yanking her arm from Isabel's, Charlisse swung it toward Kent, hoping to dissolve his smirk with a slap, but his strong grasp caught her hand, and his lips twisted into an even more pompous grin. "Ah, ah. . .no way for a lady to behave. But you aren't a real lady, are you?"

Wrenching her arm, Kent forced her to face the bay. Charlisse squeezed her eyes shut. A flood of tears empowered by old insecurities threatened to pour from them. He was right. She wasn't a real lady. Her uncle had made that quite plain.

Visions of half-naked women cooing Merrick's name from the taverns of Port Royal the first time they had ventured through the city filled her thoughts. If he truly believed she was dead, he would have no reason to be lonely for long.

Gliding one hand over her flat belly, Charlisse nearly crumbled under the agony of loss.

Shivers coiled up her spine. *Abandoned and betrayed.*

"No!" Charlisse struggled against the firm grip Kent maintained upon her arm.

Isabel yanked on the sleeve of his doublet. "Unhand her."

Releasing Charlisse, Kent bowed. "As you wish, milady. Enjoy your friend's company while you can, for I intend to find a husband for her in town."

"A husband?" Isabel pressed a hand to her stomach.

Charlisse rubbed her arm and backed away from him. "He plans to sell me as if I were chattel."

"What?" Isabel's eyes snapped to his. "How can you be so cruel?"

"Me, cruel?" Kent's features twitched as if shocked by her assessment. "Hasn't Lady Charlisse informed you of the atrocities she and her husband inflicted upon me?"

Isabel glanced at Charlisse.

"No?" Kent shook his head in mock displeasure. His eyes narrowed. "To begin with, they stole my uncle's ship—that is, after they murdered him."

Isabel's mouth fell open.

"Why, you lying knave, you are the one who stabbed my father." Charlisse gulped as pain burned up her throat at the memory. Why was he lying? To impress Isabel?

"Your husband forced my hand."

"You deceive yourself." Charlisse gave him a judicious look. "When will you learn to take the blame for your own actions?"

Kent's upper lip began to twitch. "Then, do you suppose I am at fault for being left to rot all alone in the dungeons at Fort Charles?" He shook the hair from his face. "With no one to speak on my behalf?"

Charlisse searched his eyes for any trace of deceit, but found only agony sizzling within them. She had ventured into those dungeons. A shiver raked over her at the memory. "If you were there, I'm sure you deserved it."

"For a year?" Kent's eyes blazed. "When my only crime was that I was on board your husband's ship when the authorities came upon him? Other than any misdeeds you credit me with, I had not violated any British laws—at least no more than your husband. But Merrick's powerful father freed him with a wave of his jeweled finger. And did your precious Merrick consider me? No, he had his entire crew released and left me there to fester with the sludge and rats." He turned his pained gaze to the fort's towering battlements. "Why, I'd still be there if I hadn't bribed one of the officers to release me. As it is, I had to give the thieving man every doubloon I owned."

"And if my memory serves me correctly, you were the one who had Merrick tossed into that dungeon in the first place—on false evidence that you planted on his ship."

"Ah, he barely spent a month there."

Charlisse threw her fists on her hips. "Because he escaped the first time."

"Trifling details." Kent pouted. "The point is, milady, your charitable husband left me to suffer a horrid punishment unbefitting my crimes. Now that doesn't sound like the actions of a godly man, does it?" Kent smirked.

Charlisse wrinkled her brow. Though Kent had certainly harmed them personally, no laws had been broken, at least none that warranted such a harsh penalty. She could not imagine her husband allowing Kent to remain imprisoned—even in light of his anger toward him. "I'm sorry for what you suffered, but hurting Merrick and me will not take away the pain of that year."

"Perhaps not, but it will dull it quite a bit." A wicked grin curled his lips and leeched the sorrow from his eyes.

Isabel stared at him with concern until his gaze shifted to hers and she looked away.

Charlisse snorted and turned to face the *Redemption*, trying to determine whether anyone was on board. Was Merrick pacing the quarterdeck, as he was so fond of doing? She could not make out details in the fading light, only that the ship was within a quick row of a cockboat.

*So close.*

Her eyes darted across the water below. If she jumped over the rail, she could swim to it with no trouble. She glanced at Isabel, held fast in Kent's wicked grasp. No, she could not leave her behind.

The doctor's anxious regard bore into her from where he stood below the foredeck stairs. Raising his brows, he offered her an amiable grin. Was he being sympathetic or simply enjoying her torment?

"Take one last look, milady, at your husband's ship," Kent said, drawing her eyes back to him. "For tomorrow, you belong to another man—a more powerful man—who, I assure you, will not tolerate your unruly temperament. He will tame your tongue and quell your rebellious spirit or toss you to the sharks without so much as a woeful glance."

Turning toward the *Redemption*, Charlisse screamed with all the breath her lungs could produce, "Merrick! Merrick!" She leaned over the rail and waved her hands over her head. "Merrick! Merr—"

A searing pain shot up her arm as Kent grabbed her and struck his sweaty palm against her mouth, muffling her scream and stealing her breath.

"Enough," he growled, dragging her across the deck.

Charlisse struggled against his hold, but his clench around her tender waist sent pains shooting throughout her body.

"Don't think you'll be escaping while I'm gone. It's down to the hold you go. You remember that damp, dark, rat-infested place you called home for nigh three weeks, my dear?"

Terror accompanied the pain that lanced through her. She *did* remember that horrid place. But it was not the memory of it that frightened her now. For how could she escape to find her husband if she were imprisoned below?

"Cutter, take Lady Ashton to her cabin." Kent flung an order over his shoulder to the doctor.

The last thing Charlisse saw before Kent dragged her below was the look of horror etched on Isabel's face.

# Chapter 13

# A Ship
## without a Captain

Charlisse clung to the cold iron bars and closed her eyes. *Lord, where are You? Have You forgotten me?*

A cool whiff of air struck her face. *Yes, He has left you like all the other men in your life.*

Forcing back tears, Charlisse scanned the room as her eyes grew accustomed to the darkness. Familiar shadows that lurked in the bottom of the ship began emerging like demons preparing for an assault. She drew a deep breath and immediately regretted doing so. Human waste, moldy wood, rotting food, and rat feces—the foul odors of the bilge—attacked her, strangling her breath.

She remembered her imprisonment on her father's pirate ship and how the Lord had protected her so miraculously.

*Father, I don't hear You. I don't see You. I don't feel Your presence. Where are You?*

Charlisse shivered. *He is not here. . .*

The wicked voice faded as the *thump* of boots sounded on the stairs, and Cutter emerged, his gnarled face twisting in the light of the lantern he carried. Isabel crept behind him, handkerchief to her nose. The doctor stepped to the bars and with a jingle of keys, unlocked the gate.

"We've come to help you escape."

His words floated on the kindness of his tone through the rancid air until Charlisse caught them and forced her mind to hear them again. She rushed forward. "Pray do not mock me, sir."

"It is not my desire to do so." He bowed.

Grabbing her arm, Isabel pulled Charlisse from the prison, a glimmer of hope flickering in her eyes.

Charlisse's gaze shifted from Cutter to Isabel. "But how, sir? Where's Smithy?"

"I'm afraid Smithy is quite indisposed." His warped upper lip rose into a mischievous grin. "Due to the extra four rations of rum I prescribed him—for medicinal purposes, of course." He winked.

Isabel coughed and glanced around the dark room, cringing.

Charlisse studied the doctor's silver eyes. She had learned to trust no man—save Merrick—and certainly no pirate, doctor or not. "Why would you do this?"

A chill nipped at the back of her neck. *It's a trap.*

"I turn a blind eye to many of the captain's atrocities, but I cannot abide the abuse of innocent women." Then walking toward the stairs, he peered up and gestured for them the follow. "Make haste. We haven't much time."

Charlisse hesitated, but Isabel tugged her arm. "Please, Charlisse, 'tis our only chance."

Isabel's green eyes sparkled with excitement, and Charlisse prayed for wisdom.

Offering her friend a quick smile, she patted her hand. "Then, by all means, we should take it."

Without hesitation, Isabel pulled Charlisse up the winding stairs and four decks that made up the hull of the frigate. When they caught up to Cutter, he had just stepped onto the top deck and was scanning the darkened expanse as he marched toward the starboard railing.

Charlisse nudged him from behind. "What about the other pirates?"

"Never fear, milady. Most have gone ashore, and the remainder are well into their cups." The doctor flung a rope ladder over the bulwark. "I laced both guards' drinks with laudanum." He grinned. "They should be asleep for quite some time."

A shiver ran through Charlisse, and she hugged herself, glancing behind her. Other than the muted creaks and groans of the ship rocking in the bay, a deathly silence hovered over the murky scene. Even the night air carried no breeze, either from the sea or the shore. A multitude of stars twinkled from an ebony sky like flickers of God's love in a dark world, and she prayed she was following the right course. Perhaps the doctor had plans of his own for them. Yet what choice did she have? At least this way she would be free from Kent—and so would Isabel. Charlisse gazed into her friend's hopeful eyes, seeing in them an admiration that surprised her. Who was she that anyone would look to her for strength and wisdom?

Cutter swung his legs over the rail and disappeared over the side, whispering, "When I get down, follow after me, and I'll assist you into the boat."

Charlisse leaned over to see a cockboat bobbing in the water beside the ship. "Go." She nodded toward Isabel. "Hang on tight." The girl suddenly froze. "I'll be right behind you," Charlisse reassured her and helped her over the bulwark.

Trembling, the girl clambered down the swaying ladder until Cutter grabbed her waist and helped her into the boat. Hopping down the ropes with ease, Charlisse quickly joined them, and the doctor loosened the ties and shoved the cockboat from the *Vanquisher* with his oar.

"I'll get you as far as the *Redemption*," he said, setting the lantern down and plunging the paddles into the placid sea. "I trust you'll be safe there?"

"More than safe, sir, I assure you." Charlisse smiled, imagining her reunion with Merrick and his surprise and glee when he discovered she lived. Grabbing the extra set of oars, she adjusted them in the rowlocks and joined in the doctor's efforts.

"There's no need, milady," he protested in an incredulous tone.

"On the contrary, Doctor, there's a great need for me to expedite mine and Miss Ashton's departure from this ship and her vulgar captain."

Cutter nodded.

Nothing more was said as their synchronized strokes disturbed the otherwise tranquil midnight waters, each heave pushing the boat closer to the *Redemption*.

Isabel dabbed at her forehead with the sleeve of her gown. "This heat is stifling."

Breathing hard, Charlisse shook her head and continued rowing. Her damp petticoat clung to her body and chafed her skin with each stroke of the oar, but what did it matter? With each inch of the calm water they crossed, her excitement grew. She imagined the delight on Merrick's face when he first saw her and how safe she would feel in his strong embrace once again. She could almost smell his salty, musky scent and feel the scratch of his stubble on her cheek.

How could she tell him about their son?

Out of the darkness, the crimson bow of the *Redemption* appeared. Just being so close to Merrick's ship—to him—evicted all of Charlisse's nagging doubts. Once she and Merrick were together again, they would be able to deal with the loss of their child. The lantern swinging from the foremast lit their way to the larboard side, where grooves in the hull formed steps up to the top. Smiling, Charlisse remembered how Merrick had specially built them for her comfort, but by the time they were completed, she had mastered the ropes and found the dangling twines much more adventurous.

As they held their oars above the water and the cockboat crunched against the mighty ship, a shout sounded from above. "Who goes there?"

Charlisse recognized the squeaky voice. "Rusty?"

"Aye, but announce yerself, or I'll be forced to shoot ye."

Isabel took in a breath and Cutter grabbed an oar, ready to flee, but Charlisse held up her hand. " 'Tis me, you fool." She looked up. "Permission to board?"

Silence answered her for what seemed an eternity, then a timid voice said, "Lady Charlisse?"

"Yes, go inform Merrick immediately. I'm coming up."

"But. . .but, yer dead, milady." The cock of his pistol broke the quiet night.

"Obviously I am not. Now allow me on board, or you'll have Merrick to answer to."

She heard a loud grunt. "Just you, then, till I see yer face."

After casting a reassuring glance at Isabel, Charlisse turned to Cutter. "Won't you come with us, Doctor? Surely you don't wish to stay with Kent."

"I have no choice, milady." He lifted his withered arm. "I'm afraid I scare off most of my patients. The vermin of this world are the only ones who tolerate my deformities and allow me to practice my profession."

Charlisse studied his kind eyes with sympathy. She gave him an understanding smile and gathered her skirts.

He stood, assisting her onto the first step. "Besides, if I do not return, Captain Carlton will know it was I who assisted you. And I believe you've seen how vengeful he can be."

"That I have, Doctor." She took his hand and squeezed it. "You have risked much for our sake, and I thank you."

He pressed his lips to her hand. " 'Tis an honor to be of service to so noble a lady."

Charlisse felt a giggle rise to her throat at his compliment but managed to suppress it into a gentle smile.

She took the first step. "When I signal you, follow me," she said to Isabel.

With each step up the side of the ship, the barrel of Rusty's gun grew in size until Charlisse popped her head above the railing and lifted a patronizing eyebrow at the lanky pirate. His mouth hung open.

"If you please." Charlisse touched the pistol and swung the point away from her head.

Rusty dropped the weapon to his side while Charlisse climbed aboard. Leaning over the railing, she motioned for Isabel to follow.

"What devilry is this?" With wide eyes, Rusty backed away from Charlisse.

"Faith, Rusty, I am no ghost." She approached him and grabbed his shoulders, shaking him, until he finally chuckled and threw his arms around her.

"Milady, 'tis really you! The captain will be so pleased." Then he jumped back, his ruddy complexion blooming to a bright crimson. "My apologies. I was overcome."

"I am touched." Charlisse turned and assisted Isabel aboard and leaned to wave at Cutter, but he had already shoved off and was fading into the night.

Rusty blinked and lifted his eyebrows as he glanced over Isabel.

"This is Lady Ashton," Charlisse said. "Lady Ashton, Rusty, our helmsman."

Rusty bowed to Isabel, whose glance barely perused him before shifting away. She held a hand to her nose.

"Watch over her, Rusty. I'm going to find Merrick. Is he in our cabin?" She swished her skirts in the direction of the companionway stairs without waiting for the pirate to answer, but his "No, milady" halted her quest.

She swung around. "Has he gone ashore then?"

"No, milady."

"Then where is he?"

Rusty kicked the toe of his boot against the hard deck and gazed into the night. An arrow of alarm pierced Charlisse's joyous expectations. "Is he hurt?"

Rusty shook his head.

She stomped up to him and placed her hands on her hips. "Where is he?"

Rusty's Adam's apple bobbed up and down like a nervous twitch in his throat, and his eyes flitted about, never locking on hers.

"Tortuga," a harsh voice sounded behind her.

Charlisse swerved to see Royce, a grin coiling his lips as his gaze raked over Isabel. Something devilish lurked behind the steely glint of his eyes.

"Tortuga? Without his ship?"

His eyes snapped to hers. "Aye, but ye'll have to ask Mr. Sloane 'bout that." Royce smirked and fingered his scraggly beard.

Despondency fell on Charlisse's heart like an anchor. Her hopes of seeing Merrick tonight crushed, she managed to maintain a strong demeanor. "And where might Mr. Sloane be?"

"He went into town with most of the men, milady," Rusty said.

"And when do you expect him to return?"

"I dunno."

"And I suppose you can't tell me why Merrick is in Tortuga either."

Rusty dropped his gaze. "That's not fer me to say."

Charlisse sighed. She must reach Sloane. He would tell her what was going on. "Fetch me two pistols, Rusty, primed and ready, if you please." She swerved to Royce. "Help me lower a boat."

The barrel-chested pirate leered at her through tobacco-stained teeth but did not move.

Fear rose in Charlisse's throat. *What am I doing? I can't command these ruffians without Merrick. Lord, help me.*

A cold sweat broke out on her palms.

Royce placed his hands on his hips, turned his face, and spat onto the deck. "Beggin' yer pardon, miss, but I don't take me orders from no woman."

Rusty flew down the companionway stairs. Isabel pressed close against Charlisse.

"I am Captain Merrick's wife, sir," Charlisse stormed, taking a step toward Royce. She hoped he did not notice her legs trembling. "In his absence, you will answer to me."

"He ain't here, and 'tis my guess he'll not e'er be in command o' this ship again, so as I sees it, I can do whate'er I want."

Charlisse's nerves tightened into a knot, but she knew she must not show a speck of fear or all would be lost. "Whether he ever commands this ship again should not be your concern, but rather that as long as he lives and knows you have insulted his wife, your life is worthless." She met his stare with defiance and prayed with all her might that this ragged pirate with the hawklike nose and balding head would take her threats seriously.

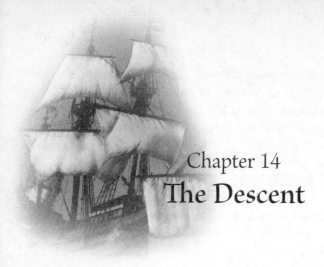

# Chapter 14
# The Descent

Charlisse squared her shoulders and bored her stern gaze into Royce's.

Shifting his stance, he chewed his wad of tobacco and studied her until finally he turned and spit a slimy, black glob onto the deck. "What's it to me if ye takes a boat? I reckon I can help ye lower it."

Charlisse opened her mouth to thank him but decided against it. "That's more like it," she said in a gruff voice as Rusty popped above deck, brandishing two brass-tipped flintlock pistols.

Thanking him, she grabbed them. "Rusty, help Royce with the boat," she ordered.

"What are you going to do?" Isabel rushed to her, wringing her hands.

"I must go ashore and find Sloane." Charlisse stuffed one of the pistols into the sash of her gown, then glanced up into Isabel's flickering eyes. "He will explain why Merrick is not with his ship."

"Surely, you don't intend to leave me with these. . .pirates." Isabel gulped as she surveyed the two men working to lower the boat.

Charlisse hesitated. Would it be more dangerous for Isabel to remain on board the *Redemption* or to chance roaming through the port at night? Most likely, she could get Rusty to escort them, but even that was no assurance of their safety. The last time Charlisse had ventured out at night into the streets of Port Royal alone, she'd been kidnapped by pirates—her own father, in fact. But that seemed a lifetime ago. *Lord, what do I do?*

"Ahoy, milady, a boat approaches," Rusty yelled, relieving her for the moment of her inner turmoil.

Rushing to the rail, Charlisse gripped it and stared out into the inky waters, broken only by the glimmer of an occasional wave catching the lantern light. She raised and cocked her pistol at the same time the two pirates did theirs. They glanced at her with wide eyes.

"Announce yerself or be shot." Royce's voice echoed across the bay.

"Hold yer fire, ye jittery old hen." The chattering of a monkey filled the air.

Charlisse's heart leapt. "Sloane!" Isabel crept up behind her.

Only silence responded, save for the splashing of the oars hitting the water.

"Who calls to me?" Sloane's scratchy voice echoed over the harbor.

" 'Tis me—Charlisse."

The rowing quickened until the longboat came into view. Sloane stood at its head, peering up at the ship. At least ten other men sat behind him.

"Lady Charlisse," Sloane shrieked. "Yer not blown to bits!"

"So it would seem." She chuckled.

As soon as the boat came within reach, a wiry monkey flew through the air, landed on the boat that Royce and Rusty were lowering, and scampered up the ropes. He jumped onto Charlisse, screeching.

Isabel screamed and leapt back, holding a hand to her chest.

"Hello, little fellow." Charlisse grabbed the squirmy animal, held him to her face, then placed him on her shoulder. She glanced at Isabel. "It's quite all right. He's harmless, really. Aren't you, Solomon?" She scratched under his chin, and the creature lifted his head and grinned. A whiff of filthy animal odors and rotten bananas struck her nose. "You're as smelly as the other critters on board this ship."

"Blast it all!" Sloane roared. "Row t' the other side of the ship, ye powder-brained carps."

In minutes, Sloane's bulky form sprang over the larboard railing and landed on the deck with an agility that defied his size. He barreled toward Charlisse and entered the lantern light bearing a wide grin that reached his eyes with a twinkle. " 'Tis really ye!" he said, clutching her shoulders and staring into her face. "Swounds, ye be a sore sight for me old eyes."

Charlisse smiled, stood on her tiptoes, and placed a kiss on his rough check. "It's good to see you, too, Sloane."

The old pirate's face turned red, as Solomon jumped onto his shoulder. Charlisse handed him her pistols. "I believe I won't need these anymore."

Smiling, he shoved them into his breeches.

Isabel inched next to Charlisse as the rest of the pirates clambered up over the side of the ship. Jackson's dark frame—barely discernable against the night sky, save for the whites of his eyes and the tan of his breeches—dropped to the deck with a *thud*. After ordering the men to lift both boats on board and tie them down, he flashed a row of stark white teeth at Charlisse, and she nodded in return.

Charlisse introduced Isabel to Sloane, who gave her an awkward bow.

"I have much to tell you," Charlisse said, taking his arm. "But first, what news of Merrick? Why is he not here with his ship?"

"Ah. . ." Sloane shuffled his feet across the deck and scratched under his headscarf. He glanced toward the shore. "We sorta borrowed 'is ship for a bit."

"I beg your pardon?"

"I came here to get the reverend, thinkin' he mebbe able to help Merrick."

"Help him do what?"

Sloane's blue eyes regarded Charlisse with apprehension. "Merrick believes ye are dead, milady."

"I know. And that is precisely why we must get word to him immediately." Uneasiness crept up Charlisse's spine. Sloane's brutal honesty had always been something she could count on, but now as he squirmed and hesitated, dread began to suffocate her hope. "What is he doing in Tortuga?" she demanded.

The thud and scrape of sodden wood against the hull echoed over the ship as the cockboats were hoisted from the water. The men heaved on taut ropes strung through pulleys that clanked in unison with their groans. As the vessels were lowered into their cradles, a jolt shook the ship. Jackson's booming voice rang across the deck, "Royce, Rusty, back on watch. The rest of ye be gone. Nothin' for ye to see here."

Charlisse pressed her hands on her hips. "Mr. Sloane?" Had he always looked this haggard, or was it simply the trials of this past week making their mark on his skin?

He shifted his gaze from hers. The monkey grimaced and flew from his shoulder up into the ratlines.

"Why would Merrick go to that savage haven?" Charlisse insisted.

"He believes ye to be dead." Sloane swallowed nervously.

"So you have said. But that does not explain why you have stolen his ship or why you believe he needs the reverend's help." Charlisse held her ground, though she didn't like the direction in which the conversation was heading or the feelings of dismay that were leaching away her hope.

"The cap'n. . ." Sloane began. "The cap'n. . ."

Charlisse studied the furrowing of his brow.

"The captain has changed. He's not hisself of late, milady."

Charlisse tapped her foot. "And?"

"He's forgotten his faith."

"Whatever do you mean?"

"He blames God fer yer death and seeks revenge on Morgan." Sloane spat the name and sighed, hanging his head. "Last I heard, he hooked up with Cap'n Collier and had done turned back to piratin'."

Merrick stood on the quarterdeck of Captain Collier's flagship, the *Satisfaction*, and felt anything but what the ship's name implied. Scattered across the deck of the forty-gun frigate lay the shadowy forms of drunken pirates, fallen where the rum they had consumed finally flooded their consciousness. Other than their snores, all was silent, save the rush of the sea against the blue hull of the massive ship. No moon graced the somber night, just as no light brightened the gloomy void in Merrick's soul.

The snap of a sail catching a contrary wind jolted the ship, and Merrick gripped the rail, steadying himself against the dizzying effect of the rum he had just downed. He'd hoped the bitter liquor would dull his senses, but found his fury and pain only further magnified.

When he had discovered the *Redemption* was missing from Cayona Bay at Tortuga, and part of his crew with it—including his most trusted friend, Sloane—he had embarked upon a rampage through the city, inflamed by his new colleague, Edward Collier, who seemed to relish in the agony of others.

Merrick gritted his teeth and stared across the charcoal sea, distinguished from the night sky by pale stars that winked at him tauntingly. How could Sloane have betrayed him—especially when Merrick had suffered so much? Now he was truly alone—without Charlisse, without his ship, and without God.

A chill came over him, though the night was muggy. *What do you need them for? You were happier when you were a pirate.*

Was he? He couldn't remember. The haze of rum snaked its way through his thoughts and memories, twisting them into a tangled mass that kept his pain at a distance. But not his anger. His anger grew daily. Like a spoiled, screaming child, it clawed its way through his soul, feeding on his fears, his misery, and his vengeance, until now it was a seething tempest with a mind of its own. Only one thing could satisfy it—revenge. And that was precisely why he was aboard this vile pirate's ship. Collier had promised him not only Morgan's head on a platter, but also that he would help him get the *Redemption* back from his mutinous crew.

Merrick chuckled. He'd taken the word of a man who used deceit as a means to an end—not the wisest course. Nevertheless, he sailed aboard Collier's ship, on his way to raid a Spanish town for no other reason than to plunder her and terrorize her citizens.

*What has happened to me?*

The *clomp* of boots sounded on the quarterdeck stairs, but Merrick could not summon up enough interest to see who remained sober enough to walk about at this hour. A bulky form appeared next to him and cleared his throat. Merrick did not move. He longed to be left alone.

"Do you remember me, *monsieur?*"

Sighing, Merrick glanced up and squinted through his blurred vision to see a tall, sinewy man dressed in a silk shirt and breeches of taffeta. His forehead sat high and wide beneath an oiled sweep of tawny hair, alluding to an intelligence Merrick doubted existed within. The man presented Merrick with his profile as if to enhance his memory.

French. Merrick returned his gaze to the sea. "I do not. Now, if you please."

"It is me, Julian Badeau." The annoying man flashed a set of jagged teeth. "I sailed under your command, monsieur, five years ago." He held a bottle up to his lips and took a gulp, drawing Merrick's attention.

"Could you spare a drink for an old friend?" Merrick asked.

Julian held out his bottle with a puzzled look; Merrick snatched it, tipped it to his mouth, and closed his eyes as the pungent fluid burned its way down his throat.

"I thought you not drink, *Capitaine*." Julian retrieved his bottle.

Merrick studied him, flipping through his foggy memories. "Ah yes, Baddo."

Julian chuckled. "It is pronounced, Ba-*doh*, but you always called me Baddo, it is true." He glanced over the choppy sea. "When you come aboard, I most happy, Capitaine. You are great capitaine and a great man."

A twinge of guilt struck Merrick, despite the rum flowing through his blood. Five years ago. . .that was after he had committed his life to God. A smile touched his lips as he remembered the exuberance, the joy at discovering that the God of the universe loved him.

*I still do, My son.*

A chilled breeze nipped at Merrick's neck, sapping his reverie. *If this is His idea of love, who needs Him?*

"Things have changed," Merrick mused.

"*Oui*, your ship. You lost it."

"I lost much more than that." Merrick shook his head and forced his mind to clear, wondering why he divulged anything to this pirate.

"Capitaine?" Julian frowned.

"Blast, don't call me that. I'm no longer your captain, Baddo. Or anyone's, for that matter."

The man hesitated. The ship bucked over a wave, compelling both of them to clutch the rail. "You always be capitaine to me, monsieur."

Merrick's gaze swerved to his, regarding his keen, solemn eyes, curious why the man held such a high opinion of him. "What happened to you, Baddo? I remember you joined France in the Dutch War, traded allegiances, eh?"

"Not for you to take personal, Cap. . .monsieur."

"I didn't take it as such. Besides, I care little for political skirmishes."

"*Après* the war, I look for your crew again." Julian took a swig. "But could not find you."

"No." Merrick plucked the bottle from Julian's hand. "I spent some time in England."

Julian's thin lips flattened into a stiff line. A pirate lying near the foredeck stairs rolled over and cursed in his sleep.

The fresh smell of dawn wafted over Merrick, carried across the water on a strong breeze. Not many men could smell the beginning of a new day, but Merrick had witnessed too many mornings at sea to deny the peculiar fresh scent.

"We come to Barracoa tomorrow," Julian announced, facing Merrick. "May I ask why you join forces with such a"—he cast a quick glance around them—"a man like Collier?"

Merrick snorted. "I am no longer above doing what I must to get what I want, Baddo. Collier has promised assistance in an endeavor of mine, and in return, I offer him my services. Beyond that, we have no association. Respect and loyalty, I have discovered, are overrated."

Badeau shook his head as Merrick drained the last swig from the bottle and tossed it into the sea. "Perhaps. But you change your mind, monsieur, after you witness the cruelty of Collier."

Merrick raked a hand through his hair and pointed at the brightening horizon. " 'Tis a new day, my old friend. Watch and see if I am not as cruel a pirate as he."

# Chapter 15
# Betrayed

Shock jolted through Charlisse, stunning all other feelings. Merrick's strong faith in God had always been a testament to her. His moral convictions and unflinching values in the face of many trials had given her strength and driven her to seek refuge in the arms of a God who had the power and love to change an evil pirate to a man of honor.

*Blames God. . .hooked up with Collier. . .turned back to pirating*—the words flew around her mind, unable to find a solid place to land.

"Edward Collier? Isn't he one of the pirates Merrick's been hunting?"

"Aye, that he is, milady. Which is hows I knew he weren't in 'is right mind, to be sure."

A muggy breeze blew in from the sea, flapping the loose sails and driving an ominous dark cloud overhead, suffocating the moonlight, leaving only the lanterns at stern and bow to cast their shifting light across the deck. A bell tolled in the distance.

Jackson approached and stood beside Sloane.

Isabel's eyes widened at his imposing stature, and a tiny breath escaped her lips.

"Stealing his ship seems a rather rash action," Charlisse snapped.

Sloane snorted. "More like borrowed, milady—to go get help."

Charlisse looked up into Jackson's dark eyes. "Are you a party to this, too?"

The massive man nodded. "Aye, ma'am. Fer Merrick's sake, it was all we could think to do." He glanced up at Rusty who leaned over the foredeck railing above them.

"You, as well, Rusty?" Charlisse asked.

He gave her a tentative smile.

"But now that yer alive, milady," Sloane piped in, "once he sees ye, all will be well again."

Charlisse found no solace in his words. How could Merrick have turned back to pirating so soon? She thought of Reverend Thomas. He was like a father to Merrick. It was the reverend who had discovered Merrick injured and bleeding in his church over six years ago, and not only nursed him to health but also introduced him to Christ.

"What did the reverend say?" Charlisse asked.

"The rev says he'll pray for 'im, but Merrick must find his own way back home. . .whate'er that means." Sloane scratched his beard.

Charlisse grabbed a wayward lock of her hair and twisted it between her fingers. She paced as disappointment fumed into flames of anger.

She glared at Sloane. "When you saw the *Vanquisher*—"

"What, milady?"

"When you saw the *Vanquisher*, was Merrick with you then?"

"Aye." Sloane cocked his head and gave her an inquisitive look. "But how did ye know?"

Charlisse motioned to Isabel. "We were held captive on that ship. Why didn't Merrick attack?"

Sloane's eyes grew wide, and Jackson flexed his jaw and looked aside. "By the powers, we didn't knows ye were on that ship! The cap'n almost attacked, he did, but somethin' came over him and he changed 'is mind." Sloane paused. "Are ye sayin' that half-witted cur, Kent, had ye all this time?"

"Yes, but 'tis a long story." Charlisse waved her hand through the air. "Meant for another time. But do tell me, Mr. Sloane. . ." She cast him a cautious glance, afraid to ask her next question, but afraid to leave it unanswered. "Has my husband found comfort with another woman?" After all, he believed she was dead, and Merrick was a man who had no trouble drawing the attention of females.

"I only saw him with one woman," Rusty yelled from atop the foredeck, his skinny frame a shadowy stick in the darkness.

With a gasp, Isabel raised a hand to her mouth and stared at Charlisse.

Sloane groaned and gave Rusty a surly frown. "Keep yer mouth shut, ye daft loon, and keep to yer watch!"

"But she weren't as pretty as ye are, milady," Rusty added before skittering off.

"Don't be mindin' him, miss," Sloane said, avoiding her eyes. "The cap'n pushed the woman from his lap right quick."

"His lap?" Charlisse growled and marched across the deck to the starboard railing, Isabel quick on her heels. Leaning over the railing, she fought back tears as she envisioned her husband in the arms of another. Wasn't it enough that she had lost her baby? Now, to lose her husband, as well?

An icy mist rose from the sea below. *Yes, indeed. What kind of loving God would allow this?*

*No.* Charlisse hung her head. A single tear slid down her cheek and fell to the choppy bay below. But that was all she would allow—for now. She'd been dead in Merrick's mind for less than a month, and already he'd entertained a woman.

Isabel's arm slid over her shoulder. "I'm sorry," she whispered, but it only forced more tears to fall from Charlisse's eyes—breaking her promise to be strong within seconds of making it.

Sloane yelled from across the deck. "Milady, we must make haste to Tortuga before the cap'n leaves."

Drawing a deep breath of the salty air, Charlisse swiped the tears from her face and turned around. "I have neither the desire nor the disposition to follow my husband's pirating carcass around the Caribbean." Truth be told, she did have the desire to find him, to find him and run into his arms and show him she was alive, but for the moment her yearning suffocated beneath the flood of her anger.

Even from where she stood, Charlisse saw Sloane's tan face blanch and the whites of Jackson's eyes glow like huge pearls inside a murky oyster.

Isabel tapped her arm. "My apologies, Charlisse, but shouldn't we be leaving before Captain Carlton returns to his ship?"

Charlisse's gaze swerved to her friend. The pleading look in Isabel's eyes sent a chill over her. In her disillusionment, she had forgotten about that villain who would have no doubt about where to search for his escaped women.

Charlisse set her lips in a firm line. "Of course."

She marched over to Jackson and widened her stance. The giant black man had always unnerved her, even though his loyalty to Merrick never wavered. His immense stature, coupled with his dark complexion, intimidated her. She had never had the opportunity to associate with men of his race in England.

"Jackson," she began.

"Aye, ma'am." He nodded.

"I fear Miss Ashton and I will find ourselves in immediate danger should Captain Carlton return to his ship in the near future." She cast an anxious glance toward the *Vanquisher*, which drifted in sleepy oblivion off their larboard side. "When will the remainder of the crew return from port?"

"It be just the eighteen of us, milady," Sloane interjected. "All aboard and accounted fer, I might add."

"Eighteen? Why so few?"

Sloane shifted guiltily and mopped his brow. "They's all who dared defy the cap'n."

Charlisse blew out a sigh. Not many men would risk taking sides against Merrick. She understood Sloane's motivation, and possibly Jackson's, but what of the others? What could they possibly hope to gain, other than taking over the ship for themselves? "Why did they join you?"

"They grew restless at Tortuga, waitin' on the cap'n while he. . ." Jackson cleared his throat. "We promised 'em that if we couldna get the cap'n back in a month, we'd gather a new crew and go piratin' on our own."

An uneasy feeling welled up in Charlisse. "Not the best sort of men to have sailing with you."

"Har, but we be needin' 'em to work the ship."

"Can she be handled with so small a number?"

"Aye," Jackson replied. "With all hands set to their tasks."

Charlisse threw a glance over her shoulder at Isabel, who remained at the rail. "May I impose upon you, sir, to make sail as soon as possible?"

Sloane and Jackson exchanged glances. "Aye, ma'am," the large man said without hesitation.

"No, we wouldn't want to be fightin' ole Kent undermanned and undergunned," Sloane said. "Not trapped like a sailfish in a net in this port neither." He flashed a gap-toothed smile at Charlisse. "And we wouldn't want to be puttin' ye and the pretty miss in any more danger than ye already been through."

"Thank you, Sloane."

Jackson turned to go but halted in his tracks. "Where to, ma'am?"

Charlisse glanced at Sloane. "Just get us out of port and head north to the Windward Passage, if you please." The treacherous passage that sliced between Hispaniola and Cuba would take them to Tortuga as well as New Providence. Once they sailed through it, Charlisse would decide which port to visit first. One glance at the troubled, exhausted features of Isabel's face told her, however, that she should return the girl to her family as soon as possible—especially in her delicate condition.

"Aye, aye, ma'am." Jackson and Sloane exchanged anxious glances before the first mate headed down the companionway, bellowing commands to send the men to their stations.

With anchor weighed and canvas spread to the light evening breeze, the *Redemption* skimmed across the shadowy waters of Kingston Harbor, attempting to slip past the *Vanquisher* undetected. The two lanterns of the evil ship glowed like demon eyes, following their every move, but soon they faded behind them into the bleak shadows of early morn.

The *Redemption* burst upon the open sea, and Charlisse stood at the bow of the ship, watching the blush of dawn tint the horizon pink as the rising morning breeze rippled through her hair. Closing her eyes, she thought of Merrick, and didn't know whether she should stifle the scream of fury or the wail of agony that simultaneously rose to her throat. Memories of him drifted through her mind like fragments of a broken dream. How often had he stood where she stood now, his piercing eyes gazing over the sea, his ebony hair gusting behind him, his cutlass hanging at his side? She could see him turn to her and offer her that sensuous grin that always sent her heart aflutter. But now all she felt was the slash of his blade as it cut through her heart.

A twinge of pain rose from her sore belly only adding to her torment. *Oh, my son.* Tears filled her eyes.

Suddenly chilled, Charlisse hugged herself. *Your husband is already in the arms of another woman. Your son is at the bottom of the sea, and you are alone once again.*

Isabel moaned, and Charlisse gazed at the poor girl standing next to her. She had refused to go below by herself and now stood staring at the sea with glazed eyes. Holding a hand to her mouth, Isabel's face paled. She swallowed.

Charlisse allowed her gaze to drift to Isabel's belly, knowing it was her child causing the nausea. Jealousy raked over her.

A chill nipped at her skin. *You should be the one carrying a child, not her. No.* Charlisse swung her face away.

Jackson's booming voice cracked the silence of the dawn. "Make haste. All hands on deck."

"What's happening?" Charlisse yelled over the pounding of boots.

" 'Tis the *Vanquisher*, ma'am. She comes about on our stern."

Lifting her skirts, Charlisse flew down the stairs onto the main deck, where Jackson stood, spyglass glued to his eye. Even without it, she could clearly see the whites of the *Vanquisher*'s sails sharp against the mountains of Jamaica, still shrouded in the shadows of early dawn.

"We can outrun them," Charlisse stated. Isabel slunk up from behind.

"Aye," Sloane said, joining them, "but fer the next few minutes, we be in range of her guns."

Jackson stomped across the deck and shouted to unfurl topsails and topgallants, and six pirates flung themselves into the main shrouds, scrambling aloft. "I want every inch of canvas spread," he yelled after them.

The blazing arc of the sun shot over the dark horizon as if hurled by the thrust of a cannon. Its emergence transformed the bulging sails of the *Redemption* into golden orange as they caught the wind with a snap and jolted the ship into a swift southerly tack.

Charlisse rushed to the railing and scanned the *Vanquisher*. White foam exploded over her bow as she plunged through the sea in pursuit. She spotted Kent standing on the foredeck, arms folded across his chest, the purple plume of his captain's hat fluttering in the wind. His angry glare pierced her, even at a distance, and she could only imagine his inflamed reaction upon discovering that she and Isabel were gone.

Isabel locked her arm in Charlisse's and shivered. "He'll catch us, won't he?"

Charlisse feigned her best smile. "No, the *Redemption* is smaller and much swifter. We need only steer clear of his broad—"

*BOOM!*

The deafening blast set the air aquiver, and Charlisse looked up to see a plume of gray smoke hovering above a minion gun on the poop of the *Vanquisher*. The four-pounder crashed through the *Redemption's* stern, tore through the mizzen, and shattered the quarterdeck railing before plummeting into the sea.

A loud thud and a moan sounded behind her, and Charlisse swerved. Jackson lay lifeless on the deck. She rushed and knelt beside him with Sloane right behind her. A spike of wood protruded from Jackson's side, blood oozing from the wound. His forehead swelled into a pink knot.

Charlisse scanned the crowd of familiar pirates swarming around the downed man and spotted the doctor, Brighton. "Smack, help Brighton; take him below," she ordered.

The men hesitated and glanced among themselves.

"Do as she says!" Sloane bellowed.

Charlisse dashed for the stern railing. Terror rose like bile in her throat, threatening to arrest the short breaths that barely escaped her mouth. The *Vanquisher* swept down upon them with all sails bulging and guns blazing. In minutes, with the wind advantage, Kent would be able to turn and loose a broadside on the *Redemption* that would sink her to the bottom of the sea.

Their leader gone, the pirates wandered aimlessly, spewing curses at their pursuer and gulping swigs of rum. Sloane appeared beside Charlisse with Solomon on his shoulder.

"What shall we do, Sloane?"

"I think we're done for, milady. Might as well surrender and dip yer colors."

Isabel leaned over the stern rail and vomited into the water below.

Putting her arm around her, Charlisse drew her close. *I cannot do this, Lord. I will not surrender this girl back into the hands of that rogue. Please help me.*

Another blast from the *Vanquisher* thundered through the air and sent the ship shuddering to her keel.

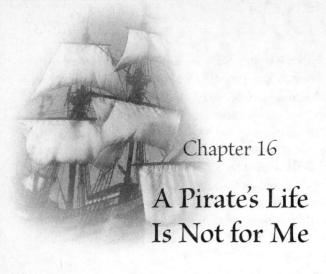

# Chapter 16

# A Pirate's Life
# Is Not for Me

Merrick stepped from the longboat onto the shore of Hispaniola, shook the wobble from his sea legs, and began trudging through the sand. Twenty men clambered from the boat behind him, weapons in hand, and rushed upon the shoreline, growling like hungry wolves. Another blast from the *Satisfaction*'s cannons thundered through the midnight sky. Merrick glanced over his shoulder to watch an eighteen-pounder tear through the fort's crumbling towers as if they were parchment. Stone exploded into fragments in all directions, carrying with them the last remnants of the town's only defense.

The fort, recently built, was undermanned and ill-prepared for the piratical onslaught—which was precisely why Collier had chosen Barracoa. Rumor had it the Spanish were hoarding large amounts of gold here in the tiny town, with barely a fort to protect it. The Spanish ruse was a clever one, but rum loosened the tongues of Spanish sailors as readily as those of any other, and word had quickly spread.

Terrorized screams blared from the town that sat just above the shore as the clank of swords and crack of muskets sliced the night air. Merrick clutched the hilt of his cutlass and shook his head. Collier had instructed him to meet him at the fort, but as he gazed at the foul captain heading his way and saw the shattered remains of the towers behind him, Merrick realized his services were no longer needed. A sense of relief spread through him, although he doubted his intentional delay on board the *Satisfaction* would have the same effect on Collier. Finding no desire to either assist the captain in taking the fort or participate in the raid, Merrick had tarried only long enough to fill his belly with rum—a necessary evil, he had found, whenever he spent any time in the captain's presence. Even now, as Collier's arrogant sneer came into view, Merrick realized he had probably not had enough of the mind-numbing liquor.

Collier jerked the horse to a stop, swung his leg over its rump, and slid off the beast as if he'd been riding his whole life. A horse-drawn wagon carrying four huge chests pulled up beside him. Three bruised and bloodied men were tethered to its backboard. A band of Collier's men surrounded them. Merrick braced himself as the pirate captain sauntered his way, wearing a look of indignation.

"Why, faith! Look who has graced us with his appearance at last. . . the great Captain Merrick." Collier rammed his face toward Merrick until Merrick could smell his foul breath and see anger flaming in his narrowed eyes.

Holding a firm stance despite the rum attempting to sway him from his spot, Merrick met Collier's gaze with equal intensity. "And yet it appears you had no need of me after all."

"Aye." Collier's eyes lit up. He flung his hand toward the spoils of his raid, the lace at his wrist fluttering in the evening breeze. "So it would seem. My skills and wit are more than capable for any task. But you, my friend. . ." Collier leaned closer. "I begin to think the rumors of your bravery and skill have been greatly exaggerated."

Merrick shifted his stance, grinding his fingers against the hilt of his cutlass.

"Perhaps you would like to test them?"

The urge to run this pompous buffoon through with his sword sent fiery twitches through Merrick's hands. In a second, he could rid the world of this monster. Instead, he offered the captain an impertinent grin.

A blast of cold air shot up from the sea. *You're no better than this man, and you know it.*

Collier studied Merrick; then a slight smile alighted on his lips. Throwing an arm around Merrick's shoulder, he said, "Let us not quarrel, my friend. We have won the city. Let us go enjoy the spoils of our victory, shall we?" Turning, he drew his sword and slashed the ropes that held the three prisoners to the wagon, then motioned for his men to seize them. After ordering two of his crew to take the gold to the ship, he handed them the reigns to his horse and started toward the city. The remainder of his men, and the prisoners, following behind.

Merrick gazed at the town perched beyond the shore—just a Spanish town, barely even a village. Until an hour ago, its citizens had slept soundly under the assumption their city had nothing to offer pirates.

A cacophony of agonizing shrieks and callous laughter carried on the breeze. A woman screamed, and Merrick clenched his jaw. He took a deep breath and prayed the liquor would drown out the sights and sounds he knew he must face. Collier had insisted Merrick join him on shore—part of their bargain, he had said—but Merrick had no desire to witness the brutal savagery of the man whom, not too long ago, he had intended to capture and bring to justice. What was he doing here with him now?

*You need him and his ship.*

Yes, he did. The best Merrick could hope for in the meantime was to prevent this madman from inflicting further harm.

"You have your treasure, Captain, why not just leave?" Merrick asked.

"Leave?" Collier chuckled. "Surely you jest? I have only just begun to pluck the fruits of this fair town." He glanced to his side. "Ah, my manners. May I introduce you to the governor of Barracoa, Vasco Nuñez de Bastidas, his lieutenant governor, Rodrigo de la Cosa, and the commander of the fort, Diego de Balboa." Collier waved at the three battered men who did not lift their eyes as they stumbled along, grappled on both sides by pirates. Blood streamed from the governor's ear, and one of his eyes was swollen shut. Mud stained his white stockings and marred his velvet coat. His graying hair hung in sweaty strands.

"What do you intend to do with them?" Merrick asked, remembering a time long ago when he had sailed under another, equally vicious, captain. Visions of the tortures inflicted on prisoners plagued him, incensing his rage.

"I believe there is more treasure to be found in this fetid spit of a town, and the governor knows its whereabouts, don't you, Governor?" Collier's lips twisted as he directed his gaze at the man.

The governor lifted his head and peered at Merrick with one eye, dulled by the sheen of hopelessness, then shifted his gaze to Collier, who immediately stopped and thrust his fist into the man's stomach. The governor crumpled to his knees with a deep groan.

Every nerve tightened within Merrick, and he looked way. "In this small town?" He hoped the fury in his voice could not be heard. "Surely you are mistaken."

"We shall see," Collier said, stepping back into place and motioning for his men to drag the governor onward. "Let's be about our fun and show these Spanish dogs firsthand what we will do to their town if they are not forthcoming with their wealth."

Marching abreast of Collier, Merrick planted his boots on the cobblestone street and braced himself for the night's madness. The scene before him burst like a nightmare, pulling from his memory a similar one at Porto Bello when he and Charlisse had fled the city on horseback. *Charlisse.* He cringed as agony clenched his heart. He needed more rum.

Pirates dashed across the street and into the main square, cursing and chasing citizens who defended their shops. The shattering of glass and the sharp crack of muskets pierced through the haze of Merrick's senses. A horde of pirates crashed into a shop across the way. The owner rushed out into the street. A pistol shot whipped through the air, and his body thudded to the ground. Other pirates, with their arms full of plunder, stumbled across the avenue, fighting amongst themselves for the treasure they carried.

An enormous blast to Merrick's right sent orange and yellow flames shooting into the night. The explosive force nearly threw him to the ground, and the scorching heat singed the hairs on his arm. Smoke surrounded him carrying the scent of charred wood and human flesh. Hacking, Merrick swatted at the putrid haze and took a step back, tripping over a dead body.

Collier motioned for the governor to come forward. "Watch, Governor, and behold what happens to your precious town when you withhold treasure from Captain Collier."

The governor scanned the hideous scene, the lines of his face deepening in obvious sorrow.

A terrified scream alerted Merrick to a woman racing across the square in her nightdress, two pirates on her heels. One of them pounced on her, toppling her to the ground, while the other grabbed her hair and began dragging her away.

Merrick clenched his fists and took a step toward them, but Collier's firm grasp on his arm pulled him back. "There are plenty of women to go around, mate."

"Please, I beg you, *Capitán*." The governor let out a strangled cry. "I know of no more gold."

Collier drew his sword, stomped to the lieutenant governor, and without warning, plunged the blade into his chest. The tall man gaped wide-eyed at Collier and gasped. Collier extracted his blade with a grunt, and the man doubled over, clutching his breast. The pirates released him, chuckling, and he folded to the road in a heap.

After wiping his sword on the dead man's coat, Collier faced the governor, pricking the man's throat with the tip of his cutlass. "Memory returning yet?"

Fury shot sobering arrows through Merrick's haze of rum, and he took a step toward the captain, flexing his fingers over the hilt of his cutlass.

The rum swirled in Merrick's mind with a numbing chill. *Killing him will not stop his men, nor will it get you to Morgan.*

The governor sobbed and shook his head.

Collier's blunt gaze swerved to Merrick's, annoyance fuming in his eyes.

The angry stomping of boots drew Merrick's attention to the street, where a mob of Spaniards barreled toward them, waving *pistolas* and swords, screaming curses at the pirates.

Collier momentarily forgotten, Merrick drew his cutlass and took on the first man who reached him, staying a furious blow with a quick lift of his blade. Another man attacked him from the side. Merrick plunged his boot into his stomach, sending him stumbling backward. Other Spaniards swept past Merrick, engaging Collier and his men. As Merrick continued battling his two opponents, he prayed the townsmen would kill Collier, free their governor, and end this senseless slaughter—even though he knew it would also mean his own demise.

The Spaniard slashed at Merrick from the right, then from above in a quick move that Merrick handled effortlessly. By his common dress and lack of skill, Merrick realized the man was no soldier—most likely a farmer or merchant. With a few well-placed blows, Merrick would have no trouble dispatching the man, whose only crime was defending his home.

"Amado," the Spaniard shouted in a panicked voice to his friend, who bumbled to his feet. *"Ayúdeme!"* Fear skipped across his darting eyes.

Amado plunged at Merrick, but with a snap of his cutlass, the captain knocked the sword from his grip and quickly turned to stave a blow from the first man.

Merrick lunged at him, pummeling the exhausted man with slash after slash until one high kick from Merrick's boot sent his sword flying into the grass beyond.

The two Spaniards gasped for breath and stared at Merrick, awaiting his final blow.

"Begone with you," Merrick said, lifting the tip of his sword at them.

After one quick glance at each other, they dashed off into the night.

The slash and plunge of swords into flesh sounded behind him, and Merrick turned to see Collier and his men finishing off the band of fishermen and farmers. Then, grabbing the Spanish commander by his collar, Collier raised his sword, his face reddening. He glanced at the governor.

"I grow tired of this. Tell me where the gold is, or I'll run him through."

The governor fell to his knees. "Capitán, all I have left is what is in my home. You are welcome to it." The muscles in his face twitched, and his hands began to tremble. He pointed to an iron-gated hacienda perched on a rise nearby.

Collier sheathed his sword, drew a handkerchief from inside his coat, and casually wiped the blood from his hands. "Now that wasn't so hard, *señor*. Bring him to the house," he ordered his men.

"What will you do with him?" Merrick asked, securing his own sword at his side.

"I'll plunder his home and make him talk, of course." His mouth curved in a devious grin. He winked and sauntered after his men.

The sting of gunpowder and the metallic odor of blood bit at Merrick's nose. Raking a hand through his hair, he glanced over the nearly deserted street. He needed more rum.

He needed to get out of here.

A woman bolted from a store along the street and dashed for a patch of forest behind the building. A pirate, lurking in the shadows, barreled after her and tossed her to the ground in the alleyway. She screamed.

Merrick darted toward them, forcing his hazy mind to clear.

Plucking his pistol from his baldric, he raced across the street and around the side of the building where the man hovered over the woman. Halting, Merrick pointed the weapon at the back of the pirate's head.

"Unhand her."

The man froze. His beady eyes took in Merrick with a quick glance. "Find yer own girl." He returned to the woman.

Merrick cocked his pistol. "I said stand off."

With a grunt, the man stood, yanking the girl up by her hair. He fingered the pistol stuffed in his belt and glared at Merrick.

The woman's wide eyes frantically searched Merrick's. She was so young, close to Charlisse's age—with the same shade of blue eyes. Merrick blinked. She was not Charlisse. Her hair was brown and her frame larger—and Charlisse was dead.

The pirate grasped his pistol, but before he could pull it out, Merrick flipped his gun and pummeled him in the head with the stock. He collapsed to the ground, and Merrick grabbed the girl to keep her from falling on top of him. She squirmed in his grasp, pushing her hands against him. "Por favor. . .let me go."

Taking a deep breath of her sweet fragrance, Merrick closed his eyes, imagining Charlisse in his rum-clouded mind.

Her skin was soft against his.

When he opened his eyes, tears were sliding down her cheeks. She trembled in his grasp.

He released her.

"You are free." He motioned toward the trees. "Go hide in the woods until we are gone."

Confusion wrinkled her brow, and she turned to run, then swerved to face him again. "*Gracias*," she said before dashing off.

Merrick watched her until the darkness swallowed her up.

*Go stop Collier, My son.*

Replacing his pistol, Merrick trudged from the alleyway and headed toward the governor's house. Drawing a deep breath, he pushed open the carved wooden door of the hacienda and stepped inside.

The stone entryway sat deep in the gloom of the night, and Merrick could barely make out a staircase that spiraled up to the darkened second story. Lantern light spilled from an open room to the right. Gut-wrenching wails emanated from within.

Bracing his hand on the hilt of his cutlass, Merrick sauntered into the lit room. The governor sat in a tall-backed, gilded chair, writhing against the bonds that held his wrists. A knotted cord stretched across his sweaty forehead and imbedded into his skin as a pirate behind him twisted a rod attached to its ends. Collier paced in front of him. He fingered the grizzled hair on his chin while two other pirates stood to the side, malice dripping from their lips.

A soft moan drew Merrick's gaze to a woman who sat on a sofa, a handkerchief raised to her red-rimmed eyes. Her black hair fell in haphazard curls over her shoulders and down onto her disheveled, partially buttoned gown.

"Ah, my friend," Collier said when he saw Merrick.

Merrick glanced at the governor. "What goes on here?" He knew exactly what was going on—they were torturing the poor man. If they continued to tighten the cord, his eyes would eventually pop out, and he would be left blind forever, provided he didn't bleed to death first.

"Why, just as I have said, I'm imploring the governor to disclose the whereabouts of his treasure." Collier thrust out his chest and nodded for the man behind the governor to continue his work.

Merrick gestured to the silver sconces, candlesticks, jewelry, and silverware the pirates had already gathered into a pile on the floor. "Surely this is more than enough treasure for you and your men."

The woman whimpered.

"Indeed," Collier agreed. "The governor's belongings are quite valuable, I'm sure." He followed Merrick's gaze to the woman. "Ah, and what a grand treasure she is, eh?"

"Who is she?"

"Why, the governor's daughter, of course." Collier glanced back at the governor, whose face by now had turned a deep shade of purple. He opened his mouth and grunted, his breath coming in rapid bursts.

Collier leaned into him. "Yes, Your Excellency? Oh, my apologies, I cannot hear you." He chuckled and glanced over his men, who took their cue to join him in his mirth.

"Perhaps he attempts to inform you of the location of his vast horde of treasure? Pity you cannot make out his words." Merrick grinned, covering the rage that churned within him.

A cool breeze flicked the candles. *Why not join him? It will give you power.*

Collier's baleful eyes narrowed. "Haven't the stomach for it, my spineless captain?" He took a step toward Merrick and crossed his arms over his chest.

"I'm merely saying that if your desire is to find further wealth, then you must allow the man to speak, but"—Merrick shrugged—"if you wish only to gain useless pleasure by torturing him to death, then by all means, continue. I had heard you to be a man of intelligence, but I perceive I was misinformed."

Collier studied Merrick with a look of cool disdain. Then, snorting, he swerved on his heels. "Untie him."

"But, Cap'n."

"Untie him. Let's hear what His Excellency has to say."

Grimacing, the pirate loosened the rope and released the governor's head, which fell to his chest.

Collier lifted the man's chin. The swollen eye had opened slightly, and his gaze shifted to the woman sitting across from him. A look of love passed between them, and she rose and flew to his side, throwing her arms around him.

Merrick stiffened and gritted his teeth.

Collier yanked her from the governor's grasp.

The governor lifted his pleading gaze. "Por favor, do not hurt her. She has nothing to do with this."

"Hurt?" Collier stroked a bloodstained finger against her cheek. "Why would I hurt such a lovely creature? No, I have other plans for your daughter, señor." He chuckled and shoved the woman to one of his men.

"I know of no more treasure, Capitán, I swear it."

"He's telling the truth, Collier. Let him go." Merrick drew closer, hoping for an opportunity to slit the pirate's throat.

The grungy pirate who held the governor's daughter plunged his face into her neck, smothering her with his slimy lips. Shrieking, she pushed away from him, and he tossed her into a nearby chair.

The governor hung his head.

"You may be right," Collier said. "But let him go? Where's the fun in that?"

He paced, fingering his short beard. "I've got it." His eyes widened, sparkling with wicked delight. "You." He pointed to Merrick. "You will kill him."

"No!" the woman screamed and jumped from the chair only to be held in place by the pirate's quick grip.

Merrick hoped the sudden alarm shooting through him did not reflect on his face.

Collier pulled a long knife from a sheath on his thigh, flipped it in the air, and handed it to Merrick. "All I have seen thus far is a cowardly captain whose religion has made him soft."

Merrick grabbed the knife and resisted the urge to fling it into Collier's gut.

Collier nodded toward the governor and stepped back. "Kill him." He smirked. "Or I will kill you."

Sobbing, the woman raised a trembling hand toward her father. Her dark swimming eyes shifted a pleading gaze to Merrick.

*Kill him. He is nothing to you but a Spanish dog.*

Merrick glared at Collier, knowing the wicked captain wouldn't hesitate to follow through with his threat. He approached the governor, the handle of the blade slick in his sweaty hand. He stopped and stared at the man who had raised his weary eyes to his. No pleading, no anger lived within his gaze—only resignation.

Merrick gripped the knife and raised it for the plunge.

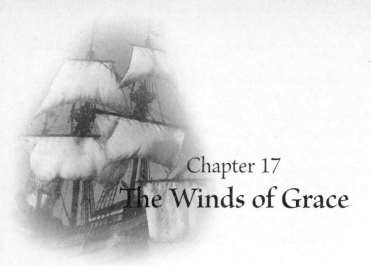

# Chapter 17
# The Winds of Grace

Charlisse leaned over the side of the ship and saw the smoking hole in the *Redemption*'s stern—just inches above the waterline. She glanced at Isabel standing next to her. Her wide eyes and pale face mirrored Charlisse's horror.

The *Vanquisher* shifted her sails, and with the wind behind her, bore down upon them, all guns blazing. In moments, Captain Carlton would be close enough to present his starboard side and loose a broadside on the *Redemption* that would no doubt plunge her into the sea.

Charlisse swerved around to see Sloane grabbing the rope to lower their flag in surrender.

"No!" she yelled.

He froze and shot her a quizzical look. Rusty stood at the helm, his usual grin replaced by a firm line of defeat. The other pirates paced the main deck, growling and loading their muskets and pistols in preparation for Kent's boarding party.

They had given up—all of them.

"Milady," Sloane protested as she turned to face their oncoming enemy. "Methinks it be a bad time to be playin' games with that slimy carp."

Grabbing Isabel's hand, Charlisse bowed her head. "Lord, I need You. Help me," she prayed, unable to think of any other words to say. She lifted her gaze to the *Vanquisher*. Bubbling foam churned at the ship's bow as Kent's crew reefed her topsails to slow her approach and prepare for the turn that would bring her guns to bear.

No surge of strength or warmth overcame Charlisse, yet she had to believe the Lord had heard her plea. She had to believe He didn't want them at the bottom of the sea, or worse, back in the hands of that villain. *Lord, what should I do?*

*Take a step in faith.*

Marching to the quarterdeck railing, Charlisse scanned the mob of pirates below and drew a deep breath, trying to steady the quivering that raked her.

"Beat to quarters, you fools. Prepare for battle," she yelled. "Who is the master gunner?"

Sloane left the flag aloft and pointed to a stout, shaggy man who looked more ape than human. "Thar he is—Gunny."

"Gunny," Charlisse barked. "Assemble a gun crew and get below. Prepare and run out the guns."

Amidst the chuckles surrounding him, the bulky pirate drew a swig from his bottle and belched, never removing his insolent gaze from Charlisse.

Just then a sweeping burst of warm air blew over her, tugging at her curls. In the clear morning sky, a dark mass suddenly appeared overhead. Charlisse looked upward. A deafening crack split the sky at the spot where the cloud stopped. The ever-present trade winds of the Caribbean abated, and a soothing peace settled over the ship. Only the creaking of the hull and the gentle slap of water broke the silence as the *Redemption* slowed on her course.

"By the powers," Sloane whispered, and Charlisse glanced at his gaping expression before shifting her gaze toward the *Vanquisher*. The mighty frigate had slowed on her turn to starboard and her sails hung impotently in the dead air.

As quickly as it had stopped, the wind commenced again, blowing this time from the opposite direction. The gust stirred up in a strong gale that fluttered the *Redemption*'s sails in excited anticipation.

Charlisse looked down upon the pirates, who stared at her aghast. "Royce, Mason, I want every stitch of canvas spread." Then she turned to Rusty. "Rusty, helm, hard aport!"

"Hard aport, milady."

"Do as she says, ye pack of worthless dogs!" Sloane howled.

Charlisse heard the shuffle of boots and turned to see Gunny bounding down the companionway stairs with five pirates on his heels. Mason, Royce, and four other men flung themselves up into the ratlines scrambling aloft like monkeys.

With all sails unfurled and tight to the wind, and a considerable list to larboard, the *Redemption* charged through the sea toward the *Vanquisher*, which was still languishing in the shifting winds. The *Redemption*'s blocks creaked and her sails rattled as the mighty ship slung close-hauled and tacked aweather.

Charlisse clutched Isabel's arm. "You should go below."

The frightened girl's eyes shifted in disbelief between Charlisse's. "How did you. . . ?" she stuttered.

"I did nothing." Charlisse shook her head, then gave Isabel's hand a squeeze. "If you won't go below, stay close to me." Lifting her skirts, Charlisse flew down the quarterdeck stairs, across the deck, and up onto the foredeck. Sloane grabbed the stunned Isabel's hand and followed Charlisse.

With the rising sun behind her, Charlisse peered at the *Vanquisher*, still floundering under slack sails. Kent stormed across the deck, shouting to his men who swung from the shrouds as they adjusted sails in an effort to catch enough wind to come about.

Sloane scratched his thick beard, chuckling. "I ne'er seen the likes o' this, milady. Only the good Lord can change the course o' the wind."

"Precisely." Charlisse flashed him a grin before returning her gaze to the *Vanquisher*, whose larboard side they now approached from astern.

Kent lifted his gaze, and his wide eyes locked with hers when he saw the *Redemption* closing in upon him. He turned, blaring orders to his men.

"FIRE!" Charlisse bellowed.

Five of the *Redemption*'s starboard cannons exploded simultaneously in a tumultuous roar, followed by the other five within seconds. A violent tremor spiked through the ship, the force of which sent the vessel listing to larboard.

Isabel lost her balance, and Sloane grabbed her before she stumbled to the deck.

Gasping for air, Charlisse coughed and glanced back at the *Vanquisher* as they sailed past her. The tips of her masts emerged from the shroud of swirling gray smoke that enveloped the ship. From within the gloom, red flashes broke, and the loud, continuous thunder of swivel guns erupted from the *Vanquisher*'s bow. A round of shots zipped over the *Redemption*'s quarterdeck, some crashing into the railing and deck. The rest, however, splashed into the water just short of the *Redemption*'s stern as she sped by out of range.

Charlisse bowed her head and thanked the Lord.

A jubilant cheer rose from the pirates. Dashing to the railings, they leaned over the bulwarks and waited for the smoke to clear so they could view the damage inflicted upon their foe.

Solomon jumped down from the ratlines onto Sloane's shoulder, chattering in glee.

"Har, littl' fellow, we done showed 'im, eh?" Sloane scratched the monkey under his chin, and the creature beamed at Charlisse.

Isabel gazed anxiously toward the battered ship.

Shock swirled over Charlisse like the acrid smoke drifting from the cannons. Had she just successfully fired upon a frigate—a forty-gun, two-hundred-manned vessel of war? What was she doing?

She hugged herself, trembling. *Yes, who do you think you are? You can't command this ship. You're nothing but a scared little girl.*

Charlisse scanned the deck and saw the pirates awaiting her command—*her* command. Swallowing down her fear, she threw her shoulders back, braced her hands on her hips, and marched to the foredeck rail. However frail she felt on the inside, she must never reveal her insecurities to these men.

"Rusty, bring us about on her port side. Let's see how she fared." She had to make sure they had crippled Kent enough to keep him from pursuing them.

"Aye, aye, Milady Captain!" Rusty yelled, and several pirates scrambled aloft to the sails.

"Sloane, have Gunny prepare the guns on our larboard side just in case."

He nodded, and Charlisse's gaze followed him as he leapt down the stairs.

With a lurching plunge, the *Redemption* went promptly about on a starboard tack, creaking and groaning before coming astern on the *Vanquisher*'s starboard quarter.

By now the smoke had cleared, and the *Vanquisher*, sitting low and heavy in the water, labored with a list to her port side. Her bowsprit hung in shattered spikes, the spritsails dragging in the water. A sharp rent splintered the quarderdeck railing in two. A gash tore across the mainmast, and two charred, smoking holes lined her hull at the waterline. Pirates rushed across her deck and up and down the ratlines in a chaotic frenzy.

Sloane returned, licking his lips. "Let's do 'em in, milady. We got 'em right where's we want 'em." The monkey on his shoulder chattered his agreement.

Kent's muscular frame marched across his quarterdeck, stopping only to lift the spyglass to his eye. He halted when he saw them watching and swerved to bark orders to his crew.

Royce popped up onto the foredeck. "Shall I give the order to fire?" he asked, bloodlust rasping through his voice.

Isabel shot an alarmed look toward Charlisse.

A shiver sped up Charlisse's spine. *Kill him. Get rid of him forever.*

"If ye aim to take 'im where it hurts, now's the time, milady, before he fires on us," Sloane added.

"Leave him be." Isabel shook her head "He can't hurt us anymore."

Charlisse nodded, confused by the pleading look in Isabel's eyes.

The sun, now a handbreadth over the horizon, spilled its warm rays over Charlisse, and she closed her eyes for a moment. The Lord had delivered her from the hands of her enemy. But was it His will that she kill him, as well?

Lifting her head, she shot Royce her best commanding look. "No. Do not fire upon him."

"What?" Royce roared. "I'll not be listenin' to no woman, says I!" He grimaced and shook his head, flinging spittle into the wind. "We can cripple 'im with langrel and board 'im for 'is treasure." He glanced over the pirates on deck, receiving their approving grunts.

Charlisse forced the quiver from her voice and met his angry stare with her own. "I said no. We have done enough damage."

With one swift move, Royce drew his cutlass and pointed the tip of its sharp blade at Charlisse's chest. Sloane reached for the pistol stuffed in his baldric.

A wave of foul, rum-laden breath issued from Royce's sneering mouth as he swerved to Sloane. "Stand off, ye lily-livered skirt kisser, or I'll run 'er through right before yer sappy littl' eyes!"

Merrick plunged the knife into the governor's side, slicing a deep gash in his skin but going no further. Aligning his mouth with the governor's ear, and with a furious grunt, he pretended to twist the knife into his flesh. "Groan and feign your death if you want to live," he whispered before he stood and withdrew the knife, dripping red.

The governor moaned. Clutching his stomach, he toppled over in the chair and fell to the tiled floor.

His daughter let out an ear-piercing screech and fainted in the arms of the pirate who held her captive.

"Faith, you do have it in you, after all." Collier snickered. "I was beginning to think otherwise." He slapped Merrick on the back and extended a hand toward his knife. "Check him, Matthews. Make sure he's dead."

The lanky pirate sauntered toward the governor, and Merrick clutched his arm, stopping him. "No need. I know where to place a knife." Merrick glared at Collier, holding the red tip of the blade toward him. "Do you doubt me?"

Collier's gaze flashed between the knife and Merrick's eyes, an evil grin writhing on his lips. His jaw twitched.

Merrick envisioned thrusting the blade into Collier's belly, daring himself to end this unholy alliance that with each second's passing he regretted more and more. His fingers tightened over the hilt, urging him onward.

A shiver snaked across his shoulders. *Then where would you be? Without a ship, how can you repay Morgan for Charlisse's death?*

Merrick pointed to the mound of treasure piled on the floor, and Matthews squirmed in his grasp. "Why not gather the spoils of your raid and be gone?" He sighed. "This town bores me." Merrick shrugged his shoulders and flipped the knife, handing it to Collier. "Surely a man of your exquisite taste and military expertise prefers more opulent and formidable game?"

Collier lifted his chin and puffed out his chest. He shifted his gaze to the wealth glittering on the floor, then to the woman, before returning it to Merrick. "I see you are a man after my own heart." Taking the knife, he wiped it clean on the pirate's shirt standing next to him, and returned it to its sheath, then gestured toward Matthews. Merrick released him.

"Pray, let us be gone then." Collier ordered his men to gather the treasure; then turning, he added, "Bring the woman to my cabin."

A spasm of wrath sped through Merrick. "Why, what is she to you?"

Collier lifted one eyebrow. "You need ask?" he chuckled. "I daresay she will provide many nights of entertainment." He strutted toward the door, yelling over his shoulder, "Don't worry, you may have her when I'm done—captain's first privilege, you know." His wicked laughter filled the entryway.

✳

Merrick paced the main deck of the *Satisfaction*, skirting clusters of pirates who were well into their drink. They gave him no trouble, but instead moved out of his way as he passed by. Collier had ordered the crew to end their activities in town, gather their plunder, and be back to the ship by dawn, or they'd be left behind. So far, only one longboat had arrived, loaded with loud, belligerent men full of rum and full of themselves after having wielded their wicked power over the defenseless victims of Barracoa.

Merrick grimaced at his part in it, no matter how unwilling he'd been.

Below, in the captain's cabin, Collier was having his way with the governor's daughter, and the thought of it caused a burning fury to course through him. Yet, outnumbered, he could do nothing. Not even *he* could take on two hundred men.

Spotting Julian Badeau on guard up on the foredeck, Merrick took the stairs in one leap and joined him. But the Frenchman kept his gaze focused on the waters of the bay.

Leaning over the railing next to him, Merrick sighed and raked his hand through his hair. "You didn't go into the town."

Julian shook his head but offered no reply.

The numbing haze of rum shielding Merrick's mind had begun to evaporate. "Got anything to drink?"

Badeau cast him a disapproving glance and gave a humorless chortle. "You did not get your fill in the village?"

Merrick gazed toward the godforsaken town. Sporadic embers still glowed in the wake of the destruction that had swept through the city like a tidal wave. No further screams pierced the night—all quelled in the silence of death or hopelessness. "I believe I got my fill." He paused. "But not of rum."

"Humph," Badeau snorted. "You are not the man I thought you to be."

Gazing down upon the dark waters, Merrick tried to block Badeau's words as they pricked at his pride but also assailed him with guilt. He huffed.

"Who are you, Baddo, to say what man I ought to be?"

Shifting his musket to his other shoulder, Badeau stared out into the darkness, avoiding Merrick's eyes. He tipped his hat and marched to the other side of the foredeck.

Merrick thought to follow him and put him in place for his insolence. Did he know who Merrick was? Of course he did—everyone knew the great Captain Edmund Merrick. Squeezing his eyes shut, he rubbed them. The ignorant Frenchman didn't understand. Merrick had not willingly taken part in any of the atrocities committed by Collier and his scurrilous crew. In fact, he had done his best to assuage their hostilities. But had he really done any good? Perhaps Badeau was right. He wasn't the man he used to be—for that man could not have stood by and watched the savagery that had occurred this night.

The ship rocked over a wave coming in from the sea, sending a cold spray over Merrick. *No, you're not that man anymore. You are a powerful, feared, and respected pirate now, back in control of your life—the master of your ship.*

Merrick opened his eyes and uttered a lifeless chuckle. Master of his ship? He had no ship to command anymore. And if he was truly the same ruthless pirate he had been before he gave his life to God, why did the heinous crimes of these men disgust him and cause every ounce of his blood to boil in protest? He shook his head. Perhaps he just needed more rum. Only by its deadening haze could he stifle the incessant bite of his soul. He had hated the pirate he had been long ago, and now his self-loathing surged like fiery lava once again within him.

*More rum is what you need.*

A scream blared up the companionway and across the deck—the scream of a woman in agony. The sound of it ripped through Merrick's heart. How could he stand by while a lady was attacked? He gripped the railing.

If he attempted to save her, he risked everything—finding Morgan, getting his revenge, and possibly his own life. Who was she to him?

It wasn't worth it. It wasn't worth it. He kept telling himself that as he clung to the railing in a death grip.

"Blast!" he swore under his breath, released the railing and swung about. Then vaulting down the foredeck steps, he ran across the deck and down the companionway stairs. No matter the consequences, no matter if Collier hung him from the yardarm, he must save this woman.

Drawing his pistol from his baldric, Merrick stopped before the massive oak door of Collier's cabin, lifted his heavy boot, and kicked it open.

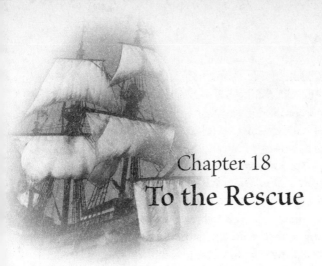

# Chapter 18
# To the Rescue

Charlisse drew a nervous breath. The tip of Royce's sword pierced the bodice of her gown. She glanced at Sloane, who had frozen in place with one hand gripping the handle of his pistol, the other on the hilt of his cutlass. His haunted blue eyes fixed upon Royce's blade, a burgundy hue of fury rising on his cheeks.

"Back off, ye flabby barracuda," Sloane spat. "D'ye mean to kill the captain's wife? He'll be having yer head fer a cannon ball."

Royce swiped the spit hanging from his beard and lifted one corner of his mouth in a crooked grin, revealing two gaping holes surrounded by brown teeth. "The captain ain't the captain no more, and that means his little doggy, waggin' 'is tail behind him, don't have no say in the matter." He shot a leering gaze at Isabel. "I can do whate'er I want."

"But I have a say," Charlisse said sharply.

Royce's narrowed, dark eyes snapped back to hers, and Charlisse swallowed a burst of terror that threatened to steal her consciousness. "You are a bigger fool than you look, Royce." She glowered at him, then glanced across the pirates who had assembled below. Raising her voice, she continued, "Perhaps you can enlighten us with your plan to board the *Vanquisher* and subdue her two hundred crew with only our eighteen?" A wave of chuckles rippled over the pirates. "And if we sink her, how can we ever hope to attack her and steal her treasure at another time when we have a larger crew?"

A spiteful respect skipped across Royce's eyes, though his intense gaze did not leave Charlisse's.

"Aye, she's right. 'Tis foolhardy to board her, ye dumb cockerel," Gunny hollered, then broke into a fit of laughter. Soon, the rest of the pirates joined him, cackling like a brood of hens.

Gritting his teeth, Royce grimaced, hatred brewing in his eyes.

He lowered his sword and sheathed it.

Sloane shoved him away from Charlisse. "Now be gone with ye. Back to work."

Before Charlisse allowed herself to breathe, she turned toward Rusty who was still standing at the helm. "Bring her about full speed."

The *Redemption* swung away from the crippled *Vanquisher*, cutting a foamy swath through the sapphire waters, then plunged through the sea, her sails billowing. The thunder of a cannon echoed behind them, sending its futile round shot splashing into the water just short of the *Redemption*'s stern.

Charlisse turned and offered Kent a taunting wave. His rigid frame stood fuming at her from the bow of his ship but slowly shrank and grew fuzzy in her vision as the sea widened between them.

After the *Vanquisher* disappeared on the horizon, Charlisse ordered two pirates to stuff sailcloth into the hole in the *Redemption*'s stern. Although the rent sat above the waterline, she hoped to avoid any water splashing into the hold until it could be properly repaired at port.

Isabel gave Charlisse a weary smile. It had been a long night—for them both. "Let's get you below to rest."

Taking Charlisse's hand, Isabel nodded, and they trudged across the deck and down the companionway stairs. "I must say, Charlisse, I'm truly amazed. Wherever did you learn how to command a ship?"

"Just something I picked up from my husband, I suppose." Although she'd watched Merrick command the ship on many occasions, she'd never expected to find herself ordering his crew around. The fact that she had done so—and during an attack—astounded her.

"And the change of the wind?" Isabel's brows shot up. "Did you learn that from him also?"

"Nay." Charlisse chuckled. "That was an answer to prayer." So the Lord had not abandoned her after all. Sprinkles of hope began to fall upon her parched soul.

Charlisse pondered what to do next as she led Isabel down the hallway. Should she go to Tortuga and search for Merrick? The thought of him pillaging and consorting with harlots sent blazing arrows through her heart. How could he do that—so soon after her death?

Her thoughts were interrupted when she reached the door to her cabin and found it bolted shut with a heavy iron lock.

Responding to her calls, Sloane barreled down the stairs. "I'm sorry, milady, but 'tis what Merrick commanded."

Charlisse huffed. "Where is the key?"

Shuffling his feet, Sloane glanced down. "Methinks it be at the bottom of the sea."

Charlisse stared at the quartermaster in disbelief, but his gaze would not rise to meet hers. "Can you hack through the bolt with a boarding ax?"

Sloane lifted his head, his eyes twinkling. "Aye, mebbe."

"Go get one, if you please, Mr. Sloane."

"Aye, aye." Sloane bounded up the stairs.

The gloomy, damp corridor swayed with the rocking of the ship, lit only by a lantern hanging in the corner. Charlisse put her arm around Isabel, drawing her near. The girl's exhausted body melted against Charlisse. "This is your quarters?"

"Yes, my husband and I share—shared—this cabin. 'Twas where I fell in love with him." Charlisse smiled at the rising memories of those days when she'd first come aboard the *Redemption*.

Soon the creak of the ship was joined by the pounding of boots as Sloane returned with Mason, the ship's carpenter. After he struck the bolt repeatedly, the iron lock thudded to the floor. Shoving the door open, Charlisse entered the cabin, groped for the table, and lit a lantern. Save for the shattered glass littering the floor and the strong scent of rum permeating the room, the cabin appeared nearly the same as she had left it. She assisted Isabel onto the bed, then turned to Sloane, who remained in the doorway. "Bring me some tea and rum, if you please."

"He couldn't be in here, milady." Sloane looked at her with sorrowful eyes. "Not without you." He glanced around the room as if it were a sacred shrine. "I ne'er seen the captain quite so. . .tormented."

Tears burned behind Charlisse's eyes as Sloane retreated out the door. Collapsing into one of the chairs, she dropped her head into her hands and began to sob.

"I'm sorry, Charlisse," Isabel whispered. "What can I do to help you?"

Charlisse lifted her head and gave Isabel a weak smile. "Thank you." She wiped her cheeks. "But I fear there's nothing you can do." Her gaze took in the cabin. So many memories filled it. Every chair, table—every inch of space—held an image of her and Merrick. This was where she'd first gotten to know him, where they'd spent their wedding night. Beyond the rum, she could smell his musky, salty scent. Could he really have been so devastated by her death that he had locked their room up forever?

After Sloane brought the tea and rum, Charlisse and Isabel forced some down—if only to settle their nerves. Soon the young girl drifted into a restless sleep, but Charlisse paced about the cabin, unable to find peace among the memories that hounded her at every turn. No wonder Merrick had boarded up the room. His voice, his scent, the lift of his saucy grin, bombarded her from all around, as visions of her must have done to him, as well. Yet, he'd thought she was dead. She realized for the first time the horrors he must have endured.

Opening the armoire, she grabbed his white shirt that was stuffed in the corner—the only one left—and lifted it to her nose. She drew a deep breath of his scent and smiled, picturing him standing in that very spot, bare-chested, grinning at her as he snatched a shirt to wear for the day. Her smile faded, and tears filled her eyes. Charlisse fell to the floor and wept—wept for the emptiness of her heart. . .and the emptiness of her womb.

As the day waned, Charlisse sifted through Merrick's things, hoping the sight and feel of them would ease her suffering. She sobbed, she wept, she chuckled, and she prayed as each memory flooded over her. Opening his Bible—the one whose margins were frazzled from so much use—she sat at his desk and thumbed through the pages, looking for answers, looking for comfort, but afraid she would find none. Her gaze landed on Romans 8, and she hesitated as the verses at the end of the chapter jumped out at her.

> *"Who shall separate us from the love of Christ? shall tribulation, or distress, or persecution, or famine, or nakedness, or peril, or sword? . . . For I am persuaded, that neither death, nor life, nor angels, nor*

*principalities, nor powers, nor things present, nor things to come, nor*
*height, nor depth, nor any other creature, shall be able to separate us*
*from the love of God, which is in Christ Jesus our Lord."*

Peace welled up inside Charlisse. The Word was clear. It didn't say
tribulations or distresses would not come, but it did say God's love would
be with her through it all. Rising, she clutched the Bible to her chest and
wandered to the bed. Then gently, she lay beside Isabel and fell asleep.

When morning broke, Charlisse snuck out, surprised to find Isabel still
asleep. Yet after all the excitement, the girl needed her rest—especially for
the baby. Standing at the bow of the *Redemption*, Charlisse basked in the
warm spray showering over her as the ship plunged and rose on its steady
course, gliding along under towering peaks of white canvas. She raised a
cup to her lips and took a sip of hot tea, feeling its warmth radiate down
her throat. How many mornings had she joined Merrick here, admiring
the way the breeze blew his wild hair behind him, the firm set of his jaw,
and those dark, piercing eyes that turned to gaze upon her when she least
expected it? His lips would then curve playfully, and he would draw her
close in a tight embrace.

She missed him.

She still loved him.

*How could he turn from You so quickly, Lord? Should I search for him?*
Quivering nerves churned inside her, bubbling up old fears. Every man
in whom she had placed her trust had rejected her. *I don't think I could
bear it if Merrick turned away from me, too, Lord.*

A dark cloud on the horizon covered the rising sun, stealing its
warmth. *Merrick will reject you. He has already forgotten you.*

She took a deep breath and closed her eyes, trying to quell her
insecurities. But she loved Merrick. Whatever mischief he was about—
however his actions may hurt her—the fate of his soul was far more
important. She knew that. Yet every fiber within her urged her to run
as far away from him as she could—anything to avoid finding herself
unloved and unwanted once again.

Charlisse smoothed a hand over her flat stomach, the emptiness
therein echoing her lonely pain. A twinge of jealousy rose within her,
tearing at her heart with ugly green claws. Why had the Lord taken her

son, created out of a loving relationship, and left untouched the unwanted baby—conceived out of violence—in Isabel's womb?

*Help me to bear it, Father.*

The thud of boots sounded behind her, and Sloane appeared. "Nice morning if I do say so, milady."

Charlisse smiled. Dark bags hung under the old pirate's eyes, but the spark in their blue depths revealed the spirited life still bursting within him. He had been a good friend to her and Merrick, as had Jackson. She had checked on the first mate last night and was pleased to hear he would soon recover.

"Where should I tell Rusty to point the ship when we clear the passage?" Sloane asked.

The main foresail caught the shifting wind in a jaunty snap, and Charlisse glanced back at Rusty, stationed at the helm. Facing the erratic sea again, she grabbed a lock of her hair and twisted it between her fingers. She knew what she had to do. Regardless of her fears, regardless of the pain it might cause her, she must trust God. She turned toward Sloane, giving him a cynical smile.

"I suppose we should go rescue that wayward husband of mine."

Sloane offered her a wide, toothless grin and turned to bellow the orders across the deck. A few moans preceded the shuffle of boots and further orders yelled up into the yards. As he turned to face the sea again, his eyes drifted over Charlisse's abdomen. He frowned.

"What happened to yer wee one, milady?" His sorrowful gaze met hers.

Charlisse swallowed hard. "I lost him when aboard the *Vanquisher.*"

The wrinkles on Sloane's face seemed to deepen. "Was it that jackanapes, Kent? Did he hurt ye?" Sloane stammered and nearly spit. "I'll kill 'im."

"I don't know what caused me to lose our son." Perhaps it was Kent's harsh shove or the stress of her predicament, or perhaps simply God's providence. " 'Twas meant to be, I suppose."

"A boy, eh?"

Charlisse nodded with a slight smile.

"I'm sorry to hear of it." Sloane gripped the railing and looked over the sea.

The fervent sentiment in his tone nearly brought tears to her eyes, and she longed to change the subject. "How is the crew faring, Mr. Sloane?"

"How's that, milady?"

"How do they feel about. . .about a woman giving them orders?"

"I think most are sceerd of ye, to be sure." Sloane laughed.

"Afraid?"

"Aye, thar's a lot of talk that ye are some powerful witch or somethin', changing the wind like ye did."

"Hmm." Charlisse took another sip of tea. "But you know better, don't you, Sloane?"

He scratched his beard. "Aye, I knows it was yer God who heard yer prayer, milady."

"Not only my God, Sloane, but yours, as well—and everyone's."

"Naw, only good-natured people as yerself, milady. Not old, grizzly pirates like me."

Charlisse chucked. "It is precisely for grizzly pirates like yourself that He sent His Son to die. He loves you, you crazy old fool."

"But He listens to ye, milady, as He listened to Merrick."

"He'll listen to anyone who calls upon the name of His Son, Jesus."

Sloane's weathered skin crinkled around his eyes as he gazed out over the sea.

Heinous laughter drew Charlisse's attention to the deck below, where a group of pirates had gathered, Royce at their center. She sighed at the interruption, having sensed a softening in Sloane's spirit. Resolved to bring up the subject at a later date, she faced the old pirate.

"What of Royce?" she asked.

"We best be keepin' our eye on him, milady. He's of a mind to be takin' o'er the ship. He always wanted to, but ne'er had the guts to attempt it against the likes o' the captain."

"How long before we reach Tortuga?"

"Two days, milady."

Charlisse nodded, knowing she had many battles to win during that time. Not only must she maintain command of the ship and keep the pirates' mutinous inclinations at bay, but she must also protect herself and Isabel from them.

As if reading her thoughts, Sloane added, "There's naught to concern ye. Jackson will protect ye and Miss Isabel, milady, when he's well again.

He can take on the whole crew by hisself, and they're plumb sceerd of 'im, too."

"I'm told that may not be for a few days."

"Aye, but I'll be doin' my best till then."

Charlisse smiled and gave his burly arm a squeeze. "And I thank you for it, Sloane, but God is on our side, too." Warmth blanketed her as she remembered the verse she'd read in Romans the night before.

"I hope yer right, milady." The corners of his eyes creased.

Whistles and cackles filled the breeze behind them, and Charlisse turned to see Isabel shuffling across the deck, holding her quivering chin in the air and ignoring the bawdy comments thrown her way.

Royce's gaze swept over Isabel, licking his lips, and then he looked back at Charlisse. Drawing a long swig of rum, he lifted his bottle toward her in a patronizing salute. Willing herself to show no fear, Charlisse staunchly returned his glare. "That crusty dawcock," Sloane protested, fingering the hilt of his cutlass.

Charlisse turned and offered Isabel a comforting smile as the girl climbed the foredeck stairs, hand over her stomach, and joined them. She hiccupped and leaned her pale face over the railing.

"Why didn't you stay below and get some rest?" Charlisse asked.

"I feel no safer here than aboard the *Vanquisher*." She took a deep breath and stared at the swirling turquoise water below. "This is just as wicked a pirate ship as the one we came from. Only there, I was at least assured protection from the crew."

Angered at Isabel's lack of appreciation, Charlisse planted a hand on her hip. "I suppose I could have left you there."

Isabel's listless eyes swung to Charlisse's. "I beg your pardon. I am not well, and I'm afraid my tongue runs away from me."

"Indeed it does, miss," Sloane piped in. "Lady Charlisse saved yer life."

Isabel gazed out over the endless sea. "Yes, you're right. My apologies."

Charlisse clutched the young girl's hand and chided herself for being cross with her. "I know you're frightened. But we will be safe. And once we find my husband, all will be well."

"We are not going to New Providence then?" Isabel's brow furrowed and tears pooled in her eyes.

"I will return you safely to your family, I assure you. You have my word. Tortuga is on the way, however, and for your safety and mine, I think it best we retrieve my husband before we embark on a much longer journey with these ruffians."

Isabel nodded. "I miss my home. I long to return and forget all the horrid trials of these past months." She scratched her arms.

"I know. And you will very soon." Charlisse hugged her, noting red blotches on Isabel's wrists. "What's this?" She took one of her hands in hers.

"A rash. Must be from nerves. I've had it for weeks."

Charlisse gently rubbed the reddened bumps. "I'm sorry you've had to endure so much."

"I fear I may have to endure more when I face my father." Isabel sighed. "He will not be pleased to find me with child."

Charlisse squeezed her hand. "But surely under the circumstances—"

"There are no circumstances when it comes to our family's reputation." Isabel shook her head. "I don't mean to paint my father in so cruel a light. He loves me, I know, and he'll be glad to see me alive, but status is everything to him."

Charlisse's heart sank as she gazed into those haggard green eyes.

Angry clouds churned in from the west, stealing the day's bright, glorious start and replacing it with gloom and restlessness. Even the tranquil sea now grew troubled without the touch of the sun upon it.

"When we get to Tortuga," Sloane broke the silence, "ye ladies need only wait while I go ashore and fetch the cap'n. Jest a few more days, and all yer troubles will be o'er."

Charlisse released Isabel. "Nay, I'll not allow you to confront my husband alone. If he's turned back to pirating and is chasing other women, I must see for myself." Despite the stories, Charlisse longed to believe that the honorable man she had married still existed. Besides, it had only been a few weeks. How much mischief could he have gotten into in that short amount of time? Truth be told, despite her tormenting insecurities, she couldn't believe he would not mourn her death longer than that.

Sloane shifted his stance and stared at Charlisse with furrowed brow. "Beggin' yer pardon, milady, but Tortuga ain't no place fer a lady. It would not be safe fer ye there."

"Please do not go." Isabel gave her a concerned look.

"Don't be silly." Charlisse pressed a hand on Isabel's back to steady her, noting the girl's pallor. "I've spent the past three years in Port Royal."

"Tortuga ain't no Port Royal, if I do say so, milady." Sloane said. "I'm afraid I must insist ye do not set foot ashore."

"Is that so?" Charlisse grinned at the endearing man. Although she'd seen him act as violently as the rest of the pirates—when the occasion called for it—she also knew she had nothing to fear from him. He was only looking out for her. On this point, however, she would not budge. "I will be going ashore at Tortuga with or without benefit of your escort, Mr. Sloane."

Charlisse flicked her hair behind her and clutched the rail.

Sloane faced the sea. "If ye aim to go, then ye need to hear this story. 'Tis a true one."

Charlisse shot him a scoffing look, but he continued, nonetheless.

"A few years back, there was a merchant who sought refuge in the bay at Tortuga from a storm. Unawares o' the type o' city it was, he brought his wife ashore to gather supplies." He glanced at Charlisse as if hesitant to continue.

"And?"

"After they hung him upside down from the rafters, they tied his wife to the bar." Sloane pursed his lips before continuing, "Well let's just say I think she died o' horror before the end o' it."

Charlisse gulped and a quiver spiked across her back.

"Sorry to be tellin' ye such a story, milady."

"No, it's alright, Sloane." Charlisse held her stomach, picturing the awful scene in her mind and feeling the agony of the poor woman. "Tortuga sounds like a dangerous place for anyone, man or woman." But she had to go into town. She must see Merrick for herself. But how? At what risk? What if he wasn't there to protect her. . . ? Her heart raced, sending a nauseous flood to her throat. She swallowed, then swerved to face Sloane.

"I see 'tis impossible for a lady to go ashore."

The taut lines on Sloane's face loosened. "Har, now yer talkin' sense, milady."

"Indeed. Fetch me some breeches."

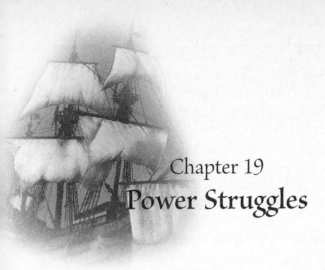

# Chapter 19
## Power Struggles

With a start, Elisa Nuñez sprang from the bed as the door to the cabin crashed open, and a man flew inside. It was the man who'd killed her father! A mixture of terror and fury surged through her as the pirate with the wild ebony hair approached. Grabbing a blanket from the bed, she held it up to cover her torn petticoat and backed against the wall.

"You killed *mi padre*." She sobbed, biting her lip.

Taking in the room with a cautious glance, he did not reply. His eyes landed on the tattered remains of her gown and bodice littering the floor, and his features tightened. "Where is Collier?"

"He left." Elisa glanced at the open door behind him, longing to make a dash for it.

"How long ago?" he asked.

"Not long—a minute perhaps." She wondered why he asked.

He closed the door and gazed up at her. "Your father is not dead, señorita."

"Not dead?" she repeated in a whisper. "But I saw you stab him."

The pirate took a step toward her.

Elisa cowered against the wall, wishing she could hide in its shadows. She raised her hand toward him. "Por favor, señor, do not hurt me."

"I have no intention of doing so." He sighed and raked a hand through his hair.

She stared into his dark eyes, her nerves beginning to calm under his sincere gaze. Tears filled her eyes. "What of mi padre, señor? Please tell me he lives." Desperation clung to any shred of hope even this pirate could give her.

"I'm sure of it," he replied, his firm jaw flexing. "I only grazed his side."

"But he fell over."

"I told him to feign his death, señorita."

Suspicion coiled through her. "*Por qué. . .*why?"

"I had no wish to kill your father. It was the only way I could think to save him."

Elisa came out of the shadows, eyeing the pirate with every step. "Why wouldn't an Englishman wish to kill a governor of Spain?"

"Though I have no liking for Spain, I have no quarrel with your father." He shifted his stance. "I am Edmund Merrick."

"Señorita Elisa Nuñez de Bastidas," she said proudly.

Merrick bowed and when he raised his head, his gaze snapped to her shoulders. He cringed. "Are you hurt?"

Elisa glanced down at the red and purple bruises and quivered, remembering the captain's brutal attack. Lifting the blanket, she covered the marks and averted her eyes as they swam with tears.

"He tried to. . .tried to. . ." She hung her head and sobbed. "He couldn't." She pictured Collier. The drunken fury that had erupted upon the captain's face after his failed attempts would forever be burned into Elisa's memory.

"Couldn't?" Merrick's eyes widened and a chuckle escaped his lips.

She darted a harsh gaze his way, finding nothing amusing about the situation.

"What do you want, señor?" She sniffed and held a hand to her nose, longing for him to leave.

"I want to help you."

"Help me?" She studied him. He made no move toward her. Nothing but concern flickered in his gaze. Was he lying about her father, or dare she hope he still lived? The cabin began to spin, and she leaned against the bed. Could she trust this pirate? Could she trust any Englishman?

"How old are you?" he asked.

Why did he wish to know? She wrinkled her brow but answered him anyway. "*Veinte.* . .twenty, why?"

Sorrow stained his brown eyes. "You remind me of someone." He looked away. Then with a sigh, he moved beside her. Surprisingly, no fear rose within her, not even when he took her hand in his. She gazed up at him, thankful for the comfort of his strong grasp.

"Señorita, stay here. I will do my best to keep the captain otherwise occupied."

She nodded, disbelief battling against hope. He squeezed her hand then marched from the room and closed the door.

Merrick had no trouble locating Collier. The roar of his cantankerous voice blasted through the ship like grapeshot. With a bottle in one hand and his sword in the other, he stormed across the deck, bellowing orders to his crew and flinging malicious insults at any of them who dared cross his path.

He stood, lifting his blade to the sky, and declared, "I am captain of this ship and commander of all the seas!" Then, dropping his sword, he swung it about him, stumbled, and nearly fell. "And any scalawag who dares to so much as look at me cross-eyed will find himself tied to the keel."

But no one dared show himself. Merrick assumed most of the crew had been smart enough to disappear below when the captain had begun his rampage. Only the watchmen remained: Badeau up on the forecastle and another pirate on the quarterdeck, both wisely keeping to the shadows.

Merrick grinned. What power Collier lacked in the bedchamber, he apparently attempted to make up for among his men. But what to do with this drunken maniac?

A young pirate emerged on deck from the main hatch, seemingly unaware of the mad shark roaming the ship. Tightening his vest around him against the evening breeze, he shuffled to the railing.

"You!" Collier yelled. "Who goes there?"

The young man swerved around, his expression lost in the shadows.

" 'Tis I, Cap'n, Kale."

Collier swaggered toward him, gulping a swig of rum. "Mr. Kale." His tone dripped with cutting sarcasm.

The pirate eased himself backward.

Collier set his bottle down on the capstan, sheathed his sword, and pointed a long, jewel-laden finger at Kale. "I know what you're up to, you traitorous, sniveling coward."

"What d'ye mean, Cap'n?" Kale's voice trembled. He could be no more than thirteen years old—neither old enough nor wise enough to plot a mutiny against such a bloodthirsty captain.

"What do I mean?" Collier marched toward the boy, backing him against the railing. "I know everything that happens on my ship. Yet you take me for a fool, don't you, Mr. Kale?"

"No, Cap'n." The pirate peered over the side of the ship as if considering a plunge into the bay a better choice than facing the drunken wrath of his captain.

Seizing his arm, Collier yanked him away from the railing. "No, you don't. You can't escape me. I know you've been plotting to take over my ship, you slimy-tongued weasel."

The young man shook his head in earnest. "No sir, I. . .I. . ."

"I. . .I. . . ," Collier mocked, snickering. "Styles, Hanson!" he yelled toward the hatch, then shoved his face into Kale's. His greased hair hung in snakelike strands to his shoulders. "I'll show you what I do with mutinous dogs."

Kale twisted in Collier's grip. "But, Cap'n, I didn't do nothin'."

Plucking a pistol from his belt, Collier pointed its muzzle at Kale's head. "I should blow your brains all over the deck." He stumbled, and the pistol grazed over the pirate's forehead like a deadly pendulum.

The young man cringed and closed his eyes.

Merrick took a step toward them, then hesitated, unsure of his next move.

"But I have a better punishment for the likes of you." Collier chuckled, lifting his hawklike nose in the air. "Styles, Hanson!"

The two pirates barreled up through the main hatch and shuffled toward their captain.

Collier belched and shoved Kale to Styles. "Take this vermin and strap a cannonball to his boots," he ordered, holding his stomach.

"No! No, I'm no traitor, Cap'n," Kale pleaded, twisting in Styles's grasp.

Merrick clenched his fists. He should stop this madness, but how could he without provoking Collier's drunken wrath? Surely if he interfered, it would not only be Kale covered with flesh-eating algae at the bottom of the sea, but Merrick would be right beside him.

Collier swayed and blinked as if he had suddenly forgotten where he was. Merrick prayed he would pass out, but he straightened himself and pointed his pistol back at Kale. "After you do that, throw him overboard. We'll leave his bloated carcass here with the Spaniards—a fitting end for a traitor."

Merrick stepped out from the shadows.

Collier looked up and squinted. A jeering smile stretched wide upon his lips. "Merrick, my good friend." He motioned for him to join him.

A line of dark blue appeared on the horizon, lifting up the black ink of night and shedding the promise of light upon the dismal scene. The predawn glow illuminated the strained creases on Collier's face and the blurry sheen of his eyes. For a moment, Merrick felt pity for the man. The slap of oars against water, accompanied by inebriated laughter, drew Collier's gaze toward the bay, where the last longboat approached.

"Ah. Good. The men can witness what I do to mutinous sharks," he hissed in Kale's ear. "I throw them to the bottom of the sea, where they belong."

Collier staggered backward, arms flailing, then stomped his boots on the deck, leveling himself. He looked at Merrick. "When the longboat arrives, assemble the men, if you please. This shall be a lesson to all." He waved his pistol in the air and nearly fell again.

Merrick cast a quick glance at Kale, still held in Styles's grasp. Terror drew all color from his face. His eyes shifted about in a haunting look.

Styles and Hanson, who exchanged uneasy glances, seemed to be of the same mind.

"Cap'n," Hanson said. "By the powers, are ye sure Kale done ye wrong?"

Collier swerved to face him. "Do you dare question my orders?" His head wobbled like a puppet's. "Would you like to join him?"

Hanson stepped back. "No, Cap'n."

The cacophony of laughter twisting around an off-key ballad wafted up from below, where the slight jolt of the ship indicated the longboat's arrival. One by one, the band of thieves climbed over the bulwarks, some landing on their feet, others crumbling onto the deck in victorious mirth.

Stepping toward Collier, Merrick threw an arm over his shoulder. The pungent scent of rum and sweat struck his nose. "This man has done nothing. Who would dare defy such a great captain as yourself?"

Merrick glanced behind him as he led the swaggering Collier to the port railing. The newly arrived pirates congregated around Styles and Hanson, who spoke to them in whispered tones.

Collier grunted in agreement.

"Why, 'tis obvious even to me, a newcomer," Merrick continued in his most flattering tone, "that your men fear and respect you. To be sure, they know what a privilege it is to be sailing under your flag."

Collier nodded and belched, showering Merrick with his foul breath.

Merrick turned on his heel and said with a loud voice for the crew to hear, "Let's hear it for Captain Collier, men. Three cheers for the greatest pirate captain on the Caribbean!"

A defiant shock silenced the men, and Merrick had to encourage them with a lifted brow and an approving nod.

"Hip hip hurray! Hip hip hurray! Hip hip hurray!" the men shouted.

"Behold, Captain, your worshiping crew. How could any of them ever plot against you?"

Collier's bloodshot eyes drifted over his men and then back to Merrick. An imperious smile lifted one corner of his mouth, and he shoved his pistol back into his belt. "Indeed."

Merrick slapped him on the back. "Have some more rum, my friend." He retrieved the captain's bottle from the capstan. "We have much to celebrate this day."

"That we do." Collier lifted the bottle to his lips.

Strutting toward the crew, Merrick ordered the longboat hoisted, and then cast a last glance at the Spanish town, still shrouded in the misery of the night. All he wanted was to sail far away from this place and forget what had happened to these innocent people.

Most of all, he wanted to forget that he had played any part in it.

He returned to Collier, who was still nursing his bottle. "All the men are aboard, Captain. Should I give the order to make sail?"

"Yes." Collier wiped the rum dripping from his lips. "To Tortuga."

He lifted the bottle. "I shall return the victor. And receive a victor's welcome."

"That you will." Merrick swallowed the disgust rising in his throat, then turned to rejoin the men.

"Let him go," he ordered Styles, who released Mr. Kale without question.

Leaning toward Kale, Merrick whispered, "Make yourself disappear for a few days, my friend." He winked, and the lad gave him a sheepish grin and flew down the companionway stairs.

A crash and a loud thud sounded behind him, and Merrick swung around to find Collier had dropped unconscious to the deck.

Merrick smiled. "Egad, 'tis about time."

Styles and Hanson exhaled deep breaths.

Taking a step back, Merrick braced his fists on his hips and scanned the crowd of pirates. Half of them were in nearly the same shape as Collier, but the other half glared at him through eyes that dripped with a greedy lust for power.

"Make sail for Tortuga, men," Merrick bellowed.

Their gazes flew between the still form of their captain lying on the deck and Merrick. Not one of them moved, save to inch their hands to the hilts of their swords.

One man in the back of the crowd threw up, and Hanson took a step toward Merrick.

"By thunder, I'll not be takin' me orders from the likes o' you!" He drew his cutlass and leveled the tip at Merrick's chest. "I says it be time we put an end to the great Cap'n Merrick."

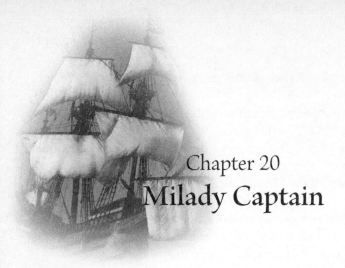

# Chapter 20
# Milady Captain

Charlisse lifted her gaze to the giggling girl perched on the bed in Merrick's cabin. Isabel's cheeks had regained a rosy color, and her laughter settled over Charlisse like a warm blanket. She had not heard Isabel laugh before, and her sweet chuckle, accompanied by a flash of pearly teeth, lifted Charlisse's spirits.

Charlisse finished buckling her belt. "And *what* is so funny?"

Isabel giggled again. "You should see yourself."

Charlisse glanced down at the baggy canvas breeches and yanked the thick belt holding them up. Underneath the oversized white shirt, she had bound her chest with sailcloth, hoping to appear more muscular than curvy. She grabbed a leather vest from the chair, swung her arms through it, and buttoned it in front for additional covering. Then, smiling at Isabel, who was still laughing, Charlisse strapped a baldric over each shoulder and sat to pull on her boots. She stood and twirled.

"How do I look? Like a pirate?" She contorted her face into her most vicious look and glowered at Isabel. "Do I scare you?"

Isabel fell back, clutching her stomach. "No, Charlisse, I'm sorry." She stopped to catch her breath. "Perhaps 'tis your long golden hair that distracts me?"

"Ah," Charlisse said, grabbing a captain's hat from the table. She bent over, tossed her hair down in front of her, twisted it up, and shoved the hat on top. Then, rising, she posed, hands on her hips.

"Oooh, now I'm scared." Isabel chortled.

"Humph."

A knock sounded on the door, and upon asking who it was, Charlisse unlocked it, and Sloane bounded in with weapons in hand. He halted, eyes bulging, when he saw Charlisse. A wide grin landed on his mouth, and he scratched his beard, circling her.

"Aye, ye just might pass fer a man, milady, as long as we go ashore under cover of night—and the pirates' eyes be clouded with rum." He chuckled. "Here's yer cutlass and pistols." He handed the weapons to Charlisse.

Hesitating to touch the odious things, she took the pistols first and stuffed them in her baldric. She grabbed the cutlass, but the blade dove to the floor with a clank, narrowly missing her foot. "I had no idea these hideous things were so heavy." Straining, she lifted the sword again and attempted to sheathe it, but floundered in frustration.

"Let me help ye, milady." Sloane rushed to her aid and slid the sword into place.

Charlisse sighed. "Well, let's pray I don't have to draw it, or I may kill myself before I have a chance to swing it at anyone."

Isabel chuckled, but Sloane's wrinkled features coiled in concern. "We may have to teach ye a few tricks. . .just in case."

Charlisse hefted the cutlass with both hands and parried with Sloane on the deck of the *Redemption*. She stopped and wiped the back of her hand across her brow. "However do you men handle these monstrous blades with only one hand?"

Sloane chuckled and lifted his sword in a feigned attack. Charlisse forced her cutlass up to meet his advance. *Clank*. She fended off his blow.

"Good, milady!" Sloane beamed.

A few claps and whistles sounded from around her.

Dropping the tip of her sword to the deck, Charlisse panted and glanced at her audience. Brighton leaned, clapping, against the larboard railing with two other pirates.

"Well done, Milady Captain," Rusty yelled from the helm.

Five other pirates, who had gathered to watch the fight, stood on the foredeck, snickering.

When she had first come up on deck, they had taken no special notice of her, but she soon felt their curious stares upon her—especially when Sloane began instructing her how to walk.

"No, not like that, milady. Ye must strut. Ye cannot, beggin' yer pardon. . ." Sloane hesitated, a red hue rising on his aged cheeks. "Ye cannot sway yer hips, or it'll draw attention to yer backside, if ye knows what I mean."

If Charlisse hadn't known what he meant, the pirates' cackles would certainly have aided her understanding. She was glad that Isabel had not wanted to join them above or Charlisse would have to endure her teasing, as well.

Although it required her total concentration to march like a man, Charlisse finally mastered enough masculinity to appease Sloane. The poor old pirate had stood, scratching his beard with a disbelieving look on his face, through the entire process. At his suggestion, they had moved on to sword training. Sloane wanted her to be able to draw and fend off a blow coming her way. But now as she felt every muscle in her body crying out in agony, Charlisse wondered whether it was worth the effort. If she found it necessary to draw her sword in Tortuga, surrounded by the Caribbean's most cruel villains, then surely she would be done for anyway.

"Again, milady." Sloane swung at her from the left.

Even though the dark clouds provided a canopy from the sun's heat, trickles of perspiration slid down Charlisse's back, and she gave Sloane a weary gaze. Muscles strained to near bursting, she swooped the blade upward with both hands and met his slash with another clank, then followed his quick move to strike her from above. He dove at her from her left, and she fended off his blow with a twist that defied her strength. Dropping the tip of her cutlass to the deck, she gasped for breath and felt a searing burn in her arms and legs.

Sloane gave her a broad smile that reached his crinkled eyes with a sparkle. "That'll about do it fer today, milady. Yer a quick learner, if I do say so." He sheathed his sword and mopped his brow. "Tomorrow we'll work on usin' just one hand."

Charlisse shot him a scorching look. "One?" She shook her head, panting. "Highly unlikely."

Solomon flew down from the shrouds and landed on Charlisse's shoulder, startling her. He chattered happily and leaned his smelly head against her cheek.

"See?" Sloane said. "Even Solomon approves."

Charlisse scratched under the monkey's chin. "Perhaps we should teach you how to fight, little fellow."

Shuffling over to a barrel, Sloane drew a ladle of grog and offered it to Charlisse.

"Now, 'ow about pistols?"

"I know how to load and shoot a pistol—one of the skills my husband taught me," she said between gulps of warm, rum-tainted water. Memories flooded over her—pictures of Merrick showing her how to prime and cock a pistol. They had stood in front of the church at Port Royal, and she had just learned her new husband must sail to England. Merrick's father was being impeached, and Merrick had to help him escape to France before his enemies killed him. Though Charlisse had pleaded to go with Merrick, he'd refused—saying it would be far more dangerous for her in England than at Port Royal with Reverend Thomas.

"Knives then," Sloane said, sloshing down a gulp.

Charlisse stretched back her shoulders, feeling the strain of tight muscles between them. "Can it wait until tomorrow?"

"We will sail into Tortuga tomorrow, milady. 'Tis best ye practice as much as ye can before then." He shuffled his feet and looked down. "Also, yer voice."

"What is wrong with my voice?" She threw her hands to her hips.

Sloane gave her a sideways glance, and Solomon jumped to his shoulder. "Well, kin ye lower it a bit, and make it more harsh?"

Charlisse clenched her jaw and scanned the ship. Her gaze landed on Rusty at the helm. The faithful man had been at his post far too long. She drew a deep breath. "Rusty!" she bellowed in her deepest voice, then glanced at Sloane for his approval. He smiled, and she turned back to see Rusty jump and look her way.

"You are relieved of your post. Get some rest."

One of Merrick's newest crew members, Smack, a man whom she had seen at the whipstaff before, stood under the quarterdeck railing, whispering in the shadows with Brighton and another man. "Smack, man the helm, if you please," Charlisse called.

With a wide grin, Rusty jumped down the quarterdeck stairs and approached Charlisse. Smack, however, was not so quick to respond.

A chilling breeze drifted up from the swirling sea. *You see, they won't listen to you.*

Swallowing a dry gulp, Charlisse stepped toward the men despite the quake in her knees. "Smack!" she yelled.

The bald man glanced at her with imperious eyes the color of the approaching storm. Brighton said something and nodded at him, and Smack headed up the stairs without saying a word.

Sloane released a long breath, but Charlisse's remained frozen in her throat.

One more day—one more day with these pirates. But so much could happen in a day. From the sly looks they cast her way and their whispers slithering around her, she had no doubt a mutinous plan brewed among them.

Feeling eyes upon her, Charlisse turned to see Rusty's cheerful, freckled face. "Don't be worrin' none. I reckon they'll get the hang o' a lady cap'n 'fore too long."

She smiled and gazed back over the ship. Brighton still whispered with another pirate as they shared a bottle of rum. Smack stood staunchly at the whipstaff. Jeremy and Mason lingered on the foredeck. The lifeless forms of three dozing pirates sprawled in the corner under the foredeck railing. The rest were no doubt sleeping or gambling below.

She sighed and felt her insides clamp. Of the eighteen men, Charlisse believed she could count on the loyalties of only three: Sloane, Rusty, and Jackson.

"How is Jackson?" she asked Sloane.

"Should be on his feet by tomorrow, milady."

So only two men for now, and two women, against fifteen mutinous pirates. *Lord, the odds are not in our favor.*

A warm breeze fluttered across her. *Remember David and Goliath?* Charlisse smiled.

Thunder rumbled in the distance, drawing her attention to angry clouds overhead.

Sloane followed her gaze. "There's naught to concern ye, milady. 'Tis not a big storm."

Lightning carved a glowing dagger into the dark sky, followed by a growl of thunder that felt like an omen of upcoming hostilities.

Charlisse frowned at Sloane as the wind nearly blew off her captain's hat. Forcing it down on her head, she faced him. "It's not the storm above us that concerns me."

"Aye." He nodded.

"Now, what about those knives?" she asked, hoping that doing something productive would keep her mind from her predicament.

"Well, it so happens that Rusty here be the best knifeman I done seen in a while."

"Indeed?" Charlisse shifted her glance to the ruddy pirate.

Rusty's face reddened, and he glanced downward.

"Well, let's be about it then."

Lifting his head, Rusty beamed. " 'Twould be my pleasure."

His ardent gaze lingered upon her longer than Charlisse felt comfortable with, and she shifted her eyes away, wondering what to make of it.

As it turned out, Rusty was quite proficient at knife throwing, and Charlisse found, much to her dismay, that either by his excellent instruction or by a talent she otherwise would never have been aware of, she possessed a natural inclination toward this horrid mode of violence. After only a few attempts, she planted a knife in the mainmast from a distance of over five yards.

"Fancy that," Rusty crowed. "Yer better 'an most o' the crew."

Sloane slapped his hat against his thigh. "Har, I knew ye had some pirate in ye."

Charlisse looked at the knife protruding from the mast. She did not want to have any pirate in her. She hated violence and never approved of its use as a means to an end.

Rusty continued his instruction and took every opportunity to touch her hands in order to position the knife. More than once, she turned her head to find him within inches of her, smiling at her with a boyish glazed look.

Although the sun had never found a way to pry back the clouds that held it captive, the fading light told Charlisse evening was upon them. The gloomy mass that had churned above had only agitated her nerves and disturbed the seas with its empty threats. No fierce storm had lashed its fury upon them—for which Charlisse was most grateful, for she had no idea how to handle a ship in a storm. Even now, the hint of a squall rising on the horizon invoked terrifying memories of the first storm she had encountered upon these seas—the tempest that had tossed her into the Caribbean and left her stranded on an island.

Charlisse leaned down to scratch her leg, chaffed from the rough canvas breeches she wore, when droplets of rain trickled from the sky. Sheathing her knife, she thanked Rusty for his kindness.

"Me pleasure, milady." He bowed. "An' would ye care to dine wi' me tonight?"

Sloane, standing behind him, cleared his throat and shook with silent chuckles.

Charlisse looked up into Rusty's cerulean eyes, too sweet for pirate's eyes. His flaming red hair, though tied behind him, sprang out like coils around his freckled face.

"I'm honored that you would ask, but I must take my supper with Isabel in the cabin."

Rusty gave her a despairing look and shuffled away.

Watching him leave, Charlisse frowned.

" 'Tis only an innocent boyish passion, milady," Sloane said. "There's naught to fear from that one."

Tossing off her hat, Charlisse raised her face to the sprinkling rain, allowing each warm drop to soak away the grimy uncertainty of the past weeks.

A piercing shriek alerted her, and she popped open her eyes to see Sloane grab the hilt of his cutlass. Another desperate cry, and Charlisse swung about to see Royce, Gunny, and several other pirates climbing onto the deck, joined by Brighton.

Royce held Isabel in front of him with a knife to her throat.

Isabel's wide eyes sparked with fear. Aside from the heaving of her chest, her body remained rigid in the pirate's grasp as he led her across the deck.

"I'll be takin' this sweet darling fer meself, if ye don't mind," Royce said, sneering. "No sense wastin' good female flesh." The men glanced at one another, uttering malicious chortles. Burying his face in Isabel's hair, he inhaled deeply. "Ye might want to know, as well." He looked up at Charlisse with twitching eyes. "I'll be takin' command o' the ship."

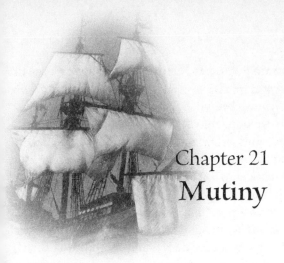

# Chapter 21
# Mutiny

Merrick braced himself for the onslaught. So this would be how it ended for the great Captain Merrick, killed by a pack of lowlife miscreants on board a villainous ship—not exactly as he'd envisioned it.

Hanson swished his cutlass through the air in front of him and licked his scarred lips. Two other pirates eased toward Merrick, drawing their weapons.

"If you kill me, you'll still be left with Captain Collier when he awakens." Merrick inched his hand toward his cutlass while maintaining a threatening gaze upon the men. He must give these pirates a reason to keep him alive. He hoped they would remember how he'd saved Kale and not want to be left at Collier's mercy.

"We can throw ye both overboard then, says I." Hanson glowered at him, flinging his stringy brown hair behind him.

Merrick studied his enemy, spotting an ignorance behind the greed in his ravenous glare. Greed for treasure. That was what every pirate wanted, even more than power.

"Very well. Who will command the ship then? You? What do you know of navigating through these seas? How many battles have you commanded?" Merrick cocked one eyebrow and grinned as the pirates began to mumble amongst themselves.

"Perhaps you've heard of my successes as captain of the *Redemption* and the vast treasure I procured for those who sailed under my flag."

Assenting grunts passed over the crowd, and the two pirates halted.

Hanson pointed a wavering sword at Merrick. "Who's to say I can't do better than the likes o' ye?"

"Hanson, ye can't find yer own behind in the dark," one pirate shouted, sending chortles of laughter shooting into the air.

Hanson's jaw tightened, and his face grew a strange shade of purple. His thinning, mud-colored hair flapped in the wind.

"I say we let Cap'n Merrick stay," one man yelled.

Concurring groans followed.

"And if Hanson wants to challenge 'im, let 'im do so by the articles."

"Aye, aye," the pirates chanted. "A fight to the death."

"A fight to the death!" The crew repeated in unison, thrusting their fists in the air.

Bracing his hand on the hilt of his cutlass, Merrick stood his ground with a smirk on his lips. He knew the cantankerous pirate would not have the courage to confront Merrick alone in a fair fight.

Hanson shuffled his feet, his slippery gaze shifting between Merrick's eyes and the cutlass hanging at his side. He bared his teeth behind scarred lips, then lowered his sword and shot Merrick a fierce look before skulking away.

"Let's throw Collier to the sharks, says I," Styles yelled.

Shouts of dissent clashed with cheers of agreement, and a heated argument broke out. Throwing Collier overboard would solve many of Merrick's problems. He would not only gain a ship of his own, but also save this crew from a murderous tyrant. Yet as he listened to the men arguing, he knew he could not bring himself to do it—at least not when the man was unconscious. Besides, he still needed Collier's association with Morgan to arrange a meeting.

Merrick let out a shrill whistle, drawing their attention. "I say let him live," he bellowed above the fading clamor. " 'Tis a coward's way out to throw a man overboard when he's too drunk to swim. If you wish to challenge Collier, then by all means, challenge him when he's awake and can defend himself."

"Aye," some men agreed, while others lowered their heads.

"Then back to your posts." Merrick hesitated, thinking of the Spanish lady below. He longed to escort her back to town—back to her father. But he could think of no one on board to whom he could entrust her safety, and he didn't dare escort her himself, for most assuredly these cretins would not think twice about absconding with the ship and leaving him stranded in the middle of an enemy town. "Make for Tortuga," he finally ordered. He'd have to find another way to get her home safely.

The pirates began to slither away, their murmurs and grumbles tapering in the evening breeze. Before too long, with all canvas spread, the *Satisfaction* flew through the glistening dark waters on a tack back to the treacherous pirate port.

Merrick stood beside the whipstaff and watched the sun climb above the horizon, flinging its gold and orange streaks over the choppy sea like paint on a dark canvas. In some small way, he felt as if those bright rays were piercing the darkness of his heart, scattering his pain with their glow and shedding light on the man he really was—the man God wanted him to be.

He had ordered two of the pirates to move Collier to the forecastle cabin, where the captain could sleep off his inebriation in peace. The longer he slept, the better it would be for Merrick—and the whole crew.

Crossing his arms over his chest, he took in a deep breath of the salty sea air, but found it did not bring him the usual comfort. Confusion twisted his now sober mind. Who was he anymore? Pirate? Nobleman? Thief? Man of God?

Only a few pirates roamed the ship—the rest of them slept off the night's debauchery, either where they had fallen unconscious on deck or below in the berth. Those who worked the sails or sauntered above nodded at him as they went about their tasks, leaving Merrick alone to sort through his jumbled thoughts.

The loss of Charlisse still burned like a festering sore eating away the remainder of his heart. He knew there would never be a cure—not even revenge. Still, whenever he thought of extracting justice from Morgan and his miscreant pirates, it seemed to cool the incessant burning in his soul. Someone must pay. Merrick had to do something. Otherwise her life, her memory, would fade into oblivion with all the other senseless deaths.

A cool breeze tugged at Merrick's hair. *Yes, she would want her death avenged.*

Merrick snorted. He knew that wasn't true. Had he ever stopped to consider what she would have wanted? Perhaps there was another way to get his revenge—another way to calm the raging storm within him.

*Is revenge really what you want, My son? Come back to Me.*

Gripping the rail, Merrick hung his head and felt that soothing voice melt through the hardened shield with which he had barricaded his soul. What price was he willing to pay to ease the pain of Charlisse's death?

*It will be worth it. You will show Morgan and the entire world that they don't dare cross the greatest pirate ever to sail the Spanish Main.*

Merrick chuckled. Hadn't he patronized Collier the same way last night, appealing to his inflated pride? Was he as much a fool as Collier?

Badeau jumped onto the quarterdeck and ventured beside Merrick. Merrick offered him a furtive glance, remembering the Frenchmen's cold manner the night before.

"I saw what you did, monsieur," Badeau said. "You saved Kale and *arrêté*. . .stopped Collier."

Merrick shifted his stance and sighed.

"And the señorita, you saved her?"

"For the time being." Merrick thought of the terrified woman below and wished he could do more for her.

"*Très beau.* She is beautiful, is she not?"

Merrick examined the Frenchman's ardent gaze. "Yes. Need I protect her from you, as well?"

"*Non, mon* capitaine." But Badeau's shifty grin gave Merrick pause. "*Mais*, you are good man. Perhaps I judge you maturely."

"Prematurely, and no, you did not." Merrick shook his head, thinking of the atrocities he had seen since joining Collier. Though he had not participated in any, wasn't it just as bad to stand around and do nothing? *"Therefore to him that knoweth to do good, and doeth it not, to him it is sin."* Shame settled over him like a stifling shroud. Closing his eyes, Merrick cursed himself.

"*Pardon*, monsieur," Badeau said. "The men. They respect you. I saw the old Merrick in you last night." He leaned toward him. "And I see it in the eyes of these men."

Merrick clenched his jaw. "The old Merrick is dead, and Collier is still the captain of this ship."

"*Pour le moment.*"

"Beware of mutinous talk, Baddo. You see where it nearly got Kale, and I doubt he was guilty of it."

"The men. They weary of Collier." Badeau paused, shifting his glance around them. "Since I join this crew, I see him murder three sailors we captured from a merchant vessel. One he hung on the yardarm for days until the weather ate his flesh, another he strapped to the keel, and a third he gutted and quartered here on the main deck."

Anger rekindled in Merrick's belly. He had heard the man was bloodthirsty, but he had no idea he was so depraved. "Why do you stay with him?"

"Why most of the men stay with him, monsieur. He makes us very wealthy. Besides, he threatens to hunt down and kill any one of us who abandon him." He nodded toward Merrick. "I am sure he now considers you one of his own."

"I belong to no man," Merrick said. "Especially not a savage like Collier." A gust of wind swept over him, and he brushed the hair from his face, raking it behind him. "I have no fear of him."

"Oui, I thought as much." Badeau paused, opened his mouth, hesitated, then closed it, studying Merrick.

Merrick stared at him curiously. The rising sun accentuated the pockmarked scars on the Frenchman's face. "Out with it, Baddo."

"The men. Some. . ." Badeau fingered his pointed beard. "Some want you to take over the ship."

"I see." Merrick squinted toward the blazing sun. "How many?"

"Near fifty. And more will join."

Merrick rubbed his tired eyes, remembering a mutiny he had led many years ago against another pirate captain just as heinous as this one. Edward the Terror, Charlisse's father. How could he do any less now for this crew?

A cool breeze slithered down Merrick's open shirt. *You still need him to get to Morgan.*

Badeau regarded Merrick with hopeful eyes. "What say you?"

"I will consider it. In the meantime, find out the exact number of men we can trust."

"Oui, Capitaine." Badeau grinned and bowed, then stepped away.

"I'm not your cap—" Merrick turned, but Badeau was already barreling down the steps.

Charlisse's breath quickened. Sloane shuffled behind her. Rusty was nowhere in sight. The two pirates on the foredeck moved to watch from the rail. Smack still manned the whipstaff.

Isabel's eyes narrowed into terrified slits. The knife bit into her neck, producing a tiny red stream. Tears slid down both her cheeks.

Terror squeezed Charlisse's belly until she felt nauseated. "Lord, help me," she whispered. Two bolts of lightning shot across the sky above Royce, forming a blazing cross. *Are You with me, Lord?*

She took a step toward the fiendish gang.

"Ah ah ah, milady," Royce said.

Charlisse swallowed hard. "Royce, if you let her go, no harm will come to you," she barked in her deepest tone.

Sloane sidled in front of her, pushing her behind him. The monkey on his shoulder wagged his bony finger at Royce.

"Keep yer bootlicker and his filthy creature away, milady, or I'll slice the girl's throat."

Charlisse would love nothing more than to hide behind this burly pirate, but she could not earn the men's respect by cowering. She slid out from behind Sloane and placed one hand on her hip, closer to the knife sheathed on her thigh.

"Why would you do that and waste good female flesh?" Charlisse asked.

The pirates snickered, and a purple hue rose on Royce's face, making his twisted features even more hideous.

Sloane drew his sword with a swish. "Put the knife down 'fore ye hurt someone, ye daft cockroach."

Two pirates yanked out their cutlasses, and another drew his pistol.

"What ye plannin' to do, old man, fight us all?" Royce said, waving his men back. "Gads, are ye so much a fool that ye'd die defendin' this wench? I'll grant ye, she's a beauty, but by the looks o' her, she's way too much fer an aged man like yerself to handle." He snarled a wicked laugh.

Isabel flinched and let out a sob that caused the knife to sink deeper into her skin.

Charlisse inched her fingers down her leg, hoping none of the pirates noticed, and wondered what she would do once she had the knife in her hand. Even if she could manage to fling it and hit one of them, the others would be on her in seconds.

"I'll tell ye what." Royce fixed his cold eyes on Sloane's. "If ye stand off quiet like, we won't kill ye."

Sloane pointed his sword straight at Royce, his gnarled knuckles reddening from his tight grip upon the blade. "Nay, ye'll have to go through me first to get to the captain's wife, mate. I gave 'im me word I'd protect her with me life."

Charlisse flung a curious glance at Sloane, unaware of such an accord between him and Merrick.

"I reckon that be the difference 'tween us," Royce said. "Ye keep yer word to a no-good cap'n who tosses it in the dung heap the first chance he gets, and I give me allegiance to no man." He sneered, shifting his sordid gaze to Charlisse. "And ye, foolish hussy, searching fer yer husband. When last I saw 'im, he was tastin' trollops all over Tortuga. Fools. Neither of ye have enough brains to fill a gnat's head. Ye deserve each other." He spat a brown glob onto the deck.

Isabel whimpered as the knife shifted.

The pirates snorted.

"Let's get on with it!" Gunny roared, licking his crooked lips. The master gunner scratched the thicket of hair that covered his broad chest.

Royce's words pierced Charlisse as if he had flung a real knife into her heart. Pain rose, threatening to fill her eyes with tears. Perhaps she truly was a fool to be searching for a husband who had forgotten her so quickly. But what did it matter now? Soon she would be dead—or worse.

Lightning flashed in the distance, and a bellow of thunder shook the ashen sky.

Images danced like scoffing jesters through her mind—images of Sloane's lifeless body sprawled across the deck, and of her and Isabel ravished by these monsters. Charlisse felt as though her heart would burst through her chest.

"Sloane, don't do this," she whispered without looking at him. "You don't have to die for me. Join them."

"Sorry, milady, yer stuck wit' me." He stood firm.

Royce nodded, and the two pirates who had drawn their swords crept forward, bloodlust in their eyes.

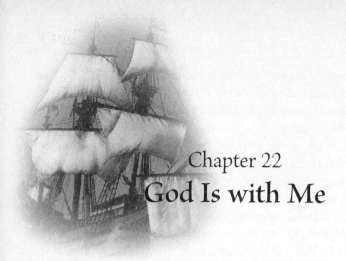

# Chapter 22
# God Is with Me

Charlisse drew her knife. The two pirates crept toward her and Sloane.

Isabel let out a stifled cry.

"Lord?" Charlisse gulped.

The pirates lifted their swords. Fiendish grimaces twisted their lips.

Above them, the dark sky folded in on itself and crouched as if ready to strike. A hissing sound charged the air. It reminded Charlisse of the sound of a sizzling linstock just as it was thrust into the touchhole of the cannon, setting off the enormous explosion.

She looked up.

A flash ignited the sky with a buzzing crackle. The muted grays of the gloomy day sparked into stark whites and blacks.

Wide-eyed, the pirates gazed upward.

Two bolts of lightning shot down from an ominous cloud, forking brilliant trails across the darkened sky. They struck the pirates' swords, setting the metal ablaze in a blinding glow. The pirates jerked violently as the lightning sparked over their swords and wrenched them across the deck.

Charlisse's body flew backward and landed on the hard wood next to Sloane's.

Instantly, the fiery shards withdrew. With hideous shrieks, the pirates crumpled to the deck. Wisps of gray smoke drifted off their twitching bodies. The stench of burning flesh filled the air.

An eerie silence followed.

Royce and three other pirates around him had also been thrown to the deck, Isabel along with them. The remainder of the pirates backed against the larboard railing, eyes wide, mouths agape, and faces as white as sails.

Stunned, Charlisse shook her head, trying to dislodge the buzzing in her ears. Sloane rose and extended a hand, assisting her to her feet. She scanned the ship. Isabel lay on the deck next to Royce. Moaning, the girl labored to sit up as Charlisse rushed to her side.

"Are you all right?" Gently pulling Isabel's arm, Charlisse swung it over her shoulder and helped her to stand.

"Yes, I think so." Isabel said in a shaky voice. Raising her hand she swiped at a trickle of blood on her neck.

Thunder growled its departure in the distance. Somber clouds dissipated, and a glorious sunset of gold, violet, and crimson sprang from the horizon.

Sloane's shocked gaze swerved to Charlisse's. Shaking his head, he grinned and approached the fallen pirates

Charlisse glared at Royce as he struggled to his feet. The tip of his beard was singed and charred blotches edged his ragged gray shirt. He gazed up at the sky, and then back down at his two friends lying on the deck and shook his head.

"They're still breathin'," Sloane declared.

"Brighton," Charlisse said. "Take these men below and tend to them at once."

The doctor stepped out from the crowd, pulling another man with him, and scurried past Charlisse, avoiding her gaze.

Her legs began to wobble as the realization of what had happened tapped on her senses. Had the Lord just delivered her—again? *Thank You, Father.*

She gazed over the pirates. They blinked at her, jaws dropped. She had to deal with them, but all she wanted to do was run to her cabin, crawl under the bedcovers, and hide—hide and cry.

But pirate captains didn't cry.

Mutineers were usually hung on the yardarm, tossed overboard, or locked in the hold. The first two options—though tempting—she could never carry out. And if she locked all these men below, who would sail the ship?

Would they think her weak if she did nothing? Perhaps not, judging by the terrified looks now distorting their faces.

Sloane came up beside Charlisse, and Isabel turned to him, holding her neck, a panicked look in her eyes. He patted her arm. " 'Tis all right now, miss."

"What ye goin' do wit' us?" asked one of the men standing next to Royce, his voice strained.

Charlisse pointed her knife at him, ignoring the nerves pinching her stomach, and then stared at the sky.

"There is none like unto the God. . .who rideth upon the heaven in thy help, and in his excellency on the sky," she quoted from Deuteronomy, wanting to make certain the men understood whose power was at work here. Her chiding gaze rolled over the band of men. "As you gentlemen bore witness firsthand today. Remember, 'It is a fearful thing to fall into the hands of the living God.' I trust you will not forget it." Some of the men shook their heads. Most would not meet her gaze.

"There'll be no more talk of mutiny aboard this ship," Charlisse said.

Royce dared a peek at her, and her eyes locked upon his. "Do I make myself clear, Mr. Royce?"

"Aye." He nodded, his face still pale.

A skinny pirate with long, wiry arms looked up at her. "Ye mean ye ain't goin' to kill us?"

" 'Tis not up to me when you die. That is for God to decide." Charlisse sheathed her knife and took a deep breath. "But God is a God of mercy." She eyed each one of them. "If you ask Him, He will forgive you and you will not be punished. So be gone with you, and behave like the men He wants you to be."

The men's ashen faces scrunched into lines of confusion at her words. Royce let out a grunt and spit onto the deck, but the others stared at her dumbfounded for a moment before shuffling away.

Later that night, Charlisse stood at the bow of the *Redemption*, arms crossed over her bound chest. She was beginning to regret her decision to grow accustomed to the binding before she ventured into Tortuga.

The tight wrapping squeezed the breath from her lungs, and beneath it, her smothered skin itched in places she could not reach. She wrinkled her nose against the stench of sweat and rum emanating from her filthy clothes. Even though Sloane had assured her they were the smallest and the cleanest garments he had found in storage below, she had no doubt she and the quartermaster had very different ideas of cleanliness. As she scratched her side, she prayed that it was just the rough fabric chafing her skin and not lice.

No matter. She gripped the rail and inhaled a deep breath of the wild Caribbean air. It was salty, spicy, and fragrant—the smell of freedom, Merrick had always claimed. Merrick. Who would she find when she got to Tortuga? Would there be even a glimpse of the man she loved, or had the wicked one swallowed him whole and dragged him once again in the slough of perdition?

"Oh, Merrick." She sighed. Tears filled her eyes, blurring the somber seas before her.

Charlisse had tried to sleep, but the traumatic events of the day skipped repeatedly through her mind and forbade slumber entrance. So she had left Isabel in bed and sneaked above to sort through her thoughts and emotions.

All the dark, ominous clouds had been swept away by a fresh trade wind, carrying with it the promise of hope. Humbled that God had delivered her in so wondrous a way, she bowed her head and gave Him thanks once again.

The ocean splashed and churned against the ship as it sliced a trail through the inky waters. When she lifted her gaze, a myriad of stars sparkled at her from a clear ebony sky, but Charlisse could barely make out the division between sea and sky on the horizon. A murky haze obscured the clear line, just as the path before her was hidden in the shadows of the unknown. "For we walk by faith, not by sight." A verse from Corinthians trickled into her mind.

Isabel crept up the companionway stairs and onto the deck. A warm breezed wafted over her, dancing through her loose hair. In her haste she'd forgotten to pin up the unruly strands. Her gaze took in the silent ship and landed on Charlisse's tiny frame up on the foredeck, and she breathed a sigh of relief. Isabel had awoken with a start from a nightmare too frightening to remember—yet she had a sensation that something horrible had happened to her friend. When she didn't find her in the cabin, terror struck every nerve.

Tiptoeing up the foredeck stairs, she slipped beside Charlisse.

"I thought you were asleep," Charlisse said.

Isabel gripped the rail and gazed across the thick blackness. "How can I sleep after what happened today?" She decided not to tell Charlisse about the nightmare. It was only a dream, after all, and the poor woman had enough to deal with.

Charlisse placed a warm hand over Isabel's. "I know what a knife feels like when it is held to your throat."

"Actually, I was referring to the lightning." Isabel grinned, the revelation surprising even her.

"Ah." Charlisse nodded. "Quite a miracle, wasn't it?"

Isabel sighed. "That is what puzzles me. I heard you praying." She scratched the rising itch on her arms and gave Charlisse a curious glance. "God answered you, didn't He?"

Charlisse squeezed her hand. "That He did."

"He exists?" Even as Isabel asked the question, she knew He must, and the thought both excited and terrified her.

Charlisse leaned her head toward Isabel and grinned. "As I've been trying to tell you."

The sliver of the moon peered above the horizon and timidly edged upward, as if assessing the safety of making another run across the sky. Isabel knew how it felt. She envied it for having a safe, dark place to crawl back into at the end of the night when its work was done. God seemed to be such a place for Charlisse. But could He be a safe place for Isabel, too?

A tear spilled down her cheek. If she admitted He existed, she had to admit that He must not care about her. "Why does God not answer me when I pray?"

"There was a time I, too, asked the same question," Charlisse gave her a weak smile and then gazed out over the sea. "For many years, after my mother died, I cried out to God to rescue me from my uncle's abuse, yet it seemed either He didn't hear me or He didn't care." The ship swooped down upon a wave, sending a sprinkle of warm water over them before Charlisse continued, "But do you know what I discovered?" Her glistening eyes darted to Isabel's. "That He'd always been with me, loving and watching over me, waiting for me to open the only door through which He could answer my prayers."

"What do you mean? What door?" Confusion stormed through Isabel. Had she missed some important ritual? She'd attended church her whole life. She'd partaken of communion and memorized the creeds and confessions. What else was there?

"The door is His Son, Jesus. He is the only way. He paid the price so we might live."

Isabel held a hand to her nose and sniffed. "But I believe that, too."

"It's more than just a belief. You must follow Him. You must *know* Him."

"But how?"

"Just talk to Him. Allow Him to change your heart."

"If I do, then God will answer my prayers, too?"

"Yes, He will. But I must warn you." Charlisse gave her a sideways glance. "Sometimes it won't be the answer you expect. Sometimes the answer is no, sometimes it is wait, and sometimes the answer comes in the form of trials that help to make us stronger."

Truth be told, that didn't sound so wonderful after all, especially in light of the afflictions that had come upon Charlisse. Isabel's glance landed on Charlisse's flat belly, and she pictured the lifeless bundle—her friend's stillborn son—being cast into the sea. "Trials such as those you have endured lately? How can those come from a loving God?" Isabel cringed at the unintended sarcasm in her voice.

Charlisse nodded and smiled. "He promises that all things work for our good and His glory. We must trust Him."

Isabel sensed torment behind her friend's faithful assurances. Laying a hand on her own stomach, she glanced down and thought of the child growing within her. How could this be for her good or God's glory?

The brave moon had now risen a handbreadth over the horizon and hung, amongst the stars, grinning at them. Its glow shimmered over the foam-capped waves, setting them ablaze with silvery light. The bubbling rustle of the sea against the ship soothed Isabel's frayed nerves, and she let out a sigh and lowered her taut shoulders. Perhaps she would try praying to God's Son. What harm could there be in trying?

"Did you see the look on those pirates' faces?" Isabel giggled, remembering the lightning strike.

Charlisse laughed. " 'Twas something, to be sure. I fancy they won't be causing us any trouble for a while."

A loud knock on the door startled Charlisse from her sleep. She jumped from the bed, wincing in pain, and grabbed a pistol off the table.

"Who goes there?"

" 'Tis me, milady." Sloane's gruff voice was muffled through the wood.

Charlisse opened the door, still holding the gun, and smiled when she saw Sloane's beaming face behind a tray. Her mouth moistened at the sight of the food. No scent wafted up from stale biscuits and dried meat, but the sight of them evoked redolent memories of sweet butter and spicy roast.

Isabel sprang up in bed and rubbed her eyes as the old pirate entered.

"Thank you, Sloane." Charlisse closed the door. "Whatever would I do without you?"

Charlisse grabbed a biscuit and slowly sat down, careful not to aggravate her already angry muscles from her sword training the day before. She took a bite and hoped her jittery stomach would accept it in peace.

"Did you inquire about the two pirates?" Charlisse asked.

Isabel eyed the food, put a hand to her belly, and got up to pour herself some tea instead.

"Aye, milady." Sloane snatched a piece of salted pork. "Brighton says the scamps will live, although he's not sure in what condition. They'll be hurtin' for quite a while, you may lay to it."

Charlisse nodded, thanking the Lord for His mercy.

"I ne'er seen the likes of it, milady. Evil, depraved men, ne'er afraid of no one or no thing, cowerin' down in the berth, plum sceered of a girl and her God." He snickered and bit off a piece of meat.

"Let's pray the fear of the Lord keeps them docile until I can find Merrick."

Sloane poured some tea and offered it to Charlisse, then took his own. "He sure saved yer hide, if I do say so, milady. Scads, I thought our sands had done run out."

Charlisse glanced at Isabel, who sat on the bed, teacup in hand. Dark circles hung beneath her half-open eyes, and exhaustion slumped her normally pert shoulders. They had not gone to bed until well after midnight, and the lack of sleep, coupled with the horrifying events of yesterday, had certainly taken their toll on the young girl.

Another knock on the door brought Sloane to his feet. He plucked his pistol from his baldric and opened the door a crack before flinging it wide. Jackson stood at its entrance.

Isabel's eyes widened at the sight of the gigantic black man.

Jumping to her feet, Charlisse winced, and waved Jackson inside. He hesitated, his glance flicking to Isabel, but at Charlisse's prompting, he limped into the room. His bright eyes carried a smile, though it did not meet his mouth until he surveyed her masculine attire. Then with beaming white teeth, he offered her the first chuckle she'd ever heard from the ominous-looking man.

"I am most happy to see you, too, Jackson. Are you well?" Charlisse asked.

"Aye, ma'am, and ready to be at yer service."

"We could have used you the past few days." Charlisse chortled.

"Har, that be the truth," Sloane added.

Charlisse grew serious. "I'm glad you're feeling better, Jackson. I'll need your help when I go to Tortuga."

"The cap'n wouldn't be likin' ye goin' into Tortuga, ma'am," Jackson's deep voice rang through the cabin.

"I know. And if the captain were here, I would have no need to go there." Bitterness etched her voice.

"Then I needs to be goin' with ye, ma'am—to protect ye."

"No, Jackson, I need you here to protect Lady Ashton. I cannot take her with me, nor can I leave her alone with these pirates."

Isabel's teacup fell to the floor and shattered across the wooden planks. "You aren't leaving me here alone," she shrieked, her eyes wide open. She jumped off the bed. "And not with. . .him!" She nodded toward Jackson but did not look his way.

Jackson studied the hysterical woman.

"Isabel, it's quite all right." Charlisse took her hand and led her to a chair, careful to avoid the slivers of china littering the floor. "You will be perfectly safe here, I assure you."

"First you drag me to this ship full of gruesome pirates who stare at me as if I were their next meal." Isabel's jade eyes sparked with anger. "Then we nearly get sunk to the bottom of the sea, then almost killed in a mutiny, and now you expect me to stay on board with these same men and guarded by a slave! I would rather have drowned in the sea or have stayed on board the *Vanquisher*." She trembled violently. Whether from rage or fear, Charlisse didn't know; she suspected it was a bit of both.

Swallowing hard, Charlisse held her tongue against a torrent of angry, critical words that would only make things worse.

Jackson growled and turned away. Sloane chomped down another biscuit.

Charlisse urged the girl to sit. "He is no slave. He is a friend. I assure you, he can be trusted." She studied Isabel's frantic eyes and grabbed her hands. "I will take you to New Providence as soon as I find my husband. You have my word."

The girl sank back into the chair, a dazed look in her eyes. Charlisse faced Jackson, who met her gaze, a look of defiance in his eyes. "Will you do this for me, Jackson? I daresay I have no one else to turn to."

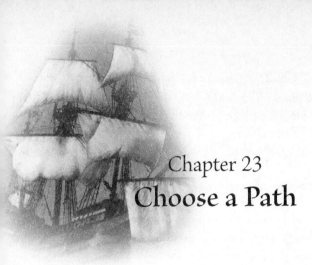

# Chapter 23
# Choose a Path

Charlisse felt a quiver race down her spine as Jackson took a step toward her. His dark eyes bored into her like two cannon balls in a sea of white foam. Towering over her by at least two feet, his dark frame consumed the small cabin, shrinking her in his shadow.

Isabel whimpered in the seat behind Charlisse.

Sloane continued his breakfast, watching with interest but seemingly unconcerned with Jackson's disgruntled attitude.

Charlisse gulped and craned her neck to meet the first mate's intense gaze. She wished she had Sloane's confidence in this man, but Jackson had always intimidated her. Ever since Merrick had rescued him from a slave ship some years back and set him free, Jackson had pledged an oath of loyalty to his captain that only death could break. Now that Merrick was no longer in command, would that loyalty extend to the captain's wife or would the first mate seize the opportunity to take over the ship?

Jackson's broad, ebony chest stretched out in front of her, hairless and glistening in the sunlight that streamed in through the window. A huge purple and red scar marred his left side where he'd been injured during Kent's attack. Charlisse could feel his warm breath upon her face. Fish and spice, tinged with rum, drifted over her. His sharp gaze jumped to Isabel and then back to Charlisse.

The corded muscles in his chest and arms fell slack.

He nodded. "Aye, ma'am, I'll stay and protect the girl as ye wish." He snorted. "But not fer her. Fer ye and Merrick."

Charlisse grinned, letting out a deep breath. "Thank you, Jackson."

The large, bald man offered her an awkward bow. The three gold earrings hooked in his left earlobe glimmered. He turned to leave just as "Land ho!" bellowed from above.

Charlisse climbed the companionway stairs and stomped onto the main deck.

"Tortuga! Two points off yer starboard bow," a voice boomed from the crosstrees.

Yanking the spyglass from her belt, she marched toward the railing, ignoring her pain. She must not appear weak in front of the men, though there was no place on her body that did not hurt—from the blisters on her feet caused by her oversized boots to the interminable ache pounding in her head. Muscles throbbed where she had not realized they existed, and her blasted sword kept hitting the floor behind her, tripping her as she hobbled along. She would have to ask Sloane for a shorter one.

Raising the spyglass, she scanned the horizon. She had never been to Tortuga, and with good reason. Merrick had told her it was hell on earth. The island, it was said, was shaped like a turtle, but as she brought the speck of land into focus, it appeared as nothing more than a green heap floating in the blue sea.

Lowering the glass, she sighed and swung about, glancing over the ship at the few pirates on deck. They went about their duties, avoiding her gaze. She climbed up the quarterdeck stairs and positioned herself to watch as they approached the wicked island. Excitement danced through her. Was Merrick here? If so, every inch of sea they parted brought her closer to him.

As they neared the harbor and the towering ships anchored in Cayona Bay came more sharply into view, Charlisse ordered the topsails reefed and the mainsails trimmed. The men scrambled to do her bidding.

"Holding steady for your orders." Rusty beamed at her from the whipstaff.

*Am I truly commanding this pirate ship?* She shook her head. *Lord, this is all Your doing.* Stuffing a wayward curl back into her hat, she smiled.

"Just bring her in easy."

Charlisse's back stiffened. What would she find in Tortuga? Maybe it would be better not to know. The rumors of Merrick's dive into debauchery had caused her enough agony. The truth might kill her. A strong instinct to turn the *Redemption* about and flee to the farthest end of the Caribbean overcame her. With one command and all sheets to the wind, this mighty ship could tack and come about without even waving a sail at the wicked port.

"Lord, what do I do?"

Forcing back tears that burned to be set free, she drew a breath and braced her fists on her hips as she'd seen Merrick do so many times when he'd set his mind on a course. She glanced over the harbor, trying to make out the ships anchored there. Her gaze landed on the town—encroaching like a brown plague upon the lush, green hills of the island.

"Come what may, Lord. I will follow You."

Merrick stood in the shadows under the foredeck railing, scanning the ship for any sign of Badeau. He was supposed to have rendezvoused with the Frenchman as soon as the sun set, which had been over an hour ago when the *Satisfaction* sailed without incident into the harbor at Tortuga. The frigate had joined at least six other ships drifting in the calm waters of the bay, none of which Merrick could make out clearly in the dusky gloom.

Several clusters of pirates lingered on the main deck and above on the quarterdeck, casting occasional glances toward Merrick. They waited for his signal. Footsteps alerted him. Badeau approached, holding out a half-empty bottle of rum.

"One hundred," Badeau whispered. "At least that."

Merrick nodded, refusing the rum. He'd had enough of the stupefying liquid while dining below with Collier. The captain had awoken late in the afternoon in a foul temper, and after bellowing orders to the crew, had disappeared below, grumbling obscenities. Later, he had invited Merrick to dine with him, and Merrick agreed, willing to suffer the captain's company in an attempt to pry information from him. Two important facts had been gleaned: Collier intended to go ashore that night, and the captain had plans to meet with Morgan at Port Royal in a month.

Merrick leaned toward Badeau. "When Collier goes ashore, have the men arm themselves and meet me here on deck."

"Oui, mon capitaine." Badeau took a swig of rum.

"And no more of that tonight." Merrick nodded toward the bottle. "I need your head clear."

Badeau snorted. "*Mon Dieu*, back to your old self so soon?"

Irksome laughter broke their evening whispers, and Collier emerged onto the deck, dressed in modish and costly silks and satins, and dragging the poor governor's daughter behind him. The more she fought him, the more jubilant his laughter became.

Merrick clenched his fists. He had hoped Collier would leave the woman behind. Of what use could she be to him, anyway—especially in town? Collier held her in a tight grasp, running his lewd fingers over her gown. She flinched, evoking more laughter as he waved a jeweled hand in the air and ordered a boat lowered.

Fuming, Merrick remained in the shadows. He glanced across the deck at the other pirates awaiting his orders—ready for mutiny. Every muscle within him tensed.

Elisa shrieked again as Collier buried his face into her neck and growled like a dog in heat.

Grabbing the hilt of his cutlass, Merrick emerged from the dark and marched toward Collier. "Where are you going?"

Collier looked up with an incredulous start. "Why, on shore as I told you, my friend." He turned to the pirates lumbering toward him. "Be quick about it, you worthless mongrels!"

Elisa's eyes locked upon Merrick's. Sheer terror shot out from them in pleading waves.

Merrick walked to the railing; then he turned to face Collier. "Yes, but why burden yourself by bringing the woman along? No doubt there are plenty in town to please you."

"Ah, I daresay you are right." Collier straightened his satin doublet with his free hand, vanity flickering in his smile. "But with this one, I intend to make a profit. Isn't that right, my dear?" He sneered, and the woman shrank back.

"I see no profit in bringing her with you," Merrick said. "She will only get in your way."

"Think, man." Collier tapped his prominent forehead. "I intend to sell her services." He ran his fingers over his glossy mustache. "Aye, she will bring a handsome price, and I will return a rich man."

Fury erupted in Merrick's gut. He glanced at Badeau, who remained in the shadows, but could not see his face. The cockboat scraped against the hull as it was lowered, grating on Merrick like a rake across his conscience. He inched beside Collier.

The woman's shimmering eyes shifted to his in a desperate appeal.

"Hurry up there!" Collier yelled to the men, then turned and groped the woman again. Twisting in his clutches, she pounded on his chest, only increasing his mirth. He threw an arm around Merrick's shoulder. "Why don't you come with me? You seem a bit unnerved."

Merrick stared out over the crooked town. A battle brewed in his soul. He should just let Collier and the woman go. His gaze roved over the ship. The forty-gun frigate was his for the taking. All he had to do was take a step back and allow Collier to leave, then Merrick could be on his way—to attack Morgan and avenge Charlisse's death.

A chill crossed his back. *Yes. You'll be a mighty captain again.*

But the woman.

The horrid fate that awaited her in Tortuga was beyond imagining. It would be worse than death.

Chest heaving, she looked at him.

*Take the ship. Why should you care about this woman? Who is she to you?*

Merrick fingered the hilt of his cutlass, releasing the tension in his hands. He wanted no bloodshed. If he struck the captain now and claimed the ship, there would be those who would oppose him, and men would die.

He must either go with Collier and keep the woman safe or stick to his original plan—take the ship and go seek the revenge he so desperately wanted.

Clenching his jaw, Merrick leveled a hard gaze at Collier. He knew what he had to do. And he knew he'd regret it later.

# Chapter 24
# The Drunken Skunk

Merrick walked in silence, checking his myriad weapons for the third time: two pistols, loaded and sheathed in his baldric; a knife strapped to his thigh; another one hidden within his right boot; his cutlass hanging at his side. Adjusting his hat, he scanned the darkened shops and warehouses lining the dirt streets near the docks of Tortuga—all boarded up against the nightly orgy. Up ahead, lanterns spread their glowing fingers out from taverns and boardinghouse windows onto the street, luring in patrons like bugs to the flame. The last time he had been in this town, rum had dulled his senses—and his wits along with them. Now, with his mind clear, Merrick remembered well the dangers of this nefarious city.

"Expecting trouble?" Collier grinned maliciously.

The governor's daughter struggled as the captain dragged her along. Five of his crew ambled behind them.

Merrick eyed Collier, desperate to wipe the smirk from the impudent man's face. "I would be surprised if we don't encounter some hostility among this crowd."

"Ah, that's the spirit." Collier slapped Merrick on the back. "Let's pray we do, for I'm in the mood for a good brawl." He forced a kiss on the woman's cheek. She wiped her face with her sleeve in disgust and then scowled in his direction.

"Getting a bit of pluck in you." He chuckled. "That's good, my dear. It'll please your customers."

Merrick looked away. *Yes, I will pray, but not for what you hope, you impotent slug.*

Gunshots echoed across the night sky, drawing Merrick's gaze to the main part of town up ahead. Shrill catcalls and whistles, accompanied by lewd comments, flew toward the governor's daughter.

"As I told you," Collier said. "I should get a fair price for her services."

One of Collier's men stepped up from behind, licking his lips at the woman as if she were a piece of meat. "How much ye askin' fer her, Cap'n?" He fingered a money purse tied to his belt.

"More than you can afford, Willis, I assure you." Collier chuckled and shoved the man aside.

Willis skulked back in step as they entered the main square.

Drunken men littered the plaza, draped over banisters, on porches, over barrels, and stumbled across the muddy street. Their belligerent boasts trumpeted over the clank of swords and the wails of the wounded. Sparsely dressed women dangled from railings and windows like ornaments on display, luring men into their traps with winks and soft coos, while others sashayed their goods across the street, then fled in feigned angst when men pursued them. Shouts and curses shot out from tavern windows, indicating it was no safer inside their rotting wooden walls than it was outside in the open street.

Elisa shrank and turned her face away.

Merrick braced himself, feeling a surge of peace he would not have expected under such precarious circumstances. He *had* done the right thing. He knew it. And he felt God's approval, even though he was not quite ready to speak to the Almighty again. Though surrounded by enemies, with each step he took, his footing grew more sure and his confidence more firm.

The sting of gunpowder and the stench of sweat bit at his nose, but another scent flowed on top of them—gardenias, Charlisse's favorite flower. Merrick drew a deep breath. The sweet, tropical fragrance did not mix with the stink of human wickedness, but somehow, the trace of it made it less foul. Hadn't God said that His people were the light of the world and the salt of the earth—in the world, but not a part of it?

*"Ye are the salt of the earth: but if the salt have lost his savour, wherewith shall it be salted? it is thenceforth good for nothing, but to be cast out, and to be trodden under foot of men."*

Merrick took another step, and pebbles crunched beneath his boot. Was he that salt that had lost its flavor?

Collier stomped up the stairs of the Drunken Skunk, the same tavern in which Merrick had first met the captain. He held his head high and scanned the crowd, waiting for recognition.

The inebriated mass parted for the two infamous captains.

"Cap'n Collier, Cap'n Merrick." Shouts tugged at them from all directions.

Lust-glazed eyes scoured the woman. Stepping to the other side of the señorita, Merrick placed a firm hand on her arm and offered her a reassuring look. She looked at him with dark, red-rimmed eyes, the delicate features of her face imprinted with terror. Her long black hair fell in disarray down the back of her bedraggled dress. A spark of hope ignited in her gaze before Collier jerked her away.

The captain sent his men for rum, then claimed a table in the back, scattering its inhabitants. He sat, forcing the woman to his lap, and buried his face in her chest, snickering.

A wave of rage surged up Merrick's back. He surveyed the tavern, cluttered wall to wall with the worst kind of vermin imaginable—pirates, buccaneers, and harlots. Several of them clustered together over mugs and whispered, pointing at Collier. Others hovered in the shadows. A fistfight broke out near the entrance, and a wiry man flew through the air, hit his head on the bar, and fell to the floor. Merrick wondered how many would come to Collier's aid should he give in to his growing urge to plunge his sword into the villain's heart and take his men out along with him.

A parrot, arrayed in bright yellow and green, landed on a rafter and looked down on Merrick, cocking its head. "Open yer eyes. Open yer eyes," it shrieked.

Merrick studied it, curiously, then looked down as a pack of men surrounded the table.

"Collier, I done heard ye sacked Barracoa," a willowy man said, wiping the sweat from his gleaming bald head.

"Aye." Collier thrust his chin to the side, flinging his greasy hair behind him.

"We heard there be gold there," another portly man beside him added.

Collier leaned toward them and cocked an eyebrow. "Not anymore." He chuckled, drawing the attention of pirates nearby, who approached, congratulating him on his victory. Collier absorbed their praises like a sponge, puffing his chest out farther with each one. Behind their feigned interest, Merrick knew, greed and jealousy brewed.

"Can you walk a bit slower, Mr. Sloane, if you please?" Charlisse darted to catch up to the bulky pirate, then tripped over a stone and would have fallen if Sloane hadn't grabbed her.

"Blast!" she said, then slapped her hand to her mouth. "My apologies, but 'tis these oversized boots. And this monstrous eye patch." She tugged at the black cloth covering her left eye. "I can hardly see."

"Sorry, milady, but yer eyes are far too pretty to pass fer a man's. The patch will help a wee bit, providin' no one looks at ye too close." Sloane peered over the darkened port and slowed his pace. "I'm just a bit anxious to find the cap'n and be gone from this place." He glanced toward a lighted area up ahead from which blared a cacophony of screams, shouts, laughter, and pistol shots. "This town makes me skin crawl."

Solomon, perched on Sloane's shoulder, prattled in agreement, and Charlisse had to admit she was starting to regret her decision to come ashore. But she had to see for herself to what depths her husband had sunk, and she didn't trust his loyal friends to be completely honest with her when they returned to the ship with him. Would it matter what he'd done if he came back repentant and still in love with her? Somehow it did, for she must know his true character, and oft times a man's true character only revealed itself in the midst of tragedy.

Rusty darted up next to Charlisse, delayed by Sloane's order to secure their cockboat.

"Can I help ye, milady?" He held out his hand.

Charlisse gave him an incredulous look. "Now how would that look, a helmsman arm in arm with his captain?"

Sloane chuckled. "Har, I done seen stranger things on this island. But she's right, you witless buffoon." He slapped his hat against Rusty's head. "She needs to be passin' fer a man, not yer lady friend." Sloane shifted a disgruntled gaze to Charlisse and shook his head. "No, milady.

Ye must strut, not swing. Like this." Placing one hand on the hilt of his cutlass, Sloane lifted his head and marched forward.

Charlisse studied him for a moment and choked down a chuckle. Why did men feel the need to prance about like peacocks? Shaking her head, she directed all her attention to ignoring her painful blisters and parading down the street in like form.

"That be it." Sloane smiled. "And ye best do as littl' talkin' as ye can get away with."

Nodding, Charlisse kept her eyes straight ahead and concentrated on her stature and her stroll, quelling the rising fear that compelled her to turn around and run back to the ship.

"Keep yer hand on yer cutlass," Rusty advised.

"Aye." Sloane glanced at her. "And keep yer chin up."

"And yer shoulders back."

"Stop it, the both of you!" Charlisse spat. "Jittery old hens." Then deepening her voice, she said, "I'll be fine, men."

Sloane groaned.

Insects swarmed around her in a buzzing clamor that grated on her already tattered nerves. She swatted at them, but to no avail. The night held a tepid saturation that dripped from the lanterns, which hung at intervals along the street. Perspiration trickled down her neck, and she yanked at the cloth binding her chest, longing to scratch beneath it.

So far, Tortuga didn't seem much different from Port Royal—just another port where sailors came to drink after a long voyage. Yet the closer they came to the center of town, the louder her nerves clamored within her. A black, chilling fog enveloped her. Wickedness lived here. No, it reigned here. She felt it in the air as thick as the night and as oppressive as the heat. Her heart clamped tight until it seemed no blood coursed through her veins.

*"Greater is he that is in you, than he that is in the world."* The verse drifted through her mind, strengthening her resolve.

Two inebriated men staggered by, lifting curious glances her way. Terror spiked through Charlisse. She sensed Sloane tense beside her. What was she thinking? How could she pass for a man? Yet the men soon dropped their gazes and stumbled onward, obviously unimpressed by the visitors.

Expelling a shaky breath, Charlisse thanked the Lord.

Not wanting to draw too much attention, she had brought only two men with her. Perhaps that had been a mistake. She had ordered the rest of the crew to remain on board the *Redemption* and patch the rent in her hull left by Kent's cannon blast. From their fearful, subdued expressions, it seemed surprisingly likely they would obey her, and if not, Jackson was there to ward off any possible mutinies. Soon it would make no difference. When she returned to the ship with Merrick all would be well.

"Now, when we get t' the tavern, walk in like yer in command," Sloane said, scratching under his headscarf. "Like ye knows ye can beat any man there. Ye must ne'er show any fear." Beads of sweat swelled on Sloane's forehead, and he reached up to wipe them.

"Don't worry, Sloane. God is with me." Charlisse gave his thick hand a squeeze and adjusted her eye patch.

"I hope so, mil—Cap'n."

"I'm with ye, too," Rusty said with a valiant look. "I'll protect ye."

Charlisse offered him a tentative grin, then turned to enter the square.

Her insides collapsed in grotesque terror.

Now she knew what Merrick had meant by hell on earth.

The monkey's hands flew up to cover his eyes. He shook his head and squealed.

Charlisse wondered how she was to endure something even a monkey was unwilling to witness. She glanced at Sloane, averting her eyes from the drunken iniquities occurring in the street. Refusing to allow her horror to reveal itself on her face, she maintained a stoic expression of boredom that seemed to please the old pirate.

*Oh Lord, help me.*

Following Sloane, Charlisse marched up to the Drunken Skunk, the tavern where Sloane thought her husband would be, and took a deep breath. Excitement and terror brewed into one big bubbling pot in her chest. Merrick had to be here. Collier's ship drifted in the bay. Sloane had pointed the frigate out to her as they paddled through the harbor on their way to shore.

Pushing through the mass of rancid humanity that crowded the entrance, Charlisse entered the haven, tipped her hat up slightly, and glanced over the hellish scene.

The acrid odors of gunpowder, rum, and human feces smothered her, and she fought down the queasiness rising in her stomach.

Merrick was here.

She knew because her heart had just skipped a beat like it always did in his presence.

Merrick leaned back in his chair as Collier's men returned with the rum and slid into seats beside their captain. A dark-skinned woman perched on Willis's lap, and the pirate ran his groping hands over her voluptuous figure. Giggling, she ignored Willis and eyed Merrick with interest. Leaning over to offer him a full view of her bosom, she licked her lips and blew him a kiss, much to Willis's dismay.

Merrick averted his eyes in disgust.

Collier placed a bottle of rum in front of him. "Drink, Merrick. 'Twill do you good."

*Yes, have some rum.*

Merrick's throat parched at the sight of the amber liquid. As he glanced over the hideous band of men congregating around them, disgust soured his belly. He could use some rum—if only to cloud the grotesque display. Yet he must keep his mind clear.

Collier shoved the bottle into his hand. "Faith, but you're in a foul mood tonight. Drink, I insist. It'll cure whatever ails you, mate."

Lifting the bottle in a salute to Collier, Merrick took a sip, careful not to swallow too much of the bitter liquid.

A warmth settled over him—at first he thought due to the rum. But then his heart began to beat faster.

*Charlisse.*

A strong sense of her presence came over him. He looked up. His anxious gaze roamed across the crowd. Had he gone mad? What devilry was this? Charlisse was dead. He rubbed his eyes and cursed. Would he ever be free of her?

"Open yer eyes. Open yer eyes," the parrot repeated from above him.

A commotion at the bar attracted his gaze. A young boy, sporting a captain's hat, stood arguing with two beefy pirates. Merrick sipped his rum, unable to pull his eyes from the squabble, even though he'd seen a thousand such altercations before.

Collier slammed down his bottle and stood, pulling Elisa up with him.

Merrick's attention snapped back. He had bigger problems than the short captain did at the bar. He must somehow protect the governor's daughter. But how?

"Gentlemen," Collier bellowed over the din. "I have a proposition for you." His greedy gaze wandered across the crowd, then landed on the woman. "I have here the daughter of the governor of Barracoa—a prize of war, if you will." He grinned. "And tonight she is for sale."

Murmurs thundered through the mob.

"Wha'dye mean, fer sale?" One brash man pushed his way forward. As wide as he was tall, the pirate carried a stench of vomit and urine that struck Merrick from across the table.

"I am offering her services for twenty minutes at a time."

The men muttered amongst themselves, ogling at the woman who closed her eyes against the salacious onslaught.

"How much?" another man asked.

"Two doubloons."

"Two doubloons for twenty minutes. That be robbery, mate!" the pirate protested.

Collier's face reddened, and he tightened his grip on the woman. She winced. "May I remind you, she is a noblewoman, not a used up old rag like these trollops you frequent." His voice belied his obvious fury with an icy smoothness.

The woman on Willis's lap scowled.

"How lovely she is," Collier added, sliding a finger over her creamy skin.

She flinched and turned away.

"Looks like she don't like ye much, Cap'n," one man said, eliciting howls from the others.

"She likes me just fine!" Collier shot at the man, spit flying from his lips. He took a breath, collecting himself, and glanced at Elisa. "In fact, we've had a grand time, haven't we, my dear?"

Refusing to look at Collier, she stared at Merrick, who met her frightened gaze with a steady nod of reassurance.

The corpulent man with the rank odor swiped drool from his lips and reached into his pocket. "I'll take her."

"Nay." Another man stepped forward. "I want 'er first. . .nice and fresh." His toothless grin dripped with desire.

"Now, gentlemen, no need to fight," Collier said. "I'll be here all night." The woman squirmed and wailed, sending a wave of laughter over the crowd.

Merrick drew a deep breath, surveying the hideous mob, their toothless smiles oozing lust. His gaze locked upon the woman's. Horror mangled her wide brown eyes into flaming pits of appeal. He must not let this happen to her.

Merrick stood, knocking his chair over behind him, and grabbed the hilt of his cutlass.

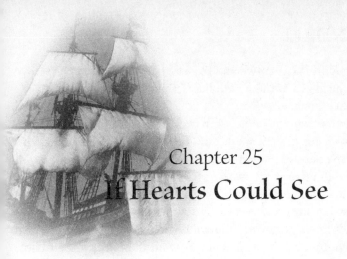

# Chapter 25
# If Hearts Could See

Charlisse sauntered to the center of the tavern, flanked by Sloane and Rusty. From there, she hoped to get a better view of the entire room, and by God's grace, find Merrick quickly and depart from this vile place. Beady eyes glared at her from the darkness, following her every move. Most of the men soon returned to their drink or their women, save a few who continued to challenge the intruders with their piercing gazes.

The rancid stench of vomit and rotting food assailed Charlisse, and she unconsciously threw a hand to her nose, then dropped it immediately. A filthy man stumbled in front of her, his drink sloshing over the rim of his mug. He bumped into Charlisse, belched, and fell to the floor, spilling his ale over her breeches. Resisting the temptation to assist him, Charlisse kicked him instead and shoved him aside with her boot.

Solomon pointed at the man and chattered in glee.

Sloane grunted. "Mebbe we should get a drink," he whispered to Charlisse. "It'll be what they're expectin'."

Nodding, Charlisse glanced at Rusty, whose cheery red face had faded to a sickly pallor. He gulped. The pirate seemed as misplaced among these thieves as she did. Perhaps she should have brought Jackson instead, but then who would have protected Isabel? Her mind writhed in confusion. A captain had to make too many decisions—too many that affected other people's lives.

Adjusting her eye patch, Charlisse headed toward the bar. Two pirates emerged from the crowd and blocked her way. Lifting her eyes to meet theirs, she glared at them with her fiercest look.

They didn't flinch.

The taller one wore no shirt, only two baldrics, stuffed with pistols, crisscrossed over his grizzly chest hair. The brown scarf tied about his neck carried the dark stain of endless sweat, and his grimy hair hung in one long braid flung over the front of his left shoulder. The shorter one made up for his smaller stature with bulk. He crossed his muscular arms over the yellowing shirt on his chest and grunted.

Charlisse's knees began to quiver. Despite the terror that clamped every nerve within her, she turned and spat on the floor by their boots and returned her steady gaze to theirs.

"And who might this be?" The tall pirate looked at Sloane and nodded toward Charlisse. "Yer pretty cabin boy, eh?"

Grimacing, Sloane stepped forward, reaching for his cutlass. "I'd be takin' that back, if I was ye. Ye don't know who this is, d'ye?"

"Should I?" The pirate cast a cursory glance toward Charlisse.

"Aye," Rusty chimed, his voice carrying a prideful tremor. " 'Tis Char—"

"Captain Charles, Captain Charles Hyde," Sloane interrupted, shooting Rusty an angry look.

Rusty groaned.

The shorter pirate studied Charlisse with interest. "I ne'er heard of 'im."

" 'Tis the man who stole Cap'n Merrick's ship, he is," Sloane announced.

Gazes shot at them from nearby tables.

Charlisse gritted her teeth. What was Sloane saying? She had hoped to hide in the shadows, not become the center of attention.

"By thunder, this littl' boy?" The tall pirate snickered. "By the looks o' 'im, he'd only be good fer two things—to fetch me food or polish me boots." He stooped and peered into Charlisse's face. "Why, swounds, he's prettier than most women I seen." Whistles and cackles flew at Charlisse as she continued to stare into the pirate's close-set eyes. He leaned back against a wide post.

She cleared her throat. "I just came fer a drink," she said, surprising herself with her baritone utterance. "Begone if ye know what's good fer ye."

The pirate tilted his head up in a loud chortle. "Begone ye say? Nay, methinks ye'll be the one leavin'. And ye best be quick 'bout it while I still have me good humor."

Sloane drew his sword.

The pirate yanked out his blade, clanging it against Sloane's.

The monkey grimaced and shook his head.

A hush settled over the crowd surrounding them.

"Step aside, old man," the pirate spat. "Me fight be wit' the pretty boy here."

Charlisse's breath halted in her throat. She glanced at Rusty, who stood frozen next to her, his eyes transfixed with horror. Visions of her two friends being beaten and flayed alive blasted across her mind, not to mention what they might do to her—especially after they discovered she was a woman.

*Lord?*

A surge of strength coursed through her, empowered by her fury. In a flash, she drew her knife from its sheath on her thigh, closed her eyes, and flung it at the pirate. A thud and a gasp told her she had hit something. When she looked up, the handle of the blade protruded from the man's arm, pinning him to the post. His cutlass clanked to the wooden floorboards.

After a stunned pause, the swarm of pirates around them broke into screeching laughter.

The pirate's lips twisted into a livid snarl. He plucked the knife from his arm without so much as a flinch. Blood oozed from the wound as he barreled toward Charlisse, aiming the bloody weapon out in front of him.

"I'll carpse ye fer that, boy!"

The tip of the blade closed in on her, propelled by the enraged pirate, whose veins bulged from his red face. Charlisse tried to flee, but her feet—overtaken by the trembling in her legs—refused to move.

Sloane lifted his blade to fend off the pirate just as Solomon sprang from his shoulder onto the man's face. The monkey's nimble fingers plucked and scratched at the pirate's eyes. Screaming, the man clutched the animal, trying to dislodge him. He lumbered forward, stumbling and cursing, yanking at the beast in a wild frenzy. His boots struck his sword still lying on the floor, and he staggered, arms flailing, before tumbling to the wooden planks with a loud thud. A moan escaped his lips, and his shoulders slumped.

Solomon climbed up into the rafters, jabbering happily.

Charlisse glanced at the man's burly friend, who stooped and nudged him a few times before turning him over. The tall pirate's bloodied eyes stared up at the ceiling, lifeless. Charlisse's knife protruded from his chest. The bulky pirate yanked out the blade and handed it to Charlisse. "I believe this be yers, Cap'n Hyde."

Charlisse took it, wondering whether he would avenge his friend's death, but instead the man stepped over the body and slapped Charlisse on the back, nearly knocking her over. "Let me buy ye a drink, Cap'n."

Grumbles coursed through the scattering pirates.

Releasing a breath, Sloane sheathed his sword and gave Charlisse a sideways glance as the man led her to the bar and ordered rum.

Thanking him, she grabbed the bottle and took a swig. The fiery liquid lit her throat ablaze, and she coughed, hacking up some of the vile potion.

The pirate cocked his head and regarded her with a furrowed brow, and for a moment, she thought he'd discovered her secret.

"Ye must be a brave one to dare show yer face with Cap'n Merrick here."

Charlisse gulped down the rum she'd intended to spit out. The amber liquor radiated a numbing warmth that did nothing to quell the quiver that overtook her. "Here?"

"Aye, I saw Cap'n Merrick hisself right o'er there." He pointed with his bottle toward the dark shadows at the far left of the tavern.

Charlisse swung about. She backed away from the bar. Her pulse quickened as she peered through the smoky room, surveying the twisted faces, each one appearing more sinister in the lanterns' shifting glow. A voice drifted to her ears, a familiar deep voice that wove a thread of comfort through the wicked shrill of the others. She took another step, focusing her gaze on a table in the back.

"I'll buy her," Merrick said, silencing the band of men that surrounded the table.

Collier glanced at him, a leering grin lifting one corner of his mouth. "Well, stab me, I wasn't sure you fancied women."

A wave of laugher engulfed the pirates.

"So be it," Collier said as he lifted his bottle and pointed it toward Merrick. "The first twenty minutes go to my friend here."

Merrick took the woman possessively by the arm. "I'll pay for the whole night, if you please."

Moans of protest emanated from the rabble.

"Faith, the whole night, is it?" Collier laughed unpleasantly and rubbed his chin. "I'll warn you, she's a wild mare, this one. . .took me a few hours to tame her."

Merrick bowed. "I daresay, I doubt I can live up to such a virile man as yourself, Captain." He shot an audacious look at Collier. "But I do feel up to the attempt."

Collier's jaw twitched. "Fifty doubloons, then."

Merrick knew that was far more than Collier would have collected for the whole night, but he had no choice. He must save the woman and return to the ship. Besides, the sooner he was on his way, the sooner he could avenge Charlisse's death.

"Naw, Collier, that ain't fair. We should all get turns wit' her," the stout pirate said.

"Curb your tongue, man," Collier barked. "If Captain Merrick wishes to waste fifty doubloons on this tart, then so be it." He regarded Merrick with a fierce look. "Do you have the coins?"

"On the ship. You shall have them when we return." Merrick glanced at Elisa. Her hopeful gaze shot to his, and she pursed her lips.

He pulled her toward him, but Collier yanked her back. "Why should I trust you?"

Merrick grinned and reached into his pocket. He pulled out a bag and poured its contents onto the table. Twenty gold coins clanked into a pile on the sodden wood, their glitter reflecting greed in the eyes of all the men, including Collier. "Twenty now. Thirty when we return to the ship. I am a man of my word."

Collier snatched up the coins and jingled them in his hands.

"Do we have a bargain?" Merrick asked.

Pocketing the coins, Collier plopped into his chair. "That we do."

Grabbing the bottle, Merrick took a swig, slammed it down on the table, and led Elisa away.

"Hold up there," Collier yelled. "Where are you going?"

Merrick stopped and turned. "Why, back to the ship, of course." He threw his arm around the woman. "To get the full value of my investment."

"Nay, I will not suffer it." Collier fingered his mustache, never taking his lofty gaze off Merrick. He slapped the chair beside him. "Come, sit, and show us your skill with the ladies. Your reputation preceded you for many years. We all long to know your secret, don't we, gentlemen?" He glanced around and received the approving grunts and nods, save for Willis, who was preoccupied with his own woman.

"Aye, Cap'n Merrick. . . Since ye done stole the woman from us, least ye can do is give us a peek a' her." A pirate next to him reached over with a grimy finger and lifted one corner of the woman's gown off her chest, peering underneath.

Merrick clutched the pirate by the wrist and tossed his arm aside, then leveled a defiant stare at Collier. A few more steps and he would have been free of this pompous bore—could have taken the woman safely back to the ship and followed through with his mutiny.

"Why, Captain, your reputation as an expert seducer is well known," Merrick said, lifting an eyebrow. "Surely you need no lessons from an amateur like myself."

A flicker of humiliation skipped across Collier's otherwise spiteful glare. He shifted in his seat.

Merrick grabbed the trembling woman again. "So, if you would be so kind, I'll take my leave now."

He turned and had barely taken a step before Collier's booming voice bellowed across the room, "You do not have my leave, sir."

Merrick swung his gaze back to Collier's, searching his eyes. Why was the captain so insistent that Merrick remain?

Collier waved a hand at the chair. "Now, if you please. We await with great impatience your sensual dalliance. Surely you will not deny these men a trifling glimpse at such a fine woman."

"Since I have purchased her for the night, I'll deny whomever I wish a glimpse of her."

Collier grinned but his eyes flared with contempt. "And yet I am your captain, and it is such a trivial request."

Merrick hesitated, wondering whether Collier suspected foul play. Or perhaps the only way for a man like him to receive pleasure from a woman was to watch her being ravished by someone else.

"As you wish." Merrick sat and pulled the woman onto his lap, giving her hand a gentle squeeze. Perhaps he could keep the depraved captain entertained until he drank himself senseless. Then Merrick could slip away.

Eyes glistening, Collier tipped his chair back. "Do carry on, my friend." He licked his lips.

Drawing Elisa close, Merrick eased his face toward her ear and pretended to nibble on it as he whispered, "Never fear, señorita. You are safe with me." Her sweet smell seeped through his skin like a tonic for his loneliness. He lifted his gaze to her brown eyes and gave her a comforting smile.

A familiar chattering sounded from above Merrick. The parrot squawked its admonition again. Merrick glanced up to see the fleeing form of a monkey jumping between the rafters. He lowered his gaze across the crowded tavern.

Charlisse squinted, peering through the smoke-filled gloom, her heart nearly beating through her chest. She took another step. Sloane slid beside her. Solomon jabbered from above, then flew through the air and landed on Sloane's shoulder.

Charlisse's breath halted. Her heart stopped. She ripped the patch from her eye for a better look.

Merrick sat at a table in the back, surrounded by a band of filthy pirates. His ebony hair hung to his shoulders, and his familiar baldric crossed his thick chest. On his lap sat a beautiful, dark-haired woman. Merrick laughed, then buried his face into her neck, kissing her.

Charlisse's heart cracked and shattered like pebbles into her boots.

Merrick lifted his face and looked her way. His eyes locked with hers. They narrowed. He stood, nearly dropping the woman to the floor.

Charlisse's eyes overflowed with tears, blurring the tormenting vision before her.

Warm waves spread over Merrick, prodding his heart into a heavy beat. As he scanned the room, his eyes landed on the same short pirate, wearing a captain's hat, whom he'd seen before. The man stood squarely in the center of the room staring at Merrick, his tiny mouth and one eye open wide. The skin on Merrick's arms tingled, and his breath came in heavy spurts. The small captain tore off his eye patch and glared at Merrick, his eyes narrowing into tiny slits.

There was something about that little man.

*Charlisse.*

No. He closed his eyes for a second and squeezed the bridge of his nose. Impossible. He must either accept her death or be haunted by her memory everywhere he went. The latter he knew would eventually drive him mad. Blinking, Merrick looked up.

Elisa slipped from his grasp.

The short pirate turned and ran out the door.

A blur of an old man and a red-haired pirate raced after him. *Sloane? Rusty?*

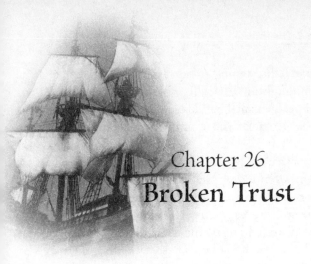

# Chapter 26
# Broken Trust

Charlisse fled down the stairs, nearly tripping over the last one. Everything was a blurry haze: the street, the pirates, the harlots. Musket shots zipped past her head.

She prayed for one to hit her.

A tall, scrawny pirate jumped into her path, blocking her way. He drew a knife. The silvery blade glistened in the light that poured from the tavern. He grinned, baring a set of pointed, brown teeth.

Charlisse lifted her arm to ward off his blow and stormed into him. She cared not whether she lived or died. All she could see was Merrick kissing that woman.

The pirate lashed at her, slicing her arm, and she threw all her weight against him, forcing him back. Sloane and Rusty rushed to her side. Sloane drew his pistol, cocked it, and aimed it at the stumbling man. He grimaced and slinked away into the night.

"Are ye all right, mila—Cap'n Charles?" Sloane came up beside her and grabbed her arm.

She yanked it from him, refusing to answer. Blood darkened the sleeve of her doublet, but she felt no pain, save for the tormenting agony in her heart. How could Merrick do this to her? How could he be with another woman so soon after he believed his wife was dead? Her head throbbed, and she reached up to rub her temples as she stumbled from the town square.

*Liar. Cheat.* Waves of anguish swept over her, like searing rods of hot iron wracking her body, threatening to burst her heart wide open. She squeezed her eyes shut, fighting back a flood of tears. She could not cry. Not here. Not now. A sob escaped her lips.

"Mebbe we should go back t' the tavern," Sloane whispered. "I think the cap'n saw ye."

"I care not whether that double-crossing reprobate saw me!" Charlisse bellowed, drawing the attention of pirates passing by. "I hope he got a good look at me, because that's the last time he'll ever lay eyes on me again." She turned away, her eyes burning.

Sloane let out a frustrated breath and scratched his beard. "Beggin' yer pardon, milady, but 'tis likely the cap'n needs ye now more than ever. He's mourning."

"Mourning? Hard to tell with that smile plastered on his lips." Charlisse pressed a hand over the throbbing in her stomach and grimaced. " 'Tis only been a few weeks since my death, after all."

Rusty kicked up dirt as he trudged beside Sloane. "Did ye see that vixen sittin' on 'is lap?" He whistled. "What a beauty."

Charlisse shot the young pirate a furious look.

Sloane slapped the back of his head. "Keep yer foolish mouth shut, ye mindless toad."

"Go to your captain, Sloane, if you must," Charlisse said. "But I'm going back to the ship."

"Nay, milady. I'll not be leavin' ye here alone in this place. And I'll not be risking yer life with just Rusty to protect ye." He glanced at Rusty. "Sorry, Rusty. But go talk to Merrick if ye wants."

Rusty shot a nervous look at the tavern. "By the powers, I'll not be goin' in there alone."

Words caught in Charlisse's throat, stifled between an agonizing sob and a wave of nausea. She darted to the side of the street, bent over, and threw up all over the bushes. Gasping for breath, she stood and wiped her mouth on her bloody sleeve. Sloane sent Rusty ahead to the cockboat and stood quietly beside her.

Enraged, she grabbed the hilt of her cutlass, turned, and took a few steps back toward the tavern. She wanted to march in there and plunge her blade straight through his heart, as he had just done to her. The overwhelming urge set her legs on fire, prodding them forward. But the thought of facing him—of seeing him with that woman, rooted her in place. She swallowed hard, shaking her head, knowing she could not bear that sight again.

A cool breeze kicked up, swirling the dust at her boots. *Leave him. He never loved you. Nobody ever loved you.*

Swinging around, Charlisse heaved, coughed, and then heaved again. She leaned over, bracing her hands on her quivering knees. Shock spread through her as the image of her husband fondling that woman fixed itself in her thoughts and refused to budge. Clenching her jaw, she straightened herself and drew a deep breath of the foul, heavy air. A tear slid down her cheek. She swiped it away and with a groan, forced back the rest—back behind the door of rejection.

Charlisse glanced at Sloane.

Solomon jumped onto her shoulder and nestled his head against her cheek. At least she could still count on the affections of a monkey.

"Let's be gettin' back to the ship, milady." The pirate lifted his brows, concern warming his old blue eyes.

Charlisse nodded and fell into place beside him.

The trip back to the *Redemption* was nothing but a blur. Clambering over the railing, Charlisse dropped her heavy boots on the deck of the ship—her ship now. At least she had Merrick's precious *Redemption*, small recompense that it was. What was *she* going to do with a pirate ship? She glanced around as Sloane and Rusty hoisted the cockboat and tied it down. All was quiet. After they'd repaired the hole in the stern, the crew must have retired below.

Charlisse plodded down the stairs to find Jackson and see how Isabel had fared during her absence. She really had no interest in dealing with the haughty girl tonight. All Charlisse wanted to do was crawl into a dark hole and cry herself to sleep.

Halfway down the companionway, Charlisse saw the cabin door ajar, spilling lantern light into the hallway. An uneasy feeling pricked life back into her callous nerves.

"Isabel!" she yelled, rushing to the open door.

Jackson's still form lay sprawled across the wooden planks. Gasping, Charlisse leapt to his side and gazed over the cabin.

Isabel was nowhere in sight.

Merrick clutched Elisa's arm and headed toward the door. He had seen Sloane and Rusty—he was sure of it. And that little captain. His eyes. They had grabbed at Merrick's heart and twisted it into shreds. Why? Who was he? No matter. The *Redemption* was here—his ship—and he intended to get her back.

One of Collier's men jumped from his seat and threw his cutlass up to block Merrick's path. Merrick glared at him. "I would stand off if I were you."

The pirate dropped his gaze and looked back at Collier.

"Pray tell, my friend, where are you off to now?" Collier's insidious voice etched icy rivulets down Merrick's back. "Why, I begin to think you are either offended by my company or you are not man enough to handle one Spanish woman."

Merrick slowly swung about and inched his fingers over his cutlass. He curved his mouth at the irony of Collier's statement. "I saw my crew. My ship is here."

"Faith, is that all?" Collier chuckled and folded his hands across his stomach. "It will be here in the morning, I assure you." He nodded toward the chair beside him. "And I insist you stay. I was just beginning to enjoy your amorous display."

Assenting grunts echoed his malicious grin.

Rage blasted past the walls of Merrick's feigned loyalty. Narrowing his eyes, he shot Collier a look of disdain. Enough. Enough of this pretentious swine. Merrick gave Elisa a reassuring glance, then pushed her gently to the side, and with a swift kick to the stomach, sent Collier's man tumbling backward to the floor. His sword flew from his hand, steel glimmering in the lantern light. Merrick caught it by the hilt and held the sharp tip to Collier's throat before the captain had a chance to unfold his hands. A trickle of red slid down his neck.

An icy breeze blew in from the window and danced playfully around the flame on the table, casting shifting shadows across Collier's sneering expression.

*Kill him.*

"What now, my friend?" Collier's lips held an insolent smirk, but fear flickered in his eyes.

The man Merrick had struck staggered to his feet, while Willis discarded the trollop and slowly rose. An astonished hush befell the surrounding crowd as more of Collier's men encroached upon the brawl, scampering out from the dark corners where they had scattered.

Would they defend their cruel captain? Merrick passed a dark gaze over them and saw nothing in their eyes but a lifeless haze of drunken curiosity.

Collier scraped his chair back against the wooden floor and non-chalantly drew a handkerchief to wipe the blood from his throat. He gave Merrick a livid stare and flicked the cloth in the air before returning it to his pocket. "This is a rather rash action, Captain Merrick, wouldn't you say?" Collier's brow grew dark with temper. "You are plainly outnumbered. Drop your sword, and I may forget this hasty affront."

Elisa shrieked beside Merrick as a pirate grabbed her from behind.

Merrick grimaced. He regretted connecting himself to this heinous monster. As he regarded Collier with cold speculation, something flashed within him, like the lighting of a torch, and he saw Collier for what he was—no longer a means to an end, but a man wallowing in a muddy slough of his own making. And for a short time, Merrick had joined him in that filthy mire.

But no more.

*That's right, My son, come back to Me.*

Merrick's hand grew moist against the hilt of the cutlass. He scanned the crowd.

Collier shot to his feet, his face in a tight pinch. He looked about the room wildly and waved a jeweled hand. "I will not stand for this. Throttle him, men!"

From the corner of his eye, Merrick saw the man to his left draw a knife and make a move toward him.

Twisting, Merrick booted a nearby chair, propelling it into the man. He swung his cutlass and struck the man's knife from his hand, sending it spiraling into the crowd. The man clutched his hand in pain. Merrick spun and grabbed his own knife. He flung it at Willis, who had just plucked out a pistol, cocked it, and pointed it at Merrick.

The knife embedded in Willis's shoulder setting off the gun with a sharp crack and a puff of smoke. Splinters of wood flew apart in the rafters. The parrot squawked and flapped its wings in protest, then flew to another spot above Collier. Clutching his shoulder, Willis howled.

Collier's eyes bulged in horrified rage. With a shaky hand, he drew his cutlass, brandishing a wicked grin. The sharp smell of sizzling gunpowder overpowered the stench that already permeated the room.

The horde crowed and cheered, slapping and shoving one another over the sloshing of ale. "He done showed ye, Collier," one man from the back yelled over the din.

The rest of Collier's men remained fixed in their spots, casting peevish glances at their captain.

Merrick pointed his sword back at Collier and drew his pistol, shifting its muzzle toward the two wounded pirates. "This is between you and me, Collier. All I want is to take the woman and leave."

Collier surveyed the throng of men that had formed around them and snapped his eyes back to Merrick. "I am your captain, and I do not give you permission to leave. You will lower your sword, or I will run you through."

"You may be the captain of the *Satisfaction*," Merrick said. "But you are not my captain, nor do you have a say in where I go or don't go."

Sweat beaded on Collier's forehead, and a trickle of blood issued from his throat. He darted his gaze around him as if looking for assurance.

"Take him on, Collier, man t' man," one pirate yelled.

"Aye, 'twill be a fair fight, an' a good one a' that," another called. The pirates grumbled in agreement.

Merrick replaced his pistol. He leaned over and blew out the lantern flame, then flung the table over, sending the lantern and bottles crashing to the floor. He stepped toward Collier and lifted his brows in a haughty invitation.

Collier shot him a smoldering look and thrust his sword at Merrick.

"Jackson." Charlisse nudged the giant man. A patch of blood stained his bald head where a knot had formed. Hearing a shuffle of boots and a gasp, Charlisse turned to see Sloane standing in the doorway. "Go get Brighton," she instructed.

The old pirate scoured the room for Isabel, shot Charlisse a look of concern, then dashed away. Grabbing a cloth and a basin of water, Charlisse dabbed at Jackson's wound and patted his face, calling out his name.

Rubbing his sleepy eyes, Brighton shuffled into the room with Sloane and Rusty on his heels. When the doctor saw Jackson, he knelt and laid two fingers on his neck, then examined his wound. The dark man stirred and mumbled.

"Jackson." Charlisse held his hand.

One eye popped open, fluttered shut, then both eyes flew open and swerved to Charlisse.

"Ma'am," Jackson said, moaning. He glanced over at Brighton, then lifted a hand to the wound on his head.

"He done took a nasty hit, but he'll be a'right," Brighton announced.

"Jackson, where's Lady Ashton?" Charlisse asked, hearing the tremor in her voice.

Grimacing, Jackson lifted his head and propped himself up on his elbows. His gaze took in the cabin. He shut his eyes, the features of his face tightening into dark lines. "I'm sorry, ma'am." He cast her an anxious look. "He took 'er."

Jackson tried to stand, and Rusty leapt forward to help Brighton lift him to a chair.

A rush of fear spiraled through Charlisse, silencing her recent sorrow. "Who took her?"

The dark man lifted his stark eyes to hers.

"Captain Carlton."

# Chapter 27
# Darkening Horizon

Charlisse bit her lip, silently berating herself for forgetting about that deviant rake, Kent. Of course he would come after Isabel. He was obsessed with her. How could she have let him slip from her mind?

It was Merrick. If she hadn't been forced to chase that perfidious mask of a man across the Caribbean, she wouldn't be in this situation, and neither would Isabel. Fuming, Charlisse paced the cabin.

"Blast!" She looked up to see if anyone would chide her for her foul mouth, but all four men stood staring at her as if awaiting her next command.

She approached them, nearly tripping over her sword, then drew it and flung it across the room. It crashed into the wall, nearly stuck by its tip, then clanked to the floor. She scanned the stunned faces of her crew before settling her eyes on Jackson. "How long ago?"

"Not long, ma'am." He touched his wound and tried to sit up straight. "I feared he would take o'er the ship, but he must o' heard ye comin' and left."

Rusty swallowed, sending his Adam's apple climbing up his neck. Sloane scratched under his headscarf and gave Charlisse a sympathetic glance. She knew what she had to do, yet a whirlwind of rage and sorrow churning within her kept her mind befuddled in inaction. She tossed off her hat, flinging it to the floor, and wiped the sweat from her brow. Drawing a deep breath, she forced down the chaos of the night and swept a determined gaze over the men.

"Brighton, wake the crew. Sloane, weigh anchor and make sail. Rusty, man the helm and take her out of the harbor."

Jackson struggled to rise. "Jackson, you rest," Charlisse ordered.

"Naw, ma'am, I feels okay." The beads of sweat on his bald head glistened in the lantern light, matching the glimmer from his earrings.

"I insist." Charlisse gave him a stern look. "Just for a few hours, if you please. I'll need you at full strength later."

"Did ye find Cap'n Merrick?" Jackson asked.

Grief shrouded over her, and she glanced at Sloane and Rusty. "Yes, we did." Charlisse clenched her jaw, trying to stifle the sobs rising in her throat. "The captain's interests are focused elsewhere at the moment. We will continue without him."

Jackson's brawny frame loomed above her. He wrinkled his brow and studied her in silence before he grunted and followed Rusty and Brighton out through the cabin door.

Charlisse dropped onto the bed, staring at Sloane.

"What be yer plan, milady?" His brow furrowed.

"My plan?" She chuckled. "To attack and capture the frigate *Vanquisher*, and to rescue Lady Ashton."

Merrick met Collier's blow with his full strength, sending the captain bumbling backward. Regaining his composure, Collier lunged, eyes wide with frenzy, and swung at Merrick from the left.

Elisa screamed.

Cheers brayed from the surrounding pirates as they exchanged coins and placed bets on their favored combatant.

Merrick fended off Collier's blow and then engaged another thrust from his right with ease.

Collier hesitated, catching his breath as the pirates taunted him onward. The parrot above him squawked, and a glob of greenish slime splattered onto Collier's satin doublet. The mob convulsed with laugher. Collier's eyes simmered like hot coals.

"Had enough?" Merrick allowed a faint smirk to cross his mouth.

Growling, Collier rushed at him. Their blades rang together, echoing across the murky tavern. Merrick's muscles strained as he forced his cutlass against Collier's and slowly pushed it back. Collier's grimacing face twisted into an enraged scarlet knot, making him look like a demon just released from hell. Spit flew from his mouth.

With a roar, Merrick shoved Collier back. Before the captain could recover, Merrick swung and knocked Collier's sword from his hand. It clanked to the floor. Howls and jeers flew from all around. Collier, chest heaving, glanced frantically over the crowd. Yet no one came to his aid. Those who knew him either slunk back into the shadows or stared at their defeated captain with chagrin.

Urgency hit Merrick. He must end this now and go after Sloane. He rushed toward Collier just as the wicked captain went for a pistol stuffed in his baldric. But before he could reach it, Merrick pummeled him in the head with the hilt of his cutlass. Collier dropped to the floor with a moan, blood trickling from his mouth.

Grumbles passed over the crowd. No doubt the pirates were disappointed the fight had ended so soon.

Merrick swerved and pointed his cutlass at the man who held Elisa. Raising his hands in the air, the stout pirate released her. Merrick clutched her arm and dragged her from the tavern.

On the stairs, he stopped, sheathed his sword, and exhaled the stale, dank air of the wicked tavern. Free of Collier at last, he lifted his shoulders, as if a huge burden had just been removed from them.

Merrick regarded Elisa. Alarm and shock flared in her eyes. He felt her trembling as he took her arm again and led her through the streets.

"You are safe now." He tried to comfort her.

"I don't know how to thank you, señor," she sobbed. "You risked your life for me."

Merrick rushed her forward, impassioned by the thought of finding Sloane and getting his ship back. He hadn't realized how much he'd missed that crimson brig. He longed to see his colors flying from the foremast again—a white cross and two golden swords. Under that flag, he had committed his life to God and to fighting evil in these turbulent seas he so loved. For the first time since Charlisse's death, he felt a lightness in his step and a quickening in his heart.

Despite the lewd comments tossed her way, Elisa felt safe leaning on Merrick's arm as he escorted her through the town and to the docks. At least her breathing came steady now, and the trembling in her legs had ceased. For several terrifying moments, she hadn't been sure this pirate would step in to protect her—especially after that beast, Collier, kept raising the stakes. Yet Merrick was truly a man of honor and bravery—a rare find in these savage seas.

He gave her arm a squeeze, and she squeezed his in return, soothed by the strength she found there. After leading her to the harbor, he assisted her into in a cockboat and shoved off from the docks.

"Where are you taking me?" A sudden fear rose at the thought of returning to Collier's ship.

Leaning over, Merrick brought the paddles forward, then plunged them into the water. He pulled back on the oars with a grunt, sending the boat gliding over the bay. "I'm seeking my ship, the *Redemption*."

Hope filtered through her. "Your ship? *Aquí*? Here?"

"Yes, you'll be safe there."

With each slap of the oars into the calm, inky waters, relief spread through Elisa. No moon graced the night, only a mass of dark clouds that hovered above them, blotting out the stars. With only the twinkle of lights from the city, and the occasional wink of a lantern from the ships at bay, she wondered how Merrick could see where he was going.

"You were very brave in the tavern, señorita," he said between the strokes of the oars.

Brave? All she could remember was being too frightened to even breathe. "You flatter me, señor."

"No. I've seen women faint in far less tremulous circumstances."

His compliment warmed her. She studied him as he lunged forward and backward.

"If you have your own ship, señor, why do you sail with Collier?" She couldn't fathom why a man like Merrick would associate with such a villain.

Lifting the paddles from the water, Merrick slowed the boat to a glide as they approached a massive hull on their right. He leaned toward it, studying it. Then his shoulders slumped before he took up the oars again and sent them on their way.

He sighed and she sensed him staring at her, though the details of his face dissolved in the darkness. "I lost my way for a while." He grunted, and their vessel took a sweeping turn toward another hull looming in the bay. In moments they were upon it, and once again, upon closer inspection, Merrick turned aside and continued rowing.

Was his ship here? Despite the nervousness that pricked her skin, she found this pirate captain intriguing. "What made you lose your way?" She knew it was a bold question and none of her business, but the sound of his voice did much to calm her nerves.

He was silent for a moment. Only the splash of the oars cracked the night. "My wife was killed," he finally said, his words flinging though the air like an arrow—an arrow that clipped Elisa's heart.

"I'm sorry." Sorrow rose in her throat. She had lost her own mother less than a year ago, and the wounds were still fresh. Should she tell him? Would it help ease his pain?

Perspiration trickled down the back of her gown, and Elisa shifted in her seat sending the boat tottering. Merrick barely noticed as he approached another ship and allowed the cockboat to coast while he examined it. After a few minutes, he moaned and plunged the oars into the water with a huge splash.

Ship after ship, he searched, and with each passing one, Elisa sensed his growing despondency. Finally, when it seemed they had swept the entire harbor, he ceased rowing and hung his head. "I fear, señorita, I must take you back to Collier's ship."

Alarm froze her heart.

He raised his gaze to hers. "Never fear. The captain has most likely not returned yet. I plan to take his ship."

"Must we go back?"

"I cannot leave you here, señorita, and I'm afraid Collier's ship is the only way out. I'll make sure he's not there before I take you aboard." His voice was calm and strong, like a soothing balm that soaked away her fears.

Dipping the oars, he began rowing again. The water purled against the cockboat, and Elisa dipped a finger into its warmth. "I'm sorry you did not find your ship."

"No more than I, no more than I."

After the boat thudded against the *Satisfaction*'s hull, Merrick tied it and assisted Elisa to her feet. She stood beside him, feeling the heat radiating from his body in a swirling mass of grief and loneliness. The vessel teetered over a swell, and she fell against him. Embarrassed, she stumbled backward, but he caught her by the waist before she toppled over. She looked up into his dark, piercing eyes.

"I lost my mother to the fever last year," she whispered.

He pressed his hand on her back and drew her nearer to him. "I'm sorry."

She fingered the collar of his shirt. "I understand what it feels like to lose someone. I thought it might help you to know." He smelled like salt and leather.

A warm tingle raced through Elisa as Merrick gazed down at her. She gulped, trying to ease the strange, exciting feelings that warmed her from head to toe. He raised his hand and stroked her cheek with the back of his finger. So gentle. Her heart raced.

He leaned down and hovered near her face. His breath fell upon her in warm puffs. Then his lips met hers. He pulled her against his firm torso, and her body instantly dissolved into his. Warm fingers slid through her hair as their lips melted together in a hungry kiss.

Then he was gone. Elisa opened her eyes as he stepped back and cleared his throat. "My apologies. I shouldn't have done that."

Disappointed, Elisa gave him a weak smile. "I'm not sorry."

He reached up and caressed her cheek again, then dropped his hands. Grabbing the rope, he hoisted himself up. "Wait for my signal."

Watching Merrick ascend the rope ladder, Elisa slid her fingers across her tingling lips.

With a grunt, Merrick hefted himself over the bulwark and scanned the deck. He expected to see Badeau and his men ready to take over the ship and make sail. Yet all was silent, save for the gurgle of the water against the hull. They must be below playing cards. Surely if Collier had returned, the ship would be in an uproar, not resting peacefully as it was.

The aroma of gardenias still clung to the air, mingling with the scent of fish and salt. He lowered a hand and assisted Elisa over the railing—the beautiful Elisa. He stared at her lips, still moist from his kiss and cursed himself. How could he have done that—how could he have kissed her so soon after Charlisse's death? Yet there she'd stood in the boat beside him staring at him with such admiration and care, reminding him so much of Charlisse—her spirit, her courage, her heart. He'd not been able to resist her. Shame tugged at him. He must not let it happen again, for it wouldn't be fair to Elisa, and it wouldn't be fair to him.

He lowered her to the deck with a smile. Doffing his hat, he raked a hand through his hair and drew a breath as he scanned the harbor again—one last time—for his *Redemption*. Could he even consider commanding that ship again without Charlisse? She had been so much a part of it. Her spirit lingered in its timbers, its sheets, and its yards. Her voice echoed through the hull; her laughter vibrated with the flapping of the sails.

Thunder rumbled in the distance, and a dark cloud slipped aside to reveal a single bright star. Staring up at the gleaming orb, Merrick allowed its milky light to shower over him.

*I am with you, My son.*

Merrick hung his head. He could not speak to God yet—not to the One who had stolen Charlisse from him. He rubbed his eyes, feeling his resolve weaken, then leveled his gaze into the darkness. The flaming lights and clamor of chaos beckoned to him from Tortuga, luring him to a place where he could hide and numb his pain with rum. It was Badeau and Elisa that kept him here. They needed him. And he needed Collier's ship—for he must find the *Redemption*.

The hairs on the back of Merrick's neck rose, and he swerved around. Pushing Elisa behind him, he grabbed the hilt of his cutlass.

From the shadows under the foredeck a dark, assuming form emerged, followed by twenty men brandishing weapons. Collier stepped into the light of the lantern, his lips twisting in a fiendish smile.

"You impudent fool." He sneered. "Did you think you could outwit Captain Collier?" He chuckled and gazed over his men, who snickered in agreement.

Merrick chided himself for delaying his return. Rage clipped each muscle into action, and he lunged forward, drawing his cutlass, but Collier's men were upon him in an instant. They surrounded him and jabbed him with the tips of their swords until he was forced to drop his.

Collier swaggered forward. "What should I do with your mutinous carcass?" He stroked his pointed beard. "Hmm, I shall have to take that into deep consideration. It should be something fitting for a man of your. . . position, wouldn't you say?"

Merrick glowered at Collier and clenched his fists. How could he have allowed this to happen?

"And you've brought the beautiful señorita back to me. How thoughtful." Collier bowed toward Elisa, who stood her ground, unflinching, although tears filled her eyes. "Take her to my cabin." He ordered, then turned to Merrick. "And lock him in the hold for now." Collier waved a hand in the air, then fingered the gash on his neck. "Let him think on the tortures he will soon endure."

# Chapter 28
# Taming the Beasts

Merrick leaned his forehead against the rusty iron bars, ignoring the hard imprint of steel on his skin. Save for the lantern hanging overhead, all was dark in the deepest part of the ship—the hold, and his prison. He had been beaten and thrown into this cage hours ago, and in that time, Merrick had rattled, pried, kicked, and punched the rods of iron that confined him, causing only more pain in his already battered body. Soon the oil in the lantern would be gone, and his light would fade, leaving him alone with the rats and the putrid smell of the bilge.

He could no longer smell the stench of human waste and rotting food that had assailed him when he first arrived, although that brought him little comfort. It meant only that he had gotten used to the foul sludge that surrounded him. Dropping to the floor, he drew up his knees and settled his back against the bars. Cool moisture from the hull soaked into his breeches, reminding him of stories he had heard of men imprisoned in the hold of ships for weeks—men whose feet had rotted from the constant saturation. He chuckled. It would be a fitting end—for a man who'd been enlightened and had tasted of the good Word of God and the powers of the world to come, and then fallen away. The verse from Hebrews scoured against his conscience.

Muffled shouts from above filtered to his ears, and the ship lurched forward, nearly toppling him. The thunderous rush of water against the hull and the moaning and creaking of timbers told him the ship was underway. He had assumed Collier would return to the city and his wicked revelry, but on second thought, why would he? His reign of fearful notoriety had been overthrown, and he would no longer receive the admiration and worship he felt was his due, at least not in Tortuga—not until time and liquor dulled the memories of those who had witnessed his humiliation.

Merrick's thoughts drifted to Elisa. He had promised her she would be safe. Now she was back in the hands of that lunatic. And Badeau and the others—Merrick had let them all down. He hung his head and reflected over the past weeks. How had he ended up here, locked in the hold of a pirate ship? How different his life had been only a month before. He'd had a beautiful wife whom he loved more than his own life, a child on the way, a ship to command, a mission from God to rid the Caribbean of wicked pirates, and loyal friends—purpose, meaning, and abundance. Now he had nothing—not even his freedom.

He'd finally started back on the right path, had freed himself of Collier, putting himself at risk for the woman and the crew, yet still things had grown worse.

The lantern flickered, and a blackness as thick as the mire in which he sat enveloped him.

Clinging to the ratlines, Charlisse balanced on the yard of the foremast high above the deck, allowing the sultry morning breeze to bathe her with its sweet fragrance. She had not attempted to climb the ratlines before, having always been too fearful of the height, but after the horrors of last night, either her courage had grown or she no longer cared whether she plunged to the deck below. She still wore her pirate attire, deciding that as long as she continued to play the part of a ship's captain, she ought to look like one. But she had tossed off the confining hat, allowing her long hair to flow behind her—the only freedom she could afford at the moment.

As the sun rose in a tumultuous gray sky, Charlisse thought of Isabel, and her heart sank like an anchor in deep water. Terror for the girl's fate clenched at every nerve and sent torrents of anxiety churning through her empty stomach.

The *Redemption* rose and swooped through the choppy seas on a steady course in pursuit of the *Vanquisher*. Black squalls swept over the foredeck, and Charlisse braced herself against another plunge into the dark waters.

Pain lanced across her forearm where a streak of red soaked through the white bandage circling the knife wound she'd received last night. If only the deep cut in her heart could be so easily patched. She glanced across the gray horizon.

*Oh Lord, how do I find Isabel in this vast ocean, and how will I rescue her against such overwhelming odds? I thought I was following You. Where did I go wrong?*

God was strangely silent this morning. Was He angry with her? Had He abandoned her, as well?

Goose bumps rose on her bare arms. *Yes. They have all left you. Your uncle, your father, your mother, Merrick, and God. You are alone and unloved.*

Merrick. She could not shake from her mind the image of him entwined with that woman. A sharp twinge of pain pierced her like a hot sword, and she clutched the ropes tightly, lest she topple over from the torment. Doubt curdled her already scalding agony. Should she have left Merrick behind? Shouldn't she have given him the chance to explain? But what was there to explain? She had seen him with her own eyes.

*He is still your husband.*

Yes, and by leaving him, she had all but ended the sacred union between them. But hadn't he done that already by his quick leap into another woman's arms? Tears swam in Charlisse's eyes, blurring the glorious vision before her into muted blues and grays. She swallowed hard. There was no time to mourn—no time to let down her guard and allow herself a good day's cry. She was the captain of a pirate ship, in pursuit of a much larger, more heavily gunned frigate, on a mission to rescue a girl from a vicious villain. She winced at the incredibly odd turn her life had taken. She would never have imagined herself in this position a month before.

The *Redemption* had been Merrick's ship, but as she hung among the lines she realized the name no longer seemed to fit. Besides, now that she was in command, she could rename it whatever she wished. *Lord, what do I call her?* She thought of her journey thus far on this mighty brigantine, of the battle with the *Vanquisher*, the attempted mutiny, and the fears and insecurities she'd had to overcome in order to take command. She'd accomplished more than she ever thought possible, yet she'd not been the one who'd done any of it. All the victories that had been won, all the wisdom she'd possessed, and all the strength she'd received—all had been wrought by the hand of God. All she'd had to do was rely on Him.

Taking a deep breath, she climbed down the ratlines, and planted her feet firmly on the rolling deck. She called for Sloane to approach.

"Can the ship's name be changed?" she asked.

He gave her a curious look and scratched his beard. "Well, seein' as yer the cap'n, I suppose ye can call it whate'er ye wants."

"But can we repaint the name on the hull?"

"Aye."

"While at sea?"

Sloane's blue eyes held a gleeful luster. "Har, with some ropes we could keep a man in place at the side, providin' no storm arises." He glanced at the angry sky in the distance. "What name d'ye have in mind, if I may be askin'?"

Lightning flashed across the eastern horizon, and Charlisse watched as another glowing spire followed.

"*Reliance*," she said, darting her eyes back to Sloane's, "For reliance on God and on His love has brought me this far, and He will most assuredly see me through to the end."

"*Reliance*." Sloane nodded. "I like the sounds o' it, milady—I mean, Cap'n." He winked.

"Have it done then, if you please, Mr. Sloane. But first call the men together. I wish to speak to them."

Sloane's eyes glinted in amusement. He cocked his head and gave her a quick "Aye" before rushing off.

The men shuffled onto the deck, some clambering up from below and others trudging down the foredeck and quarterdeck stairs. Charlisse's heart pounded in her chest, and trickles of perspiration slid down her back. She balled her fists on her hips and allowed her stern gaze to jump from man to man, bringing their names to memory.

Rusty beamed at her through white teeth, in stark contrast with the fiery red of his hair. His jittery frame nearly made her chuckle. The boy could never stand still. Brighton stood next to him, wearing that infernal brown patch over his left eye. Charlisse wondered whether any damage truly existed beneath it. Or was the doctor simply attempting to appear fierce? If it was the latter, he had succeeded. Gunny, the master gunner, stood off to the right, his barrel chest bare to the wind. The thicket of hair upon it fluttered like weeds in an open field. With face lowered, he kept his eyes on the deck. Mason, a young boy with oiled hair that he tied behind him, shifted his feet nervously and glanced across the sea. Charlisse recognized Smack, next to him a shifty-eyed slip of a man with a square jaw and stubby fingers. Royce lingered off to the side, arms folded over his thick chest. All the hair on his head seemed to have migrated down to his chin in a furry blond mass. The rest of the pirates she didn't know by name.

A sudden gust of rain-laden wind blew from the east, blasted past the men, and pummeled Charlisse with the smell of unwashed bodies and rum. She stifled a cough and surveyed her crew, most of whom would not meet her gaze. Fear was a powerful ally for a captain, yet Charlisse didn't want these men to attribute the recent miraculous happenings to any magic they thought she possessed. She must give the glory to God, no matter the consequences.

"Men," she shouted in her deepest voice. "We are in pursuit of Captain Carlton's ship, *Vanquisher*. I intend to take her as a prize." A few snorts shot at her from within the mob. "For your loyalty and cooperation, you will receive your fair share according to the articles you signed with Captain Merrick." Charlisse grimaced as she spoke his name, but she had to ensure the pirates' loyalty, and the only way to do that was through their greed.

Grunts of approval rippling across them confirmed her assumption.

All except Brighton. "Beggin' yer pardon, Cap'n, but how are we supposed to capture the *Vanquisher*? By thunder, she's a forty-gun frigate!" he exclaimed. "Not that I wouldn't want to plunder her hold to be sure, but 'tain't worth me life to do it."

Some of the pirates scratched their heads while others narrowed their eyes upon her. "Aye, what's yer plan?" Mason asked.

Charlisse feared this question would be raised—expected it at some point, but truth be told, she had no answer to give that would ease their minds. She felt like David with his slingshot and three stones going up against the giant. All he'd had was his faith in God and his belief that he was following what the Lord had told him to do. And that's all she had, as well, for she knew in her heart that God wanted her to rescue Isabel and that He would provide a way.

"Leave the planning to me, gentlemen," she said with as much authority and confidence as she could muster, praying they would acquiesce to her assurances. "I'll fill you in on the details when we find the *Vanquisher*."

With squinted eyes and moans, they scowled at her.

"However," she continued, "I intend to make some changes on this ship." Charlisse paced in front of the men as she had seen Merrick do on many an occasion.

Royce continued to stare at her.

Sloane's expression twisted in confusion.

"First of all, every man on board this ship will bathe daily."

Groans passed from man to man. Some of the men shot skeptical looks her way before lowering their eyes again.

Royce took a step forward. "By thunder, that be goin' too far."

"And your clothes are to be cleaned once a week, as well," she added, ignoring him.

The pirates squirmed, and grumbles of dissent spat her way.

Rusty continued smiling at her, and Sloane scratched his beard, tugging at the smirk planted on his lips.

Solomon sprang to Charlisse's shoulder and began scolding the men.

"Do you wish to remain filthy, repugnant beasts, fit only for the company of trollops and pigs?" Charlisse raised her brows and gave them a motherly look of reproof. "Or would you prefer to look and behave like gentleman, deserving of the fortunes you will acquire and the attentions of true ladies?"

Some of the men blinked wide-eyed at her. Others, with furrowed brows, nodded sheepishly. Royce spewed a string of foul curses.

"Still yer tongue," Sloane bellowed. "There be a lady present."

"She ain't no lady—she's our cap'n," one of the men shouted, sending chortles through the mob.

Royce didn't laugh. His unflinching glare burned through Charlisse. He turned and spat onto the deck "By thunder, ye won't be turning me into any fancy man, if I have a say in it."

Charlisse faced him and drew a breath of strength. "You don't have a say in it, Mr. Royce. Not unless you wish to spend some time locked in the hold, where I should have put you anyway, after your futile attempt to take over my ship."

She turned away before seeing his expression or giving him a chance to retort. "Which brings me to my last point." She scanned the men, knowing this next task might be the hardest for them to swallow. "We shall have Bible readings right here on deck every morning."

"Naw, Cap'n," one man mumbled.

" 'Twill be a cold day in hell," another protested.

Further grumbles weaved their way through the men.

Smack laughed. "Ye'd have to sober me up first."

Charlisse took a step toward him, crossing her arms over her chest. "Then I suppose I must ration your nightly drink."

Smack's face paled, and he gave her a look as if she'd just insisted he be thrown overboard.

"Every true gentleman should read the Bible and know its contents." Her eyes drifted over the crew. "Whether you believe it or not is up to you, but I'll have you know any power you've witnessed on board this ship comes not from me, but from God above. So it would be for your own benefit to get to know Him."

Charlisse studied their faces and braced herself against the expected defiance. Bathing was one thing, but Bible reading would definitely go against the crusty grain of these pirates. Yet surprisingly, aside from a few grumbled curses, most leveled their eyes to the deck and kept silent.

*Thank You, Lord.* Charlisse breathed a sigh of relief.

Sloane offered her an approving wink, and Rusty's fatuous smile reached his eyes with a gleaming look of admiration. Only Royce remained in a defiant stance, rubbing his stubby fingers over the hilt of his cutlass.

Charlisse swung her fierce gaze to his. How long must she deal with this insolent man?

He turned to the crew. "How can ye sissies allow this woman to turn ye into merry Andrews, ye spineless eunuchs?" He grimaced, glowering over them.

" 'Tain't no harm in getting a bit o' culture," Mason spoke up.

"Har, I ne'er had no one want t' teach me nothin' before," Brighton announced.

"A gentleman, I like the sounds o' that," another man added.

Fuming, Royce began to march away. "Ye bunch o' soft skirt kissers," he hissed under his breath.

"Hold up there, Royce," Charlisse said. "Now's as good a time as any to begin those Bible readings." She gestured for him to return. He stopped, swung around, but remained where he stood with arms crossed over his chest and eyes fixed on the horizon.

Charlisse turned to Sloane. "Would you be so kind as to fetch my Bible?"

With a nod, the old pirate rushed down the hatch, and Charlisse quietly thanked the Lord, while maintaining an unyielding eye upon the crew.

When Sloane returned, Charlisse chose a passage from Isaiah: "All we like sheep have gone astray; we have turned every one to his own way; and the Lord hath laid on him the iniquity of us all. He was oppressed, and he was afflicted, yet he opened not his mouth: he is brought as a lamb to the slaughter, and as a sheep before her shearers is dumb, so he openeth not his mouth. . ." Charlisse looked up. Some of the men listened with rapt attention, while others shuffled their feet and glanced around the ship. But at least they were hearing the word of God. She continued her reading with zeal: "He was taken from prison and from judgment: and who shall declare his generation? for he was cut off out of the land of the living: for the transgression of my people was he stricken."

After gently closing the Bible, Charlisse instructed Mason to prepare a barrel of water down in the berth for bathing, and she ordered two other pirates to paint the ship's new name, *Reliance*, upon her bow. Then she dismissed the men to their tasks.

Exhaustion dragged Charlisse down to her cabin. She spent the rest of the morning on her knees, praising God, not only for the strength He had given her, but also for causing the men to submit to her authority—at least for the time being. All save Royce. He had been a thorn in her side since day one, and the way he had stared at her today with such hate-filled eyes set her nerves on edge. She wondered if she should lock him up below before he had a chance to rally the crew against her again. *Lord, what should I do with him? Please give me wisdom.*

*Pray for him. And pray for Merrick.* The words came to her so clearly, she popped her head up and glanced around, expecting to see the Almighty standing before her in all His brilliant glory. But all she saw were gloomy reminders of Merrick.

Sobbing, she dropped her head onto the bed again. The bedcovers still held the smell of him. "Lord, I'll pray for Royce, but please don't ask me to pray for the man who has torn my heart in two."

Charlisse rose and plopped down in a chair, wiping the tears from her face and forcing back with them all thoughts of Merrick. She must focus on Isabel. A slight chuckle reached her lips when she thought of how much the young girl would have enjoyed seeing the pirates' reactions today to Charlisse's speech. She missed her. It had been nice to have a friend, even for a short while. *Please keep her safe, Lord, until we can reach her.*

When she emerged from the cabin hours later, it was to a "Sail ho!" blaring at her from the crosstrees. Plucking the spyglass from her belt, she asked in what direction, and the answer, "Three points off the larboard bow," shouted in return. Lifting the glass, she quickly brought into focus the mountain of sails bobbing on the horizon.

Sloane slid beside her. "Who is it?"

Shaking her head, Charlisse handed him the glass. "I don't know, but they appear to be in a bit of a hurry." Her nerves teetered on the cliff of excitement. Could it be Kent's ship? She hadn't expected to come across him so soon.

"Can you make her out?"

"Aye, milady." Sloane lowered the glass and shifted his troubled gaze to hers. " 'Tis the *Vanquisher*."

# Chapter 29
# Deliverance

Merrick paced the iron cage, counting the steps it took to cross the expanse of darkness that now made up his world. Three. Three steps before the metal stronghold prevented him from escaping from the sludge and filth to the light above.

Tiny red eyes glowed at him from the corners of the dark hold, shifting across the inky gloom, peering at Merrick from every direction—the rats' sharp squeaks raking over him in whispers of his demise.

Seizing the bars, Merrick shook them with the fury of a wild animal, feeling the sharp flakes of rust cut into his skin and a jarring pain spike through his cracked ribs. As if in answer to his agony, the ship creaked and groaned under the swell of a wave. The gurgle and slosh of water against the hull reminded him he was beneath the surface of the sea— already in a watery grave. He would have preferred it if Collier had sewn him into a shroud and tossed him overboard, rather than to endure this hell. For this must be what hell was truly like—a dark void, all alone, save for the agonizing onslaught of regrets and the excruciating thirst for a death that would never come.

"Oh God, what have I done?" Merrick cried, sliding to the floor. How quickly he had slid from the path of light into the surrounding darkness, how quickly he had turned his back on the One who had rescued him from the clutches of the enemy—from an eternity of torment. He had not deserved so much as a glimpse from Almighty God, yet the Lord had given him so much more. Merrick dropped his head into his hands.

Sometime later, the creaking of timbers and the forward lurch of the ship woke him from his daze of misery. Lifting his head, he rose and hung onto the bars as the ship lunged to the port side.

A dark mass with a pair of fiery eyes skittered across the cell and crawled up Merrick's right boot. With a kick, he flung it aside, hearing the beast hit the bars and fall to the floor with a thud before it scampered away. The vile creatures grew braver the longer he was down here, and the longer he went without food or water, the weaker he would become. Soon he would be defenseless against their overpowering numbers, and they would swarm over him and gnaw upon his flesh.

Merrick began pacing again, the thud of his boots against the wooden planks drumming a countdown to his destruction. Though his body weakened, it was his soul that gasped for its last breaths. Without the nourishment of God's Word and the daily communication with his Father, Merrick's spirit had languished, and the dark spiritual forces of this world seized the opportunity to penetrate his dwindling armor.

He halted and stared into the blackness. "God, help me," he whispered.

A chill snaked across his shoulders. *Why call to God? It's because of Him Charlisse is dead and you are in this prison.*

"No." Merrick rushed across the cell, coughing back the stench the sudden exertion forced into his lungs. He shook his head. "No. I won't listen to your lies anymore."

Something touched Merrick, and he swerved, flinging his arms out in front of him.

Nothing.

He sensed a presence. A shifting black form, thicker and darker than the surrounding gloom that hung above him. Another mass appeared to his right, and the two phantoms swung at him, uttering guttural murmurs. As they passed by him, a cool mist prickled over Merrick's skin.

He swung around. Deep, rasping howls echoed through the dark void. Or was it just the rumble of the sea against the hull? *Am I going mad?* He rubbed his temples as a blast of icy wind struck him. The black shadows swirled above him, hovering like vultures awaiting his death. Hissing whispers from a thousand voices filled his ears.

*We won't let you go. We won't let you go.*

An overpowering sense of evil and utter hopelessness consumed him. Tortured, moaning screams blared from all around.

"Oh God." Merrick fell to his knees and covered his ears against the wicked onslaught. "I am in hell!"

*I'm here.* A quiet voice spoke in his head. *Come home, My son.*

*Charlisse is dead. Charlisse is dead. . . .* The shrilling voices hissed.

Squeezing his eyes shut, Merrick fought back the fury, the sorrow, the emptiness of the past three weeks. He felt as though he was in the fiercest battle of his life, fighting not on the seas with cannon and swivel gun, but on the ravaged plane of his soul. *How can I ever trust You again, Lord?*

*I am trustworthy, and I love you.* He could hardly make out the voice over the pulsating chants.

*You must be in control. You must get revenge.*

"No!" Merrick bellowed and threw his hands together, wringing his sweaty palms. "No. Look what has happened to me since I have listened to you. God is my refuge and strength, a very present help in trouble." Merrick bowed his head. "And in Him, and Him alone, will I place my trust."

The whispers ceased.

"I'm sorry, Lord. I'm so sorry." Waves of shame and regret swept through him. "Please forgive me."

Merrick heard a rush of wind and the sound of a door slamming shut. Then all was silent save for the slap of water against the ship.

A sudden warmth shoved aside the chilled air, and a spark of hope glowed in Merrick's soul. Peace, like he'd never felt before, showered over him. He sat back, drawing his knees up, and smiled for the first time in quite a while.

But then guilt washed over him, drawing to his memory each horrid thing he had done and each vicious word he had spoken. He repented of them all, one by one, and found his shoulders lightened and his breathing eased with each turn of his heart toward the Light.

But Charlisse was still gone.

He hung his head, his eyes moistening. "Why, Lord? Why did You take her from me?"

No answer came, only the comfort of God's presence.

Merrick did not want to lose it again, not even as he realized it wasn't

Morgan or any other pirate who had killed Charlisse. God had allowed it. Merrick's revenge on Morgan would not only be misplaced it would be useless. *Should I fight You then, Lord?* He shook his head.

Beady red eyes glowed at him from outside his cell, but for some reason they wouldn't cross the threshold of iron bars. Something—or Someone—prevented them. God protected him. Merrick looked up. "I don't deserve You. I don't deserve Your love."

Merrick lowered his head and grunted. Trusting God meant giving up all control again and placing himself at the mercy of the Almighty. He glanced over his dark prison and chuckled. *I've been such a fool.*

Verses from Proverbs floated through his mind: "He that trusteth in his own heart is a fool: but whoso walketh wisely, he shall be delivered." And "Trust in the Lord with all thine heart; and lean not unto thine own understanding. In all thy ways acknowledge him, and he shall direct thy paths."

"I don't understand, Lord. What purpose could Charlisse's death have served? Yet Your word says to trust You whether I understand or not."

Merrick rose to his feet. "So be it, Father. Whatever Your will is, I must believe it is for the best." He grabbed the bars and shook them. "Even if I remain in this prison. Even if I die, I am Yours."

A surge of warmth rose within him, tingling each nerve. Merrick felt as though he rode on the wings of angels, no longer trapped in a prison of iron, but soaring over the turquoise waters of the Caribbean. Though his body was confined, his soul flew free.

He was home again.

Thudding footsteps on the stairway and a slight glow from a lantern alerted Merrick that someone approached. Friend or foe, it mattered not. He would be content with either, having placed his providence at the mercy of God. But when Badeau emerged from the darkness, Merrick offered a silent prayer of thanks.

The slight curve of a smile lifted the corners of the Frenchman's thin lips as he raised his hand to reveal Merrick's cutlass and pistols. He yanked a set of keys from his belt and jingled them in front of the cage. Then placing the lantern down, he unlocked the bolt, and swung open the door.

"What news, Baddo?" Merrick said, rushing forward and clasping his arm in a warm embrace.

"The men. They are still with you, mon capitaine." He lifted the lantern, sweeping it across the dark room, scattering rats in its lighted path. Wrinkling his nose, he faced Merrick and handed him his weapons. "Collier drinks again. Something happened with the woman."

Merrick's stomach knotted. "Is she hurt?"

Badeau shook his head. "*Je ne sais pas.* He left his cabin last night in a fit of rage and does not stop his drink since. This morning, he orders the crew to make sail and then goes back to his cabin."

Merrick strapped on his cutlass, baldric, and pistols, and dashed past Badeau. "Gather the men who are with us on the main deck. I'll meet you there after I take care of Collier."

"Oui, mon capitaine." The Frenchman barreled up the stairs behind him. They parted ways at the captain's door.

No sounds came from within the cabin. Merrick feared the worst. Bracing himself, he thrust his shoulder against the oak barricade. The heavy slab swung open, pounding into the wall behind it.

Elisa jumped. She bolted from the bed, but upon seeing Merrick, relaxed and let out a ragged breath. He crept inside and gave her a questioning look. She nodded. Merrick followed the shift of her eyes to the window, where Collier lay curled up in the sun on the ledge like a sleeping panther.

As he approached Elisa, Merrick kept an eye on Collier. "Are you hurt?"

He studied her haggard, pallid face, the dark circles beneath her red-rimmed eyes, and then noticed a garish bruise forming on her right cheek. Gently, he moved her chin to one side to examine it.

Her eyes flooded with tears and she fell into his embrace.

"He hit you."

She nodded against his chest.

Fury hammered through him. What kind of monster would hit such a precious lady? Merrick took a step back and clasped her hands. "Did he hurt you otherwise?"

"No, it was the same as before." She glanced at Collier. "He becomes angrier each time." Her large brown eyes looked up at him in desperation. "I'm frightened."

Raising his hand, he brushed a curl from her forehead and placed a kiss upon it, then wrapped his arms around her. "Never fear, I will not let him harm you again." He felt her relax in his arms and remembered how many times Charlisse had done the same.

Merrick pushed her back with a sigh and turned toward Collier. He studied the unconscious man on the ledge and surprised himself when a twinge of pity tugged at his heart. Without God, it was no wonder Collier turned out the way he did. Nonetheless, Merrick had a mutiny to orchestrate and a ship to find, and Collier must go.

He swung his gaze back to Elisa. "I'm taking command. As soon as I find my ship, I promise to take you back home."

"Home?" She bit her lip and smiled, hope lifting her features, and something else—admiration. "You are a good man, Merrick."

Merrick shook his head. He'd been anything but good as of late, but thanks be to God, that was about to change. "Stay here. You will be safe." Then, marching to Collier, Merrick clutched the pirate captain by the arm and dragged him off the ledge.

Bumbling, Collier staggered to his feet, muttering curses. Merrick stripped him of his weapons before he could protest. He swayed, wiping the drool from his beard and squinting at Merrick.

"Who. . .what?"

" 'Tis me, your old friend. Or have you forgotten me already?" Merrick grabbed Collier's right arm and twisted it behind him. Collier winced.

"I protest."

"You may protest all you wish, Captain. But if you would be so kind, you are wanted on deck." Merrick shoved him through the door and up the stairs, feeling as though he were pushing a sick horse up a mountain.

When the two captains emerged above, it was to a burst of cheers. Badeau had assembled a group of at least a hundred fifty men, all brandishing weapons. Upon seeing their former captain restrained, they began hurling insults at him.

Squinting in the blaring sun, Collier scowled at his crew and thrashed in Merrick's grasp. The fresh air and howls seemed to have had a sobering effect on him. "What's the meaning of this?"

"The meaning of this, Captain," Merrick said, "is that I have taken command of your ship."

"You worthless—"

Merrick jerked Collier's arm in a snarled twist, and he cried out in pain.

The men laughed, mocking him.

"And as for the rest of you." Merrick lifted his gaze to the crew and then scanned the decks above, where others crowded the railing. "Either accept me as captain, or join Collier for a swim."

For a moment, no one moved. Merrick felt a quiver lance through Collier's arm. The wicked captain snorted and gazed across his mutinous crew.

"After all I've done for you, you traitorous pack of sniveling dogs," he spat. A few of the men looked away. Others shuffled their feet uncomfortably. Kale stared down at his boots. "Come on, Captain." Merrick yanked him toward the starboard railing. "I'm hoping you can swim."

Struggling, Collier shot a fiery gaze over the men. "As the devil is my witness, I'll remember each one of you for this! You'll not live a day without looking over your shoulder in fear of finding me there, ready to twist a knife in your gut!" He glanced up on the foredeck, where Hanson and Styles stood leaning against the rail.

"Hanson, Styles, you will be the first to go," he howled.

Hanson's eyes narrowed into smoldering slits. Styles gulped nervously.

As they neared the railing, Merrick nodded at Badeau, and he and two other pirates came forward. They ran a plank over the gunwale and lashed it down. Merrick released Collier. The former captain snapped his arm back and rubbed it, sneering, as the rest of the pirates came forward, swords drawn and pointed.

Merrick braced his hands on his hips and offered Collier a grin. He nodded toward the green mound fading on the horizon. " 'Tis about three knots to Tortuga. Perhaps the water will cool your temper along the way."

Hatred emerged from Collier's bulging eyes. "We had a bargain. I took you on board my ship."

"For which I am greatly indebted." Merrick bowed. "But a pact with the devil can never be considered binding, I'm afraid."

"You gutless worm. I shall hunt you down if it's the last thing I do."

"Come now," Merrick replied with an insolent smirk. " 'Tis mercy I'm offering you. If I left it up to your crew, they'd have strung you up on the yardarm and let your body rot in the salty breeze."

The men growled and one of them shouted, "Let's tie him to the keel like he did t' Jamie!"

"Aye, aye," echoed the agreement.

Sword tips poked at Collier, and fear flickered in his cold eyes. His face paled, but he maintained a stern gaze upon the crew.

"If you please." Merrick flung an arm toward the plank. "The longer you wait, the farther you must swim, Captain."

Collier took a deep breath. He peeled off his silk doublet, tugged off his white lace neckerchief, and kicked off his boots, then clutched the railing and paused, looking at the blue-green waters rushing some twenty-five feet below them.

He stepped onto the plank as the mob of pirates flung jeering curses his way.

"Begone with you now," Merrick said in a mocking tone. "Enjoy your swim, Captain."

After one last furious glance toward Merrick, Captain Collier took two steps onto the plank, hesitated, stared at the retreating landmass in the distance, then took two more steps before he tumbled into the water below.

Merrick leaned over the railing as the pirates rushed forward to see the fierce captain rise to the surface and gasp for air. The mob let out a cheering howl, shaking their fists and swords at him until his bobbing head faded from view.

After receiving congratulations from the crew, Merrick tested his new authority by ordering them to their tasks. The fifty or so who hadn't joined the mutiny at first now seemed content with Merrick's command—at least for the time being. Even Hanson took up his duties as first mate without question.

"Well done, mon capitaine." Badeau approached Merrick with a grin and a slap on the back. "I'm pleased to have you in command again."

"Thank you, Baddo, but 'twas you who made this happen. I'd still be rotting below if you hadn't come to my rescue."

"And us, we would still suffer with the cruelty of Collier." Badeau grinned and fingered his pointed beard. "I say we celebrate. We have rum. We have a woman. It is enough."

With a chuckle, Merrick shot him a judicious look. "You may have your rum, Baddo, but the woman is off limits. Do I make myself clear?"

"Oui." Badeau scowled but amusement glinted in his eyes.

Leaving him, Merrick jumped up the foredeck stairs and planted his boots at the bow of the *Satisfaction*. He crossed his arms over his chest and allowed the morning breeze to wash over him, blasting off the filth of the past weeks. Taking in a deep breath, he filled his lungs with the scent of spice and salt—the smell of freedom, then bowed his head. He thanked God for the bloodless mutiny and for the true freedom that came only through Christ.

After a few moments, he looked up again and scanned the turquoise horizon. The *Redemption* was out there somewhere. He must find her. He wanted nothing more than to be back in command of that mighty ship and continue the work God had called him to do. He sighed, raking a hand through his wind-tossed hair as his thoughts drifted to Charlisse. The *Redemption* held so many memories of her. Would he be able to sail aboard her again? He didn't know. But he had to try. The *Redemption* was more than just a ship to him. She was home. She was God's gift to Merrick, and he couldn't imagine sailing the Caribbean without her.

The ship thrust boldly into the next roller, sending a showery spray over Merrick.

"Father, where is she? Lead me to her."

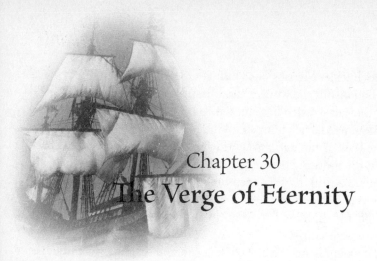

# Chapter 30
# The Verge of Eternity

Charlisse snatched the spyglass from Sloane. "Are you quite sure?"

"Aye, milady. I knows that knave's ship anywhere—especially after he near sunk us."

She peered through the glass. The *Vanquisher* sped swiftly through the Caribbean two knots off their starboard bow. "Thank You, Lord. You've brought me right to her." Charlisse lowered the glass and looked at Sloane.

Nodding his head, he pointed upward. "By thunder, He always answers yer prayers." He smiled, further creasing his leathery, sunburned face.

"Not always." Charlisse turned away, thinking of Merrick. Her eyes moistened, and she swallowed a flame of rising sorrow.

"If ye be meanin' Merrick, methinks you'll be seein' 'im 'afore long. It ain't over yet."

Charlisse shot him an icy glance. " 'Tis over for me." Yet even as the harsh words flew from her mouth, she knew they sprang from her anger and not from her heart.

Then, spinning on her heels, she shouted aloft to unfurl the topsails and topgallants. "I want every rag of canvas stretched on the yards!"

"Rusty!" she bellowed, lowering her gaze to the helm. "Bring her. . ." Charlisse studied the position of the speeding ship. "Twenty degrees to starboard. After the *Vanquisher*!"

A round of cheers erupted from the men.

Leaving Sloane, Charlisse flew up the foredeck stairs and took her spot at the bow of the ship. She clung to the railing as the *Reliance* soared and lunged over the growing swells. "Lord, please help me. I don't know how I'm going to rescue Isabel with just one ship and eighteen men." The only reply was a thunderous boom from the blackening clouds roiling on the horizon, and Charlisse had to believe that was God's way of assuring her He would be with her.

As the morning waned, so did Charlisse's strength, and if she had to admit it, her faith, as well. The *Vanquisher* had disappeared into a thick, dark cloud shaped like a giant leviathan. Bolts of lightning shot out from it, followed by a roaring belch of thunder. Perhaps the villainous ship had given the beast indigestion. Now the skies spewed down their torrent of rain, soaking not only Charlisse, but her spirits, as well.

Rusty came up beside her and held out her hat. His burst of copper hair dangled in twisted, drenched ropes, but his ivory smile beamed wide.

Grabbing the tricorn, she shoved it atop her dripping hair as Sloane and Jackson approached.

"We've lost the *Vanquisher*, ma'am," Jackson said.

Sloane inched beside her and clutched the rail just as the *Reliance* careened down the other side of a sweeping wave. Bracing her boots on the slick deck, Charlisse balanced herself against the shifting timbers. A wall of water shot up over the bow and slapped her face. Seawater poured down her throat. She hacked and gasped for air. The sharp tang of salt burned in her nose. Her legs began to wobble and swirl with the sea beneath them, and she would have tumbled over had Rusty not caught her. Still sore from her sword training, her legs now withered under the strain of trying to stand for hours on a heaving deck.

"The storm, milady." Sloane turned his soggy face to her. Water pooled on his lashes and dripped from his beard "It be growin' worse. Ye should get below."

"I'm the captain of this ship," she shouted above the tempest. "When there's a storm, I should be on deck."

Jackson's dark form leaned toward her ear. "Nay, ma'am. I's able t' handle it. The cap'n. . .Cap'n Merrick that be, always lets me, if it just be a small one like this."

Rusty still held onto Charlisse's arm. "I'll take ye below, Milady Cap'n." he said, water dripping from his lips.

She glanced at him, then at Sloane, who nodded.

"Very well, Mr. Jackson. You have the helm. Call me if the weather worsens." She headed down the stairs with Rusty. What was she saying? She had no idea what to do in a squall. Always when a tempest had arisen, Merrick had confined her below until the sea quieted. Yet somehow she felt responsible for this ship and its crew—as though she indeed *were* the captain.

Once settled in the cabin, Charlisse dismissed Rusty, despite his offers to stay and keep her company. Although she found the young pirate's infatuation charming, she did not want to encourage him, nor was she in any humor to deal with his puppylike advances.

Lighting a lantern, she searched the armoire for something dry and warm to wear. One of Merrick's shirts flowed back and forth with the rolling of the ship, just like his shifting affections. She tore the taunting fabric from its hook, crumpled it up, and tossed it to the floor, then stomped on it with her sodden boots, marring the white cotton with imprints of tar and grime. She snorted and grabbed a gown—the only dry garment she had left. Sitting, she yanked off her boots and poured out the water that had collected in them. Then tossing her hat aside, she peeled off her wet clothes and donned the silky dress.

Finally dry and warm, she plopped onto the bed—the bed she and Merrick had shared—and fought back the urge to weep. She had been rejected by her uncle, her father, and at one time she'd thought by God, but this pain she felt now bested them all. Perhaps it would have been better to stay on deck in the midst of the storm, with waves and wind as companions, than to shelter herself below, alone with her tormenting memories.

The ship listed, and Charlisse clung to the bedpost. She thought of Isabel and her delicate constitution and wondered how the girl fared in these wild seas.

A tap on the door brought a welcome interruption, and Charlisse jumped up to admit Sloane, who carried a tray of cold rummed-tea and biscuits.

"Thought ye might be needin' somethin' to settle yer belly, milady." He stepped inside and set the tray down. "Ye look a mite pretty, if I do say so—in that gown an' all."

Charlisse closed the door and glanced down at the flowing emerald garment, spreading out the silky folds with her hands. "To be honest, it feels a bit strange to be attired as a lady again." She flounced over to a chair and sat, while Sloane poured some tea.

"It do make ye walk differently, if ye don't mind me sayin'." He grinned, handing her the cup. "Sorry, the tea's cold due to the storm, and a bit weak I might add."

"Thank you, Sloane. I'm sure it will be fine." She took a sip. "But I'll be back to looking like a captain tomorrow." She winked at him and noticed that his saturated waistcoat and trousers dripped on the floorboards. "Don't you wish to change into something dry?"

"Naw, milady. I'm used to it. Besides, I'll be goin' up on deck again soon."

Charlisse nodded, then saw her own pirate clothes dripping in the corner. She wondered if it paid to be a woman in today's society—for women must depend on men, and men seemed to always let them down.

"Perhaps I will remain a gentleman and a pirate for a while," she declared. "It seems to hold a better prospect than being the wife of one."

Raising his brows, Sloane squished into the other chair. "Beggin' yer pardon, milady, but seems to me ye should be trustin' God fer things to be workin' out fer good—even with Cap'n Merrick, eh? Isn't that what yer Good Book says?"

Conviction nudged at Charlisse as she studied the lines on Sloane's leathery face. He was right, of course. But to hear it from his lips surprised her. Had he actually been listening when she'd quoted scripture and rambled on about the goodness of God?

"So you believe in God now?" Charlisse cocked her head and gave him an inquisitive look.

Sloane folded his thick hands over his prominent belly. "Aye, how could I not, seein' all that He's done fer ye?"

A spark of hope scattered the gloom that hovered over Charlisse's heart. Here sat a man on the verge of eternity—a man she cared deeply about.

She sipped her tea, trying to hide the excitement growing within her. "Then do you understand how we all are separated from God and why

He had to send His Son, Jesus, to rescue us?"

"Aye, I been thinkin' on it a bit. . .on what ye told me."

Charlisse felt a flutter in her spirit. An idea popped into her head. " 'Tis similar to Isabel—how she's been captured by an evil man and held captive aboard his ship. That's what happened to mankind."

Sloane nodded and steadied the tray as the ship tipped to the port side. One of Charlisse's boots tumbled across the floor.

"We are on our way to rescue her," Charlisse continued. "And if need be, I will offer my life to do so."

Sloane shot forward in his chair. "Nay, milady, I won't allow it."

"But don't you see?" Charlisse could hear the excitement in her voice. "That's what God did. He loved us so much that He allowed His only Son to die in order to rescue us."

The old pirate tossed a wet strand of hair from his face. "Har, makes some sense."

The lantern's glow drifted across Sloane with the sway of the ship as if light and dark battled for preeminence over him.

Charlisse inched to the edge of her seat, staring at the swirling liquid in her cup. "Then He defeated death and rose again so that we who follow Him will also rise again." She lifted her eyes to Sloane's.

A blast of thunder rumbled in agreement.

He scratched his beard and peered at her with eyes the color of a hazy day. "Aye, there be no denyin' the things I seen 'tween ye and Merrick. . . the changes in ye both and the power of God to save ye when ye cry out to 'im."

Charlisse reached out and grabbed his hand. A flash of lighting etched across the window. "Won't you give your life to Him? All you have to do is ask Him."

Snatching a biscuit, Sloane stood. "I'll be thinkin' on it fer sure, ye may lay to it, milady." He glanced toward the window. "Seems the storm be passin'. Ye best be gettin' some rest."

Charlisse's heart sank. She wanted to say more, wanted so desperately for Sloane to see the light. But she knew it wasn't up to her. *He's in Your hands, Lord.*

She rose. "Thank you for the tea."

He nodded.

"And for your friendship."

A crimson hue rose on his face. He looked down and shuffled his feet. "Aye, 'tis me pleasure, milady." Then plopping the biscuit into his mouth, he turned and scampered from the room, leaving Charlisse alone once more.

*Swish-thud.*

*Swish-thud.*

Charlisse sauntered over to the mainmast and plucked from it the two knifes she had just tossed into the wood. Her target was a face she'd carved, complete with eyes, nose, and mouth—Merrick's face, and this morning she found intense enjoyment from flinging blades at his visage.

"The men be ready fer their Bible readin'." Sloane's smiling face intruded on her vengeance.

How could a pirate who wasn't a Christian cause her so much discomfiture? She shot a patronizing look into his bright gaze. The sides of his eyes crinkled as he squinted in the morning sun. A radiance glowed from within them, and the smile perched on his lips seemed somewhat lighter this morning.

"Thank you, Sloane." She sheathed her knives and scratched her coarse breeches, still damp from yesterday. Solomon flew down from the shrouds and landed on Sloane's shoulder. He chattered in glee as the men assembled en masse on the main deck. Jackson came forward and stood near the front of the group, his muscular arms planted across his chest. She wondered how the portentous man would take to her mandatory Bible readings.

Sloane handed her the Bible, and she glanced across the swarthy faces before her. A morning breeze flowed past them over Charlisse, and she held her breath against the incoming pungency. Yet instead of sweat, rum, and foul breath, she smelled only the sharp scent of lye intermingled with the salty air. One more glance revealed crisp, bright clothes, occasioned only by a few wrinkles and stubborn stains. They had followed her orders.

Stifling a smile, she studied their faces. Some returned her gaze with interest, others looked down at their boots or gazed off to the side, while Royce and Gunny stared at her with a defiance that stiffened their stances.

Fear skittered through Charlisse, and she drew a breath, hoping to hide her uneasiness. Opening the Bible to the Gospel of John, she began to read:

"Then said Jesus unto them again, Verily, verily, I say unto you, I am the door of the sheep. All that ever came before me are thieves and robbers: but the sheep did not hear them. I am the door: by me if any man enter in, he shall be saved, and shall go in and out, and find pasture. The thief cometh not, but for to steal, and to kill, and to destroy: I am come that they might have life, and that they might have it more abundantly."

When she looked up, it was to Solomon who grinned at her from Sloane's shoulder, but when she glanced over the men, all save Rusty—who gazed at her with a sheepish grin—stood staring at her with glazed eyes and slack jaws. Well, at least the monkey was getting something from her reading.

After dismissing them, Charlisse stomped up on the foredeck to survey the choppy azure waters for any sign of the *Vanquisher*. The morning had blossomed in bright shades of saffron and coral that had transformed the blue sea to a lustrous aquamarine. Now a handbreadth above the horizon, the sun cast its golden rays upon her, sweeping away the chilled misery of the night before. A light breeze played with a tendril that had escaped from her hat, tickling her neck.

"A ship, Cap'n!" Smack yelled from the crosstrees.

Charlisse swung about, shielding her eyes from the sun, and gazed across the horizon. "Where is she?"

"Directly off our stern," came the booming reply.

Charlisse flew down the foredeck stairs and across the main deck, pulling out the spyglass as she ran. Up onto the quarterdeck she marched, then halted, lifting the glass to her eye as Sloane rushed to join her.

"It's not the *Vanquisher*." She adjusted the glass and studied the frigate, searching for a name on its hull. "But who, then?" She handed the glass to Sloane.

He peered through it for what seemed an interminable amount of time, his lips contorting first in confusion then in widening excitement.

Lowering it, he grinned and cast her a sly look.

" 'Tis the *Satisfaction*, milady."

# Chapter 31
# The Chase

Captain Merrick positioned himself on the foredeck of the *Satisfaction*, spyglass pressed to his eye. Badeau and Kale stood by his side. Slamming the glass shut, he turned to Hanson, standing on the main deck below them.

"Helm, three points to larboard. Set the topsails," he ordered the first mate. So far, the man had obeyed his orders, but rebellion leaked from each glance he shot toward Merrick.

Hanson snapped his gaze away and marched across the deck, repeating the orders to the men. Four of the crew clambered into the shrouds, and the frigate veered to the left as the rudder obeyed the turn of the whipstaff.

"That is the ship you seek?" Badeau asked, when Merrick once again turned his gaze forward.

"Yes, that is the one, *mon ami*." Raising the glass, Merrick braced himself as the ship tumbled down a choppy swell. White foam exploded over the bow, depositing pearly bubbles onto the deck. Although he couldn't make out any details, he knew his ship—the hue, the shape. It was the *Redemption*. No doubt.

A flash of white caught his eye, and he peered through the spyglass to see the *Redemption*'s topgallants being raised and spread to the wind. The brig turned into the warm gust, filling her sails to near bursting, and sped through the rippling waters, trailing a long, creamy wake.

"She flees," Merrick said, not quite believing his own words. It had not occurred to him that Sloane and any of his old crew who'd remained with the *Redemption* wouldn't want their captain back.

As if reading his mind, Kale offered Merrick a reassuring glance. "Mebbe they's not 'specting ye to be in command o' this ship?"

"Yes, of course." Merrick shook his head. "They don't know it's me." Even with his flag lowered in a friendly salute, they would not trust him—especially not Sloane, who knew Collier for the miscreant devil that he was.

"*N'importe*, mon capitaine." Badeau slicked back his oiled, tawny hair. "With the wind advantage, we shall be close soon. Then they see you."

Merrick nodded and braced his hands on his hips, watching with an eager gaze as the breadth of sea shrank between the two ships. Yet after several minutes and well within range of recognition, the brigantine made no move to reduce sail and put her helm over.

Holding the spyglass steady, Merrick focused it upon the deck of the *Redemption*—or was it the *Redemption*? Something odd caught his eye, and he shifted the glass forward. The word *Reliance* stood out in deep black against the crimson bow as it pitched and lunged in the frothy sea. Confusion strangled his excitement. *Reliance?*

He scoured the ship, zooming in on each familiar detail. No, indeed, it was the *Redemption*. A flicker blazed across his vision, temporarily blinding him, and he swerved his glass until it landed on the round glare of a spyglass pointed back in his direction. Holding it was a short man wearing a captain's hat.

A tremor crossed through Charlisse, reaching her legs in a faltering wobble. She drew a hand to her breast and gasped for the air that had rushed from her lungs.

*Merrick.*

There he stood on the foredeck of the *Satisfaction*, brazen and commanding—hands on his hips. Unbound, his ebony hair blew behind him in a wild dance. One side of his white shirt fluttered in the breeze, teasing her with peeks at his brawny chest. The other side was held down by a baldric, housing two pistols. His cutlass hung at his side, the golden hilt glittering in the morning sun.

The remaining pebbles of Charlisse's broken heart crushed into sand beneath his piercing gaze. She lowered the spyglass. The sky began to swirl around her in mixed shades of ivory and cerulean. The solid deck beneath her boots suddenly melted, and she stumbled.

Jackson's strong grasp clutched her arm. "Are ye all right, ma'am?"

Charlisse drew in deep breaths, trying to calm herself, as some of the men gathered around. "Yes, quite all right, Jackson. Thank you."

An image of Merrick fondling the dark-haired beauty blazed through Charlisse's mind, sending a wave of fury across her tottering senses, bolstering them with determination. She broadened her stance and forced down the sharp pain that tried to subdue her.

" 'Tis Merrick," she spat, lifting the spyglass to her eye again. This time, Merrick also held up his glass, its focus directly upon her.

"He sees me."

Sloane stepped beside her. "But he won't know ye—dressed as ye are."

Charlisse spun around and brayed orders to the two men aloft and then to Smack manning the helm. "I'll outrun him." She faced Sloane and flattened her lips together.

The old pirate raised both gray brows. "He's got the wind on 'is side, milady." He glanced at the *Satisfaction*. "By thunder, he'll be on us in no time."

Snorting, Charlisse faced the oncoming ship and braced her fists on her hips.

"And he outguns us by more'n double."

"Merrick won't fire on his own ship. I know him."

"Aye, mebbe." Sloane nodded. "But why not just see what he wants?"

"He wants his ship back." Charlisse tugged at a wayward lock of hair tickling her forehead and shoved it back under her hat. "But I'm not going to let him have it."

Merrick slapped the spyglass across the palm of his hand. Surely, whoever it was had recognized him by now. Yet he'd just seen that short captain swing about, gaze aloft, and seemingly shout orders to his crew that sent the *Redemption* on a swift tack to larboard, stealing farther away from Merrick.

Merrick pummeled down the foredeck stairs and marched across the main deck, fury and confusion warring in his soul. Who was this dwarf commanding his ship? How could Sloane and the others have replaced him so quickly—and especially with a boy who was obviously beneath Merrick's station and most likely as deficient in skill and wit as he was in height? And the impertinent runt dared to run from him!

Gritting his teeth, Merrick stomped to the railing, nearly tripping over Hanson, and raised his glass again. The *Redemption* cut a wide *V* of creamy froth through the turbulent waters a half knot off his larboard bow. He spotted Sloane's gray thatch of hair bristling from under his purple headscarf. The traitorous quartermaster followed quick on the heels of his captain, like a hound on its new master. Merrick grunted and flicked the glass to see Jackson's immense frame looming on the quarterdeck and Rusty at the helm.

His men. His ship.

The reek of sweat and rum assaulted Merrick's nose, and he knew before he looked up that Hanson had joined him.

The first mate belched, spewing a foul cloud that covered Merrick with the stench of rotten fish. "What's on yer mind to be chasin' down this slip of a ship?"

Merrick lowered the glass. "I aim to take her," he replied without looking at him.

"There be treasure aboard her then?"

The muscles in Merrick's back tensed. He remained quiet, his focus on the *Redemption*. Perhaps if he ignored him, this rat would scamper back to the shadows.

"I'm not of a mind to be wastin' me time when there's no treasure to be taken." Hanson's course voice rasped with menace.

Letting out a sigh, Merrick spun about, his gaze taking in the burly man. Adorned in a worn and weather-stained coat accented with silver buttons, he made a pretense of civility, belied by the deep scar of a cutlass slash across his lips, setting them in a permanent frown.

Shifting his stance, Merrick glared at him. "Your job requires neither you have a mind, nor if you do, to have anything upon it. Your job is to obey my orders."

Willis slinked up beside Hanson, who took a step back. His upper lip curled in a seething snarl, revealing a rotting hole in his gums.

Annoyance joined Merrick's battling emotions. *Pirates.* How he tired of their insatiable greed.

Willis licked his lips, his eyes darting between Hanson and the captain. Merrick knew Willis lacked the courage to confront him on his own but wouldn't hesitate if his friend took the initiative.

"If your purpose is to challenge me," Merrick said, grabbing the hilt of his cutlass, "then be about it. Otherwise, stand off." He eyed Hanson and saw fear jitter across his gaze.

Seizing a quick glance at the *Redemption*, Merrick faced Hanson again with an idea to appease the villain. "Whatever treasure is aboard my ship, I intend to split fairly among the crew, I assure you."

The pirate gave a nod of his head. "Aye, that be more like it."

"Capitaine," Badeau yelled from the foredeck. "We approach firing range."

Merrick swung around, no longer needing the spyglass to see the activity on board the *Redemption*.

"Hanson, dip our colors, if you please." Perhaps now the crew of the *Redemption* would clearly see that it was him and that he wished to board in peace.

Hanson turned and shouted the order aloft.

Merrick stuffed the spyglass in his belt and gripped the railing, tensing his muscles. A shower of saltwater sprayed over him as the *Satisfaction* plunged over a wave, bearing down on the *Redemption*. With sails full to the wind, the brigantine made a valiant run, but within minutes the two ships would be side by side. Despite the cold reception, Merrick intended to board his ship again and make things right with his shipmates. As for the new captain, he would either absorb the diminutive man into his crew, if the midget was worthy, or leave him on an island with many a day to ponder whether he'd embarked upon a wise course when he stole the ship of Captain Edmund Merrick.

"Reef the top and gallants," he bellowed to Hanson. "Shorten the main." He needed to slow down the *Satisfaction*, or they'd soon fly past the *Redemption* without so much as a by-your-leave. He darted his gaze back to his ship. The little captain stood on the main deck, glaring at him, fists planted on his hips. Sloane and Jackson stood on either side of him.

Merrick waved, hoping to allay their fears with a friendly gesture. In reply, all six gun ports flew open on the *Redemption*'s starboard side, and the charred muzzles of six cannons poked through their darkened holes.

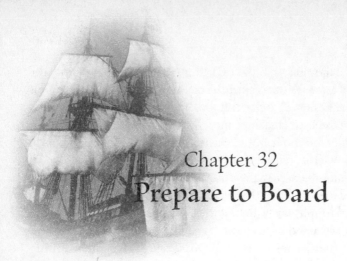

# Chapter 32
# Prepare to Board

"Fire!" Charlisse shouted, strain cracking her voice. Four of the six cannons exploded in a thunderous roar, followed within seconds by the remaining two. The *Reliance* trembled under the fierce quake as the cannons recoiled. A billowing cloud of smoke saturated the air between the two ships, and Charlisse bent over, coughing. The acrid fumes filled her nostrils and burned her eyes. Frenzied shouts and angry curses shot at her from the *Satisfaction*. She peered through the haze, suddenly afraid she may have hit the ship.

Sloane took a step toward the rail and swatted at the dissipating smoke.

Jackson barreled up from below, where he had governed the undermanned gun crew. His gaze riveted on the *Satisfaction*.

"Well done, Jackson," Charlisse said, then glanced toward the helm. "Rusty, hard to larboard," her voice echoed across the ship, bouncing off the smoky mist.

One look at Jackson sent the first mate marching over the deck, ordering the men up in the shrouds to adjust the sails for the tack. Perhaps the warning shots would give sufficient notice to Merrick that he was no longer wanted on his ship and he would halt his pursuit.

Sloane groaned, and Charlisse snapped her gaze to see the *Satisfaction* through the clearing smoke. A twinge of relief assuaged her taut nerves. The twelve-pounders had plunged harmlessly into the sea yards short of the ship as she'd instructed. Pirates scurried across her deck, but Merrick remained steadfast, arms folded across his chest, glaring at her. She wondered what he was thinking. Did he have any idea who she was?

The *Reliance* swept over a rising swell, and Charlisse clung to the railing as they veered to port, spitting a gush of foamy spray off their starboard quarter toward the *Satisfaction*.

Brighton rushed forward. "D'ye want me to blast 'em with our stern chasers, Cap'n?"

Charlisse squinted toward their adversary. "When they are out of range, fire warning shots across their bow."

"Warnin' shots is all?" Looking rather disappointed, Brighton adjusted his eye patch and flung his bristly hair behind him.

Charlisse offered him a blunt gaze. "You heard me."

The doctor grunted and shuffled up the quarterdeck stairs.

Charlisse wished no harm to anyone on board the *Satisfaction*—including Merrick. Despite the pain and anger that now consumed her, she could never willingly hurt him. All she wanted was for him to sail away and leave her be—at least for now. *Lord, please make him go away.* But when she glanced back at the *Satisfaction* and saw the ship's ivory sails gorged and looming off the *Reliance*'s stern, she knew this particular prayer would not be answered.

Sloane turned to face her. "By the looks o' it, she'll be back on us afore we can spit out a tune." He regarded her with raised brows.

"That seems to please you, Mr. Sloane." Charlisse cocked her head, noting the patronizing gleam in the old pirate's eyes.

"Naw, milady. I just be thinkin' ye may want to talk wit' 'im. Let 'im know who ye are, 'tis all."

Charlisse studied Sloane's pleading blue eyes. He and Merrick had been good friends. No wonder he wished the best for his captain—perhaps even hoped to have him in command again. And very well he might be, someday. But not today. She could not face him today.

"I have no intention of revealing my identity to Captain Merrick." Charlisse threw her shoulders back and looked away, feeling tears rising to her eyes.

Sloane shuffled his feet. "He's still yer husband, eh?"

Charlisse shot her gaze back to his, intending a clever retort, but Solomon leapt upon her shoulder and nuzzled his face into her cheek. "If Merrick had half the loyalty of this smelly creature, we wouldn't be in this position."

The monkey chattered happily and grinned.

Charlisse let out a deep breath. "Merrick can have this bloody ship, and you can have your friend back, but first we must rescue Isabel and bring her home. Then you may drop me off at Port Royal and seek out your captain." Charlisse gave Sloane a questioning look. "What do you say to that?"

Grapeshot blasted from the stern chaser. Brighton had complied with her orders. But no sooner did the pounding cease than the doctor yelled over his shoulder. "She be on our tail again, Cap'n."

Flying up the quarterdeck stairs, Charlisse stopped behind Brighton as Sloane edged past her and grabbed the stern railing. Solomon jumped on the old pirate's shoulder.

Wasn't it enough that Merrick had so quickly tossed her memory aside for another woman? If Charlisse had truly died, her body would not yet be cold in the grave. What more did he want, to come and stomp the remaining pieces of her heart to dust? Of course, he didn't know it was her. Would he still chase her if he knew? Or would his shame thrust him back into the arms of his dark-haired beauty? Charlisse didn't want to find out—couldn't bear to face that sight again.

Charlisse hung her head. *I can't. Don't make me face him, Lord. Please.* She squeezed her eyes shut against the legion of tears advancing like an army and listened to the splash and roar of the sea against the hull, the creaking of the ship's timbers, and the cranking of the tackles and spars—sounds so familiar, so soothing. Yet when she opened her eyes, all she saw was the *Satisfaction* rising and plunging through the sea, angry foam bursting over its bow.

She wiped a wayward tear and looked over to find Jackson eyeing her with concern. For once, she hadn't heard the giant man approach. Had he seen her give in to her sorrow?

She cleared her throat from the lump of pain. "Prepare the guns, Jackson." If Merrick insisted on chasing her, she'd be forced to fire another warning volley.

He nodded. "Aye, ma'am." The muscles in his massive jaw clenched. He turned to leave, then halted and faced her again.

A spike of fear darted through her. Would he defy her? She'd been surprised when he'd agreed to fire upon the *Satisfaction*—with Merrick in command. Her husband inspired great loyalty among his crew. Charlisse gave Jackson an understanding nod. " 'Tis not my intention to harm your captain."

Sweat glistened in the sunlight beating on his thick dark chest. "Yer me cap'n now, ma'am." The stark whites of his eyes shifted to the *Satisfaction.* "Methinks he just wants to talk wit' ye."

Charlisse's eyes burned again at his sudden loyalty and care.

"Thank you, Jackson." She gulped. "But ready the guns, if you please."

The big man cast her a look of unease, then marched away.

Sloane remained by the stern, his back to her, gripping the railing with head bowed. *Was he praying?* Solomon scampered across his back to the other shoulder, trying to get his attention, but he remained unmoving.

Beyond him, the *Satisfaction* flew down upon them, all sails bursting like white clouds against the cerulean sky. The monkey pointed a wiry finger toward the oncoming ship.

She caught glimpses of Merrick through the flapping spritsail at the bow of the *Satisfaction.* His image teetered in her vision with the heaving of the ship. Sorrow wrenched her heart. *Please, go away. Go back to your new woman.* Charlisse ran a hand over her flat belly, now covered with coarse breeches and waistcoat, and felt so alone. She shook her head. No, not alone. *I always have You, Lord. You'll never leave me.*

A warm gust of wind danced over her, trying to dislodge her hat. She held down the rebellious tricorn and shoved it further on her head.

The stomping of several pairs of boots sounded behind Charlisse.

Royce lumbered up beside her. "Yer goin' t' get us sunk t' the bottom of the sea. Merrick's the best I seen at warfare. Ye don't stand a chance." He turned and spat a black wad on the deck.

"Thank you, Mr. Royce. That's very helpful." Charlisse planted her fists on her hips, shooting an apprehensive glance at Sloane.

"Best be surrenderin' 'fore he bears a broadside on us," Royce continued.

"Aye, aye," the other pirates squawked.

Charlisse swung about to face them. "He will not fire upon his own ship." She gazed over the men. "Are you pirates and gentlemen, or are you cowards and landsmen?"

The crew grumbled and looked away.

"We be pirates!" one man yelled.

"Pirates learnin' t' be gentlemen," Mason added, chuckling.

Charlisse grinned. "Then let's be about it, gentlemen. Royce, Smack, man the swivels, if you please. When he comes in range, deter him with another warning shower of grapeshot."

Merrick clutched the mainrail head at the bow of the *Satisfaction* and peered around the flapping spritsail toward the retreating *Redemption—Reliance*—whatever the blasted ship's name was. No matter. It was *his* ship. When that pygmy of a captain had loosed a broadside upon Merrick, it had taken him quite by surprise, but soon afterward, his fury had risen like the fiery smoke between them. Merrick's colors had been lowered as a sign of his peaceful intentions. Didn't the runt know that to fire—even warning shots—upon a ship approaching in peace went against all rules of naval decorum? But what upset him the most was that his old crew had allowed it. How could they have shifted their loyalties so soon?

He would teach them a lesson. With full colors raised and all sails unfurled, he soared through the agitated sea, fully intending to overtake, cripple, and board his mutinous ship.

*It was your loyalties that shifted, Merrick.*

Merrick sighed. *Nay, Lord, it was they who stole my ship.*

The *Satisfaction* plunged through a huge roller, sending salty spray back over the bow, showering Merrick. Shaking the moisture from his face, he stared at the stern of the *Reliance*. Sloane stood, face bowed toward the frothy wake churning behind the ship. Brighton manned the stern chaser, and the little captain stood behind them. Even the monkey, perched on Sloane's shoulder, taunted Merrick with his wagging finger.

How dare they challenge the great Captain Merrick? What power did this puny captain have over Merrick's crew to cause such betrayal?

*It was you who betrayed them.*

Images skidded across Merrick's mind—of the tavern in Tortuga and his good friend Sloane urging him to have no dealings with Collier and return to Port Royal. Guilt pricked at Merrick's pride. Egad, if his quartermaster hadn't been right. What misery had befallen him by that foolish association?

Badeau approached and stood beside him. "Your crew. They no longer wish you in command, mon capitaine?" He lifted his scarred eyebrow.

"So it would seem." Merrick glanced up to make sure all sails were raised and filled to capacity, and then leveled his gaze back toward the *Reliance*.

Badeau grinned at him through pointy teeth, and the scent of rum wafted over Merrick.

"Good to have the old Capitaine Merrick back."

"What gives you cause to say that, Baddo?"

"That light in your eyes. It shines again." Badeau looked away, rubbing his furry chin. "There was death on you before. Like a *maladie. . .*a sickness."

Merrick crossed his arms over his chest. Yes, he had felt like dying, to be sure. "I've returned to following God again."

Badeau nodded. "It shows, Capitaine." He gazed at the *Reliance*. "Your God. Does He wish you to attack your old ship?"

Drawing a deep breath of the sea air, Merrick shifted his back against the sun's fiery rays. *Do You, Lord? Why am I insistent on reclaiming my ship? Is it pride? Anger? Or perhaps a bit of both?* Shame smothered Merrick's fury, and he flexed his jaw, unable to believe he'd fallen so quickly back into the trap of arrogance and control.

Looking up, he smelled, rather than heard, Hanson approach from behind.

"We'll be within firin' range soon, Cap'n."

*Lord, whatever Your will is. Let it be so.* Merrick shot a probing gaze at the *Reliance*, then pivoted to face Hanson. "Bring us along her starboard quarter. Ready the guns with chain shot."

Nodding, Hanson flew down the stairs, barking orders. Men, already swinging from the ratlines, clambered aloft to trim the sails.

The helmsman pulled the tiller, and the *Satisfaction* tipped and luffed alee of the *Reliance*, rushing upon her starboard side. The creak of blocks and snap of billowing sails filled the air.

A shattering explosion of rapid gunfire sounded across the ship. Merrick gazed over to see two of his old crewmen pointing the *Reliance*'s swivel guns just off the *Satisfaction*'s bow. Wisps of gray smoke hovered above them as their shots splashed into the sea—more warning shots. Whoever captained his ship had no intention of harming Merrick or his men, but apparently he also had no intention of allowing him to board either. Flying down the forestairs, Merrick landed on the main deck. Pirates swarmed all around, plucking the pistols from their braces and aiming them toward their enemy.

"Do not fire upon them!" Merrick yelled. Then turning to Hanson. "Blast the crossbar at their riggings!"

"Aye, aye, Cap'n." Hanson plunged down the main hatch.

The scrape of the gun trucks and groans of the men elevating the cannons reached Merrick's ears from below. The chain shot, properly aimed, would only damage the yards and masts.

Badeau darted to his side. "Mon capitaine. They ready their cannons again."

Merrick spun to face the *Reliance*'s starboard side. The muzzles of six cannons taunted him from blackened portholes. Men flitted behind them with burning linstocks in hand, preparing the iron menaces to spew their cannonballs.

"As soon as we fire on them, turn us hard to starboard," he ordered Badeau. "Ready the men at the sails and helm."

Badeau tipped his hat and darted off.

If Merrick could cripple the *Reliance*'s sails, and then make a swift turn and come about on their larboard side, perhaps he could board her and bring a swift end to this improvident battle.

"When you are ready to fire, Hanson, do so!" Merrick howled down the hatch.

Almost instantaneously, the *Satisfaction* roared its broadside in a deafening blast that sent a violent shudder through the ship, testing each timber and tackle. The chalky haze of smoke gorged the air, diffusing both the sound and scene of the destruction.

"Helm, hard to starboard!" Merrick grabbed the capstan and held on as the mighty frigate whipped to the right, sending booms whining and masts groaning under the strain. The *Satisfaction* plunged into the sea with a roar just as red sparks flashed in the gloom behind him. The thunder of cannons exploded in the distance, hurling twelve-pounders across the *Satisfaction*'s larboard quarter and splashing into the sea.

Merrick raced to the quarterdeck and plucked out his spyglass to view the *Reliance* through the dissipating smoke.

Her shattered bowsprit hung in a mass of cordage athwart her bows. The ship's rigging on the foresail fell in a tangled web to the deck, and the mainsail, sprinkled with gaping holes, floundered in the wind. The crew dashed across the deck, scrambling up the shrouds and picking up wreckage. The *Reliance* wallowed in the breeze, powerless to maneuver.

Hanson popped up on deck, and a band of men approached the stern. Upon seeing their success, the pirates cheered and congratulated one another.

"She lowers her flag, Capitaine," Badeau yelled, "and raises a white one!"

Merrick turned to Hanson, allowing a confident grin to play upon his lips. "Heave to and bring us alongside her." He glanced back toward the hapless vessel.

"Prepare to board."

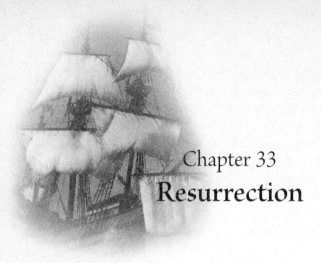

## Chapter 33
# Resurrection

Grapnels!" Merrick yelled.

Four pirates whirled the iron hooks above their heads and then tossed them across the gap betwixt the two ships. They struck the deck of the *Reliance* with a clank and a scrape of splintering wood.

Sloane stood on the main deck, arms crisscrossed over his barrel chest. Jackson, armed to the hilt, stood by his side. They both stared at Merrick with apprehension.

The pirates aboard the *Satisfaction* heaved the ropes, groaning under the strain as they wrenched the ships together with a thudding crunch that sent both vessels aquiver.

Merrick scanned the deck of the *Reliance* and spotted Rusty, Brighton, and Royce up on the quarterdeck, eyeing him from behind the railing. Gunny, Mason, and Smack huddled together on the foredeck. None of his crew seemed pleased to see him, but why should they? These were the men who'd stolen his ship. If anything, he would expect no emotion save fear—fear of his retribution for their mutiny. Certainly dread flickered on some of their features, but there was something else present. Guilt, perhaps? No, it was more like expectation. A shiver crossed his shoulders. Perhaps he walked into a trap.

He searched for the short captain—the man who'd either been the instigator of the mutiny or had later taken command of a ship that clearly was not his. Perhaps the coward had skulked off to hide.

"Merrick." A soft voice called to him, and he swerved to see Elisa weaving her way through the pirates in his direction. He held out a hand to her, beckoning her near, amazed that she braved coming on deck by herself. Her long black hair fluttered over her lilac gown, and her dark eyes met his as she took his hand in hers.

"You shouldn't be up here, señorita." Merrick said. "It isn't safe."

"I couldn't stay below any longer, Capitán. I heard the hooks catch, and I thought you might have found your ship." Her glance took in the *Reliance*.

"That I did." Merrick grinned, giving her hand a squeeze. "But please go below. I assure you, I'll bring you aboard when it is safe."

"Please take me with you. I cannot bear to be on this ship another minute." Her pleading eyes flickered between his.

Bullock and Hanson approached and drew their cutlasses, waiting for his order to board.

Merrick glanced at them. "There'll be no need for weapons. The ship is undermanned and its crew quite temperate, as you can see."

Hanson smacked his lips together and snarled as his eyes darted over their conquest. "Are ye sure we can't kill someone?"

"Nay, sorry to disappoint you." Merrick grimaced and gave Hanson a patronizing look. "You'll not harm anyone if you want your share of whatever treasure you find on board."

Hanson sheathed his sword with a snort.

The pounding of boots sounded behind him, and the chortles and curses of pirates blared at Merrick's back. He shot a look over his shoulder and saw a mob of at least seventy men crowding on deck in preparation to board.

"Keep the men here until I give the signal."

Merrick glanced at Elisa and back at his ship. It appeared safe enough. No weapons were visible, and certainly she'd be safer with him than on board the *Vanquisher* without him.

With a nod in her direction, Merrick jumped onto the railing and assisted her up beside him. Then grabbing her waist with one arm and clutching a ratline with his other hand, he swung them over to the bulwarks of the *Reliance*. He shot a tentative smile at Sloane, who gave him a curt nod in return. Then he leapt onto the deck. The feel of her sturdy oak planks beneath him again gave him a moment's pause as he thanked his Father before turning and helping Elisa down.

Merrick took a deep breath, balled his hands on his hips, and surveyed the crew. The sting of gunpowder still tainted the salty air. But another scent rose on the wind—lilacs. Was it possible after all this time that Charlisse's scent still clung to the ship? He shook his head. Heaviness gripped him, dragging him down. *Lord, I don't know if I can do this.*

Leading Elisa, he moved cautiously toward Sloane, trying to appear as unassuming as possible. The old pirate's gaze teetered between Merrick and Elisa with apprehension, but the closer Merrick came, the wider the grin on Sloane's lips grew until Merrick saw his friend's shoulders relax and his arm reach out to meet his. Grasping it firmly, Merrick studied Sloane's blue eyes. An unusual glow shone forth from behind them.

"It be good t' see ye, Cap'n."

"And you, my friend."

Jackson cleared his throat. Merrick released Sloane's arm and nodded toward the dark man. "Jackson."

"Cap'n," he responded.

"May I introduce Señorita Elisa Nuñez de Bastidas." Merrick gestured toward Elisa.

Sloane offered her a tentative smile. "Me pleasure, Miss." His accusing gaze then shifted to Merrick, but he quickly looked down and shuffled his feet. "We thought ye might be a bit rattled 'bout us takin' yer ship."

Grunts and curses emanated from the band of pirates waiting on the *Satisfaction*, and Merrick shot a steely glance over his shoulder to silence their impatience.

"Hey, Cap'n!" a voice boomed from the quarterdeck.

Glancing up, Rusty's red face beamed down at Merrick. He returned his smile, relief spreading through him at the welcome.

"Rest assured, your mutinous behavior will not go unpunished," Merrick said. He shifted an austere gaze from Sloane to Jackson. "But at present, I'm much too pleased to be on board my ship again to be overly vexed. What was the meaning of firing upon me?" Merrick furrowed his brow. "Didn't you see it was me?"

Sloane's gaze darted apprehensively toward the larboard railing. Jackson shot a glance in the same direction, then looked back at Merrick, his black eyes burdened with distress.

Merrick looked over and spotted the short captain standing amidships, facing the sea. "Sloane, will you watch the señorita for a moment?" he asked and glanced at Elisa who nodded her assurances.

Clearing his throat, Merrick laid a hand on the hilt of his cutlass and approached the thieving imp. With each step he took toward him, Merrick's insides coiled in a frenzied knot. Bewilderment and discomfort engulfed him. He halted behind the man. The tip of his tricorn reached just below Merrick's chin, and beneath the damask waistcoat lingered a feeble frame. How could such a tiny man have commanded his scurrilous crew? How dare he ignore Merrick and not give him the respect due a conquering captain?

"Captain, if you would be so kind as to face me like a man."

A tremble crossed the man's back, and Merrick detected a quiver in his legs. Who was this gutless cur?

A wisp of blond hair escaped from under the man's hat and danced in the light breeze across his pale, scrawny neck.

Merrick's heart jumped a beat. A tingle ran down his limbs.

The man reached up and lifted the tricorn from his head, releasing a cascade of golden curls to flutter in the breeze. With excruciating slowness, he turned and faced Merrick with crystalline blue eyes sparking with fury.

Merrick staggered.

Shock clamped every muscle, every nerve. His breath constricted in his throat. His hands went numb. He gasped and stared at the creature who looked just like his wife. His mind raced through a multitude of possibilities that would make it so.

The wind ceased its endless blast.

The ship stopped rocking.

The rustle of water against the hull, even the obscene noises from the pirates, all fell silent. The only sensation remaining was the sizzle of the sun on Merrick's back, shooting its fiery rays into the fortress of ice around his heart.

It began to melt.

"Charlisse?"

Her pink lips wrinkled into a tight frown. "Of course 'tis me, you fool."

The honey-drenched voice soaked through him, soothing his pain and filling his heart with joy. "How? What? I thought. . ."

Charlisse glared at him, flaming darts flinging from her eyes. She raised a brow and crossed her arms over her chest—that rounded chest. Merrick's gaze took her in. Although she'd tried to hide her curvaceous figure beneath baggy garments, it was like trying to hide a treasure chest on a ship full of greedy pirates.

Merrick stepped toward her. All he wanted to do was hold her—touch her—to ensure she was no vision conjured up from his agony-ridden mind. He opened his arms to receive her embrace.

Charlisse retreated. The muscles in her delicate jaw clenched. She bit her lip, wrinkling her brow.

"Charlisse?" He shook his head and smiled, unsure why she hesitated.

She searched his gaze, the hard sheen over hers melting into a soft blue glow. The hint of a smile alighted on her lips. Then something caught her eye, and she looked over his shoulder and froze. Her chest began to heave, and she narrowed her harsh glare upon him again.

Merrick cast a quick glance behind him and saw Elisa standing beside Sloane. With a groan he faced Charlisse, intending to explain who the woman was, but before he could say a word, Charlisse raised her hand and struck his cheek. His head swung away under the biting slap. The sting radiated across his face. Raging emotions stormed within his soul: anger, confusion, joy, relief.

But nothing else mattered anymore.

Charlisse was alive.

He faced her, giving her a compassionate, questioning look.

The stern expression on her face dissolved as her eyes filled with tears. She turned and dashed away from him and flew down the companionway stairs.

Charlisse stormed into her cabin and slammed and locked the door behind her. Stumbling to the bed, she collapsed in a heap, releasing a gush of tears.

"Lord, why? Why did you make me face him with his woman?" she sobbed, gasping for breath.

His eyes—those dark, piercing eyes—had looked at her with such shock, but also such love, just as they used to do.

"How am I to bear it? How can I allow him to look at me like that when I know he's been with another?"

*Oh God, help me.*

Charlisse curled into a ball and wrapped her arms around herself. Tormenting sorrow consumed her heart as visions of her husband taunted her—that handsome face, strong and commanding. Yet wasn't there a hint of sorrow tugging at his eyes?

He had reached for her—had opened his arms for her embrace. Oh, how she'd wanted to run into them, to feel his strength and assurance surround her again.

A chill crossed over her. *Those same arms have held another. Those lips have kissed another.*

Charlisse sprang up and grabbed the nearest thing she could get her hands on—an unlit lantern on the table beside the bed. She hurled it across the room and watched it shatter into a thousand pieces against the armoire, splattering down the mahogany in slippery streams of putrid-smelling whale oil.

Falling to the bed again, she wept. *Oh Lord, what should I do?*

*Talk to him.*

Squeezing her eyes shut, she shook her head. *I cannot. Don't ask me to do that, not yet, not now.*

Yet he had seemed pleased to see her, hadn't he? Or maybe it was only his guilt when he realized how quickly he'd moved to another.

Charlisse hugged the pillow to her chest. What did it matter now?

Hours passed as she lay on the bed, too dazed to move, until the thump of boots on the deck and pounding on the stairs startled her. Nearly forgetting she was no longer in command, she shot up and reached for her pistols on the table. But her mind slowly recalled that the *Reliance* was not her ship anymore. Her husband had returned to claim it. But he would never hold claim to her again.

She rubbed her eyes, squeezing the remaining tears from them, and sat back on the bed. Her thoughts sped to Isabel. How could she rescue her without a ship?

Trudging to the looking glass by her vanity, she gazed into it and barely recognized the girl who stared back at her. Her hair sprang out around her flushed face in a disheveled, tangled mass. The skin around her eyes swelled in pink, fleshy mounds. She took a deep breath and swallowed any remaining tears. Then grabbing a few pins from her vanity, she bound her hair up in a loose knot.

Isabel needed her. She must convince Merrick to help rescue the poor girl. Then he could deposit them both at New Providence and go on his way.

But how could she face him?

*Lord, this isn't fair.*

Merrick turned to rush after Charlisse, but a strong hand grabbed his arm and held him back.

"Swounds, man, let me go!" He swerved to see Sloane's aged features set in determined lines. Elisa stood next to him.

"Best be leavin' her alone for a time, Cap'n."

Merrick glanced toward the companionway stairs that had swallowed up Charlisse's golden curls and heard the slam of the oak door to their cabin.

Charlisse. She was alive! Shock still held his reason captive, unwilling to allow him to truly believe he had just seen his wife. He touched his cheek where the sting of her slap reassured him that indeed he had. But why had she struck him? Why had she been so angry?

He studied Sloane's indignant gaze and yanked his arm from the older man's grasp.

"I need to talk to her."

"There be some things ye best be knowin' first." Sloane raised his shaggy, gray brows.

"Your wife is alive, señor?" Elisa gripped Merrick's arm and smiled, her eyes moistening.

"Yes, but I fear she is not too happy with me at the moment." Why had the sight of Elisa so instantly changed his wife's demeanor? She'd never been jealous of other women before. His gaze dropped to Elisa's soft pink lips and the memory of their kiss sent a ripple of warmth through him, followed by a tidal wave of guilt. But Charlisse didn't know—she couldn't know. Forcing down his shame, Merrick glanced over the ship. Jackson stood by the foredeck stairs. The rest of Merrick's men remained on the upper decks, shooting him looks of disappointment and anger. His jittery crew on board the *Satisfaction* stared his way, their grins dripping with greed as they waited for his command to board and plunder the ship.

Merrick looked back at Sloane. A thousand questions filled his mind, begging for answers. How had Charlisse survived the explosion at the church? Why was she in command of this ship? Why did she fire upon him? He'd wanted to ask her himself, but now after observing her reaction and the outraged expressions of his crew, he thought better of it. Perhaps he should allow his wife some time to calm down.

But the thought of her being so close—right in their cabin—set every part of him on fire. For too long, he'd thought he'd lost her. For too many agonizing nights, he'd thought he'd never feel her soft skin against his. He longed to hold her—to make sure she was indeed real.

As if reading his mind Sloane cast him a wary glance. "She won't be goin' nowhere."

Nodding, Merrick turned to Elisa. "Please allow Mr. Sloane to escort you to the Master's cabin. I'll have some food brought to you later."

Elisa brushed a curl from her face. "Of course, Capitán. Gracias." She touched Merrick's arm and gazed into his eyes, the exchange not going unnoticed by Sloane who moaned.

"This way, miss," he said, gesturing for her to follow while tossing a scolding look in Merrick's direction.

With a swish of her gown, Elisa turned and followed him down the stairs.

Merrick trudged over to Jackson and explained the situation on board the *Satisfaction* before motioning for the pirates to clamber over the railings.

"There's not much treasure aboard, Cap'n," the first mate exclaimed, disgust souring his voice.

"It'll be enough to appease them for now." Merrick watched the horde of beasts scale the bulwarks and sweep out across the deck. "Then I'll send them on their way." He faced Jackson, but the dark man only uttered a fierce grunt and looked away.

When Sloane returned on deck, Merrick motioned for him to follow and then led him up to the foredeck, stopping near the main headrail.

"Pray tell what miracle has brought my wife back to me?"

Sloane offered Merrick a hesitant look and scratched his beard. "As it be turnin' out, she weren't in the church when it got blowed up."

Confusion churned through Merrick. But he'd left Charlisse there and seen it explode only minutes later.

" 'Twas Kent," Sloane continued. "He partook in that raid wit' Morgan and planned to trick ye by makin' ye think ye'd lost yer wife."

Kent! A hot arrow spiked down Merrick's spine. He'd thought he'd seen the last of him. "Continue."

"He took Lady Charlisse aboard 'is ship, but she escaped—her an' another o' his mistresses."

Alarm pricked at Merrick. Had Kent touched Charlisse? "Another?"

"Aye, Lady Ashton."

Merrick thought of the baby. Panic seized him. "Did he harm Charlisse?"

"Naw, methinks no harm was done t' her, Cap'n. Leastways, not in the way yer thinkin'." Sloane grabbed his arm. " 'Tis all right. God protected 'er."

Merrick's gaze darted to Sloane. Since when did his friend give credit to God for anything? A new twinkle gleamed in the old pirate's eyes.

Raking a hand through his hair, Merrick glanced over the turquoise sea. His thoughts returned to Charlisse. "I must go to her."

"I tells ye, she's had a hard time of it, Cap'n. It might be easier if ye leave 'er alone a bit."

Ignoring him, Merrick stormed off.

Sloane cleared his throat. "She knows about yer lady friend."

Halting, Merrick slowly turned around. "My lady friend?"

"Aye, we saw ye at the Drunken Skunk."

The Drunken Skunk. Visions of the tiny captain shot through his mind—of her standing there gawking at him from across the room, then racing out in a huff, two flashes of gray and red hair bobbing out after her. "You. . .you and Rusty were there?"

"Aye, 'twas us, to be sure, and Lady Charlisse."

"Why didn't she come. . . ?" Merrick didn't need to ask. He knew why she hadn't come over to him that night. Elisa had been perched in his lap, and he was entertaining Collier with his feigned affections for her. Merrick rubbed his cheek where Charlisse had slapped him. When he glanced up, Sloane's accusing glare bore into him.

"Ye pimpish fool, how could ye do that t' 'er?"

Merrick felt his blood boil at the insult. "'Twas not as it seemed." But even as he said it, he knew that wasn't completely true.

Sloane grunted and crossed his arms over his chest. "It be a sore temptation to think otherwise."

# Chapter 34
# Consequences

*B*am, bam, bam!

Charlisse shot up in bed, where she had finally given in to exhaustion and fallen asleep.

*Bam, bam, bam!*

Her heart beat a rapid jaunt. She reached up to rub her swollen eyes. "Who goes there?"

"Your husband," came the stern reply.

"Go away," Charlisse bellowed, feeling her face flush at the sound of his sultry voice.

"Open the door this instant!" *Bam, bam, bam!* "I am your husband, and I insist on speaking with you."

Charlisse bit her lip and slowly approached the door. Through it, she heard snickers in the hallway and Merrick's loud "Be gone with you." Well, at least he was receiving the mockery he deserved.

"Charlisse." His voice softened. "Unbolt the door, if you please. I wish only to speak with you for a moment."

A tremble passed over Charlisse. She didn't want to speak with him, didn't want to even see him. Just the sound of his voice set her emotions whirling. But Isabel needed her, and she needed his ship. She must put aside her own pain for the young girl's sake.

She heard shuffling outside the door, and Merrick's low, deep voice wove through the cracks in the aged oak. "I should suppose you'd want to admit me freely rather than have me blast down the door and shatter your privacy."

Charlisse wiped the hair from her face, lifted the latch, and unbolted the door. Turning, she sauntered toward the bed. The door creaked open. A slight breeze wafted into the room, carrying with it the strong scent of salt and musk.

*Merrick.*

She heard his heavy boots clomp inside and the door shut. The cabin suddenly seemed too small.

"Thank you." His deep voice slid across the room like butter on a hot biscuit, threatening to melt Charlisse as it grazed over her skin.

*Lord, help me.*

"Are you going to look at me?"

With a sigh, she threw back her shoulders and turned.

Something akin to shame alighted on his features when he saw her face. Her heartache, she feared, could not be hidden behind her red, swollen eyes. She hated that he knew she'd been crying, but there was nothing to be done about it now.

He had pulled back his hair and tied it behind him, cavalier style, but a dark tendril had escaped and hung next to his cheek, taunting her as it waved across his strong, stubbled jaw. He seized the back of a leather chair and gazed upon her. His eyes landed on her stomach, and his features wrinkled. He took a step closer, examining her belly and looked up, distress written on his face. "The baby?"

Searing pain clenched Charlisse's heart. Of course he didn't know. Glancing down, she ran a hand over her empty womb, before looking up, unable to stop the tears pooling in her eyes.

"Our son is dead."

Agony twisted Merrick's face. He opened his mouth, but no words came forth. Raking a hand through his hair, he cast his stormy gaze back to Charlisse. "Kent?"

Charlisse forced her tears back, allowing only a single one to escape down her cheek. "Nay, Kent did not touch me. I suppose it was just the stress of losing you and being on his ship that caused me to. . . ."

Merrick gritted his teeth. "I shall make him suffer for this."

"Make him suffer? Is that all you can say?" Charlisse backed against the bed, fuming. "What of my suffering? Do you know what I endured while you were out pirating and doing God knows what else?" Somehow she couldn't even bring herself to voice her suspicions.

Merrick took a breath and looked down. Leaning over the back of the chair, he wrung his hands together. "I didn't know you were alive. I didn't know you were suffering. I'm sorry." He looked up. "It was a boy?"

Charlisse said nothing.

A sheen of moisture glistened in Merrick's eyes. He skirted the chair and plopped into it, lowering his head to his hands. "I'm so sorry, Charlisse," he mumbled. "I should have been with you."

"Yes, but obviously you were otherwise engaged."

Merrick sat up and gave her a stern look. "If you mean Elisa, I can explain."

Waves of heat radiated through Charlisse. "Elisa, is it? Her familiar name so soon?" Her heart sank in a mire of jealously, but she forced her feelings aside.

"A boy." Merrick mumbled. "My son." He looked up at her, his eyes swimming. "Where is he?"

"Kent allowed me to give him a proper burial at sea."

Merrick looked down at his boots and ran a hand through his hair.

Memories sprang into Charlisse's mind—memories of the reason for Kent's anger toward Merrick. "Why didn't you arrange for a proper trial for Kent?"

Merrick frowned. "A trial?"

"Yes. He told me you left him to rot at Fort Charles."

"Nay, 'tis not true. I spoke to the officials myself."

Charlisse nodded. She knew he wouldn't have done such a cruel thing—even to an enemy.

"Are you saying that scoundrel did all of this because he believes I abandoned him to the noose?" Merrick's brow wrinkled as anger smoldered in his gaze.

"Yes, I suppose, along with other grievances his demented mind has conjured up against you."

With a growl, Merrick placed his arms on his knees and leaned forward.

"What does it matter now?" Charlisse flung her hair behind her. "What's done is done. State your business, if you please, for I've some business of my own."

Looking up, he gestured toward the other leather chair. "Won't you sit down?"

"I'll stand." Charlisse returned his penetrating gaze. Her heart quickened under his intense perusal.

"Very well. Since you will not state your business, I shall state mine." She looked away and began to pace in front of the bed. "I would ask a favor of you."

"Anything."

His easy compliance startled her, but she did not look his way. "Kent has captured a young lady—a friend." Charlisse gazed toward the window, noting the sun setting in its usual brilliant swaths of fiery orange and yellow. "I was on my way to rescue her when you attacked me."

"If I may remind you, you fired upon me first."

Charlisse shot him a smoldering glance, noting the sardonic grin curling his lips. Was he enjoying this? *Rogue.* She shifted her gaze away.

Merrick stood and approached her.

Charlisse swerved and held up her hand. "If you would be so kind."

Merrick stopped, eyes widening. "I have no intention of hurting you, Charlisse. I only wished to touch you."

"Your touch would hurt me." She swallowed, still holding her hand up. "Please."

Merrick cringed and shot her a look of despair. "There is no other, Charlisse."

No other? Did he think her blind? "What sort of fool do you take me for? I saw the woman you dragged aboard my ship."

"She is but a friend."

Charlisse turned away and swallowed a burst of rage. Rubbing her tender eyes, she faced him again, trying to avoid his piercing gaze. "Do you love her?"

Merrick grabbed the bedpost. "Allow me to explain about Tortuga. I was trying to save Elisa from Collier."

"Save? Yes, of course. I could see that." Charlisse shot him a patronizing look. "From where I stood, the only fiend she needed saving from was you." She stomped to the window and gazed out, trying to shake the vision from her thoughts, then faced him again. "You didn't answer my question."

Merrick hung his head. His thick chest heaved beneath his shirt.

He shifted his stance. "I've been a fool, Charlisse. I thought you were dead." He raised his eyes to meet hers. "I turned my back on God, but not on you. I don't love her. She brought me some comfort, 'tis all."

"What sort of comfort?" Her heart froze, ready to burst in agony at his answer.

"She consoled me with kind words, and"—he flattened his lips and swallowed—"a kiss."

The room began to spin, and Charlisse leaned on the window ledge for support. A kiss? Her heart crumpled within her. Tears welled in her eyes, and she spun around. "So soon after my death?"

"I'm sorry, Charlisse. It was just one kiss. I never touched her again."

Turning back around, Charlisse could not stop the tears sliding down her cheeks. "It's not the kiss," she sobbed. "It's that you mourned for me so little."

She heard him step toward her. "It was because of my mourning that it happened—because I felt like I would die from the agony of losing you."

Charlisse turned to face him, but found no deception in those eyes she knew so well. Shaking her head, she raised one hand to wipe the tears from her face. She couldn't think about this right now—didn't know what to believe.

"I no longer wish to discuss this." She rubbed her temples where a headache began to pound. "Will you help me rescue Lady Ashton or not?"

"Of course I will help you." With stooped shoulders, he trudged to his oak desk in the corner. He shuffled through his papers scattered across it, and fingered his sextant, pen, and bag of jewels. Then he glanced toward the armoire, where white lace peeked from a crack in between the doors.

"Why don't you put on one of your gowns? No need to dress like a pirate anymore." He opened the doors, still dripping with lamp oil and rubbed his fingers together, raising them to his nose.

"But I am a pirate now. Forced to become one in order to find you."

Merrick looked down. Following his glance, Charlisse saw his soiled shirt lying in a heap—filthy boot prints smeared all over it.

"I can see how much you missed me," Merrick said.

He took a step, and his boots crunched over shattered glass. A tremor crossed his broad shoulders. "Did we have a problem with a lantern?"

Charlisse snorted. "We had many problems since your desertion."

"May I remind you, 'twas Sloane who took off with my ship." Merrick turned and raised a cocky brow.

"To help you. . .to find Reverend Thomas." Charlisse shook her head.

Astonishment alighted on Merrick's expression. He crossed his clenched fists over his chest. "You found Sloane at Port Royal?"

"Yes."

"And then you went in search of me?"

Merrick's brow darkened, and he flexed his jaw, but Charlisse remained silent, battling with her conflicting emotions. He seemed sincere in his remorse, and the love still flowed from his eyes, but she could not shake the image of that woman in his arms and the way he smiled at her. She knew that smile—the one she thought he only reserved for her.

"Now, if you please. You may take your leave."

A hint of pain tainted Merrick's gaze. "This is my cabin. This ship is my home. I know you're cross with me, Charlisse, but I don't know what else to say to make you understand." His eyes swept over her as he gave her a disarming smile. "I cannot tell you how happy I am to see you."

Charlisse's heart leapt. Her pulse raced under his warm smile and inviting gaze. She stiffened, forcing down her weakness, and raised her chin. "Please go." She gulped, hearing the tremor in her voice. "You may have your ship back after you assist me in rescuing my friend. Then you may leave us at New Providence and be on your way."

Merrick stepped toward her, opened his mouth to speak then stopped. "As you wish." He sighed, pain reflecting in his eyes, then marched from the room and closed the door behind him.

Charlisse folded onto the window ledge and wept.

*Lord, I'm sorry. I don't have the strength to endure this. Why do You force his assistance upon me?*

*What is the name of your ship, My daughter?*

Charlisse looked up. "You know, Lord, *Reliance*."

*Aye*, came the silent reply.

# Chapter 35
# Pride

Merrick stormed from the cabin, fighting to contain the overwhelming agony and rage battling within him. He didn't know whether he was angrier with Kent, Charlisse, or himself. How dare his wife treat him as if he truly had been unfaithful to her. Had he? He had to admit he'd been attracted to Elisa, had enjoyed their kiss, had found comfort in her embrace. But did that make him the scoundrel Charlisse thought he was? Perhaps so, for it was a matter of the heart after all, and when his heart should still have been mourning his wife, he had set its affections on another.

He pounded up the companionway stairs and onto the main deck. The evening breeze flowed over him, helping to cool his temper. Pirates lingered in snickering clusters across the deck. A waft of spicy rum floated past his nose. He could use a drink right now. But he knew very well that potent liquid would only add to his problems. An off-key ballad drifted down from the quarterdeck:

*"Old Cap'n Silly, jilted by yer filly,*
*Thars plenty more where she came from.*
*Yer face be all red, all alone in yer bed,*
*Ye best be gettin' back to yer rum."*

Merrick clenched his fists. It was time for these pirates to return from whence they came.

Badeau tromped down the foredeck stairs. The grin on his face faded with each step he took toward Merrick.

"Trouble with your lady, mon capitaine?"

Merrick glowered at him, then stared off into the black sea.

Badeau shook his head. "*Femmes.* Who can understand them?" He leaned toward his captain and winked. "If you like some advice, Monsieur Capitaine, I have vast experience with women."

The light from the mainmast lantern drifted over the pockmarks on the Frenchman's face.

"That won't be necessary, Baddo." Merrick braced his hands on his hips. "I'm making you captain of the *Satisfaction*. Can you handle her?"

Badeau's eyes sparked. "Oui, mon capitaine. It is great honor. *Merci.*"

"And Hanson?" Merrick asked. "Can you handle him, as well?"

"Oui, but he is unhappy with the treasure found on board." Badeau cast a glance behind him. "He complain to all the men."

"I expected as much." Merrick sighed. "Tomorrow we set sail in search of the *Vanquisher*. That should cheer the men up. In the meantime, Baddo, would you select twenty of your crew and have them report to Jackson to assist with the repairs? And round up the rest and return to the *Satisfaction*."

Badeau bowed. "Oui, mon capitaine."

Heading toward the bow of his ship—his favorite place to think—Merrick leapt up the foredeck stairs, past a horde of pirates, whom he ordered back to the *Satisfaction*, and halted before the railing. Their grumbling protests retreated behind him. He stared out over the charcoal sea spanned by clusters of waves christened in silver by a half-moon.

Charlisse was alive.

Merrick still found it hard to grasp the fingers of his reason around that fact. The thrill of seeing her again, of knowing she was safe, sent waves of elation through him. There could have been no better news. Yet equal in intensity to his happiness was the pain of her rejection.

Kent. It was all his fault. A chilled breeze gripped the hairs on Merrick's neck. *Revenge. That is what you need.*

*No.* Merrick clutched the railing. Hadn't he given all that up to God? Why then did the urge for vengeance still burn so strongly within him?

His thoughts drifted to Charlisse and the horrors she must have suffered, captured by that madman, held aboard his ship, and believing her husband had abandoned her. Then losing their child, Merrick's son—a part of them both. No wonder she wasn't herself.

*Lord, why?*

Footsteps sounded behind him, and he took a breath to collect himself before turning to see Sloane standing at his side. The old pirate gazed toward the dark horizon.

Silence loomed between them until Sloane cleared his throat. "Are ye all right, Cap'n?"

"As well as I can be."

"Lady Charlisse will come around, Cap'n, ye'll see."

"Yes, but why does she have to be so stubborn?"

"Aye, she's got a bit of pluck in 'er, that one."

"Indeed." Merrick stared out over the inky expanse, listening to the purling of the sea against the hull. How soothing it sounded compared to the storm raging in his soul.

"She found you at Port Royal?" Merrick asked, wondering at the turn of events that had brought Charlisse aboard.

"Aye, by thunder, her and Lady Ashton climbed straight up onto the deck of the *Redemption*—in the thick o' the night, too."

A sudden warmth covered Merrick at the sound of his ship's name. Yet visions of the word *Reliance* painted on the crimson bow flashed into his mind. "Did my eyes deceive me or does my ship now carry the name *Reliance*?"

"Aye, Charlisse changed the name after. . .after seeing ye at Tortuga."

"I see." Merrick grimaced, forcing down his annoyance.

Port Royal. Hadn't the Lord urged him to go there? Right after the storm and before he'd seen Kent's ship.

*Kent's ship.*

A numbing spasm of shock coursed through Merrick. "Blast!" Merrick struck the railing and swerved toward Sloane. "When we saw the *Vanquisher*, Charlisse was aboard her."

"Aye, Cap'n. Quite a shock t' me, too, when I heard it."

Closing his eyes, Merrick squeezed the railing until his fingers ached. He could have avoided this whole nightmare had he followed his instinct to attack that blackguard Kent instead of drowning himself in rum and self-pity.

Sloane scratched his beard. "Kent attacked us when we set off from Port Royal."

Merrick shot an anxious glance at his friend.

"Jackson got hisself hit right off," Sloane continued. "And milady Charlisse took o'er the ship—handled her like a real cap'n, says I."

"She defeated him?"

"Aye, she did a' that. You'd a been proud o' her, Cap'n." Sloane's eye held a twinkle that sparkled in the moonlight. "Though methinks she had some help from above." He shot a glance upward. "If ye knows what I mean."

Curiosity leapt within Merrick. Apparently there was much more to Charlisse's adventure than he knew. "How did she defeat such a formidable captain?"

"Naw, best hear it from yer wife." Sloane yawned. "I need t' be gettin' some sleep."

"I doubt I will hear much of anything from her. The lady no longer wishes to speak to me."

Sloane slapped him on the back. "I wouldn't be worryin' too much 'bout that, Cap'n. The good Lord will be showin' her the error o' her ways in no time."

Though dumbfounded by Sloane's confidence in God, Merrick kept silent and nodded as the old pirate lumbered away.

Merrick drew a long breath. *Father, I hope he's right.* The scent of tar, salt, and soggy wood filtered to his nose, and a shroud of helplessness settled over him, leeching away his strength.

*God, I've given You all control. Yet, why do I feel so out of control?*

Leaning back against the foremast, Merrick propped one boot up against it and studied the multitude of stars peering at him from behind the darkening curtain of night. He was back in command of his ship again. Yet was he? His men cast him furtive glances. His wife treated him with flippant disregard.

Indignant fury burned within him. Why, he ought to march down there, burst into his cabin, and insist on sleeping in his own bed—with his own wife. What kind of a pirate captain was thrown out of his cabin? How could he command the respect of his men if he allowed a woman to rule him? He'd already heard his crew ridiculing him behind his back. Humph.

*Trust Me.*

A warm breeze scented with rain danced over him, and Merrick shook his head. What was he thinking? Hadn't he learned anything at all during the past month? When he'd taken the control of his life away from God and handed it over to his selfish pride, he'd only caused himself and others more pain. Now he saw it was his own disobedience that brought him to this humbling place. He bowed his head. *Father, whatever is Thy will.*

A loud shout sent Merrick bolting from his sleep. He sprang from his spot on the foredeck, reached for his pistol, and tried to focus his bleary eyes. Two pirates below him clashed swords in a mock battle, chortling and cursing as they swung blades glistening in the morning sun. Releasing a breath, Merrick relaxed his stance and felt an ache spike down his back. He reached behind and rubbed it, stretching the stiffness from his tired body. Sleeping on the hard wood had taken its toll on him. Up above him, pirates clambered back and forth, balancing on thin ropes, repairing the foresail rigging and hoisting a new mainsail.

Merrick lumbered down the foredeck stairs, rubbing his eyes, and nearly toppled over Sloane, who was on his way up with a cup of tea.

The old pirate handed him the steaming mug with a grin. " 'Tis a fine morning, Cap'n, and a new day."

Merrick grumbled but accepted the cup with thanks. He followed Sloane to the main deck, where several pirates congregated, flinging leery glances in his direction. Two of his men, Shanks and Murdock, stumbled up from below, barely able to put one foot before the other. Red splotches stained their faces and arms, and every move they took seemed to steal their breath from them.

Solomon scrambled up from the main hatch and leapt onto Sloane's shoulder. The monkey scowled at Merrick, waving a scrawny finger.

"What happened to Shanks and Murdock?"

Sloane chuckled. "That be another long story, Cap'n. I'll tells ye after the reading."

"The read—"

A stomping of boots sounded, and a hush fell over the normally unruly mob. A mass of golden curls appeared at the top of the companionway stairs, glittering as the sun's rays touched each strand. Merrick swallowed a burst of desire as his wife emerged from below. Her blue gaze grazed over him before she looked away and strode to the front of the throng of pirates, holding her chin in the air as she passed him.

Merrick cast Sloane an inquisitive look, but his friend kept his attention riveted on Charlisse. She halted and opened the Bible in her hands.

Clearing her throat, she glanced across the pirates. Those who wore hats removed them sheepishly under her intense gaze. Then, looking back down at her Bible, she began reading.

Merrick recognized the passage from Romans, but it wasn't the Bible lesson that enthralled him, nor was it that Charlisse taught it. It was that these brutal men listened with such quiet respect.

Something else was amiss. He couldn't quite place it. He scanned his raucous crew, examining each face. Some of the men had shaved. Perhaps that was it. His gaze skipped to Brighton. The skin on his face shone bright and tawny, no longer hidden beneath smudges of filth. Then his eyes landed on Mason, whose face and arms glistened in the morning sun. Indeed, all the men appeared freshly scrubbed, including their attire. Even Jackson, who stood toward the back, arms crossed over his swarthy chest, lacked his usual layer of grime.

Raising his nose in the air, Merrick sniffed. No scents, save salt and timber flowed past it. He leaned into Sloane and took a deep breath. Only the foul odor of the monkey struck him. "What miracle has washed the filth from my pirates?" Merrick whispered into his friend's ear.

Sloane didn't answer, but tossed a "shush" toward his captain, disturbing Charlisse, who stopped her reading and glared at Merrick.

She cocked her head to one side. "I realize the holy scriptures hold no interest for you any longer, Captain, but perhaps you could feign a show of reverence whilst they are read in public."

The bite of her tone took a chunk from Merrick's heart.

The pirates gave him looks of reproach. All except Royce and Gunny, who seemed quite pleased with the interruption.

"Gads, woman. I do protest. Of course I revere the Word of God."

" 'Tis not only the revering of it but the following of it that matters," she retorted.

Merrick's blood boiled. Enough of this woman's impertinence. He started toward her when Sloane's hand landed firmly on his arm. He glanced back at the old pirate, who gave him a stern look. Merrick stopped, took a deep breath, and turned to face Charlisse.

"I beg your pardon, milady." He offered her a bow, sending a chuckle across the mob. "Carry on, if you please." He waved his hand in the air.

With a snort, Charlisse returned to her reading. When she had completed the passage, she lifted her gaze, closed the Bible, and dismissed the men.

Sloane faced Merrick. "Yer wife's idea—the readin' and the bathin'."

"I have no doubt." Merrick glanced at Charlisse, who stood talking with Jackson, the sight of her still warming every part of him. "But what confuses me is how she got the men to agree to it."

Merrick listened intently as Sloane relayed to him the story of Royce's attempted mutiny, the lightning strike upon Shanks and Murdock, and the ensuing fear of God—and of Charlisse—instilled in the men afterward. From the corner of his eye, he saw Badeau hop over the two ships' bulwarks and head toward him. But as Sloane continued his story, Merrick found he could not remove his gaze from his wife.

She stood, hands on her shapely hips—still curvy despite her obvious effort to hide them in men's clothing—talking with Jackson and Rusty. Her golden curls cascaded down her back and danced in the light morning breeze. Even attired in breeches and waistcoat and strapped with a cutlass, she was a vision of beauty. And the more he heard from Sloane, the more his heart burst with admiration. Despite formidable odds, she had commanded a crew of ruthless pirates, fought and defeated the *Vanquisher*—a frigate nearly twice her size and with twice her gun power—and staved off a mutiny that would surely have left her and Sloane dead.

" 'Twas the good Lord," Sloane continued, "and His power that came to her aid each time."

Merrick glanced at his friend, then back at Charlisse. With or without God, he would never have been able to tame these pirates into listening to the Bible and keeping themselves clean. Moisture blurred his vision as he studied his wife with newfound respect. He'd always loved her, but not until now did he truly appreciate her determination, strength, and faith. When tragedy had struck, he'd give up on his faith. But hers had only grown stronger.

When Sloane finished his discourse, Badeau cleared his throat. "What are your orders, mon capitaine?"

Merrick gazed toward the *Satisfaction*, still clinging to the *Redemption*—the *Reliance*, he reminded himself—in a tight embrace of ropes and iron claws.

"Make ready the ship. We set sail within the hour." Merrick noted the twinkle in Badeau's eyes, most likely from the excitement of his new command. "Pick thirty of your men and send them over. We are undermanned." Badeau nodded and marched away.

Charlisse looked up, her eyes locking with his. He felt a chill run down his back at her icy glare. Jackson and Rusty sauntered away, and she headed toward him, shifting her glance away from him and onto Sloane and the monkey until she halted before him.

"What are your plans, Captain?"

Merrick cringed at her formality. She crossed her arms over her chest, her rosy lips crumpling in a tiny pout. How he longed to take her in his arms, to hold her and love away all the pain and horrors she had endured. And then to swat her on the behind for being such a whelp.

"What are you staring at, you knave?" She shattered his desire with her harsh tone.

"I beg your pardon, milady, but I have trouble keeping my gaze from your beauty." He bowed, giving her his most amorous grin. "As I have always had difficulty in doing."

"Well, might I suggest you apply the same amount of effort with which you tossed aside my memory."

Merrick grew livid under her cold demeanor. "We set sail in pursuit of the *Vanquisher*, at your request."

Charlisse gave him a curt nod. "You have my sincere gratitude."

"And yet, it is so much more that I desire from you."

Charlisse shot him a look of scorn, her lips twisting in a scowl. "I fear your wait for anything more will be in vain."

Solomon sprang from Sloane's shoulder onto Merrick's, chattering gleefully into his ear. "Well, at least Solomon still finds my company tolerable."

A piercing pain suddenly gripped Merrick's right ear. He reached up to grab the hairy beast, but the monkey dashed from his shoulder and leapt up into the ratlines.

"That blasted monkey bit me!" Merrick roared, holding his ear and glaring above at the creature that jabbered accusingly at him from the yards.

Merrick glanced at Sloane, who shrugged his shoulders, and then returned his gaze to Charlisse.

A flicker of amusement flashed in her eyes. "Seems he finds your company as intolerable as I do, after all."

Merrick frowned. Every muscle in his body roasted with anger and humiliation. He forced down a blast of pride that threatened to set his tongue loose with words he would regret. "Perhaps in time I will grow on you again?"

Sloane's gaze shifted between them, a slight grin on his lips.

A twinge of hope began to quell Merrick's temper as he saw a smile appear on Charlisse's delicate lips.

"Perhaps," she said. Then her face instantly regained its contemptuous demeanor. "Perhaps you will grow on me like rot on the keel of the ship."

"To cling to you so closely would satisfy me." He grinned.

Merrick found his first mate standing on the quarterdeck. "Jackson. All hands on deck. Prepare to set sail. Gunny, get ready to release the grapnels."

Both men faced Merrick but made no reply. Uncertainty clouded Jackson's otherwise stolid expression. The first mate's eyes swung to Charlisse. Gunny stopped tying the rope he held and also glanced her way.

Charlisse cocked an eyebrow at Merrick before turning to the men. "Do as he says, and be quick about it."

Humiliation swept over Merrick. His men—his crew—had obeyed his wife's command, not his.

Hands on her hips, Charlisse clomped across the deck in her oversized boots. "Men!" she bellowed, drawing the attention of the entire crew. Merrick had never heard such a loud, guttural voice come out of his wife.

"Captain Merrick is your captain now. You will obey his orders."

Some of the crew nodded. A few grumbled. Then all returned to their tasks.

Merrick longed to sink into the wooden planks of the deck, anything to escape the embarrassment of receiving his authority from a woman.

A shuffle of skirts and flash of violet drew his attention from his inner turmoil to Elisa who'd just come on deck. Charlisse stiffened instantly. Dropping her fists, she clenched them at her sides and spun on her heels to face him.

"How dare you keep your woman aboard my ship!" She stormed toward him, her creamy white skin turning a bright shade of red.

Horror twisted Sloane's aged features.

"In the first place, she is not my woman," Merrick began, anxious to set things right, but fearful he wouldn't be able to.

Charlisse turned her face away, but not before he saw her eyes moisten.

"And secondly, I cannot in good conscience leave her on board a ship full of pirates."

Merrick took another tentative step toward her, but she swung around. "I am most grateful for your help in rescuing Lady Ashton," she said. "But I beg for your discretion while I am still on board this ship." Her voice cracked.

Elisa inched toward them, a look of anguish on her face.

Merrick held a hand up to stop her. He faced Charlisse. "Then you shall have it."

Sloane started toward Charlisse, but she halted him with one look of warning.

Turning, she marched across the deck, nearly tripping over her cutlass, and disappeared down the companionway stairs.

Merrick motioned for Elisa to approach. "Sloane, would you show Señorita Nuñez around the ship and make sure she receives a proper lunch."

Sloane gave him a doleful look and nodded.

"I'm sorry for the trouble I am causing you, Capitán." Elisa clasped her hands in front of her.

" 'Tis not your fault, señorita."

"I will speak to your wife, if you wish."

"Most kind of you to offer." Merrick grimaced, glancing at the companionway. "But I fear she is not ready for that just yet." He smiled at Elisa. "Now, if you'll excuse me."

Merrick watched as Sloane escorted Elisa across the deck, then he paced the ship, unable to escape the torment raging inside him. Perhaps bringing Elisa on board had not been the most prudent decision. Yet how could he have left her to the evil devices of those pirates? He'd kept pursuing what he'd thought to be the right course of action, yet each decision, each word he spoke, seemed to plunge him deeper into trouble, and further away from Charlisse.

When all the repairs and preparations had been made, and final orders given to Badeau, Merrick commanded the grapnels released and all canvas set to the wind. The sails caught the breeze in a jaunty snap, sending the ship on a speedy course through the sea. Foamy spray showered over the bow as Merrick stood gazing at the *Satisfaction* just abaft their starboard beam. Together, they would find the *Vanquisher*, and then Merrick would deal with that rapscallion Kent and retrieve Charlisse's friend from his vile clutches.

He sighed. Perhaps by then, her heart would soften toward him.

*Father, I can't lose her again.*

# Chapter 36
# Restoration

Merrick leaned on the taffrail and stared glumly into the frothing wake bubbling off the *Reliance*'s stern. The churning in his soul matched the fuming of the foamy indigo sea. Charlisse's face, contorted with anger and pain, kept appearing in his mind. Though the hole in his heart caused by her purported death had now been healed, another one, equally painful, had formed. At least when he had believed her dead, he took comfort in the knowledge that she had parted this world with all the love he had given her. Now, to have her spew nothing but bitterness toward him, to see her so closed to his affections, was a pain worse than death. It would have been better to have died himself, taking with him to the grave the fond remembrance of her adoring love.

Lifting his gaze, Merrick watched the *Satisfaction* plunging through the choppy sea a half mile off the *Reliance*'s starboard quarter. With sails billowing, the two ships had glided next to each other all day in search of that nefarious pirate Kent Carlton. Just the thought of him ignited rage inside Merrick. From the moment he'd taken him aboard his ship nigh six years ago, Kent had caused him and Charlisse nothing but trouble. Visions of slicing him to bits with his cutlass and tossing his shredded carcass into the sea passed through Merrick's mind. He sighed, knowing it was wrong to think such things, but found himself unable to stop. Truthfully, he didn't know what he would do with Kent when he found him. *Lord, I will need Your strength.*

Merrick crossed his arms over his chest and braced himself as the

*Reliance* surged over a swell. The sun, now a brilliant golden orb in the west, grazed the ocean with a sizzle, shooting out arrows of red and orange across the horizon.

With a new foresail hoisted and mainsail and rigging repaired, the *Reliance* soared across the Caribbean with the ease and grace of a mighty gull. Planting his boots firmly on the deck, Merrick listened to the familiar creaks and moans of the ship's booms and tackles and drew in a deep breath of her wood and pitch. On this ship, he'd given his life to God. On this ship, he'd captured many a wicked pirate, relieving the Caribbean of their vile ravaging. And on this ship, he'd given his heart to Charlisse. He was home again, not only on the *Reliance*, but also in his heart with God.

How could he make Charlisse see that he still loved her—that he always had, and always would? He clutched the railing. Blast her foolish notions and mistrust. He must go see her.

A crisp breeze nipped at him. *Yes, how dare she defy her husband?*

Chattering alerted Merrick to Solomon climbing on the shrouds above him. Even the monkey no longer showed him any respect.

Merrick swerved about and glanced across the ship. He hated feeling helpless. He had been too long without Charlisse. She was still his wife and therefore under obligation to obey him.

Marching across the quarterdeck, he ignored Rusty's greeting and nearly knocked over Sloane as he barreled down the stairs. He would make Charlisse understand. He would not spend another night without her in his arms—in his bed.

Stopping before the massive oak door, he hesitated, then without a knock, lifted the latch and burst into the room.

Charlisse whirled, her unbound curls swirling through the air around her. She wore nothing save oversized breeches, a lacy chemise, and a look of horror on her face.

Merrick gaped at her, mesmerized by the creamy luster of her bare skin.

"How dare you?" She bolted toward the table, where one of her pistols lay, and snatched it just as Merrick lunged and plucked it from her grasp.

He retreated and closed the door before anyone saw his uncovered wife. Her beauty had always captivated him, but now without her pirate regalia, and with her curves so graciously exposed, his heart quickened, and the room grew suddenly warm. He swallowed and took a step toward her.

"What are you staring at, you cad?" She retreated and glanced over the cabin.

Following her gaze, Merrick noticed her cutlass, a knife, and one other pistol lying on a chair. He quickly gathered them and set them on his desk, then leaned back against the top. The point of his cutlass scraped over the wooden legs. He crossed his arms and tried to squelch the tremendous urge to rush at Charlisse and take her into his arms.

Grabbing her shirt from the bed, she held it up to her neck. "What is your intention? By the look in your eyes, 'tis not a noble one." She glanced away. "Isn't one woman enough for you?"

Merrick crossed one boot over the other. "One woman is more than enough for me."

He studied her unsettled expression. Where was the strong, defiant captain he'd seen only moments before? She blinked at him through red-rimmed eyes. She'd been crying again. "I do not wish to distress you." Merrick softened his voice. "No need to cover yourself, Charlisse." He gestured to the shirt she clutched to her chest. "You are my wife."

"I am your wife in name only."

Her words struck him deeper than any sword, and Merrick hung his head and gripped the edge of the desk. When he lifted his gaze, Charlisse had turned slightly, and he noticed a wide gash on her right arm. He rushed to her side.

Glancing up, she recoiled at his advance.

"What is this?" Merrick grabbed her arm and examined the wound. The scent of lilacs floated around him.

Sobbing, Charlisse tried to pry her arm from his hands.

"A deep cut," he said.

"I know what it is, you fool." Charlisse turned her face away, and Merrick felt a tremble pass through her. He stood within inches of her and could feel the heat radiating from her body. His blood warmed. He leaned toward her hair and drew a deep breath.

She fixed her fiery, moist eyes upon him and yanked her arm away. " 'Tis nothing. . .just another wound you have caused me."

Merrick stared into her ocean-blue eyes. The last rays of the sun filtered through the window and glittered on a wayward curl that had fallen across her cheek. He reached and moved the golden tendril aside, grazing his hand over her bare shoulder. She flinched and closed her eyes. Merrick's body responded to the silky feel of her skin, and his breath deepened.

"Please, Charlisse." He pulled her toward him.

"No!" She pushed against him, allowing her shirt to drop to the floor. Tears filled her eyes and spilled down her reddened cheeks. "Why do you torture me so?"

She turned her back to him. "Please leave me alone, Merrick," she sobbed. "Please."

Merrick stared at his wife, trembling and weeping, and realized how selfish he had been. He dropped his gaze and offered her a slight bow. "I'm sorry." He shook his head. "I'm sorry, Charlisse. I will bother you no further."

Turning, he trudged from the room and closed the door behind him, leaning back against the oak slab. A burst of sobs emanated from the cabin, cutting him to the quick.

Charlisse collapsed to her knees, dropped her head into her hands. She slid her fingers over the spot on her arm Merrick had clutched, then over her shoulder where his warm touch had sent every nerve quivering. She raised her fingers to her nose and smelled his scent upon her: musk, salt, and leather. Her body still tingled from his closeness. Why wouldn't he leave her alone? Why didn't he go to his Spanish lady?

Fury rose within her, extinguishing her heated nerves and smothering her sorrow. She shot to her feet, took a deep breath, and swiped the tears from her face, berating herself for appearing so weak in front of him.

Donning her shirt, she retrieved her weapons and latched the door. Next time, she would be better prepared.

A loud knock sounded, and she nearly jumped from her skin. "Go away!"

" 'Tis me with yer tea, milady." Sloane's scratchy voice echoed through the thick oak.

Charlisse rushed to unbolt the door, then stopped to listen. "You are alone?"

"Aye, milady, just me and the rats."

Unlatching the door, she admitted him. He strolled in, carrying a tray of steaming tea and warm biscuits. There was a lightness to his step and a smile on his face even amidst the tension still lingering in the cabin.

"Thank you, Sloane."

Charlisse lit a lantern, hoping to dispel the gloom that had blanketed both the room and her heart, and gestured for Sloane to take a seat and join her.

"Don't mind if I do. Thank ye, milady." He plopped into a chair, poured tea into a cup, and handed it to her, eyeing her with suspicion.

Charlisse accepted it and sat in the chair next to him. She attributed his wary looks to his overhearing the discourse between Merrick and her. The sturdy-looking walls on a ship often betrayed the confidences whispered within. But truthfully, although she knew she should be embarrassed at such a personal display, there wasn't much about her and Merrick that Sloane was not already privy to, and she longed for his opinion.

"I suppose you saw the captain leave the cabin?"

Sloane poured himself some tea and sipped it, then grabbed a biscuit. "Aye, that I did."

He chomped on some bread and stared out the window. Night had finally cast its dark shroud over the swarming seas, trying to stifle their savage tendencies. Sloane shifted his gray eyes to Charlisse. "I knows yer hurtin', milady, and I hate to see ye so distraught." He glanced away.

Was that moisture in his eyes? Charlisse's heart warmed at his concern.

"By thunder, I'll not be denyin' I's mad at the cap'n, too." Sloane clanked his cup down on the table, nearly shattering it. "He done lost his senses is all, and went off on a fool's errand to be sure." He took another bite from his biscuit, crumbs flying from his mouth.

Charlisse settled back into the chair, sipped her tea, and allowed its warmth to soothe her agitated humors. She smiled, pleased that finally someone else was as angry at the illustrious Captain Merrick as she was.

Sloane grunted. "I've a mind t' be teachin' him a lesson meself fer acting the dolt and hurtin' ye. But. . ." Sloane swallowed his bread and glanced at Charlisse. "The good Lord done reminded me that I done some foolhardy things in me life, as well."

Charlisse examined Sloane's aged face. His frequent mention of God of late piqued her curiosity. "I should rather suppose that *you* learn from your mistakes, Mr. Sloane, and don't keep committing the same ones over again."

"Aye. I like to be thinkin' that's true, milady."

"Apparently, your captain is not as wise, for he entertains his woman on board, flaunting her right before his wife's eyes."

"Naw, milady. Ye be mistaken. The cap'n has not called on the señorita—not once since she came aboard."

"Then where did he sleep last night?"

"On the foredeck. And he's pretty sore from it." Sloane chuckled. He reached out and grabbed Charlisse's hand. The rough surface of his hands felt like a warm, old rope against her delicate skin.

A glimmer of hope nestled within her barren heart. "I beg you not to make a fool of me for his sake," she said.

"Nay, I wouldn't be doin' that." He squeezed her hand. "Leastways, 'tis not right to be lying."

Charlisse studied his face, now reddening under her intense perusal. "Do my eyes deceive me or do I detect a change in you, Mr. Sloane?" A spring of elation welled up within her at the recognition of the gleam in his eyes.

Sloane tugged his hand back and scuffed his boots across the wooden planks. "Mebbe." He gave Charlisse a sideways glance. "Mebbe I called out to yer God like ye told me to."

Charlisse put down her tea and leapt from the chair. "This is wonderful news!" She knelt beside him, grabbing his hands again. "You've accepted Christ as your Lord?"

Sloane flashed her a grin that sparkled despite his grungy teeth. "Aye, that I did, milady. And I 'ave to say, naught's been the same since."

Overcome with excitement, Charlisse begged Sloane to disclose every detail of his conversion. Afterward she kept him long into the night talking about the goodness of God and what wonderful things he'd already experienced in his newfound faith. But as the night continued to drop, so did Sloane's eyelids until finally, yawning, he excused himself.

As soon as the oak door thudded shut, the solemn emptiness of the cabin smothered Charlisse once again, and the agony of her heart battled for preeminence over the good news of Sloane's redemption.

After gathering her weapons and laying them beside the bed, she blew out the lantern and crawled under the covers, drawing them over her head. She longed to disappear, to be invisible—invisible to Merrick, invisible to the pain, invisible to herself. She yearned to go back to the way things had been between her and Merrick before Porto Bello. But even if that were possible, she doubted she'd ever be able to trust him again. He had been the one man she had trusted with everything, and he had let her down.

Charlisse sobbed, remembering the verse in Romans: *"For all have sinned, and come short of the glory of God."* Perhaps she was being too harsh on Merrick. Pondering these words and human weakness, Charlisse drifted to sleep with the rocking of the ship.

Terrified screams blared into Charlisse's hazy mind, frantically jarring her awake. Rolling over, she yanked the pillow over her face, muffling the shrieks, thinking perhaps it was her own soul finally gone mad. But the wails continued, clamoring like warning bells until she sprang up in bed, her eyes darting around the dark room. She saw nothing save the filtered moonlight shimmering through the window and the murky shadows of furniture around her.

Another horrified scream tore through the ship. Boots pounded outside her door. Charlisse jumped off the bed and lit a candle. She quickly donned her shirt and breeches and bolted from the cabin. With candle in hand, she crept down the now silent companionway, the candlelight casting shifting shadows over the walls of the rolling ship. The moist wood beneath her bare feet sent cooling ripples up her legs. A splinter tore her flesh, and she winced.

Creeping forward, Charlisse turned a corner and saw the Spanish woman's door ajar, flooding the hallway with light. She halted when she heard Merrick's voice. Jackson emerged from within, nodding at Charlisse as he passed. The whites of his eyes gleamed in the darkness, but he said nothing.

A soft, feminine voice with a Spanish accent flowed like silk from the room. Tiptoeing forward, Charlisse stopped just before the doorway.

"Gracias, Merrick. I'm sorry to disturb you."

"It is understandable after what you've been through." Merrick's deep voice penetrated the darkness. "I beg your leave, señorita. Rest well."

Charlisse turned to flee but heard Merrick step into the hallway behind her and close the door. Her candle shed a circle of light around her, giving her away.

His heavy boots thumped, and a tingle ran down her back as he passed her and tipped his hat. "Milady." A slight smile lifted one corner of his mouth. "What brings you out of your cabin this late?"

"I heard a scream."

"Yes, Señorita Elisa had a nightmare." He glanced at her door. "She's been through a terrifying ordeal for one so young."

Charlisse hadn't even considered what the woman must have endured on Captain Collier's ship. A wave of guilt flooded over her.

"Would you like me to escort you back to the cabin?" Merrick asked, holding out his arm.

"No thank you. I can manage."

With a nod, he strutted down the hall until the corner took him from her sight.

Charlisse tapped lightly on the señorita's door. Whatever had happened between this woman and Merrick—whatever feelings existed between them, Charlisse must put that aside and offer her what comfort she could.

The door opened. Elisa's puffy eyes widened when she saw Charlisse.

"May I come in?" Charlisse asked.

The woman nodded and stepped aside, closing the door after Charlisse entered. The tiny cabin contained only a small cot built into one wall and a slab of oak extending from the other, which served as a table. Setting the candle down, Charlisse turned to face Elisa. Her long dark hair cascaded over her shoulders to her waist, and her gentle brown gaze took in Charlisse with nervous expectation.

"I heard you scream, señorita, and I wanted to make sure you were all right."

Elisa's brows furrowed for a moment, then letting out a sigh, she walked to the cot and sat down. "*Sí*, I am fine, gracias, señora. I have no chair to offer you. Would you care to sit?" She gestured to a place beside her on the cot.

Charlisse shook her head and tried to smile. Elisa's beauty sparkled, despite the bags under her eyes and her disheveled hair and gown.

"I am sorry to awaken you," Elisa continued. "I fear it will be quite some time before I can forget the horrors of Captain Collier."

"How did you come to be on his ship?"

"He raided my town, Barracoa. He and Mer. . .your husband." Her gaze lowered to the floor.

Charlisse gulped. Merrick on a raid? So it was true. He had turned to pirating. "I'm sorry for what you must have gone through." Dare she inquire as to the specifics? Perhaps it was best left unsaid. "Is there something I can get for you?"

"No, señora, you are very kind." Elisa dropped her head into her hands and sobbed.

Pushing her jealousy aside, Charlisse eased beside her on the cot and gently placed an arm over her shoulders. "There's nothing to fear anymore, señorita. You will be safe on this ship."

"Please call me Elisa," she sniffed and gazed at Charlisse with glassy eyes. "I know. I hardly shed a tear when I was with Collier, but now that I'm protected, I find I cannot stop weeping like a baby." A sorrowful giggle escaped her lips.

"That's to be expected." Charlisse rubbed her back, remembering all the times she'd broken down and wept after she'd survived a terrifying event. "Go ahead and cry. You'll feel much better."

And cry Elisa did—for the next hour—pouring out in between sobs and sniffs the story of her kidnapping, Collier's attempts to ravish her, the times he'd struck her, and finally how he'd dragged her to the Drunken Skunk in an attempt to sell her to the mob.

Charlisse cringed. "How horrible! I can't imagine how frightened you must have been."

"Your husband. He saved me. He pretended to buy me for the whole night, but that beast Collier would not let him go."

Images of Elisa on Merrick's lap flashed through Charlisse's mind. He had been trying to save her just as he'd told Charlisse, but still she could not forget that look in his eyes as he'd buried his face in Elisa's neck. She glanced down at the woman's lips and thought of the kiss Merrick said they'd shared. Pain squeezed her heart.

"My husband is a good man," Charlisse said, trying to focus on the fact that he had risked his life to save Elisa.

"Sí, señora, you are very lucky."

"You care for him." Charlisse stated, sadly, instead of questioned.

Elisa let out a tiny whimper and pursed her lips. "I do, señora." She shifted her gaze away from Charlisse. "But I would not have allowed such feelings to grow if I'd known you were alive. Please believe me. Besides. . ." She folded her hands on her lap and looked down. "He loves only you."

Tugging on a lock of her hair, Charlisse twirled it around her finger and watched the candle flickering across the room. Elisa's last words pierced through the dark shroud around her heart.

"It is true." Elisa grabbed Charlisse's hand. "I see it in his gaze when he looks at you."

Tears burned behind Charlisse's eyes, but this time they weren't tears of anguish, but tears of joy. Perhaps Merrick had been hasty in his affections toward another, but what did Charlisse know of the sorrow he had endured when he believed she was dead? Could she forgive him?

"Go to him," Elisa urged her. "Go to your husband." Her excited smile held the hint of sorrow.

Charlisse squeezed her hand and gave her a big hug. "Thank you." Then jumping to her feet, Charlisse stepped to the door, turned, and smiled at Elisa before opening it and darting down the hallway and up the companionway stairs.

She scanned the deck, searching for Merrick. Pirates stood in clusters by the larboard railing. On the foredeck up ahead, a tall silhouette loomed. A half moon draped its milky light over him, setting him apart from the shadows of rigging and mast.

Charlisse rushed to the stairs, taking them in two leaping bounds, then softly walked toward the dark figure until she stood beside him. She glanced at him. His arms crossed over his thick chest, and his hair blew behind him in ebony strands. With firm jaw, he stared over the raucous ocean.

She turned her gaze to the sea, as well. The moonlight dabbed sparkling light on chosen waves, brightening their journey through the dark world.

"I spoke with Elisa."

"You did?"

"She's very sweet. I see why you like her."

A hint of a smile toyed upon Merrick's lips. "But I love you, Charlisse."

"So she told me."

He snorted and shook his head, offering her a sly glance. "I would hope you would be able to see that for yourself."

Charlisse grinned and inched closer to him, feeling his warmth dispel the chill of the evening. "I should have. I'm sorry."

"I was so miserable without you." Letting his arms fall, he turned toward her. "I didn't know what I was doing." He pulled Charlisse into his embrace.

She fell against his chest and allowed his warmth to engulf her. Melting into him, she took a deep breath of his scent, and for the first time in a month, let her guard down, releasing all the tension within her in tears that spilled down her cheeks.

"I'm so sorry, Charlisse. I never meant to hurt you." He stroked her back and ran his hands through her hair, kissing her forehead. "Please don't ever leave me again."

She stood back. "It was you who left me, if you remember."

Merrick pushed the hair gently from her face and ran his thumb over her cheek, wiping away her tears, his dark gaze riveted to hers. "A mistake I intend never to make again."

The *Reliance* lunged over a swell, and Merrick steadied himself and grabbed Charlisse. She buried her face in his chest and sighed, feeling safe at last, surrounded by his strength. Her body warmed, and she gazed up at him.

Instantly his lips were on hers, drawing her into him. Charlisse's heart melted. When he pulled back from her, his breath came deep and hard, and his gaze roved over her.

Leaning down, he swept her up into his arms and marched across the deck and down the stairs. Ignoring the snickers around them, he descended to their cabin. With one thrust, he kicked the oak door aside and gently placed Charlisse on the bed, before closing and latching the door. He turned and sauntered toward her, unbuttoning his shirt, a grin playing on his lips.

Charlisse could resist her husband no longer. Nor did she want to. A warmth stirred within her, spreading over her in waves, and she opened her arms to receive him.

## Chapter 37
# Stolen Treasure

Isabel sat on the window ledge in the cabin and gazed over the gloomy, turbulent sea. A half-blackened moon cast its paltry light upon the dismal scene, only increasing the hopelessness that had taken residence within her heart. It had been five days since Captain Carlton had stormed aboard Charlisse's ship and stolen Isabel, once again dragging her back into the nightmare she had previously endured for so long.

Since then, the captain had been naught but kind, offering her every comfort and never forcing his attentions upon her. His visits had become less frequent, and she sensed an uneasiness in his demeanor that frightened her. Perhaps the cost of maintaining his gentlemanly facade was taking its toll on him, and soon he would revert to the lecherous brigand he truly was. It was in his nature, after all—in the nature of all those born common.

As the arduous days and nights passed, Isabel had resigned herself to her fate—to be the captive of a pirate captain for the rest of her days. No one knew where she was, save Charlisse, and why would Lady Hyde risk her life for someone she barely knew? By now, surely she had reunited with her husband and they were beginning their life anew.

The idea of Charlisse's God hounded Isabel day and night—not the god Isabel had learned about in church. This God was different, full of power and love. Was it possible He loved Isabel, too, just as Charlisse had claimed?

One night, when the reality of her situation had pulled her into a mire of despair, she'd called out to Him. But although she'd felt some peace and a sprinkle of hope that lifted her spirits, her situation hadn't changed. Whether God had heard her prayer or not, she determined to remain strong and not allow Kent's feigned benevolence squirm its way through the bitter casing around her heart.

And she had much to be bitter about. Isabel clutched her stomach. The child would make himself known to the gazes of others in only a few months. She loathed the babe growing inside her—a pirate's child.

The grating of the latch sounded, and the door creaked open. Kent swaggered in, pocketing the key, and eyed her with concern. He doffed his hat and bowed, loosing a strand of his dark hair across his cheek. Tossing it back, he perused her with a tender gaze that leeched her resolve.

"I trust you are feeling well, milady."

Isabel snorted and turned away from his dauntless figure. "As well as can be expected."

"Oh, come now, surely you have been treated like nothing short of royalty aboard my ship."

"Pshaw, you know nothing of the finer things in life." She glared at him. "Your measly attempts at presenting a table a true noblewoman would enjoy are laughable." No sooner had the words escaped her lips, than Isabel wished to recall them, as fury stormed on Kent's face, causing his upper lip to twitch.

He shifted his gaze away and tossed his hat onto the table.

"And yet your food has been the finest ever served aboard this ship." Spinning, he marched to the desk and began rummaging through drawers, slamming each one in turn.

His salty, spicy scent wafted over Isabel.

Kent pulled out a bottle of rum, uncorked it, and drew two huge gulps from its mouth. He sighed, closing his eyes. "Why do I always feel the need for rum in your presence?"

" 'Tis not me who causes it, but your own weak nature that draws you to the vile potion."

Chuckling, Kent opened his eyes and took another swig. "Egad, your mouth spews a more deadly blast than any broadside."

"Then perhaps you should avoid setting it off."

"Here, here." Kent pressed the bottle to his chest. "You have cut me to the quick, milady."

Was that a shimmer in his eyes, or was it only the rum taking effect?

Isabel glanced down, wrapping her arms around her belly. She heard the liquor slosh inside the bottle. Was he going to drink it all?

Tears burned her eyes as she thought of her home in New Providence, of her father and mother and the dreams she'd once had of marrying a rich nobleman, of living a life of wealth and luxury. Now, even if she could get free from this villain, what true gentleman would have her, defiled and sullied as she was?

The thud of boots on the wooden floor drew her gaze upward to Kent, stumbling toward her. He set his half-empty bottle on a table and settled the tottering flask before continuing his approach. His eyes shone with the haze of alcohol and something else Isabel could not determine.

She backed against the window and cringed, her breath quickening. Visions of the captain's assault upon her two months ago twirled like phantoms in her mind. It had happened so quickly, and he had been so benevolent since, that if not for the child growing with her, she would have thought it only a nightmare that had assailed her thoughts one restless night.

He stopped before her. She lowered her head, unable to meet his searching brown eyes.

The pungent odor of rum stung her nose, and she twitched it, trying to loosen its grip on her senses.

Placing a finger under her chin, he lifted her head until she could not avoid his intense gaze. "What is it you find so repulsive about me?" His deep voice simmered.

Isabel gulped, and she detected a tremor cross the thick muscles of his chest beneath his open shirt. Was he jesting? After what he'd done to her? "You need ask?"

Turning his back, he balled his hands on his hips and looked down. The waves of his long umber hair spiraled down his back from the tie that held them in place. "I never meant to harm you," he said without facing her.

Isabel swallowed her curt reply, wondering at the twinge of sympathy that broke through her bitterness.

The captain spun around and offered her a pleading gaze. "Is there nothing I can do that will please you?"

Isabel furrowed her brow at his humble entreaty. The tenderness in his voice caused tears to fill her eyes and hope to spark within her. A teardrop escaped down her cheek. "I want to go home."

Kent fingered his mustache, his jaw flexing. He shot her a look of grievous defiance. "I will not let you go. I cannot."

Squeezing her eyes shut, Isabel held back a flood of tears. "Then please leave me alone."

Daring not to turn her back on him, she simply hung her head and wept, no longer ashamed of such an outpouring in his presence. She heard his heavy boots thump away and saw his blurred form grab the bottle of rum and exit the room, closing the door behind him.

Plodding down the hallway, Kent grabbed the main hatch railing and hoisted himself up the stairs. He released his fierce grip on the iron banister and shook the ache from his hand as he stormed up onto the main deck. A slap of rain-laden air struck him. He drew a deep breath, hoping it would cool both his temper and the longing that set his senses on fire whenever he was near Lady Ashton.

*Isabel.* The woman infuriated him. Her tongue, like a sharp cutlass, could cut a man in two before he even realized she'd drawn the vile weapon.

Bounding up onto the quarterdeck and onto the poop deck, where Kent felt most in command, he marched with rum in hand, nodding at a few of the pirates who still lingered above. When he reached the stern of the frigate, he gripped the railing with one hand and tipped the bottle to his lips with the other, pouring a full draught down his parched throat. Perhaps the numbing fluid would ease the pain lancing through his heart.

Lightning flashed in the distance, brightening the sky for a moment with its forked silver light. As the night progressed, the seas had become more restless. A storm approached. Kent snorted and plopped down to the hard wood, shoved his legs through the rails, and hung them over the side.

A storm approached, indeed. One he did not think he would survive.

What was wrong with him? Why couldn't he just force himself upon the blasted woman as every ounce of his body ached to do? His father had taught him to take what he wanted in life—to demand it, in fact.

But Lady Ashton. Surely she had cast a loathsome spell upon him, some delusion that had temporarily absconded with his reason. For there was no other explanation for the way his courage withered under her sharp gaze, the way he fumbled with his words like an untutored bumpkin in her presence, the abject insecurities that overtook him, and his inability to do anything to harm her. He felt nothing, save a desperate care for her—one that superseded even his fleshly urge to bed her.

A low rumble of thunder shook the sea, matching the burgeoning malaise in his soul.

He downed another swig of rum and glanced through the railings to the wake churning off the ship. Draped in moonlight, it bubbled into a creamy white froth—creamy and white like Lady Ashton's skin. And her eyes, those jade eyes, the same color of the Caribbean on a summer's day. He shook his head. Why couldn't he keep her from his thoughts?

He heard his father's guttural laugh. *You ninny. You've always been nothing but a weak little boy—a disappointment. Letting a woman rule you. You should force her to be yours if that's what you want.*

Gulping down the rest of the rum, Kent tossed the bottle into the sea and watched it splash into the inky waters, bobbing up and down before settling on its side and sinking into the depths.

Finally the haze of alcohol sped through his mind, knocking out his senses, leaving nothing but a dull throb of agony. He leaned his head on the railing, feeling the rough wood against his skin.

He loved her.

But if this was what love was like, he wanted no part of it, for he could not subdue it—could not conquer it. It slinked around him like an invisible enemy, taunting him with delicacies he could never taste. Love was nothing but a ghost ship filled with treasure that would always be beyond his cannons' reach. He'd tried all he knew to capture it and offer the prize to Isabel, but for all his efforts, she'd done nothing but refuse him.

He must let her go. He knew that, for he could no longer bear to see her so unhappy. The thought of releasing her cut like a hot knife into his heart, sending searing waves of pain throughout him. But for once in his life, someone else's happiness meant more to him than his own.

Lightning darted across the inky expanse, drawing Kent's attention to the horizon. The smoky shadows of two ships, dark against the bright flash that illuminated the sky, flickered across his vision. Then they were gone. Kent shook his head and peered into the darkness.

Nothing. Must be the rum.

# Chapter 38
## Safe in His Arms

Merrick leaned on his elbow, propping his head in his hand, and gazed upon the beauty sleeping next to him. Her gentle, deep breaths told him she slept soundly, although her long eyelashes fluttered upon her cheeks as if she were involved in some grand adventure deep within her slumberous mind. He hoped he played as big a part in her dreams as she did in his.

Golden curls cascaded over her bare shoulder and onto the sheet that covered her. Merrick longed to stroke her soft, silky skin—never tiring of the feel of it beneath his hand—but he didn't dare wake her. She'd been through so much on his account, and he'd kept her up well into the early morning hours. *Father, thank You for bringing her back to me. I am blessed above all men to have such a woman as my wife.*

Charlisse moaned and twitched her pink lips. Merrick smiled.

The hazy glow of dawn swept through the cabin window, diffusing the shadows and brightening Charlisse's delicate features. He could not keep his gaze from her, nor was he inclined ever to do so again.

Thunder rumbled in the distance. Boots pounded on the deck above, and Merrick wished they would all cease, at least for a day—the sounds, the people, the problems. Then he could lie beside Charlisse and hold her until any remembrance of the ache of losing her finally dissipated.

But that was not the life he'd chosen, not the quiet life of a country gentleman. He was a privateer, and a privateer's life did not allow for such peaceful repose. The *Reliance* swooped over a wave, jarring the bed. A booming voice bellowed above.

Charlisse's eyes cracked open, and she grinned, stretching her arms above her head. "Do my eyes deceive me, or is there a handsome pirate in my bed?"

"Not only a handsome pirate, but as your good fortune would dictate, your husband, as well."

Charlisse giggled. "Ah, I see the humiliation of your recent debauchery has not tempered your vanity in the slightest." Then her expression fell serious, and she ran her hand across the stubble on his jaw, her eyes moistening. "I missed you, Merrick."

Merrick smoothed the wayward curls from around her face, trying to quell the burst of emotion rising in his throat. He gazed into her ocean-blue eyes. As they searched his, they sparkled with joy, admiration, and yearning just as they used to, and Merrick felt his insides melt. He shook his head. He didn't deserve such happiness. Not after he'd turned his back on God. Quietly, he thanked the Lord again, knowing it was only by His grace Merrick was here with Charlisse and not rotting at the bottom of the sea.

Charlisse's brow furrowed. "Something troubles you. What are you thinking?"

"Nay, my love, I'm not troubled at all. Quite the opposite."

Smiling, Charlisse stretched like a cat on a warm blanket. "Perhaps we should get dressed and be about our business. I daresay we have a villain to catch."

But Merrick wasn't thinking about pursuing villains or anyone else, save his lovely wife. "Perhaps I should see what writhes beneath these sheets." He gave her a taunting grin and lifted one corner of the covers, peering underneath. "I perceive some beast has taken shelter here."

Slapping his hand away, Charlisse clutched the covers to her neck. "The only beast in this room is your insatiable desire. Egad, haven't you had your fill?"

Merrick cocked an eyebrow. "Never." He pounced on her, nestling his head in her neck and kissing her repeatedly.

Charlisse giggled, pushing him back.

"Never enough," he said, smiling. Then touched her lips with his and took her in his arms.

*Bam! Bam! Bam!*

Muffled voices sounded from outside the door, but Merrick ignored them.

Sloane's scratchy whisper seeped through the oak. "Ye must not disturb them."

Jackson's deep voice responded. "But the cap'n told me to tell him when I spot a ship."

*Bam! Bam! Bam!*

Pulling back from Charlisse, Merrick sighed in frustration and jerked from the bed. He jumped into his breeches and yelled through the door, "I'll be up presently, Jackson."

"Aye, aye, Cap'n," came the solemn reply.

Boot steps shuffled away, and Sloane's voice echoed in the hall. "Now look what ye've done. Don't ye have no sense o' romance in ye, ye crabby stiff-necked barnacle?"

Grabbing his shirt, Merrick glanced at Charlisse, who, with sheet wrapped tightly around her, searched for her clothes. "Why so modest around your husband?"

Charlisse faced him, and a coquettish smile alighted on her lips. "You think me modest after last night?" She picked up her breeches. "Nay, we have business to attend to, and I don't want to divert your attentions."

Merrick nodded. "Not only beautiful, but wise." He stepped to the armoire, selected one of Charlisse's gowns, and held it up. "Perchance you would honor me by dressing like a lady again?"

"If I won't be too much of a distraction."

Merrick gave her a teasing look. "That I cannot promise regardless of your attire."

A few minutes later when they stepped up onto the foredeck, Merrick released Charlisse's hand with a kiss and marched to Jackson, who held the spyglass to his eye.

The first mate handed the glass to Merrick. "Four points off the bow, Cap'n."

Bracing himself against the jostling of the ship, Merrick spotted the tall, three-masted vessel tottering on the rising waves of an incoming storm. He focused the glass on the name painted on the bow of the ship, trying to keep it steady upon the plunging target. A swish of skirts sounded beside him.

"The *Vanquisher*," he stated, lowering the glass.

"Aye," the first mate concurred.

Charlisse rushed to the railing, her golden hair dancing against the back of her tawny gown. Merrick swept her with his gaze, enjoying the way the dress clung to her curves. A sizzling warmth stirred within him. Perhaps he should have allowed her to don the baggy breeches as she'd wanted.

She glanced back at Merrick, her eyes aglow. "The Lord has led us to her."

"That He did." Merrick nodded and returned her smile, as anxious to deal with Kent as his wife was to rescue her friend. "Jackson, all hands about ship. Unfurl all topgallants, and set a course"—Merrick raised his gaze back to the *Vanquisher*—"twenty degrees north-northwest."

"Aye, aye, Cap'n." Jackson turned on his heels and began roaring orders across the deck, sending men scurrying up the ratlines. Smack gave the whipstaff a slight turn to port, and the *Reliance* veered into the wind, her sails snapping.

Thunder bellowed from a darkening sky in the east, and Rusty jumped up on deck, followed by Sloane, his countenance beaming. Solomon chattered a tune from the old pirate's shoulder, his tiny beady eyes flitting from Charlisse to Merrick.

Rusty approached Charlisse and halted beside her at the railing. The red-haired pirate leaned toward her, speaking softly in her ear. The intimate action torched fiery coals within Merrick. He started toward them, but Sloane raised an arm. "No need, Cap'n, 'tis naught but simple admiration."

"Admiration or not, I daresay the man will not be so familiar with my wife." He charged forward again, but Sloane further restrained him.

Charlisse giggled and cast a glance over her shoulder at Merrick. A trace of mischievousness darted across her expression when she saw her husband. Still smiling at Merrick, she leaned closer to Rusty and whispered something in the pirate's ear.

Merrick clenched his fists as a swell of jealousy threatened to drown him with fury.

Sloane chuckled. "It be a hard thing when the cutlass be on the other hip, eh, Cap'n?"

Merrick shot his friend a steely gaze. Yet Sloane was right. Hadn't Charlisse witnessed Merrick in a far more seductive embrace back at the Drunken Skunk—one she'd thought was real? After last night, he had no doubt as to her affections toward him, yet even this jesting display curdled in his gut. Merrick let out a deep sigh, swallowing another stab of pride.

Charlisse took Rusty's hand in hers and gave it a squeeze before releasing it.

The pirate, whose face now matched the color of his hair, bowed and dashed away, avoiding Merrick's fuming eyes.

Crossing her arms over her chest, Charlisse approached Merrick, a teasing look upon her face. "Are you jealous, milord?"

Merrick snorted. "Hardly." Solomon jumped onto his shoulder, chattering and nodding his head, and Merrick flinched, holding a hand over his ear. "But pray tell, what did my helmsman want with you?"

"He only wished to know if you were treating me well, and if not, for me to let him know so he could put you in your place."

Merrick flexed his jaw. How long must he suffer this constant humiliation? "And what, may I inquire, was your reply?"

"That I would certainly call upon him at your slightest affront." Charlisse grinned, raising her chin in the air. "But that you have been nothing short of a gentleman thus far. . . ." She gave him a coy glance. "Well, perhaps not entirely a gentleman."

Sloane's aged face blossomed a deep maroon, and he glanced away, clearing his throat.

Merrick sighed, flattening his lips, and smiled at the monkey playing on his shoulder. "Are we friends again, little one?"

The creature prattled with glee.

"Seems I must win your favor, milady, to receive any respect aboard this ship at all." He offered her a slight bow.

Sloane nodded toward the main deck, where several pirates were congregating. "The men await the Bible readin', milady."

Charlisse glanced down, eyebrows raising. "Of course, how could I forget?" Swerving, she stared at Kent's ship, growing larger on the horizon and looked back at Merrick.

He met her beseeching gaze. "We have time. Read to your crew, milady. We'll prepare for battle when you are done."

Nodding, she flew down the stairs while Sloane and Merrick took their places at the foredeck railing, looking down upon the scene.

"T's a mite happy 'bout ye and milady gettin' things worked out, Cap'n."

Merrick slapped him on the back. "No happier than I am. 'Twas all by the Lord's grace."

"Aye."

Merrick gave Sloane a questioning look. "Charlisse informs me you have given your life to Christ?"

"Aye, by thunder, would be foolish not to, after all I seen, eh?"

Merrick smiled. "Indeed." He shook his head, running a hand through his hair. Charlisse had been able to reach the old sea dog after only a week when Merrick had been trying for years. "I can see the difference in you already."

"Aye, 'tis a whole new life." Sloane's eyes moistened, and he looked away.

After the reading, the men dispersed, and Merrick's deep voice blared over the ship, issuing orders for the ensuing confrontation. Off their starboard side, nigh just a half a knot behind them, the *Satisfaction* flew through the turbulent waters, following his lead. With two such mighty ships, Kent didn't stand a chance. It would be to his advantage to simply raise the white flag and avoid any bloodshed. But Merrick knew this scamp, knew his temper and his insolent pride all too well. Most likely, he would not go down without a fight. Bowing his head, Merrick offered a quick prayer to the Lord for the safety of all—especially Charlisse.

A ragged bolt of lightning etched the darkening sky, warning of the storm to come. The newly risen sun darted, cowering, behind the black, threatening clouds. Merrick stood on the foredeck, boots planted next to the mast, and turned to see Charlisse sidle up next to him. She gave him a loving glance, then wove her arm through his. A gust of warm wind flowed over her, tossing her hair behind her in a chaotic golden mass. The tangy scent of rain and the sting of lightning struck Merrick's nose—both subdued by the soothing fragrance of lilacs.

He patted Charlisse's hand. "Don't dismay. We will save your friend."

"I know you will." Charlisse smiled and leaned on him. A loud "A sail, a sail!" howled from above.

Releasing Charlisse, Merrick stormed down onto the main deck, scanning the horizon. "Where away, Smack?"

"Right off our stern, Cap'n. South-southeast!"

Clutching the spyglass from his belt, Merrick barreled up onto the quarterdeck, hearing Charlisse following close behind him. He raised the glass to his eye, immediately spotting the stark white sails brimming against the stormy horizon. Who dared to follow him?

Lowering the glass, Merrick approached the taffrail as Jackson and Sloane jumped onto the deck and rushed toward him.

"Do you know who she is?" Charlisse asked, holding out her hand for the glass.

Hesitating, Merrick stared at his wife with astonishment, then handed her the instrument.

Pressing the glass to her eye, she adjusted it, holding it in place for several seconds.

Merrick glanced at Sloane and Jackson, who stared ahead, undaunted at Charlisse's commanding air.

"The *Bandit d'Or*," she announced, handing the glass back to Merrick. "Do you know her?"

Merrick peered toward the pursuant again, alarm clanging within him. Yes, the *Golden Bandit*, he knew her. It was the ship of that feeble Frenchman, Jean Doglar, known to join forces with Collier from time to time. He lowered the glass. "Yes, but 'tis who commands her that gives me concern."

"We'll be knowin' that soon enough," Sloane offered, scratching his beard. "She bears down on us faster than a trollop on a newly shored sailor."

"Jackson," Charlisse said, turning to the first mate. "How long before we are in firing range of the *Vanquisher*?"

Casting an imposing glance at his wife, Merrick swung about to face his first mate and saw the *Vanquisher* tumbling through the riotous sea off their larboard bow.

"Less than an hour, ma'am," the dark man replied.

Merrick gazed back at the *Golden Bandit*. He'd seen her in the harbor at Tortuga. Could that wretched scoundrel, Collier, have made it to the shore and commandeered Doglar's ship to pursue him?

Solomon sprang from Sloane's shoulder and skittered up into the shrouds above them, wagging his bony fingers toward the pursuing menace.

Merrick peered through the glass again and spotted a man on the foredeck, tall and dark-haired, his arrogant stance immediately familiar. " 'Tis that snake, Collier." Merrick slammed the glass shut. "Blast! I knew I should have killed him!"

A gentle hand touched his arm, and he turned to see Charlisse's calming gaze upon him. "She's but a schooner. Surely, we can outrun her?"

"We cannot." Merrick sighed. "She'll reach us before we can attack the *Vanquisher*."

Sloane arched his gray eyebrows. "Mebbe the *Satisfaction* can handle 'er without us, Cap'n."

"Yes, but with the damage to our fore and mainsail we cannot take the *Vanquisher* alone—especially undergunned." Merrick raked his hair and began to pace. "Only with the aid of the *Satisfaction* can we assure our victory."

Jackson clutched one of the pistols in his baldric. "We must stand together and fight Collier."

"But we'll lose the *Vanquisher*." Charlisse swerved her desperate gaze to Merrick. "Who knows when we'll find her again." She rushed to his side, grabbing his arm. "We can't leave Lady Ashton with that monster another minute."

How could he resist those pleading blue eyes? He would give her the world if he could. Yet now, with sinking heart, he knew he could not grant her request. "What would you have me do? I need both ships to confront either enemy, and the one pursuing us will be upon us first. I have no choice."

"Yes, you do." Charlisse pointed at the *Satisfaction*. "Cannot the *Satisfaction* defeat the *Vanquisher*? Are they not equally matched?"

Merrick nodded. "I suppose, yes, but do you trust a ship full of pirates to rescue your friend and keep their hands off of her until we can join them?"

"No, but I trust you would do so."

Warmed by her growing faith in him again, Merrick also feared the implication behind her words. "What are you suggesting?"

Charlisse's eyes brightened. "You take the *Satisfaction* and rescue Lady Ashton. I will command the *Reliance* and stave off the *Golden Bandit* until your return."

"Nay, I will not allow it!" He stormed across the deck and gripped the railing. Thunder roared in outrage, and a blast of wind tore through his hair.

"It's the only way, Merrick." He heard his wife's voice behind him, and he turned to face her. She gave him the same pleading look she'd given him that night at the church in Porto Bello. Her eyes swam in moisture and flickered back and forth between his. "We must save Isabel." But all he heard was, "We must save the children," the same words she'd used to urge him to leave her just before the church had been blown to bits, and her along with it.

He could not do this again—*would* not do this again. "We shall deal with the *Golden Bandit* and then return for Isabel."

Charlisse took a step toward him. "It may be too late then." She reached out her hand, her delicate brow wrinkled.

Scattered images flashed in Merrick's mind—Charlisse in the church, baby in her arms, begging him to leave her, assuring him she'd be safe. Then the explosion, the orange and yellow flames licking at the sky, the pieces of stone and wood blasting past him. The agony of believing she had died. "I will not lose you again."

"I can do this, Merrick. God will take care of me."

Jackson, arms pressed over his chest, stared at Merrick with a grim expression. Sloane pursed his lips, his eyes sparkling with anticipation; Smack waited at the helm; a cluster of pirates stood at the ready on the main deck. All eyes were upon him.

Lightning flashed, sending a white glow flickering over Charlisse's face. A chill raked up Merrick's spine, spiking across his shoulders and down his arms. *This time she will die. This time your God will not save her.*

Charlisse squeezed his arm. "Trust God, Merrick. Whether you're with me or not, my life has always been in His hands."

He clutched Charlisse's shoulders. "I must keep you safe. Don't ask me to leave you again."

"I have commanded this ship for a week. God has been with me. He will not let me down now." She glanced toward the oncoming ship. " 'Tis but a schooner. We outgun her."

"But what if God chooses to take you from me?"

"Then it will be for the best."

Merrick shook his head and turned away, feeling his eyes burn.

Looking up, Merrick gazed toward the *Vanquisher*. What should he do? But he already knew the answer. It was a miracle of God they had found the ship in the first place. Lady Ashton must be saved. And Charlisse had proven she could handle the *Reliance*. He must do the right thing and trust God with the result.

But he didn't know if he could.

He swung about and studied the *Satisfaction* sailing nigh three ship's lengths off their starboard side and the *Golden Bandit* swooping over the swells behind it, gaining on them by the moment. He hung his head. The fiery weight of decision burned like a furnace within him. *Lord, give me strength.*

Thunder rumbled and an icy spray of seawater showered over him.

*If you leave her, she will die.*

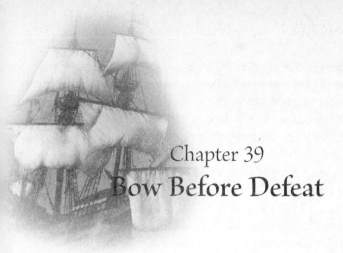

# Chapter 39
# Bow Before Defeat

$M$errick slowly turned around, his gaze scouring over his crew and finally landing on Charlisse. Her sweet smile warmed every part of him. He must do the right thing and trust God no matter what befell them. Even if some further tragedy took Charlisse from him again, he would never serve any other God.

Merrick swung his gaze to the first mate. "Jackson, signal the *Satisfaction* to come alongside."

Jackson's white teeth gleamed. "Aye, aye, Cap'n."

Sloane nodded, approval glinting in his eyes, before turning to assist the first mate.

Merrick looked back upon Charlisse. She stepped to him and melted into his arms. "It will be all right. You will see."

Grazing his lips over her forehead, Merrick took a deep whiff of her hair, already regretting his decision.

Standing on the main deck of the *Reliance*, Merrick clung to the rope that Badeau had tossed from the top of the *Satisfaction*'s mainmast. The mighty frigate tumbled over the swirling sea just eight yards off the *Reliance*'s starboard side, and Merrick must hurry before either of the ships lost its pace. His gaze swept over his crew. Charlisse, dressed in her pirate clothing once more, stood right beside him. The graceful features of her face held a confident peacefulness that he envied. Sloane, Jackson, and Rusty stood behind her. Up on the foredeck, Royce stared at him, his lips twisting in their usual snarl. Gunny and Mason clung to the ratlines. Brighton adjusted his eye patch as he stood beside Smack at the helm. Other pirates lingered in clusters across the deck.

Merrick's stern gaze swerved back to Jackson and Sloane. "Take care of her."

Sloane grunted. "There's naught t' concern ye, Cap'n. God will take care o' us, to be sure."

Cursing reached Merrick's ears from the pirates aboard the *Satisfaction.* "I fear these pirates have not had the benefit of your fine Biblical tutelage." Merrick grinned at Charlisse.

She glanced their way. "A motley crew if ever I saw one. You have your work cut out for you." She returned his smile, but a trace of sadness lingered in it.

The rope jerked in Merrick's grasp'as the ships dove down a massive wave, showering the deck with foamy spray. He nearly lost his grip on the coarse fibers that chafed his hand.

"Monsieur Capitaine! You must jump now!" Badeau boomed.

A light rain began to sprinkle upon them, and Merrick leaned down and placed his lips on Charlisse's, ignoring the taunting jeers and whistles flying at him from all around. "I love you, Charlisse," he whispered near her cheek.

"And I, you." Her eyes brimmed with tears. "Now, begone. Go and rescue Isabel, and may God be with you." She swiped at her cheeks and took a step back.

Jumping onto the bulwarks, Merrick tipped his hat toward his crew, winked at Charlisse, then clutched the rope and swung himself over to the *Satisfaction.* His boots landed with an ominous thud on the main deck. He turned and watched as his wife took command, ordering the *Reliance* to tack toward their oncoming enemy. His gaze locked with hers as wind and sea drove them asunder. He thought he saw a smile flicker upon her lips before she turned and shoved her captain's hat down upon her head.

Derisive snorts from the pirates behind him and Badeau's silly face grinning at him forced Merrick back to the task at hand—the *Vanquisher.* He clasped the Frenchman's outstretched hand and surveyed Captain Carlton's ship as it plunged through the sea at full sail off their larboard bow.

Badeau released Merrick's grip and nodded toward the fading *Reliance*. "Ah, I see you and your lady. You've solved your differences?"

"Resolved, yes, we have, Baddo. And I am obliged for your kind hospitality in taking me back on board."

"Your wife. She is *très belle*."

Merrick eyed him with suspicion. "And she is *my* wife, Baddo. I'll thank you to remember that."

Fingering his beard, Badeau grinned. "Of course, Capitaine."

The crew of the *Satisfaction* continued their work, casting furtive glances at Merrick. Hanson skulked by, scowling as he tugged on a rope that led to the mainmast.

Merrick certainly had not expected a warm welcome from the pirates, but something in the Frenchman's demeanor gave him pause. Had the heady lure of being in command already begun to inflate the man's ego?

"I assure you, Badeau, it is not my intention to take over your ship. I wish only to assist you in subduing the *Vanquisher*, rescue a lady the captain holds aboard, and return to my ship as soon as possible."

"It is nothing, mon capitaine. You are welcome."

Badeau's voice carried the tone of respect and camaraderie Merrick had learned to recognize from his friend, putting Merrick immediately at ease.

"We rescue a lady?"

Merrick chuckled and nodded.

Turning, he plodded across the deck, booming orders, which Badeau quickly repeated, sending pirates scurrying to their tasks. Cannons were prepared, powder measured, and sails were trimmed as the pirates armed themselves with pistols, swords, and boarding axes.

Planting himself on the foredeck next to Badeau, Merrick studied the *Vanquisher*, now nearly within firing range. He could no longer spot the *Reliance* off their stern, and the loss of her cut deep into his soul. He prayed for a swift battle, an easy defeat, and a minimal loss of life, but not before he prayed for Charlisse and the crew of the *Reliance*—that God would preserve them unscathed until he returned.

"You have concern in your eyes," Badeau said, dousing Merrick with a cloud of rum-drenched breath.

Merrick sighed, sorry to see his friend's inability to abstain from the foul liquor. "Yes, Captain Carlton is a formidable foe." He cocked an eyebrow toward Badeau. "I'm afraid I taught him myself."

"Ah, oui, then to beat him, we must be smarter than you."

"I daresay based on my recent behavior, that should not be a problem."

Thunder boomed from above, sending a tremor through the ship, and the sharp tang of rain scented the breeze. Merrick ordered the guns run out and the decks cleared for battle. Within a minute, they'd be within firing range of the *Vanquisher*.

Instantly, Kent's ship swung hard to port in a turn so sharp Merrick thought the ocean would flood in over the bulwarks and her masts would snap in two.

"Fire!" Merrick shouted, hoping to hit her before she shifted out of range, but by the time the cannonballs blasted forth, the *Vanquisher* presented naught but her skinny stern for a target. All but one round shot splashed into the sea. Stinging smoke gorged the air as the cannon's recoil sent a jarring spasm through the *Satisfaction*.

Captain Carlton open fire with his two stern chasers. Grapeshot belched from their muzzles, sending a hail of death and confusion over the *Satisfaction*'s deck.

Dashing amidst the incoming rounds, Merrick ordered the ship to come about on the port quarter of their enemy, where they quickly seized the weather gauge. With a swift maneuvering of sails, they caught up to the *Vanquisher* and fired a broadside upon her. The roar of the guns thundered across the fuming skies. Through the clearing smoke, two charred and blackened holes appeared, both in the larboard hull of the *Vanquisher*, but neither below the waterline.

Before the wind could sweep the *Satisfaction* out of range, Kent returned fire. Twenty cannons blasted, sending the air aquiver. Only three of the iron balls struck the *Satisfaction* as she flew by. The ship shuddered from stem to stern, and screams sliced through the billowing smoke. Two shots blasted over the bulwarks and across the deck with minimal damage. Another exploded into the mizzenmast, sending sheets and tackles to the deck in a tangle of rope and a shower of splinters. Two pirates lay unconscious on the deck and another held his arm, blood oozing from beneath his hand.

Crippled, the *Satisfaction* languished in the wind.

Merrick ordered the injured to be taken below where their wounds could be attended, while he sent ten men to repair the mizzen as best they could and bring all the remaining sails to bear. Then storming across the *Satisfaction*, he leapt up onto the poop deck, with a cursing Badeau quick on his heels. Grumbles emanated from the pirates, and Merrick heard Hanson shout from across the deck.

"That cuckoldy milksop's goin' to get us all killed, by thunder."

Ignoring them, Merrick pressed the spyglass to his eye and scanned the *Vanquisher* and her master. Gloating upon her quarterdeck, Kent stood with arms crossed over his chest, a sardonic grin plastered on his twisted lips. Beside him stood a woman—a beautiful woman in a green gown—struggling in the grasp of another pirate. He lowered the glass.

"Lady Ashton."

Badeau lifted his scarred eyebrow. *"Qui?"*

"That must be Lady Ashton," Merrick repeated, pointing toward the woman. "But why would Captain Carlton put her in such danger up on deck?"

Grabbing the glass, Badeau took a peek, while Merrick glanced over his shoulder at the repairs being made. It would take days to repair the mizzenmast and hoist her sails once again. With the remaining two masts, the *Satisfaction* could sail, albeit slower, but she had lost her ability to turn sharply. Within seconds, the *Vanquisher* would be upon them, and although they could return fire, they would not be able to position their shots effectively.

Merrick's heart sank. He had let Charlisse down again. And not only her, but himself, his crew, and Lady Ashton. He stomped to the railing and gripped it until his fingers reddened and his knuckles grew white from the pain. *Lord, why?* In all Merrick's days at sea, he had never been defeated this badly. He'd been crippled and forced to flee on occasion, to be sure, but never to the point of surrendering or sinking. Now, to be beaten by the very man whom Merrick had trained himself was insufferable and demeaning. Just another blow to his already butchered pride. *Where is Your justice, God?*

Badeau approached him. "What do you order, mon capitaine?" His voice held a hint of disdain.

Thunder grumbled, echoing across the ship, and Merrick prayed it was indeed thunder and not the sound of distant cannons. *Charlisse*. He must get back to her. Too late to turn and flee, too crippled to win a fight. Should he surrender? None of these options returned him to his wife.

"Blast!" Merrick struck the railing. *Father, I trusted You with Charlisse.... Please protect her and bring her back to me.*

He cast a quick glance at the *Vanquisher*, surging through the choppy seas and coming within yards of their starboard quarter. He faced Badeau. "We must fight. Order the guns—" Something flashed in the corner of Merrick's vision, and he looked up to see the white flag of truce being raised and lowered on the main truck of the *Vanquisher*.

Confusion swirled in his mind. Why would Kent surrender when he clearly had won?

Following Merrick's gaze, Badeau's forehead wrinkled as he looked up. "*Mon Dieu.* He surrenders?"

"So it would seem. But he also signals us to heave to." Doffing his hat, Merrick began to pace, fidgeting with the wet tricorn. It must be a trap. But how? Halting, his stern gaze landed on Badeau. "Lower all sails. All hands on deck. Have the men fully armed and ready for a fight."

"Oui, mon capitaine." Badeau nodded and marched off, leaving Merrick to stare at the oncoming frigate gliding to a stop beside them. Kent remained at his spot on the quarterdeck, still wearing an insolent grin. It made no sense. Why would he risk losing his men in a boarding party when he could have sunk them to the bottom of the sea with a few strategically placed broadsides?

Merrick raked a hand through his hair. It began to rain, first in small drops, then it pounded down upon him, and he slapped his hat back on, allowing the water to slide off in tiny rivulets. *Father, give me wisdom.* As if in reply, two bolts of lightning cut across the gray sky, zigzagging over each other and leaving a glowing cross imprinted in Merrick's vision.

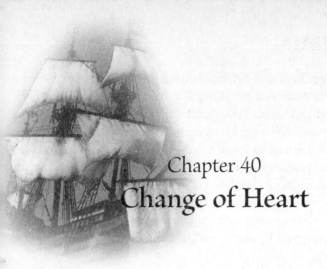

# Chapter 40
# Change of Heart

Thunder rumbled as the hulls of the two mighty ships slammed against each another in a crash that sent Merrick and his crew staggering. Grapnels were hurled and their ropes pulled taut until there was but a few gaping feet between the frigates. Merrick stood, hand on the hilt of his cutlass, at the head of his band of men. Numbering well over one hundred, his pirates covered the deck like flies on refuse, leaving barely a speck of the wooden planks beneath them in view. They growled at their adversaries in a defiant chant that assured them they would not go down without a bloody fight.

In a challenging reply, Kent's men lined the deck of the *Vanquisher*. Like monkeys, some hung from the ratlines and shrouds, howling down insults upon their defeated foes; others stood on the bulwarks and railings, brandishing cutlasses and pistols, grimacing through brown teeth in anticipation of battle.

Rain drizzled upon them in a chilled mist, casting an eerie foreboding of carnage, and inciting an uneasy dread within Merrick. He had seen too many of these brutal fights, had witnessed too often the decks of ships pooled with blood. And for what—treasure, power?

An hour ago, Merrick believed all had been lost, but now, for some reason unbeknownst to him, Kent had given him a second chance. Yet even though victory was possible in hand-to-hand combat, Merrick did not relish the blood that would be shed.

Lightning flashed, followed by another boom of thunder as Kent sauntered down onto the main deck, the pirate behind him holding the woman in tow. He motioned for Merrick to come aboard.

"He wants a parley." Badeau shifted his feet nervously on the slippery deck. "*Mais pour quoi?* Why does he not charge at us?"

"Why, indeed." Merrick rubbed his fingers over the hilt of his cutlass, feeling the tension chisel through his arm and across his shoulders. Kent's tactics had always been predictable. But these recent actions were rash and unorthodox—two characteristics of a man afflicted by madness or love. Oftentimes, the one condition could be attributed to the other.

Merrick glanced over the men standing behind him. "Bullock, Styles, come with me."

"You go?" Badeau's face twisted.

"Yes." Merrick clutched the fore shrouds. "Wait for my order to attack." He glanced back, making sure the men he'd selected were following. "Unless, of course, I am killed." He raised a teasing brow toward Badeau. "Then you may attack at will."

Badeau nodded grimly.

With one hop, Merrick jumped onto the bulwarks of the *Satisfaction*, and then leapt over to the *Vanquisher*, hearing the thuds of his men's boots behind him. Growls and curses shot their way as Kent's pirates surged toward them, but with one wave of their captain's jeweled hand, they halted and grumbled.

Merrick approached Kent, keeping his eyes riveted upon the knave's familiar dark gaze. He'd not seen the pirate for nigh three years, and the boy had filled into a man in both height and breadth. A new confidence swelled around the young scamp, though he still wore the expression of a pompous brat. Kent's twitching lips curved into a smug grin.

Fury raged in burning shards through Merrick when he thought of the pain this rogue had caused him and Charlisse. Perhaps he should challenge him to a duel right here and finally rid the world of his fiendish ways.

"Welcome aboard, Captain." Kent bowed, doffing his plumed hat. "It has been far too long."

"Not long enough to please me." Merrick fixed him with a hard gaze.

"Ah, I see your temperament has not improved since I last made your acquaintance."

"What is it you want, Kent?" Merrick flexed his jaw.

"That's Captain Carlton, if you please."

Merrick released a heavy sigh. "I'm in no humor for your trifling games."

"It saddens me to hear that. Been ill disposed as of late, lost something perhaps?" Kent snickered.

Gripping the hilt of his cutlass, Merrick longed to draw the blade and thrust it through the impudent fool's heart—if only to wipe the smirk from his lips. "My disposition is none of your concern, though it has been quite cheerful recently."

A flicker of confusion crossed Kent's expression. "Indeed." His beady eyes were alight with cruel intelligence as he narrowed them upon Merrick. "Perhaps I misread your strong affections for your wife."

"You know as well as I that Charlisse is alive and well."

The young woman in the pirate's grasp let out a sob. She began to struggle against the grip of the pirate who held her captive, drawing Kent's attention. Her pleading look shifted from Kent to Merrick.

Kent's gaze instantly transformed back into a sneer when he faced Merrick again. "It displeases me to hear my charade was so quickly spoiled." He crossed his arms over his damp leather jerkin. "I should suppose you wish to kill me for the trouble I've caused you?"

"I would love nothing more, and given the chance I will do just that." Merrick shifted his stance. "But alas, my purpose for attacking you lies elsewhere."

Kent flung a hand in the air, lace bursting from his sleeve. "Perhaps, but 'twas I who defeated you, was it not?" He glanced over his crew. "I bested the great Captain Edmund Merrick." He strutted across the deck like a peacock, eliciting cheers from his band of pirates.

Burning rage ripped through Merrick, but he kept his tongue, resisting the urge to show this pretentious slug who the best pirate really was. "Which brings me back to my question." Merrick let out a sigh. "What is it you want, Kent?"

"*Captain Carlton*," Kent spat through gritted teeth. Then his face relaxed. "Hmm, I see how this unexpected rendezvous perplexes you." He turned and nodded toward the pirate, who dragged the woman forward.

Drenched, she sloshed across the deck. Her green gown clung to her, drawing the eyes of most of the pirates. Her auburn hair had collapsed upon her shoulders in saturated strands.

But it was the change in Kent that caught Merrick's attention. His overbearing, insolent facade faded, his shoulders stooped slightly, and the smirk disappeared from his lips.

Lightning blazed across the eastern sky as Lady Ashton gazed at her captor from beneath sodden lashes. Her green eyes pleaded with Kent as the two of them exchanged a knowing glance.

A blast of thunder roared, sending a tremble through the ship and over Lady Ashton. Kent reached for her, but she cowered away. He withdrew his hand and turned to Merrick.

"May I present—"

"Lady Ashton, I presume?" Merrick interrupted, offering her the bow he had not honored Kent with earlier.

Flinching, Kent raised his brows.

Isabel took a step toward Merrick, but the old pirate who held her tugged her back. She winced. "You are Charlisse's husband?"

"That I am, milady." Merrick nodded, trying to give her a reassuring smile. "At your service."

"And, pray tell, what service is it you offer her, hmm?" Kent's mouth curved as irony laughed in his eyes. "You'd be rotting at the bottom of the sea with the rest of your spineless minions if it weren't for me."

"I beg you to do me the honor of trying to put me there now." Merrick clutched the handle of his blade, yearning for Kent to draw his. "I tire of your mawkish dalliance. State your business with me, or by God, I'll finish mine with you."

The ship lunged over a wave, sending a salty spray over the deck. The spicy scent of rain mingled with the stench of the soggy pirates and the trace of gunpowder still lingering in the air.

Kent stepped toward Merrick, his dark eyes flashing, and started to draw his sword, when Lady Ashton yanked herself from the pirate's grasp and dashed in front of him.

"Please, Captain, please. Let me go with him." Her trembling voice echoed across the ship.

The rain faded to a light drizzle.

The rage in Kent's eyes dissolved as his gaze swept over her. With a sigh, he tossed his head, flinging back his wet hair and reached toward her. Then hesitating, he withdrew his hand once more. Turmoil writhed upon his features.

Lady Ashton gripped his arm. "Please, if I stay with you, I will die."

Kent gazed at her for a minute longer, then looked up at Merrick. "Take the woman and leave." He retreated from her, a tortured expression on his face.

Shock swept through Merrick. Never before had he seen the insolent pirate surrender anything—not a battle, a duel, an argument, nor especially a woman.

Grunts and curses shot out from the horde of pirates surrounding them.

"What d'ye mean, leave?"

"Aye, what 'bout the treasure?"

Drawing his cutlass, Kent swung about, pointing it across the mob. "There'll be no treasure today, gentlemen." His deep voice boomed. "If you aim to challenge me, be quick about it!" With red face and throbbing veins, he scanned his crew, and Merrick believed, in Kent's present state of mind, he would take on every last one of them if he had to.

The pirates muttered, cursing under their breath, but none stepped forward. Merrick could see his former first mate had become a formidable captain.

Kent sheathed his sword and slowly turned around to find Lady Ashton still standing before him. The fury left him, and a pained surprise took its place. "What delays you, milady?" He gestured toward Merrick, flicking his hand in the air. "You are free to go."

Scattered rays of sunshine made their way through the vanishing clouds above and landed in glistening patches upon the saturated deck. Drops of water fell from the sails and rigging in pitter-pattering sounds over the wooden planks.

Clutching her damp skirts, Lady Ashton turned and inched her way toward Merrick. She reached his side and faced Kent again.

Despite the warming air, the hairs on the back of Merrick's neck pricked. Something was amiss. "What will prevent you from firing upon me as soon as we set sail?"

Kent's gaze landed on Lady Ashton and remained there. "You hold a treasure far more dear to me than the conquest of any ship—even *your* ship."

Isabel's eyes softened and looked into his inquisitively.

Merrick gently took hold of her arm. "And why should I not blast you from the sea as soon as our ships separate?"

Kent shrugged. "Because I will take your word on it, and you are a man of honor." His gaze shifted to Isabel. "Take her safely home to New Providence, for I cannot. I have many enemies lurking in those waters."

Merrick retreated, keeping his eyes on Kent, and ordered his men back to the ship. He handed Lady Ashton to Badeau who eagerly grabbed her by the waist and hoisted her aboard the *Satisfaction*. Then Merrick leapt over the bulwarks.

"Release the grapnels," he ordered, thinking it best to make a speedy exit while the captain was so obliging. The haunted look in Kent's eyes did nothing to assuage Merrick's fear that any second he would change his mind.

Three pirates rushed forward to unhook the iron claws from the deck and toss them back to the *Vanquisher*. When the sails had been unfurled, Merrick watched as the two ships began to part.

"Do you trust him, mon capitaine?" Badeau stared at their departing enemy.

Merrick glanced at Lady Ashton, who stood beside him. A twinge of sorrow flickered in her eyes. The *Vanquisher's* sails filled with a burst of wind, and the ship jolted. Kent gripped the railing and returned Isabel's gaze with equal intensity before the ship sped off through the sea.

"As long as we have her on board"—Merrick leaned toward Badeau—"I don't believe he'll do us any harm.

Isabel's green eyes darted to Merrick. "Nay, he loves only himself." A tear escaped the brim of her lashes, and she swiped it away as if in doing so she could swipe away the memories of the past few months.

Isabel stared at the dark, retreating form of Captain Kent Carlton. His imperious gaze drew her to him like a rope between the ships. A sadness seeped from his eyes that she sensed even at a distance and one that she had clearly seen on board his ship in those final moments before he let her go with Captain Merrick.

He had let her go.

There was goodness in him, after all, and even his small display of kindness began to dispel the bitterness in her heart toward his one heinous act. Tears burned in her eyes. What was wrong with her? She was finally safe and no doubt would be going home soon to the sanctuary of her father's estate, where everything was secure, regimented, pristine, and predictable—so unlike her time with Captain Carlton.

With a huff, she wiped the string of wet hair from her face. Of course he was naught but a cruel pirate. She was glad to be finally rid of him. Yet hadn't she sensed something behind his cruelty, something that tore at the sympathies of her heart? Strangely as his ship sped from view, she wondered if she'd ever see the ignominious captain again.

Gliding her fingers over her abdomen, a sob rose in her throat. How could she face her parents, how could she face society, with the illegitimate child of a pirate growing within her? The shame of it. Her life would never be the same. But at least she was alive. At least she was heading home.

She turned to Captain Merrick. "I cannot thank you enough for saving my life."

Merrick glanced at the young woman, confused by the intense emotions toiling in her gaze. "My wife's idea, milady. You may thank her when you see her." Merrick's utterance sent a blaze of hope through him, although he recognized the doubt that crept behind it.

Distant booms echoed across the clearing sky, giving Merrick no doubt as to the source—cannons, not thunder.

*Father, please keep her safe until I can reach her.*

# Chapter 41
# Reliance

Charlisse peered through the spyglass. A torrent of rain poured down upon them like a curtain, concealing their advancing enemy. She focused the instrument through the gray haze, swiped the drops from its lens, and squinted upon a fleeting dark shape. Several bright orange lights flashed through the gloomy vapor.

"All hands down!" Charlisse roared across the deck.

The thunder of the ensuing booms confirmed her fears. The twelve-pounders struck the *Reliance,* blasting through her sturdy hull and pummeling through sails, masts, bulwarks, and taffrail. The ship shuddered under the violent hammering.

One mighty ball zipped past Charlisse with an eerie whine before it crashed into the bulwarks beyond. She tumbled to the deck as shards of splintered wood flew in all directions. Screams cracked the billowing smoke. Stunned, she lay unable to move. The rough deck scraped against her cheek as the odors of sodden oak, gunpowder, and blood assailed her. Her heart pounded in rhythm to the thump of the frenzied chaos around her.

She must get up. She was the captain. These men depended on her.

Her thoughts jumped to Elisa below, and she prayed she had not been hurt.

Shaking the ringing from her ears, Charlisse stumbled to her feet and rushed toward the railing. She slipped on something slick and flopped to the deck beside Gunny. He lay on his side in a pool of blood. She swung her glance off the starboard railing. The *Golden Bandit* jabbed through the mist, like a demon emerging from hell.

Dread consumed her. She alone carried the responsibility of the ship and every soul aboard. She had hoped only to tease Collier and keep him occupied until Merrick returned—certainly not to engage him. Rising, Charlisse tossed back her shoulders and turned to her crew.

"Brighton, Smack, take Gunny below, if you please."

The two men nodded and picked up the limp man. He moaned, and Charlisse let out a breath of relief.

Pirates dashed across the deck, hurling curses toward their enemy. Fear contorted their features as they armed themselves and took positions at the minions and swivel guns perched at the railings.

"Hold steady, men," Charlisse shouted, trying to calm them. "Jackson, run out the starboard battery. Wait for my orders."

With a nod, the huge man lunged down the companionway stairs.

Darting to the railing, Charlisse eyed the *Golden Bandit* as the wind caught her flaxen sails in a southerly tack that would bring the enemy vessel about on her starboard side.

Sloane appeared next to her, coughing and holding his arm. Red splotches stained his stubby fingers.

"You're hurt." Charlisse swung about, trying to peek under his hand.

"Aye, milady, just a flesh wound, 'tis all." He grimaced; then he glanced over her shoulder, and his eyes widened. Tossing his arm around Charlisse, he forced her to the deck.

Booms quaked the ship as four pounders zipped over their heads. Only one found a target on the larboard railing, smashing a section to bits. The others splashed harmlessly into the sea.

Thanking Sloane, Charlisse pushed herself up from the deck and gazed at their enemy. Smoke curled up from the *Golden Bandit*'s guns on her stern. They didn't have much time before the heinous ship would complete her turn and bring her starboard cannons to bear.

Charlisse took a step back and rubbed her temples. "What damage to the ship? Can she sail?"

"Two shots hit our starboard bow, milady," Sloane answered. "One below the waterline. The other took out one of our guns."

Pressing her lips together, she began to pace. "Have the men repair—"

"They be on it already, milady." Sloane offered her a pained grin, then nodded to his left. "The mainmast be damaged, too."

Charlisse looked over his shoulder and saw a thirteen-inch groove scoured into the thick pole, chunks of the light-colored wood jutting from within it. She glanced above at the heavy yards, booms, and sails, and wondered how long the damaged mast would stand.

Sloane shuffled his feet. "And some o' the booms and tackles are tore up on the fore."

Charlisse returned her gaze to the black menace soaring over the choppy waves. Damaged so, the *Reliance* would not be able to gain enough speed to outrun her. "How did Collier sneak up on us so quickly? He caught the wind advantage and was on us before I knew it." She chided herself, knowing Merrick would not have been fooled so easily.

"That Collier. I 'eard he be a master at sea tactics."

Charlisse clenched her teeth, and waves of chilling doubt washed over her confidence. What had made her think she was capable of staving off such a notorious pirate?

*Yes, who do you think you are, little girl?*

She hung her head. Had it simply been her pride prompting her to command this ship again? If so, she had put all these men's lives at risk for nothing but to satisfy her own ego.

*You will die along with your crew, and you will never see your precious Merrick again.*

A chill coursed through her, and she glanced at Sloane.

His old weathered face wrinkled in concern. Then he tilted his head and regarded her intently. "Methinks by the look on yer face, you be listenin' to the wrong voice."

Charlisse examined his wise old eyes and smiled. He was right. Where was her faith? *Father, I trust You.*

Turning, Sloane gestured toward Collier's ship. "His aim was low. The powder-brained ape means to sink us and take no prisoners, if ye knows what I mean."

"What are yer orders, Cap'n?" Brighton and another pirate darted to her side, their chests heaving.

*What were her orders?* Charlisse faced the *Golden Bandit*. Lightning spiked white across the stormy sky, illuminating the evil ship's starboard quarter as she veered to the right. Biting her lip, Charlisse flung a look up to the quarterdeck. "Rusty, helm, hard aport." At least she could present as small a target as possible to their enemy.

"Hard aport, Cap'n!" The helmsman repeated.

As the *Reliance* swerved, the wind shifted, and the snap of sails drew Charlisse's attention above where she saw the foretopsail flapping idly in the wind. The yards and booms to which it should be attached hung in shattered spikes.

Sloane followed her gaze. "We cannot outrun her fer sure, milady."

Royce appeared beside Brighton. "I told ye she don't know how to cap'n a ship. She's goin' t' get us all killed!" he yelled across the ship.

Ignoring him, Charlisse brushed past him and marched across the deck, avoiding the patches of blood in her path. She swallowed the bile rising in her throat at the thought of the men injured on her account. The rest of the men—those not attending the cannons or the wounded—awaited her orders.

Once again she found all eyes upon her, expecting some brilliant strategic plan, or perhaps another miracle from God—expecting *her* to save their lives. But no clever ideas formed in her mind, nor did she feel the power of God upon her. All she felt was terror etching its way up her body, and she knew if it reached her mind, she'd be unable to accomplish anything.

Examining the puddles of blood around her feet, Charlisse looked up and her eyes locked on Smack. "Sand the deck if you please," she ordered, trying to sound calm, but hearing the quiver in her voice.

"Aye, aye, Cap'n." He scurried away.

Charlisse glanced across her men. Some she had grown to care for, others remained a thorn in her side. She had no idea what to say to them now, but knew they needed to see their captain dauntless and unfaltering. "We face an enemy who intends to sink us, gentlemen. Are we going to let him?"

"No!" The pirates growled in one accord and thrust their weapons in the air above them.

"Brighton, Mason, command the swivels," Charlisse ordered. "When we come into range, shoot at will." The men nodded and darted to their posts.

"Jackson!" she bellowed, and the dark man poked his head up from the main hatch. "Fire the guns as soon as you have a target."

"Aye, aye, Cap'n." He grinned and his bald head disappeared below.

Returning to Sloane, Charlisse gripped the railing and glared at the black demon flying through the water. With the wind on her quarter, the *Golden Bandit* would be upon them in seconds. As for the *Reliance*, she was bilging fast with an ominous list to starboard. Lowering her head, Charlisse began to pray silently.

Sloane grabbed her hand. "I'll pray with ye, if ye don't mind."

She nodded. "Lord, You are the only One who can save us from our enemies. Please come to our aid. But if You choose to take us home, then let Your will be done."

"Amen," Sloane added, giving her hand a squeeze.

When Charlisse opened her eyes, the *Golden Bandit* was but a half mile off their starboard quarter. The menacing ship surged over the stormy swells, licking her foamed lips in anticipation.

Collier's dark form stood on the foredeck, his pompous stance taunting her. Did he know Merrick wasn't even on board? Probably not, nor did she think it would stop him—not from what she'd heard of his cruelty.

Charlisse turned to Royce. "Tell Jackson to fire as soon as we are within range."

Scowling, Royce mumbled something about everyone dying and headed down the hatch.

The *Golden Bandit* continued its descent upon them. Thunder howled as the beastly vessel swept into place beside the *Reliance* and presented her starboard gun ports. The muzzles of seven guns jutted from their blackened holes.

As Charlisse stared at the instruments of death being prepared to blast her to pieces, she thought of Merrick and how glorious their last night together had been. *Father, please help him accept this as Your will. Help him not to turn from You again.*

Tears filled her eyes, and Charlisse squeezed them shut, waiting for the final blasts that would sink her and all her men to the bottom of the sea.

*Boom! Boom! Boom! Boom! Boom!*

An enormous volley shattered the air, followed by the sound of rending timbers, screaming tackles, and fallen masts.

Yet the *Reliance* did not tremble under the blasts. The echo of the thunderous booms faded into an eerie silence that blanketed the ship.

*We must be dead.* The shots must have been so strategically placed that the ship had simply exploded, leaving neither trace of timber nor flesh to mark its passage. Charlisse waited in anticipation for her move into the world beyond.

But then she heard Sloane draw in a deep breath and exclaim, "By the powers!"

Charlisse popped open her eyes and gaped across the troubled sea. The *Golden Bandit* was ablaze, its topmasts thrusting above a cloud of smoke. Fire licked at the mizzen, and black smoke poured from a hole in the hull. Her shattered foremast hung in slivers to the waist below. Sailing low and heavy, she was listing to starboard.

Disbelief froze Charlisse in place. The scattered rays of the sun began to pierce the dark clouds. Then slowly, the blue hull and square sails of the *Satisfaction* emerged from the haze and plunged across the churning waters, showering spray back over her deck in all the brilliant colors of a rainbow. Merrick raised his flag upon her mainmast, and Charlisse saw his tall form standing fast upon the foredeck.

Letting out a yell of victory, she flew into Sloane's arms and was delighted when the normally reserved pirate returned her strong embrace. Laughing and crying, they hugged each other as the other pirates approached, thrusting their weapons in the air with victory cries.

Releasing Sloane, Charlisse swung her gaze over the crew. "Seems we have been saved, men." She cast a glance at the helm. "Rusty, bring her about, if you please. Let's see if we can assist the *Satisfaction*."

"With smilin' pleasure, Cap'n," Rusty yelled.

Solomon scampered across the deck and pounced onto Charlisse's shoulder, jabbering happily.

"Oh, now you show up, little one." Charlisse scratched him under his tiny chin, chuckling. "When the battle is already won."

Though still listing heavily and taking on water, the *Reliance* inched toward the *Satisfaction*. Charlisse noted with each passing wave the blackened, crumbling remains of the *Golden Bandit*. With one well-placed broadside, Merrick had crippled Collier's ship to the point where she could no longer fire her cannons on the starboard side, nor maneuver to fire the larboard battery. Merrick's crew now boarded her and began roaming through the sinking ship, absconding with all her treasure.

Charlisse watched as Merrick rescued the survivors and sent them below. A hideous-looking man of medium build with long hair curled on the ends stood before him, struggling in the clutches of two burly pirates. Finally, jerking from their grasp, he bowed, snatched his captain's hat from one of the pirates, and was escorted below. A chill ran down Charlisse at the sight of the man she assumed to be the infamous Captain Edward Collier.

After all the survivors and treasure were removed, Merrick set the ship on fire, so that by the time Charlisse and her crew arrived, the *Golden Bandit* was nothing but a blazing hull sinking fast into the deep waters.

As the last tip of the *Golden Bandit*'s mainmast disappeared beneath the Caribbean, Merrick's gaze shot to hers across the twenty yards between the two ships. Though she could not make out the details of his expression, she felt his smile upon her, along with a yearning that bridged the gap between them.

He turned and bellowed an order, and the *Satisfaction* veered slightly, making its way toward the *Reliance*. Ordering all sails furled, Charlisse awaited his arrival. A woman appeared next to him on the main deck and Charlisse's heart leapt.

*Isabel.* Merrick had saved her!

With a thud and a quiver, the hulls of the *Satisfaction* and the *Reliance* thumped against each other, and the pirates rushed to tie the two ships together.

Before they even finished securing the ropes, Merrick bounded over the railings and gathered Charlisse into his arms. She clung to him, unable to say a word.

Sloane stood beside them, grinning. Solomon chattered happily from his shoulder. Jackson stood at a distance, arms folded over his massive chest, beaming.

"Uh-hmm." A heavily accented voice disturbed Charlisse, and she peeked over Merrick's arm to see a tawny-haired pirate with a pointed beard, grinning at her. Her eyes shifted to the woman beside him.

Charlisse flew toward Isabel and hugged her. "I'm so glad to see you again."

Isabel sank into Charlisse's arms. "Thank you for remembering me."

"Of course. How could I forget you?" Stepping back, Charlisse examined her friend, noting her red, swollen eyes, the dark circles beneath them, her normally perfect hair hanging in saturated threads around her pale face. "I'm so sorry I couldn't protect you from Kent." She hugged her again. "But you're all right now."

Tears welled in Isabel's jade eyes. She shook her head. " 'Twas not your fault." She glanced at Merrick. "I am forever in your debt for saving me, Captain."

Merrick bowed and smiled, then motioned to the man next to her. "Baddo, may I present my wife, Lady Charlisse Hyde."

Charlisse offered her hand to the tawny-haired pirate who snatched it up and pressed a moist kiss upon it. *"Madame, mon plaisir."*

Retrieving her hand from the Frenchman's grasp, Merrick shot him a scolding look, then gazed across the deck. "Now what have you done to my ship, woman?" He swung about, surveying the damage. "I leave you with a perfectly good vessel for but a few hours, and when I return, it is a mass of shattered timbers and frayed ratlines. He pounded across the deck. "I believe she takes on water, as well."

Placing her hands on her hips, Charlisse swaggered toward her husband. "What kind of captain leaves his wife in charge of a crippled ship to defend herself against one of the most notorious pirates ever to sail the Caribbean?" She glanced over the smiling faces of the crew. "Why, you should consider yourself fortunate, sir, that I obeyed your orders and staved off the villain, or it would be your ship in such dire straights." Charlisse studied the *Satisfaction*, noting the shattered mizzen and torn sails. "Although it seems that fortune favored you no more than me."

Chuckles filtered through the crew.

Merrick raised a brow and cast her a playful grin. "Nevertheless, I'll ask you to remember that it was I who rescued you from certain defeat."

Turning, Charlisse took Isabel by the arm and led her toward the companionway stairs. She cast a sarcastic glance over her shoulder toward Merrick. "We shall discuss this matter at a more opportune moment."

Escorting her friend below, Charlisse thought her heart would burst with happiness. "Thank you, Lord."

"I also prayed to your God," Isabel whispered. "When I was trapped on board the *Vanquisher*."

"You did?" Charlisse grinned. "And what was His answer?"

Isabel smiled. "When I thought all was lost, He brought your husband to rescue me."

Charlisse squeezed her hand. "I am most happy to hear it. Did I not tell you He is a faithful God?" Stopping before Elisa's door, she tapped lightly and led Isabel within.

Standing on the foredeck of the *Reliance*, Charlisse leaned back against her husband. He wrapped his strong arms around her and gave her a squeeze, placing a kiss upon her cheek.

A warm salty breeze danced over Charlisse as a waning moon cast its silver reflection upon the calm, inky waters. The *Reliance* bobbed upon the sea. The sound of the water purling against the hull soothed Charlisse almost as much as the scent and feel of her husband cradling her against his chest.

"How is your friend?" Merrick's deep voice broke the night air like a sultry song.

"Warm and safe. She and Elisa are getting along quite well."

Silence overtook them again, save for the creak and groan of the ship.

Charlisse nestled against Merrick's chest. "She carries Kent's child."

Her husband sighed, his warm breath flowing over her cheek. " 'Tis more than a woman should have to bear." Then reaching down, he ran his hand over her belly. "We shall have another."

Charlisse nodded, sorrow catching the words in her throat. She swallowed hard, wondering if she would ever be able to carry a child again, and if so, should she dare bring a new life into such a violent world? At one time she'd thought that was all she wanted—a home, a husband, and lots of children. But now. . .

"What are your plans?" she asked Merrick, both excitement and apprehension rising within her.

"I will take Lady Ashton back to her home in New Providence, and return Señorita Elisa to her father in Barracoa. Then it is my intention to turn over that wretched brute, Collier, to the authorities at Port Royal to do with as they please."

"Hmm. Then I trust you intend to continue your mission to rid the Caribbean of murderous villains?"

She felt his body tense. "Nay, it's always been your desire to settle down and raise a family. And naught but my own selfishness prevented it. There'll be no more roving over the dangerous sea for me, nor for my beautiful wife."

"No more roving?" Charlisse turned her head slightly and gave him a teasing grin. "Surely you jest!"

Squeezing her more tightly, Merrick rubbed her arms and rested his chin on the top of her head. "You are more important to me than any quest."

Charlisse heard the sincerity in his voice, but with it, a trace of sorrow. "But 'tis God who gave you that quest. Who are you to disobey Him?"

" 'Tis God who gave you to me—to protect and to love. That is where my priority lies."

"Nay, I no longer wish to settle down," Charlisse spat in an insolent tone.

"What?" Merrick swung her around to face him.

"I'm afraid I have some pirate in me after all." Charlisse gave him a sly look. "After I've commanded this ship, subdued a crew of scurrilous cutthroats, and fought off vicious pirates, do you actually think I would want to settle down to a quiet life in the country?"

Merrick's brows rose. The evening breeze caught his ebony hair, flinging it behind him. "Do not play me for the fool, woman."

"I doubt anyone could ever do that."

Excitement flickered across Merrick's face, then dwindled into somber lines. "Nay." He took her in his arms. "I will never put you in danger again."

Charlisse reached up and rubbed the stubble on his jaw. "Have you learned nothing at all? Didn't God keep me safe when you thought me dead? He is faithful, Merrick. Nothing can harm us, save He allows it."

A daring grin lifted one corner of his mouth as he ran his thumb over her lips. His dark, piercing eyes scanned hers.

"He is reliable, Merrick. That's why I called the ship *Reliance*. He will never let us down."

Merrick nodded. "That He is. He never gave up on me, though I turned my back on Him." His eyes held a twinkle as he looked at her. "Truth be told, it would be hard to abandon these seas and my mission, for I believe He not only wants me to stop these murderous pirates but point them to Him, the only One who can truly help them."

"I believe I can assist you with that, Captain." Charlisse smiled.

"Yes, you've more than proven your skill in that area."

Tears of joy flooded Charlisse's eyes, and she fell into Merrick's arms. He showered her forehead with kisses, then absorbed her lips in his.

Waves of tingling warmth flowed over her as his embrace grew tighter.

He pulled back from her. "Shall we roam these seas together?"

"Aye, Cap'n. That we shall."

Merrick's brow furrowed. "But alas, I fear we have a problem."

Puzzled at his sudden change in manner, a twinge of alarm coursed through her. "What problem?"

"We cannot both be captain of this ship." His mouth curved in irony.

"Ah, 'tis true," she said, placing a finger on her lips. "But how to resolve it." Her gaze shot to his. "A duel, perhaps?"

"Nay." Merrick shook his head, squeezing the muscles in her arms. "It would not be to your advantage." He ran his fingers through her hair, a rakish flicker crossing his eyes. "Perhaps we should join forces."

Raising her chin in the air, Charlisse shot him a saucy look.

Without saying a word, Merrick swung her up in his arms and carried her across the deck.

"I protest, sir. Unhand me at once." Charlisse struggled. "Where do you think you're taking me?"

"Why, down to my cabin." He grinned, winking at her. "To discuss our new alliance."

Chuckling, Charlisse clung to her husband and closed her eyes, thanking God for bringing Merrick back to her and for the adventurous life before them. Most of all, she thanked God for being so faithful—for she now knew she could rely on Him forever.

## Author's Historical Footnote

Edward Collier was a real pirate who took part in several expeditions with Henry Morgan. He commanded one of the pirate ships in Morgan's 1668 raid on Porto Bello and soon after captured a French ship, which he renamed the *Satisfaction*. It is said he was crueler than any of the other buccaneer captains at that time, delighting in inflicting vicious and unnecessary tortures upon his victims. The Spanish never captured him, and the British authorities refused to press charges against him. Apparently, he never repented of his evil ways and continued to sail with Captain Morgan on several other raids, including Rio de la Hacha and Panama, where he tortured and slaughtered several Spaniards and murdered a Franciscan friar in cold blood. He spent his later years on his estate in Jamaica.

There is no record that he ever dared to cross paths with Captain Merrick and Lady Charlisse again.

# M. L. TYNDALL

MaryLu Tyndall spent her early years on the shores of South Florida, where she grew to love the sea and the tropics. After attending Oral Roberts University in Tulsa, Oklahoma, she moved to California and graduated from San Jose State with a degree in math. During the next fifteen years, she worked for a software company, got married, and started a family. She also began pursuing a writing career, and her love of history sent her delving into the past through books and movies in search of fascinating stories and heroic characters. MaryLu now writes full-time and currently lives in California with her husband, six children, and three cats.